MERCY

A Ball & Chain Thriller

Book 1

By
John W. Mefford

One

Eighteen years ago

The single streetlight illuminated water dripping off the leaves of two weeping willows. The humidity was so thick it was as if Mother Nature was squeezing a sponge across the entire North Texas region.

The man stuck his hand out the open window of his parked car. Not even a hint of a breeze. In the hottest summer on record in Fort Worth, even a warm wind would bring some relief. But cool weather was as elusive as a peaceful mental existence. He felt like he was forever stuck in the confines of Hell, where the relentless heat that pounded on him day after day was only surpassed by the purgatory that held his mind captive.

Relief. He had prayed for it, rode his bike, swam, ran, even trained for a mini-triathlon. No results. If anything, the stress from work, from home, from the world had skyrocketed even more. He learned about yoga, so he poured himself into that practice. The mantras made sense, but he couldn't stop repeating them. One minute would turn into five minutes. An hour later, he'd find himself trapped in a redundant cycle of saying the same words, hoping that some higher being would help him break free of the chains that bound him to his unrelenting mental anguish.

But the freedom never happened. And the anxiety continued to cultivate like a parasite inside his body. It grew to the point where he thought he'd have a heart attack and die.

Either there wasn't an entity that controlled the universe or he'd been designated NIE—not important enough.

Desperate for even a brief respite from the paralyzing anxiety, he researched every homeopathic remedy he could find. He tried about half a dozen, including experimenting with three different types of teas, lemon balm, and various herbs. He'd even burned lavender candles, based upon a study that called it an emotional anti-inflammatory.

His wife thought he was nuts. He couldn't argue the point, although he routinely had urges to literally rip the skin off her face, especially after she would unleash a string of insults, adding a double dose of depression and bitter self-loathing.

"If you made more money, our kids would have a loving parent at home with them," she would bark at him repeatedly. "But you're not capable of that, are you? So our kids have to be raised by strangers in some sterile daycare facility. Do you like that? Do you?"

That's when he'd typically take a walk around the block. Up until this point in his life, he'd somehow contained his impulses to lash out at his wife and two young kids.

Consider that a fucking miracle.

But those urges had finally reached a peak. He felt as though a stake had been driven right through his skull, and the only way to relieve that stress was to take that stake and bury it into something else.

Hence, tonight.

He emerged from his car and quietly shut the door. The street was void of vehicles and people. A few of the homes had lights on inside. It was like the night was whispering a message to him. *"Do it. This is your time to finally take control of your life. There's no other way."*

Yes, a voice had spoken to him. Where that voice came from, he couldn't say. Nor did he analyze it much. He heard it. There was no mistake. Now was not the time to sit back and ponder consequences. Fuck the consequences. It was time to act.

He lumbered across the street—he lumbered almost anywhere he went. His size wasn't something he could hide. Ridiculed his entire life for looking like Shrek, an ugly ogre, the man knew there was a benefit to his mass. A natural strength that made carrying a weapon unnecessary.

He checked the time and knew he had five minutes to reach his destination. He wasn't worried. He'd completed this part of the task several times. Anything to relieve the stress.

He moved between two trees, stumbled over a root in the grass, and caught himself just before falling to the ground. "Fuck," he muttered as his pulse peppered his neck.

He was on edge, needed to get this done. He pulled around a house and heard movement. His pace slowed. There was moaning and then a metal bang. His sights swung to the right. A boy and girl were making out on the hood of a car. He instantly thought about his wife, back when they'd first started dating. They couldn't get enough of each other. He'd thought it was a love so great that it would last five lifetimes. He'd been so wrong. Was he just a bad judge of character?

"We've got company," the girl said, straightening her skirt and sitting up.

The man tried to ignore them and walk across the street.

"Are you homeless?" the girl asked.

Her comment initially bit into his flesh. How dare her! He stopped and wondered if he would change his plans. Two for the price of one, maybe? He turned slowly in their direction.

"Sorry if that offended you," the boy said.

They looked to be college-aged. Maybe a little drunk.

"I'm fine." He couldn't believe that he'd spoken. He glanced down and realized he was wearing a T-shirt with holes in it, cut-off shorts, and his toes stuck out of his sneakers—the raggedy clothes he wore to cut the grass. He'd started it earlier but given up midway. He'd given up on life, so why not the lawn?

"It's okay if you don't have a place to sleep. Nothing to be ashamed of, especially in this economy." She and the boy stood up.

"Hey," the boy said, approaching him.

The man scanned the area, looking for other people. All clear. He could grab the skinny kid and break his neck like a twig in seconds. She would probably faint from fear. And then…well, then the fun would really begin.

"All I got is twenty bucks. But I think that will get you a room at the Como Six motel off Allen Avenue." The boy held out a crumpled twenty-dollar bill. "Come on. Take it. You need it more than we do. We'll just spend it on beer or something stupid."

The man was stunned. He reached out and took the money. "Thank you."

"No prob. Have a good one." The boy walked back to his girlfriend. They held hands and headed toward the house.

The man continued on his trek, although his mind was confused. More than one voice was vying for control.

A few minutes later, he was crouched behind bushes in the shadows of a dark side yard. If history repeated itself on this Friday night, he'd see a…

Headlights stole his attention. He hunkered even lower and watched the pickup pull to a stop near the streetlight. The engine hummed for a minute or two. He was sure the young couple was making out one final time. This had been their MO for a good couple of months. He'd stumbled upon this very same scene one night when he was out walking. That had been when he saw the girl get out of the truck and walk all by herself down the street.

Something about her isolation had ignited a flurry of feelings within him.

Control. That's what he craved. He wanted—needed—to control something. Someone.

The passenger door opened, and the girl slid out of the truck. She walked around the pickup, gave her boyfriend one more smooch through the open window, then slipped her backpack over her shoulder and walked down the street. The man started to lift up and follow, but the pickup didn't drive off.

Dammit. That wasn't supposed to happen. The boyfriend needed to leave. He'd done so the previous seven times the man had watched. It was obvious they were trying to hide their relationship from the girl's parents. Or maybe just hide the fact that she was seeing him so often. It didn't matter to the man. He only wanted to see the pickup drive off.

Seconds felt like minutes. Perspiration dripped off his forehead and nose. He could feel his shirt stick to his back. The fucking heat wave was unrelenting—over ninety degrees, even at this late hour. But he also knew his internal temperature was on the rise for another reason. The anticipation of releasing his demons.

The pickup's engine rumbled louder, then it slowly pulled away from the curb and executed a U-turn.

The truck drove off. The man watched until it disappeared around the corner. Blood coursed through his veins. Everything was happening the way it should.

Then, it was as though he'd spread his wings and a wind lifted him up and glided him down the street. The girl was strolling casually just up ahead, a little bit of a hip wiggle in her walk. Not a care in the world. Maybe thinking about her boyfriend. It didn't matter. The man was reaching a near-euphoric state. She was alone. It was dark and still. They might as well have been the last two people on the planet.

Soon it would be just one.

The breeze gently set him on the concrete about ten feet behind her. He started to pick up his pace and lifted his arms so he could put one arm around her mouth, the other around her torso. He'd hold her like a loaf of bread and carry her into the woods across the street. And then he would demonstrate his creative side.

Now at six feet and closing fast, he lunged in her direction. Suddenly, he was plunging uncontrollably to the road. He'd tripped over his shoelace. *Fuck!* He was such a klutz! His knees and elbows were bloodied, and the top of his nose was scraped.

"Are you okay?"

He looked up to see the girl staring down at him. "Uh…" was all he could say.

"You scared me for a second. If you want, you can come to my house. My mom's a nurse. She loves taking care of people."

His mind scrambled for a direction.

"You must really be hurt."

She leaned closer and inspected his knees.

"You might have tiny rocks in your skin. That could get infected."

"I'll be okay." He slowly got to his feet. His eyes were darting around, just like his mind. She was right there. *Grab her. Take her into the woods and show the world what you can do. What you were meant to do.*

"Well, if you're not going to let my mom help, I need to get going." She turned to leave.

He leaned toward her, envisioning his arms around her body, her flailing like a fish out of water, and then the desperation in her eyes.

Before she'd taken two steps, she stopped. Had she heard his breath hitch? What was she doing?

She bent down, picked something off the road, and extended her hand. "I think you dropped this."

It was the twenty-dollar bill. "Thank you."

"Sure. Have a good one. Be sure to get those wounds cleaned up."

She walked another block, then went inside her home.

The man looked at the twenty-dollar bill. He thought about the acts of kindness that had come at just the wrong time.

Were they a sign? Did he have it all wrong?

He headed back to his car, mulling over the unanticipated turn of events. This night had been memorable. It would alter the course of his life. But he also knew that it would only be temporary. Weeks, months, maybe years from now, his true self would reemerge. And that's when his destiny would play out. It was inevitable.

Two

Present day

Cooper

Ever chipped a tooth before?

I've done it twice, now. The first time happened while I was in college. I was nineteen years old and playing golf with my buddies…drunk.

We were on the seventh hole of Tennyson Golf Course in South Dallas. I had downed six shots of tequila and three beers. And that was before I'd teed off on the first hole, a duck hook that sent me into the woods. At least I got a chance to take a pee. Relief. Then, I'd hacked my way out of the woods and hacked even more for the next six holes.

On hole number six, a shapely "beer girl" offered me two whiskey sours if I could chip in from twenty yards out. I missed the hole by about thirty feet. She was nice enough to give me a fist bump. I couldn't restrain myself from asking for her phone number. She laughed and drove off to tease the next foursome. Then, of course, my buddies razzed me relentlessly. I would have expected nothing less.

Anyway, I was standing on the tee box of the seventh hole—a

162-yard par 3—and was cleaning my nails with the end of my tee. Why? Who knows? But I was shit-faced and patiently waiting my turn to tee off when I heard what sounded like a gunshot. My reflexes moved at the speed of a slow-motion replay. I looked to my left and saw a car spewing fumes on an adjoining road. Probably nothing more than a backfire. When I turned my head around to check out my buddy's tee shot, I instead ate his Mizuno 5 iron. Somehow, I'd lost my sense of space and stood far too close to my buddy, who was equally as drunk. It felt as though my entire head was rattling like a tin can full of coins. Stunned, I swallowed the chip of a tooth. Even though I was plastered, the sudden spike of pain was unworldly.

The second time I'd chipped a tooth—as in about thirty seconds ago—I wasn't numbed by inebriation. My tongue felt the rough edges of the tooth as blood pooled in my mouth. I had no idea where the chipped-off part had gone. Still down on one knee, I touched my lip. It had to be cartoonish huge.

A baritone grunt-chuckle brought my gaze upward to see Elan Sachen adjusting his brass knuckles while about twenty muscles twitched in his chest and arms. Actually, I wasn't sure if it was Elan. Standing next to him was his twin brother, Milo. They were mirror replications of the other, right down to their red muscle shirts. I called them the Sack Brothers, because I wasn't good with pronouncing names. Regardless, their mission statement was to make my life a living hell—until they actually sent me to hell. Was now that time?

"Check it out, Milo. I chipped off one of his teeth." Elan and his twin ogre did some type of high five by hooking their elbows together above their heads. Weird.

They laughed and grunted, happy in my misery.

"I'm glad you guys are getting your jollies today." Did the word "jollies" come out as "jowies"? I sounded like a drunk Rocky. Or was it a sober Rocky? Actually, I could use someone with his skill set right about now, not to mention the last six months. These two beasts had followed me across the country.

"Cooper, man, when are you going to learn?" Milo pounded his sledgehammer fist into the opposite hand. "You don't fuck with the Sachen Brothers. And you def...uh, def-i-nite-ly, yeah, definitely, don't fuck with Dr. V."

You'd think English was their second language. It wasn't. The Sack Brothers, whose ancestors were from somewhere in eastern Europe, were born and bred in Jersey. Their form of communication was usually grunting and one-syllable words.

"Right, don't fuck with Dr. V." As the two men-children grunted and chuckled and chest-bumped, I tried to think of an option for escape.

The Sack Brothers had grabbed me off the sidewalk after I left a local coffee shop and literally picked me up and dropped me onto the concrete in this alley. It was void of any living thing, although I think I saw a rat scurrying off when I hit the ground. The brothers not only stood between me and the single opening of the alley back into the street, but they also blocked the early morning sun. Their shadows stretched a good ten feet beyond me, angling up a brick wall that was coated with a gray filth.

I froze. My eyes had just spotted a lead pipe sticking out from under a trash bin. I knew I was no Colonel Mustard, but I took a quick glance at the brothers—they weren't paying me much attention. Not surprising. I was boxed in by two Russian tanks, even if they did have the attention span of first-graders.

My mind ran through a swift scenario of me bolting out of my stance to reach the lead pipe before they could pounce on me. But even with a weapon in my hand, did I have the fighting skills to crack their skulls and escape? I was no Jackie Chan. Hell, I was probably closer to a Jackie Gleason—yes, I know he was a famous comedian; hence, the comparison.

"Don't even think about it, Cooper," Elan said.

Damn. I pushed off one knee and lifted to a standing position. My legs felt like cooked spaghetti. "Think about what?"

"I see that pipe over there. You think you can take us down with that little thing? That's like bringing chopsticks to a nunchuck fight." He hee-hawed at his lame joke and banged elbows with his brother.

I didn't really get his analogy, but who was I to question it? Okay, I guess I was. "But I like Chinese food, so I'm rather proficient with a pair of chopsticks."

They looked at each other, then turned to me. No one spoke for a few seconds. Their blank stares had me wondering how much time it took their brains to decipher a three-syllable word.

"You think we're fucking stupid?" Elan erupted, taking a step closer to me.

That's when I hooked my elbow behind his massive arm and spun around him before he had a chance to bat an eye. One down, one to go. Milo widened his stance and smiled. "Come at me, bitch!" he snorted like a velociraptor about to devour me.

I swallowed, then did my best juke—my go-to move when I played college basketball. Milo crossed his feet; I saw my opening and I took it. One step and Elan snatched me from behind by the collar of my shirt, yanking me backward as though he were cracking a whip.

"Get your ass back here, Cooper. We're not done with you. Not until you pay up."

Fifty grand. That's how much I was in the hole. Technically, it had started at thirty grand. But compound interest being as it is among the illegal-gambling crowd, the debt had taken on an additional twenty grand.

I patted the front and back pockets of my jeans. "Forgot my checkbook, guys. But my bank is just down the corner. Let me run off to the ATM, and I'll be right back with your money." I tried to move, but Milo grabbed me by the back of my neck and pulled me straight up, my shoes barely scraping concrete.

"Hey, what's going on in there?"

I looked up and saw a Dallas cop. Salvation! And then I thought ahead to what would happen if I ratted out the Sack Brothers. Even if I could get the cop to arrest them on assault charges, they'd be out on bail before dinner. And the next time they found me, they'd probably pull my appendages off one by one and sell them on the black market.

"We're just having some fun. Right, Coop?"

Milo lowered me to the ground and patted me on the shoulder like an old pal.

"Yep. We're just practicing a scene."

The cop, who'd started walking into the alley, stopped and adjusted his hat. "A scene?"

"Yeah," I said, scrambling for an idea. "Uh, we're working on a movie that's being shot here in Dallas."

The cop popped a brow. "Seriously?"

I paused a second, reconsidering the idea of the quick-and-easy path to freedom. Throw the brothers in jail. I could run the entire time while the Sack Brothers worked their way through the legal system, but they'd hunt me down. Dr. V's network was too extensive for them not to find me. Nope, not an option.

"Yep, it's an action-thriller."

"But I don't think I've seen you in the movies before," he said, narrowing his eyes.

"Ever seen Bradley Cooper?"

He raised part of his lip, as if a rotten stench had passed by. "I got eyes. You're no Bradley Cooper."

I was almost offended. My mom had actually told me I looked like Bradley Cooper. I never believed her, of course. She was always showering me with unwarranted praise, like I was still a baby-faced toddler.

"Never said I was. But the guys with the money in Hollywood

think I'm the next Bradley Cooper." I shrugged and gave him that aw-shucks smile. I was quite proud of my ability to think on my feet. It came naturally most of the time, although each life-threatening situation was its own animal. Or in this case, two animals.

The cop's radio squawked. He grabbed the shoulder mic and spoke into it, then he looked to us. "Hey, I gotta run. Good luck with the movie." He scooted off.

"Nice work, Cooper. You can lie with the best of them," Milo said.

"Lying is awfully harsh. I call it 'embellishing.' Do you think I look like Bradley Cooper?"

He growled. "You're going off topic again. Back to our fifty grand."

"Oh, right. I'll have it all in a week."

He scoffed. "You've been giving us that same line of bullshit for the last six months. Why should we believe you now?"

I held up three fingers. "Scout's honor."

"Huh?" Elan asked with confusion all over his face.

"I'm saying that you can count on me."

"You're so full of shit." Milo put his paw on my shoulder. I thought he might crack multiple bones.

"I swear. One of the reasons I moved back to Dallas was to be near family and friends. So, I'm working two angles to get my fifty grand."

In all reality, Dallas wasn't much of a home base. I was a corporate brat, moved at least a dozen times in my younger years, including once to Hong Kong.

Elan poked my chest. "That's what you don't get. It's Dr. V's fifty grand, bitch."

"Yeah, bitch," Milo chortled. "You're going to be our bitch unless you turn over fifty grand in one week."

"Would that make this a Russian bitch hunt?" I smiled.

Elan turned his head like a dog that had just heard a high-pitched sound. "You're making fun of us again." He punched me in the gut. I let out an "oomph" and doubled over, trying to find some air.

"I got your Russian bitch hunt right here," he said, grabbing his crotch. The brothers chuckled and started to walk off. Then Milo twisted around to face me and said, "One week, Cooper. That's your last chance to pay up. Fifty grand, or you'll have to pay the price."

They left me alone in the alley. My lungs unfolded, and I took in a few breaths. I had zero chance of securing fifty grand in a week. But at least I had a week to figure something out.

I heard a church's bells go off. "Fuck, I'm late for work."

I headed to the bookstore, where I made minimum wage. While I jogged, I realized I'd have to work five thousand hours before I could repay my debt. I could do the math. Outside of some type of time-traveling technique, I couldn't squeeze five thousand hours into a 168-hour week.

Yep, Cooper Chain was, once again, in a heap of trouble. The kind that could finally get him killed.

Three

Cooper

The jogging lasted for no more than a few steps. I became dizzy, and my brain felt like it was cracking into pieces. Elan's brass-knuckle punch to the face had probably given me a concussion.

I walked into Books and Spirits—adding a bar to their space had been a huge draw in the North Dallas area—looking like there was no urgency. Brandy, my snooty manager who just loved to put her thumb right on top of you, stepped into my personal space before I could come up with an excuse for my lateness.

"You look like a drunk who slept on the street." The top of her head barely reached my chin, but intimidation was her middle name. And despite her undersized body, she had the fight of a pissed-off grizzly.

I wet my fingers and slicked back my hair. Like that would do much for me. I'd ripped a hole in my jeans, and my lip felt like it had tripled in size.

"I haven't had any alcohol. It's ten in the morning, Brandy."

Her eyes, already the size of dinner plates, bulged out like that of a bullfrog. "Oh. My. God."

A customer walked up, saving me from further scrutiny. "Where can I find books about World War III?"

Brandy and I both did a double take. "I'm sorry?" Brandy went from bitch manager to helpful customer service person in a heartbeat.

"You know, WWIII. The big war that *will* happen."

Brandy and I exchanged a glance. I shrugged, then a thought hit me. "Are you looking for post-apocalyptic books?"

"Yeah, I guess that's what non-believers call them."

Non-believers?

"Here," Brandy said, "let me walk you to that section." They tottered away.

Cool. Freedom. I made my way to the employee breakroom and punched in so I could start earning that fifty grand. Instead of allowing my mind to drift into considering my next big feature story I wanted to write, or even a great book idea, I decided to spend my entire eight-hour shift working on how to get out of this debt dilemma. Hell, you can't work retail for minimum wage and not think about something else most of the time without losing your sanity.

I walked into the bathroom and flinched at my reflection in the mirror. I cleaned some dried blood off my lip and splashed cold water on my face to try to break through the mental cobwebs.

"Ready to make it a great day, Cooper?" I said with as much sarcasm as I could muster, pumping my fist in the air. The fact is, my one-liners rarely gave me much satisfaction unless I had an audience. As of late, though, my audience had dwindled severely, given my cross-country jaunt to escape Dr. V. and his legion of doom, as well as searching for a place where I wasn't considered a leper. Talking to myself was a tad more exciting than chatting it up with Brandy or any of my esteemed colleagues, most of whom were either in college or tap-dancing into retirement. Me? I was right in the middle. Thirty-nine years old. I should be nearing the apex of my career, kicking ass and taking names. Instead, I had about three hundred bucks in the bank and could no longer legally vote. And that was the good news. My personal life was even more depressing, especially since the Sack Brothers had given me a week to live.

I tossed a paper towel in the trash, emerged from the bathroom, and made my way across the breakroom. Brandy marched into the room so fast I stumbled back a couple of steps. Even then, she stuck with me like an All-Pro defensive back. "Cooper, what the hell is going on?" she asked, folding her arms across her chest.

"Green eggs and ham."

She shook her head like a wet dog. "What?"

"You had one of your egg-and-ham sandwiches for breakfast. I assume the eggs weren't green, though." I waved a hand in front of my face. She seemed to get the picture, and she backed off.

Brandy was an interesting individual. She'd recently earned a master's degree at Southern Methodist University, which was just down the road, but was managing a bookstore. Yes, an actual brick-and-mortar bookstore. Probably had something to do with her father running a major telecommunications company.

In reality, though, I was the stupid one. She had a fallback plan, even if it was her parents' net (worth). I took this job not only because I couldn't get any other job (long story), but also because I'd heard through the rumor mill that local literary agents and magazine publishers frequented this bookstore. Just thinking through the odds that any rational person would put on running into one of those very few people made me question my sanity.

"Whatever. Figures you'd quote a children's book." She rolled those voluminous eyes. It was like watching a white eclipse.

I decided not to remind her of the Freudian messages Dr. Seuss had allegedly offered through his children's books.

"So, I've washed the blood off my lip. I'm good to go." I clapped my hands as though I were thrilled to have the opportunity to run out into the store and start doing the retail thing.

She tilted her head forward and squinted. "What happened to

your tooth?"

I glanced off to the corner and spotted one of those inspirational signs she'd put up so that the employees could draw some inspiration: *"Life is like a mirror. We get the best results when we smile at it."* I noticed the author was "unknown." No good wordsmith would ever associate their name with such a lame saying.

"Your tooth," she said, pointing a finger at my mouth. "What happened to your tooth?"

I smiled, which made her wince. "It's kind of a weird story. Probably not something you'd want to hear about."

"I can only imagine." She released an audible sigh then started tapping her foot. "I took a chance on you, Cooper. How many people are going to hire a convicted felon?"

Apparently, just one. I knew the job sucked major donkey dicks, but it was still a paying job. Something I couldn't find in New York City. "I appreciate the opportunity you're giving me, Brandy. You ready to go sell some books?"

She bit the inside of her cheek and stared at me. Those manhole-sized eyes nearly made me quiver. I tried not to whistle while she debated my fate. "You can go on a delivery run."

"Delivery? Like a pizza guy?"

"You know, the bridal magazines that we deliver to all the wedding businesses."

I had no recollection of this information, but I nodded anyway. "Oh, right. Bridal magazines."

"You'll find the boxes just inside the closet by the back door. I'm assuming your car is running?"

I was assuming she didn't want to know the truth. My car was sitting just outside of my garage apartment, as it had been for the last three weeks. This morning I thought I saw blades of grass poking up against the back fender. "I'm as reliable as a postal delivery guy," I said with a wink.

Even though I couldn't see it, I just know she rolled her eyes after she turned to walk out of the room.

I followed. "Hey, can you recommend a cheap dentist?"

"Maybe. How cheap?"

"Free cheap." I tried not to smile, but somehow that Bradley Cooper grin showed itself again.

She turned away while giving me the hand. "Just deliver the magazines, please."

I was all too happy for the break from retail hell.

Four

Cooper

I walked a good two miles while carrying three boxes that had to weigh at least fifty pounds. The poor slaves who'd built the World Cup facilities in Qatar had to have been treated better.

I was joking, of course. Brandy had her issues, but she wasn't in the same galaxy as the people who ran FIFA, the poster-child organization for greed and corruption. But the corruption in FIFA was about more than fixing games and paying dirty money to bribe both public and private officials. It had led to thousands of people being brought in from other countries with promises of paying jobs but then literally being forced to work for food and water. Definitely a story worth telling at a deeper level. That was the kind of feature sports story I'd grown accustomed to writing over the last fifteen years. Until my world imploded six months ago.

I stopped for a second and wondered if I'd gotten lost. My knee was throbbing, and it felt like I'd undergone an ice-pick implant in my lower back.

"Screw it." I dropped the boxes by the curb and sat down on a bus bench. Even though it was close to sixty degrees outside, I wiped sweat from my forehead and rubbed my bum knee.

"Hey, that's not allowed."

I looked up and, through the glare of the sun, saw a man who looked like a gray porcupine. His spiked head of gelled hair didn't capture my attention for long because the man had more wrinkles than a shriveled prune.

"I'm sorry. What's not allowed?"

"Those of us who take the bus might trip over your boxes. And we all need a seat."

I looked around. No one else was standing nearby. "There's plenty of room on the bench. I'll just be a minute. Need to rest for a sec."

"You're young. Why do you need to rest?"

Did I really need to explain my life to this old guy? "Just trying to figure out where a bridal shop is."

"You talking about Posh Bridal Couture?"

"Yeah, that's it."

"One block that way," he said, pointing down the block. "Highland Park Village. You heard of that, haven't you?"

I should have known. Highland Park, surrounded by the city of Dallas on all sides, was the most affluent zip code in Texas. "Uh, yeah." I got to my feet, arched my back. "Thanks for the tip."

"Any time. Just don't sit on my bench, okay?"

"Roger that." I lifted the boxes and tried to summon my second wind. I was sucking air by the time I swung open the door to the bridal shop and a lady in a flowing blue dress quickly approached me.

"You must have the wrong place, sir," she said, grabbing my elbow and trying to usher me back outside.

"Nope." I let go of the boxes, and they landed with a thud that drew about a dozen stares. All women. I gave them a mock salute. "No shots fired. All good," I said with a smile.

The lady said, "Who are you with?"

"Books and Spirits. Just delivering your magazines," I said while checking the place out. Soft elevator music, lots of white, and almost everyone was holding champagne flutes. It wasn't even noon. Posh Bridal Couture had the buying experience down pat—get them drunk, tell the brides they looked beautiful, and then charge ten grand for a dress.

The employee put her hands at her waist and stuck out her prominent chin. "I thought you'd know better."

"Know what better?"

"All deliveries should be made through the back, so as not to interrupt the heavenly ambiance for our guests in the showroom," she said in a velvety voice.

"Sorry. My back and knee are killing me. Mind if I just take them to the back from here?"

A sigh. "Well, if you must, but please be quiet and don't speak to anyone," she said with a huff.

I bit my tongue and lifted up the boxes again. I walked ten steps, then heard a bunch of women gasping to my left. I swung my sights in that direction and stopped moving.

I'd either had a stroke and was hallucinating, or…it was real.

"Sir, did you hear me?"

I ignored the devil in the blue dress and stared at the woman spinning around in her wedding dress for all her friends to admire. Then she looked up and caught my awestruck gaze.

"Cooper?"

The voice sounded like her. The hair, up in bun with curls spilling everywhere, was the same montage of fall colors. But it was those damn eyes—eyes of maple sugar—that made my knees buckle.

The next thing I heard were the boxes tumbling to the floor.

She walked in my direction, reached out and touched my arm. "Cooper. It's really you."

I almost stuttered. "Willow?"

Then she punched me in the shoulder. Hard. Yep, it was Willow Ball. My old college flame. From the power in that punch, I knew I was in more deep shit.

Five

Willow

The last person I expected to see—wanted to see—a week before my wedding was Cooper Chain. So why was I hurriedly changing back into my jeans and Oxford shirt while he hung out with my lady friends?

Oh, yeah. I wanted to kick his ass.

"Hey, Willow, the ladies are waiting." It was the sing-song voice of Alli, my long-time friend and maid of honor.

"Just a second." I put my hand over my chest; my heart was racing. Why? He meant nothing to me. Well, maybe a little resentment still lingered. Throw in the timing of his grand entrance, and I guess it made sense why I was so…on edge?

I pushed the curtain to the side and spotted Cooper chatting up two of my friends and a cousin. They had no idea of our history, and he was the only male in the whole place. By the look on his face, he was soaking it up. He was a magnet to women. Or was it the opposite? Not sure. My brain seemed foggy and confused.

He nodded a couple of times, offered a few words in response, although I couldn't hear the conversation. But more than anything, he looked engaged, as if their stories were important. It was a prominent skill, one that I was certain he was born with. A combination of wit and charm that could be used for good or evil. I'd seen both in action. Once, when two mountain-sized bikers had pulled a blade on an innocent teenage kid who'd accidentally touched one of their precious motorcycles, Cooper convinced them that the kid wasn't worth their time. I can still recall the fear in that boy's eyes. Hell, my insides had been trembling as well. But Cooper talked them out of it, and no blood was shed.

On the evil side of the ledger—well, my definition of Cooper evil, anyway—he could use his aw-shucks smile and self-deprecating humor to pretty much have his way with almost any woman. In fact, it was happening right now!

I could feel my arms swinging and my legs marching in their direction before my brain had caught up with the involuntary movement. What was I doing? Hell, what was *he* doing?

"Oh, hey, Willow. We were just introducing ourselves to your friend Cooper," my cousin Marion said. Her smile had "smitten" written all over it.

"Wonderful," I said with not an ounce of enthusiasm.

Marion conspicuously leaned closer to me. "He's kind of cute. Is he taken?"

I could feel one of my recently sculpted eyebrows inch higher. I wanted to say either, "How the hell would I know?" or "Only if some girl had been drinking his spiked Kool-Aid." Instead, I casually shrugged. No big deal, right? "For all I know, Cooper is running from the cops."

The girls and I chuckled, but Cooper's smile never made it to the laughter state. That's when I saw something that sent a memory shockwave through my body. His tooth.

I gently touched his elbow. "We're about to walk out the door, but do you have a quick second?"

"Uh, yeah. I thought that's why you wanted me to stick around." He was trying to catch up to me as I walked judiciously over to the rack of bridesmaid dresses. I flipped around, flashed a smile at anyone watching, then spoke with a clenched jaw.

"What is this?" I tapped my front tooth with my fingernail.

He slowly moved his hand to his mouth.

"And your lip. Did you get in a fight? It's like we're back in college when you were hit in the mouth with that golf club. Wait, didn't Alli's brother swing that club?"

He opened his mouth, but no words came out. Was Cooper actually tongue-twisted? I stared at the chipped tooth. Was it fake?

Suddenly, the dots on this whole scene magically came together and I started laughing, although the sound of my own voice shocked me. It had a sinister edge to it. "This…this appearance out of nowhere, this elaborate charade could only be the work of the ultimate prankster, Alli's brother. He's trying to get me riled up by making you wear makeup and this fake chipped tooth, right?"

I didn't let him respond. "I'm sure of it. That must be it. It's been eighteen years, but old Benjamin must have put you up to this just to get me frazzled before my wedding. Is he hiding around here somewhere, catching all this on his phone?" I scanned the main area. "Knowing my luck, he'll post it all over social media just to make me and Harvey look—"

"Harvey?" Cooper's expression was like a big question mark.

"Don't mock him. He's the man I love."

He moved his shoulders and head as if he were confused. "I don't understand the point of what you're suggesting."

"What? Are you naïve? Or are you still sticking with the script Benjamin gave you?"

"Actually, I've only seen him once since I got back. He dropped by the bookstore."

I went still. "Got back," I repeated, my brain still playing catchup with what he'd just said.

He nodded a single time.

"Bookstore? Wait, I thought I heard you were some type of

big-time writer." Almost instantly, my state of mind went back to my pre-Harvey days, and the comparison horse raced out of the barn.

"Something wrong?" he said.

"Nothing." I turned and started shifting dresses on the rack.

"Willow, I had no idea you'd be here."

I tried to ignore him and not replay my demoralizing fall from the perch of respect and normalcy.

"You're upset."

"I'm not upset, Cooper. Don't give yourself that much credit. It's been eighteen years since you just walked away."

"But—"

"Willow, everything cool?" Alli's voice made me flinch.

I turned my head, and her eyes shifted to Cooper and back to me.

"Yeah, all good. Just catching up." I wanted to ask if she knew anything about Benjamin's prank, but now I was doubting my intuition. Dammit, I hated when Cooper made me do that!

"Okay," she said. A mischievous grin lit up her face as she strummed her fingers together. "All of us are dying to start phase two of your twenty-four-hour bachelorette party."

"I'm curious, but I'm wondering if I should also be afraid." I could feel my forehead begin to furrow. "I don't want Harvey thinking that I'm some kind of rabble-rouser."

Cooper muttered something under his breath while scratching the back of his head.

"Did you say something?"

"Oh, me? No, just talking to myself."

I gritted my teeth as I turned my sights back to Alli. "I'm eager for phase two as well. Just one more quick second."

"No problem. It's your day." As she turned around, she glanced at Cooper. "Good seeing you, Cooper."

"Yeah, you too, Alli."

She walked off.

"She hasn't changed much," he said. "Just as aloof as ever."

"Only to you," I said, tilting my head. *Damn, that was cold.* "Did I just say that?"

"Yeah, you kinda did."

I took a deep inhale and released a long breath. "Lots going on with the wedding. Just never expected you to show up."

"I get it. No apologies necessary."

"I never said I was sorry."

He smirked, and I touched a nail to my front tooth again. I couldn't help myself.

"Cooper, what's going on?"

"You tell me. You're getting married, and life has been perfect since eighteen years ago."

If he only knew.

"Willow!" the girls yelled as a group.

"Hey, I need to run. But if you're still going to be in town, you want to meet for lunch tomorrow?"

Did I really just suggest that?

"Where at?" he asked too quickly before I could walk back what I'd said.

I slowed down my emotional responses and just looked at him for a moment. Outside of his swollen lip and chipped tooth, he seemed…off. Was it something as simple as him being older, maybe a little more mature? My Cooper compass couldn't pick up a definitive reading. That made me curious and, if I were being honest with myself, a little worried too.

"How about that little sandwich shop off Mockingbird?"

"I remember it well," he said with his patented wink.

"We can catch up and maybe have a more proper way of finalizing our relationship."

"Look, I'm not sure—"

"I'll see you at noon."

I was out the door before he could utter another word.

Six

Cooper

I asked Brandy if I could work a double shift, and her response was classic Brandy: she gave me a devilish smile. You know, the same kind that your old coach would give if you'd just blurted a curse word in the middle of a student assembly.

Funny how life's experiences come full circle in some ways.

I did my best to ignore her passive-aggressive behavior toward me and went about completing the tasks of my job, as mundane as they were. For once, I actually stayed focused on the work at hand. I didn't drift off into fantasizing about getting the red-carpet treatment in similar bookstores as my publisher picks up the tab for my wildly successful book tour. And, surprisingly, I avoided thinking about Willow. For the most part.

"Can't keep living in the past, Coop," I said to myself as I stocked the shelves of the Self-Help and Relationships section. I paused a second, staring at a book I was holding. The title was *One Man's Story: How I Learned If I Still Loved My Old College Sweetheart.*

Did that just happen? I lifted my sights to the ceiling as if that had all the answers. My dear mother carried the religious torch in our family. I was raised Catholic, but in my young life, I mostly just practiced the religion of rebellion. I took another glance at the book. Yep, my eyes hadn't transformed the book title. It was still the same.

I huffed out a breath and momentarily allowed my thoughts to drift into a quick montage of Willow images—most carried her signature smile, but some also captured her serious side, especially when she was competing at anything. Her shoulders weren't large—the torso of her tall, slender frame was on the small side—but her muscles rippled like a mountain range on a 3-D map. Still, she always said she had chubby thighs. I begged to differ. Those thighs had the squeezing power of a twenty-foot viper, but they were not chubby.

Willow Ball. The first woman I'd ever loved. As much as I didn't want to admit it, I could feel something churning inside. But I was in no mood for sifting through the remnants of my life right now. Maybe ever. Too many pitfalls and potholes going down that ugly path.

The chime from the front door jarred my attention, and I eased back into stocking the shelves.

People came in and out of the bookstore as day turned to night. Some just wanted to find a quiet spot to read—we had a few couches and lounge chairs in the corner. A few made their way over to our bar (thus, the "Spirits" in our store name, Books and Spirits) and enjoyed a cocktail or beer. Others would peruse a book here and there as if they were just biding time. And a handful would actually purchase a book. Truth be told, we also sold a fair amount of junk, the kind of little trinkets you'd get from your grandmother for Christmas.

"Mr. Chain…"

I turned to see a little old lady peering up at me. If she wasn't hunched over, I'd probably only stand a foot taller than her. Right now, you could add at least three or four inches to that.

"Hi, Mrs. Kowalski."

She had a blue leather purse hooked in the crook of her arm, which matched her yellow and blue hat and a dress that seemed more suited for church than our bookstore.

"I didn't know you were working today...well, and tonight, apparently. Your car still isn't running properly?"

Mrs. Kowalski was my landlord. She lived alone in the big house, the one that might be as old as her, and probably had just as many stories woven into its history. She usually kept a close watch on my comings and goings; my apartment was situated above her detached garage.

"I'm sure it just needs a new battery. I've been too busy to mess with it. I can push it behind the garage if it's too much of an eyesore for the neighborhood."

She was so close she was almost under my chin. "Mr. Chain, I've told you how many times that you're welcome to borrow my old DeLorean?"

Yes, Mrs. Kowalski actually had one of the very few DeLorean sports cars—the ones made famous in the *Back to the Future* movies. She paid a mechanic to come to the house to perform monthly maintenance. She said she couldn't bring herself to let go of the old car. It was a classic, just like her. When I first started living on her property three months ago and she told me that her husband was deceased, I'd made the mistake of asking if that car used to belong to him. Her response told me everything about her.

"That asshat never appreciated anything fun or exciting about life."

At first, I was stunned, and she must have read my body language.

"You think I'm a bitter old woman. Well, I actually divorced his ass before he died," she'd said. "I found him in bed with my neighbor with his head between her legs. And after she left, he had the gall to think I'd have to stay with him because I was reliant on him. Screw that. I went back to school, received my JP degree, became a county judge, and practiced law on the side for thirty-two years. Stashed away a nice sum of money. But I also pledged to never be dependent on a man to meet any of my needs."

I heard people laughing, and I turned to see what looked like a father and a teenage daughter standing near the magazine section. They had the same tapered jawline and long neck. My mind snapped back to more memories. What was this…"shock Cooper" day?

"Mr. Chain?"

"Uh, yeah. I appreciate you offering up the DeLorean. It's very nice of you. But I don't have insurance on it."

"That's hogwash. You can drive a car, can't you?"

"But that's no average car. I'd be nervous the moment I pulled onto the road. Now, you might catch me in the garage occasionally just sitting in it and pretending I'm flying through the air like Marty McFly."

Her face lit up. "Now that's more like it. If you can't dream a little, what's life worth living for?"

I smiled at the fact that I was being instructed to never stop dreaming by an eighty-eight-year-old woman.

She checked her watch. "I think you get off in about fifteen minutes, don't you?"

I gave her a straight-lipped smile. I thought she'd recall that I wasn't into accepting charity rides. It felt too much like being a teenager, when I had to rely on Mom to be my main mode of transportation.

"Hold on, mister. You think I forgot that you don't like me to be your chauffeur?"

"No, I figured you remembered," I said, trying to save face.

"Good. I'm just timing our exits. I'm meeting a new male friend for a quick drink before the bar shuts down."

My eyes went wide. She never ceased to amaze me, this woman.

"Now, don't worry about me. I met him in the Biography section a couple of weeks ago. He's nice, quite funny, and he's easy on the eyes."

My mouth fell open to match my wide eyes. To be honest, I'd met Mrs. Kowalski here at the bookstore. That was how I learned she was renting out her garage apartment. But that was different. Very different.

"Don't be so surprised, Mr. Chain. A woman has needs, even at my advanced age."

Did she just share that? Tell me no. "Well, I need to check in with Brandy and see what she needs me to do tonight for closing," I said, scanning the bookstore for Brandy or anyone else who might need my help.

Mrs. Kowalski started giggling. Well, it was more like a happy cackle. And it didn't stop. "Well, since you don't need a ride home, I might just hang out with my new friend a while."

"But we close in just a few minutes."

"You're kind of slow at times, Mr. Chain. He tells me he has a large SUV. Plenty of room for little old me."

Before I could beg her to stop, she walked off while whistling some happy tune.

She'd made me sweat but also offered a little perspective. Life was all about your attitude.

If you start whistling Broadway show tunes, will that drop fifty grand in your lap so you can avoid being pummeled by the Sack Brothers?

The shot of realism punctured my happy bubble. I worked another forty-five minutes to help close the store and then walked out the front door.

"Help a man who's down on his luck?"

I looked to my right and saw a man, who I assumed was homeless, sitting against the wall. A cardboard sign that was leaning against his knee read: *Money for food please.* His ill-fitting clothes had holes at the elbows and knees. The bags under his eyes could have cradled a quarter, and he looked like he hadn't shaved or bathed in weeks.

As I searched my pockets for loose change, two college-aged guys walked up while holding beers.

"Hey, look at this pathetic loser," said the guy with a green sweater tied around his waist. "You have to beg for money just because you're too damn lazy to get a real job?"

He and his buddy both busted out in laughter.

I could feel my internal temperature rising by the second. I gave them another quick once-over. Both wore jeans that had the casual worn look, but I knew they probably cost north of two hundred bucks. Same for the shoes and their preppy sweaters. One wore a watch that looked like something you'd see on a retiring executive, while the "Bif" character with the green sweater twirled a set of BMW keys in his hand. They were living the life—on Mommy's or Daddy's dime, most likely.

I had no knowledge of this homeless guy's background. I only knew about the statistics. Many suffered from severe mental illness. During my stint as an investigative sports reporter for the *New York Daily News*, I'd come across a lot of stories that were tragic and had no happy ending, and some included athletes or family members of said athletes who'd found themselves living out of the back of their cars, or even asking for a few dollars from passers-by. That experience not only became the pinnacle of my journalistic career, it opened my eyes to a world I'd never witnessed or thought a lot about. And given my recent demise, I wasn't very far from falling into the same situation. If there was anything that I'd learned, it was once you experienced adversity, suddenly your perspective changed a great deal.

I took a step toward Bif and his sidekick. "Guys, just leave the man alone. He's not doing anything to you."

"Who the fuck are you?" Bif sneered, moving within inches of my face. His beer breath billowed across my space. It was all I could do not to back up or push him away. But I was determined to do neither.

"I'm just a guy working retail who sees someone who could use some help." My voice was nice and calm, although, admittedly, I could feel that little flutter inside. The one that knows there's a strong possibility this could quickly turn into a physical confrontation. It was like a barometer.

Out of the corner of my eye, I could see his beer bottle dangling from his hand. I could likely snatch it from his grip before he knew it. He might tackle me, but I was sure I could swing him off me and crack the bottle against his head. Then there was his buddy. He was probably just as drunk, so his response time would be impaired. But there was also an element of unpredictability. Would he turn and run? Not likely. Stand there in awe? Maybe. Try to hit me with his beer bottle? That was an option, and one I might be able to thwart. But what if he was one of those so-called tough guys carrying a concealed handgun—just because he could. Bad shit could happen to me and others.

I moved around Bif, pulled some loose change out of my pocket, and dropped it in a tin can next to the homeless man.

"Hey, bro, I think he just dissed you," the other guy said.

Bif turned around with a scowl on his face. I thought he might crack the bottle over his own head. "Fuck you," he said, pointing at his buddy. "And fuck you!" He shot me the bird.

He then removed a wad of cash from his front pocket, plucked out a hundred-dollar bill, and stuffed it in the can. "No one makes me look bad. Let's get the hell out of this place. It smells."

He and his beer buddy walked off.

"Dear God, it's a gift from above. I don't know how to thank you," the man said with emotion in his voice.

I glanced over my shoulder to make sure the boneheads were really leaving, then I turned back to the man. "I'd find another place to do your thing. The next set of characters might get violent."

"Yes, sir. I'll do that. Have a great night."

"You too." I quickly scooted away from Books and Spirits. My psyche could be permanently damaged if I saw Mrs. Kowalski crawling into the back of some guy's SUV.

Seven

It had been eighteen years, four months, and twenty-one days.

And the man wept.

He had friends who'd kicked a drug habit or alcohol addiction. They counted days. It made them feel good about making it one more day. Many of them said that counting the days of their sobriety kept it relevant in their minds and allowed them to live a humble existence. They knew that one line of coke or one shot of vodka could end it all. And then the counting would start all over again. And that was only if that one mistake didn't snowball into drinking two bottles of vodka within three hours and their brains shutting down for good.

Initially born from disillusionment with society, the man's feelings and belief system had evolved over the years. He had witnessed cruelty and hatred on a level that he never thought humans were capable of. At least not under normal circumstances.

But what about this world over the last eighteen years has been normal?

A sharp intake of air. He wiped tears from his face and released a long, deep breath. The emotional episode had been somewhat liberating because he knew his mind was now clear on what needed to happen.

He pulled a picture from his pocket and tilted it toward the glow of the full moon. He focused on the person who stood out from the crowd, not just for her captivating smile and sparkling emerald eyes, but because he could practically feel the kindness flowing from her.

It made his heart soar. At the same time, it also made his heart feel like it was being squeezed to bursting like a supernova. He thought about the polar-opposite emotions swirling through his brain. Some might think he was conflicted about the world, about how to respond to the near-constant barrage of attacks. Social media was the worst, but it wasn't the only medium of dysfunctional cruelty. Much of it was woven into our institutions—locking up kids in cages like they were animals just because they were born a few hundred miles south. Other forms of cruelty were direct and confrontational, meant to create separation: *I'm better than you.* That was the underlying message of the many people who seemed to swim in the pool of cruelty.

And it was one big fucking pool. A cesspool.

He heard a car door shut and lifted his torso to see the woman clumsily walking away from one of those Uber cars. The four-door Camry sped off, and she stumbled her way around the corner of the apartment building. Taking a quick scan of the complex, no one was outside. If someone happened to be glancing out a window—and who would be doing that at almost two in the morning?—they'd see a pizza delivery man with a red and blue cap on his head carrying a pizza pouch.

He walked swiftly across the open space, ducked under the low-hanging limbs of a live oak, and entered the cove where the woman was just now opening her door.

Perfect timing.

"Hey, there. I got the pizza you ordered," he said, holding his pouch up to his eyes.

She awkwardly turned around while stumbling inside her darkened apartment. "I didn't order a frickin' pizza."

"Well, this is apartment 108, correct?"

"Yep. But it wasn't me."

He stopped and adjusted his cap. "Well, if you don't want it, I guess I'll take it back to the store. I probably messed up. My manager will chew my ass out." He started to turn to walk away.

"Wait. Hold on a second. I don't want you to get into trouble. That's crazy."

His extremities began to tingle, and it was all he could do not to quiver with excitement. He slowly turned around to face her.

"Come on in," she said, setting her purse on the table and sifting through it. "What kind of pizza is it?"

"It's the works. All meats, all veggies, and even extra cheese." He quietly shut the door and ambled into the small foyer. "Nice setup you have here."

"Thanks." She kept her head down while fishing through her purse. "A pizza sounds good after a night of debauchery and drinking." She glanced at the man and giggled.

"I'm sure you were just having fun," he said.

"I probably had a little too much fun. I might pay for it tomorrow, but maybe this pizza will soak up some of the alcohol." She paused, putting a hand to her chin.

"What is it?" He could hear a bit of panic in his voice. Things couldn't go awry at this point. Not after waiting eighteen years, four months, and twenty-one days.

"Dammit. I think I left my wallet in my friend's purse. Or did I toss it up on the stage when…?" She pressed her lips shut.

"When…?" he prompted.

"Oh, nothing. I'm sure it will turn up. I'll call my friend, all of my friends, tomorrow. Wait. Hold on for a second," she said, lifting a finger. She walked over to what looked like an urn sitting on the mantle. "I used to hide cigarettes from my ex. Little did he know he drove me to smoking. All that's in the past now. Thank you, Jesus!" She lifted up on her toes and reached a hand into the urn. "I think I stashed a spare twenty-dollar bill in here."

"Cool. I'll get your pizza out." He set the pouch on the table and pulled back the Velcro.

"You're welcome to have a slice if you're hungry. I'm sure I won't be able to eat the whole thing myself."

He didn't respond.

"Don't tell me you don't like pizza," she said. "There. Got it!" She held up the twenty-dollar bill and flipped around. He was standing inches in front of her, a wide smile on his face.

She flinched. "Oh! You scared me."

"You have no reason to be scared," he said, his voice subdued and calm.

For one second, her face relaxed. He would always remember that face.

Before she could move, he threw the bag over her head and pulled the rip cord. It snapped taut against her neck.

Then he hugged her. She struggled to move her arms for a moment. But then she went to sleep. In his arms. Peacefully. Just the way it was meant to be.

A single tear rolled down his face. Relief. Finally. After eighteen years, four months, and twenty-one days.

But when the sun rose in the morning, he knew he couldn't start counting the days again. There was much more to accomplish.

All in the name of mercy.

Eight

Cooper

The brisk walk across town was uneventful—no sign of the Sack Brothers. Not that I expected to run into the twin numbnuts, but I knew firsthand that whenever Dr. V was in the mix, terms and conditions of this one-week extension could change in an instant. And in a very volatile manner.

I arrived at the sandwich shop before Willow. That was my first surprise. She was like a programmable robot when it came to keeping her life and anything that touched it organized. Clean freak? Check. Obsessive-compulsive? Double check. She was so anal that the cans in her pantry all faced forward. Perfectly spaced too.

"Boo!"

I flinched and turned around to see Willow struggling to smile, a hand to the side of her head. Her eyes were hidden behind a pair sunglasses. Were those ROKA sunglasses? Those frickin' things cost over two hundred bucks!

"Thanks. I needed that. I really did," I deadpanned.

"Uggh. I shouldn't have raised my voice. Feels like I put my head in a blender."

I smiled and led the way toward the shop's front door. She

grabbed my arm. "Let's sit outside. I need the fresh air."

"Works for me."

We found a table in the shade of a street-side live oak. I noticed her attire—loose-fitting sweat pants, a purple and black Lycra top that hugged her body, and a sweat jacket tied around her waist.

"So, how was phase two?" I asked as I grabbed a menu and looked for the cheapest option.

She adjusted her glasses. "Phase two?"

"Alli said at the wedding dress place that you and your girlfriends were about start phase two of your bachelorette party."

"Oh, right. The phases kind of ran together." She held up a hand, and a waiter walked over. "Can I get some water please?"

Water was free, so I was on board. Just wasn't sure who would be picking up the tab. "I'll take a water as well."

"But," she said, holding up a single finger like she was an elementary school teacher, "do you happen to have any Evian?"

The guy quickly looked at me, then swung back to her. "Not sure. I'll have to check the fridge."

"Well, just bring me the best bottled water that you have."

"The best?"

"You know, the highest alkaline level."

"Alka-what?'"

"Seltzer," I said, doing a quick drumroll and rimshot on the table. "*Ba-dum. Tshh.*"

"Please don't rattle the table, Cooper. My head is pounding."

"Sorry." I could see she was in pain. I could be a sarcastic ass, but whenever the women in my life were in pain, I instantly turned into a softie. I looked up at the man. "My friend's in a lot of pain, so just bring out the best bottled water you have."

"Roger that."

He started to walk off.

"Oh, sir," Willow called. "Could you also give me some lemons?"

"Sure."

"One more thing. Make sure they're cut into small wedges so I can drop them in the bottled water."

He turned his eyes to me. I knew what he was thinking: this was a sandwich shop, not some five-star swanky restaurant you might find in Uptown. "I appreciate you helping us out," I said.

He shrugged and went inside.

"So," I said, turning back to Willow, "did anyone get arrested last night?"

"What the hell is that supposed to mean?"

Oops. I'd accidentally stepped on a mine. "It was just a joke, Willow. You doing okay?"

"I'm fine. It's just this headache. Sorry. I guess I'm kind of cranky." She peered over my shoulder, apparently looking for the waiter.

"If he's not out here with some type of water in a minute, I'll go check on it."

"Thank you." Her voice was calm and kind. I wanted to look into those eyes, but the tint on her damn glasses was too dark.

Then I thought again. Perhaps it was best for her to be cloaked behind a shield.

The waiter brought out two bottled waters. I wished I had asked for a simple glass of tap water. Free water. But I didn't want Willow to think she was having lunch with a cheapskate, even though she was.

Willow scrunched up her nose. "Dasani? That's the best you have?"

"That's all we got." He set the bottles on the table.

"What about the lemons?"

"I've got our lemon chef working on that right now." He put a hand to his face and quietly chuckled while giving me the eye— as if this were a guy bonding moment. I resisted the urge to pile on. Point for me.

Willow wasn't laughing. He quickly saw her straight face and said, "I'll go grab the lemons. You guys want to order or just drink bottled water?"

We ordered sandwiches, and the waiter walked off. A minute later, he returned with the lemons, then scampered away again.

"So, Cooper…" She paused, pulled a plastic container from her purse, removed a pill, placed it in her mouth, and chugged a few gulps of water. Then she squeezed two lemons into the bottle.

"What was that?"

"Vitamin B6. The best thing for a hangover."

Should have figured the woman with the nursing degree would know that.

"You never told me how you got all of this," she said, waving a hand in front of her mouth. She was referring to my chipped tooth and swollen lip, which didn't look that bad today.

"I ran into a door."

She shook her head. "The real story, Cooper."

"What is this…*True Detective*?"

"Funny."

"I thought this lunch was supposed to be our way of burying any resentment and parting ways with a clear conscience."

"You're deflecting again."

I was tempted to offer a retort, but I could see that would only escalate into a confrontation. Despite what some might think, I wasn't big on confrontations, especially with people I cared about. I just didn't respond.

She looked off, sipped her water, and crossed her legs. Then she started kicking her top leg—a sure sign that something was bothering her.

"You just left me, back in college. One quick phone call, and then you were gone."

"That was a sudden turn down memory lane," I said with a smile.

She didn't smile back. Her head was still being held upright by her hand.

Okay, here we go. "I thought about writing a note and slipping it under your door, but—"

"Are you fucking serious?"

"But I didn't do it, right? I called you on the phone because I didn't want you to think that you didn't mean something to me."

"A two-minute conversation and very one-sided." She went back to kicking, and the waiter arrived with our sandwiches. Mine was a BLT. I took a crunchy bite, then chased it with some water. She just kept kicking that damn leg.

I put my napkin on the table and leaned toward her. "Hey, Will."

She turned, opened her mouth, then closed it. "No one has called me 'Will' in eighteen years."

I'd forgotten that had been my pet name for her. Back in the day, she'd thought it was endearing, but that was a long time ago. "I didn't mean to offend you. You're no guy, that's rather obvious." I tried laughing, but it was a little awkward. I released a deep breath and gave it another shot. "I'm sorry I left without talking to you more about why I made that decision."

"To go play basketball," she said, as if playing Division I basketball was the same as twiddling my thumbs.

"It was a D-I offer, Will. I couldn't pass it up. When you're twenty-one and you don't really have a clear direction in college, and you get a call from your old high school coach who's now an assistant at the D-I school, you take it. You just do."

She nodded and kicked the leg. "I thought we had something pretty special."

I looked at my food. I'd suddenly lost my appetite. I wasn't particularly good with being cornered on the decisions I'd made in my life. I felt the itch to get up and walk out.

"You want to leave, don't you?"

"Are you a fucking mind reader?"

"'Cut-and-run.' That should be your nickname. Cooper 'Cut-and-run' Chain." She swallowed, then uttered under her breath, "Just like Dad."

"Ouch."

I recalled her telling me something about her father leaving when she was young. She'd hated him for it. I wondered if they'd ever reconnected. I got the feeling she hated me for leaving as well.

Her phone chirped, and she pulled it from her purse. She quickly got lost in some inane text or post for a good minute. I looked around. Yes, I was searching for an exit, figuratively and literally.

She giggled, and I turned to look at her. She'd just lifted her glasses, and her eyes made my heart bounce like I'd been hit with a pair of shock paddles.

I grabbed my water and downed a gulp. "What's so funny?"

"Just some pictures from last night. Alli and Jennie were a riot."

"Jennie, your sister. How's she doing?"

She tilted her head. "She's like the rest of us. Been through some rough spots. She got married and divorced within a year quite a while ago. Doing pretty good these days, I guess. But she's just a book nerd now. She reads three, four books a week. I think that's her substitute for having ten cats. Or even one man."

We both laughed.

"You were a good writer in college, Cooper. Not surprising that you made it a career."

"How would you know I was any good?"

She twisted her lips in a playful way. "I kind of peeked in your journal."

"Really?"

"I was curious."

"Did you think I was keeping a secret girl on the side?" I asked with obvious sarcasm.

"While you do have the playboy persona—at least you did when we met—I was pretty sure I had you tied around my finger."

"You think so, huh?"

"No?"

I sighed. "Actually, you're right, and you know it. Honestly, it kind of scared me."

"And that's why you ran off?"

"It was all about basketball. I worshipped that sport, even more than you at the time."

She didn't respond, but she did put her glasses back on. She might as well have put on a straightjacket. On me.

"Honestly, I didn't know it would work out at Canisius College. I hate winters. And going to school in Buffalo…well, I just didn't have high hopes I'd make it one semester."

"But then you hit the big shot. And the rest is history."

That 'big shot' came at just about the sweetest time for any college basketball player. But it only came after a series of unpredictable actions, starting with my old high school coach taking an assistant's job at Canisius. Not exactly a basketball hotbed. But the head coach had known Coach Rossie's father, so there was a connection.

When my high school basketball days ended, I'd received a few sniffs from junior colleges in Texas, but nothing materialized. Like most six-one guys with only a decent game, my sports days were over. Or so I'd thought. Coach Rossie called me up at the end of my first semester in my junior year at Texas Christian University. Willow, who also attended TCU, and I had been dating for about a year at the time. And she was right. We were something pretty special. We'd even begun talking about what our combined future might look like. The problem was she had a path—she'd wanted to be a nurse for years. I had no such path. So how can you combine something where there's basically a void on one side of the equation? Not a very balanced team.

When Rossie said the starting point guard at Canisius had suffered a career-ending knee injury and he wanted to bring me up and challenge for the starting point guard spot, I suddenly saw a future. I didn't necessarily see the NBA as part of that journey, but it was still a push in one direction. And I relished that push. So I took the chance and traveled north.

I clicked with the coaches and my new teammates. And I really clicked on the court. Not sure why things were so different. Maybe I didn't feel any pressure, or I'd somehow developed this go-for-it attitude, not focusing on how I could fail and instead focusing on how well I could lead our team, whether I scored two or twenty points a game. I was just excited as hell to be playing Division I basketball. At the time I became a starter, we were 1-5. By the time the regular season ended, our record was 19-7. We won the Metro Atlantic Athletic Conference post-season tournament with a win over Monmouth, punching our ticket to the Big Dance—the NCAA Tournament.

Little old Canisius, with a student population of three thousand, was in the tournament for the first time since 1956. Life couldn't get any better.

We won our first game—an upset over Villanova. But it was the second game that gave me my fifteen minutes of fame. Trailing by two against Duke with just over four seconds to play, I took the inbound pass, weaved through three defenders, and then put up a running half-court shot with someone's hand in my face. The ball banked in, and the place exploded. I was mobbed, and it was the best feeling in the world. We lost our next game, but that didn't matter. I'd carved out a very small piece of basketball history for myself. CBS even included my game-winning shot in its "One Shining Moment" tribute at the end of the tournament.

I wrote everything about my college experience in my journal, starting with my first day at TCU and all the way through Canisius.

And that chronicle is what helped me land my first sports-writing gig.

"You're right, Will. It is history. Behind me. That game, my shot was a long time ago. No one remembers or cares. And so here we are again after eighteen years."

I could feel a lump in my throat. Dammit! Her glasses weren't even off, and I was acting like a fifteen-year-old kid who'd just fallen for his Spanish teacher.

She didn't say anything, so I did. "Are you still holding a grudge?"

"Pfft. I think you're giving yourself a little too much credit. I haven't been sulking or sitting around stabbing needles into a voodoo doll."

I rubbed my backside. "You sure? Kind of feels like I've been gouged."

She gave me a half-smile, but it was enough to cut the tension.

"So," I said, "if you're shopping for a wedding dress in Highland Park Village, life must be treating you pretty well."

She made a scoffing noise. "I'm not sure what to make of you, with the chipped tooth and busted lip, but you're also a famous writer. Champagne and caviar, am I right?"

I'd decided I wasn't going to give her a full-blown lie. Why not be honest with Will, of all people? "Caviar is for people who live in Highland Park." Okay, I chickened out. But it takes me a while to warm up.

She lifted her glasses again. *Dammit!*

This time, though, those eyes were peering into my soul. And I was back in the corner again. "So, wait, are you actually living in this area now?" she asked.

"What makes you think that?"

"Deflection," she said in monotone.

"You sound like an attorney."

She cleared her throat.

I held up my hands. "Okay, okay. Yes, I recently moved back to the area. I've thought about you, but I figured you'd moved on with your life, a good life. And I think I was right on that front, from what I can tell. Honestly, if anything, I thought you'd be living in Fort Worth."

"You thought I'd live right next to TCU?" she asked with a giggle.

'Well, I never expected to see you at that wedding shop. Actually, why haven't you married before now?"

Her eyes shifted to my hand. "Same could be asked of you."

"Touché."

"But no answer."

"I think we're both deflecting a little bit, aren't we?"

Her phone chirped. "Is that a sign that we should just avoid discussing our pasts?" She picked up the phone and looked at the screen for a quick second before snorting out a laugh.

"You ever heard of Randy the Master Blaster?" she asked.

"Sure. He was a defenseman for the Philadelphia Flyers."

She rolled her eyes—even that made my heart flutter. What the hell was wrong with me?

"You said that with such confidence I almost believed you, and I knew it was a lie," she said.

"What can I say?" I shrugged and smiled.

"Anyway, my cousin Marion—you met her at the dress shop—insisted on dragging us to this disgusting male strip club."

"You know all those guys are gay, right?"

"How would you know?"

"Funny. It's just a rumor."

"A rumor you probably heard when you were fifteen. Anyway, there's this picture of her on stage right next to Randy the Master Blaster, who's slinging his junk." She dropped her head she laughed so hard. "Oh God, that hurts, but it was so frickin' funny."

"You know, before yesterday, I don't recall you mentioning

Marion."

"She's a distant cousin. We were never close growing up. She's been through a lot. Twice divorced, just broke up with an overly possessive boyfriend."

"So why is she in your wedding?"

She rolled her eyes. "Ma made me include her."

"You—"

She held up a hand. "Don't go there. I know I shouldn't let my mother walk all over me. It's not like it used to be. But there are some battles just not worth fighting, especially when it's your wedding. And I don't want anything to smear the wedding to the man I love."

"And his name is Harvey."

"Cooper Chain, don't you dare say a derogatory thing about my future husband, not unless you want to be able to use your shoulder," she said with a wry grin.

"Good point. Sounds like a great guy."

"What? I haven't told you a thing about him."

"Exactly."

Her phone chirped. "Oh, crap."

"What?"

"I forgot I have to meet the girls at the club for a team tennis match."

"The *club*?"

She shoved her phone in her purse, then pulled out a wallet. She opened it up. "Double crap. It's Marion's wallet. I forgot she gave it to me last night. I need to run."

"So now who's the queen of cut-and-run?"

"Stuff it. You didn't drive here, did you?"

"How do you know everything?"

"I can read you, Cooper. We'll drop off Marion's wallet first, I'll drive you to wherever you need to go, and then I'll head to the club. On the way, you can tell me more about what's been happening in your life."

I pulled out my credit card, hoping I wouldn't have to use it. I was pretty sure it was maxed out. "It will take a little bit of time to pay the bill."

She grabbed thirty bucks from her purse and tossed it on the table. "Let's go."

Nine

Willow

"**D**amn, Will. I had no idea nursing paid like you were getting hush money from the royal family," Cooper said, running his hands along the leather seats of my BMW.

I shook my head but kept my gaze on the road. "It was a gift from Harvey."

"What the fuck?" Cooper blurted.

"Glad there aren't any kids in the back."

"You sure there aren't any kids in the oven?"

I could feel my eyes squinting. "What's that supposed to mean?"

"Pretend I didn't say that."

"Yeah, right."

"So, I'm guessing that Harvey must be one of those doctors who specializes in 'enhancement surgeries,' and the two of you met while you were assisting him in surgery."

"You're living in a fictional world, Cooper." I stole a quick glance at him as I pulled up to a stoplight. He was nodding, his eyes seemingly searching for a safe landing spot. It was as though he had taken my comment in a different way—a deeper way, perhaps? There was something else bothering him. Or had he simply changed? He'd been avoiding all my questions up to now. Mr. Deflection. Yes, I'd done a little bit of dodging of my own, but his was at another level. Life-altering was the sense I got.

"Are you going to tell me why you moved back home?"

"Is that what this is? Home?"

"Well, you went to high school in Arlington, college at TCU. Your mother still lives here."

"How do you know Mom still lives here?"

"Ma."

"Your mother's been interacting with my mom?"

He seemed authentically agitated. Another layer he didn't show often.

"Yeah, long story. But back to why you're here. You've been writing all these years?"

He looked out the window. "Yep."

I was waiting for more, but I never got it. Shadows splashed through the windshield as I drove down a tree-lined street. Cooper had gone back into his shell. I guess he couldn't exactly jump out of a moving car, so the walls had gone up. He was in self-protection mode, it appeared. But was he truly wounded or just feeling sorry for himself?

I pulled into the apartment complex and found a covered spot with no cars on either side.

"I take it you don't want any dings on your new car," Cooper said as we shut our doors and walked onto the sidewalk. "Or did Harvey give you that edict when he handed you the keys?"

I stopped in my tracks. He wasn't looking where he was going, so he plowed right into me. I poked a finger in his chest. "Stop it with the Harvey cut-downs. You haven't even met the guy yet."

"Yet. So, you're planning to introduce me? You could say, 'Harvey, I'd like to introduce you to the douche bag from college who ran off with his head between his legs.'"

I rolled my eyes. "My head is starting to throb again."

"Hey, that's the line I used to give you in college." He started laughing before he could say more.

But it did send me back to those days. Damn, he was right. Had I subconsciously kept that one-liner in the back of my mind all this time? And then what would happen after that? *Oh, woman. Don't go there.*

I left him standing where he was and walked around the building toward Marion's apartment. Cooper quickly caught up to me. "Did I push it too far?"

"When don't you?"

"I have my moments."

"I guess we all do."

He got in front of me, and I stopped. He lowered his head while looking at me.

"What are you doing you, freak?"

He started fluffing his hair. "Nice mirror," he said.

I removed my sunglasses. "Better?"

"Much."

He paused, and our eyes locked. Gone was his smirk. I heard a bird chirping in a nearby tree, and then it faded away. For a few seconds, I could feel a flutter inside my chest. Something I hadn't felt in a long time, possibly not since…

"Maybe too much," he added.

I blinked a few times. "I'm sorry? Too much what?" I asked, trying to recall how we'd gotten into this… *What is this exactly?*

"You basically asked if it was better when you took off your glasses."

"Why too much?" As soon as I asked the question, I knew. Or at least I thought I knew.

He broke the gaze, found a rock, and tossed it about thirty feet, popping it off the side of a tree trunk. "I still got it."

I continued my trek on the sidewalk, and he kept pace. "Now you're telling me you could have played pro baseball? Sheesh. You have a pretty high opinion of yourself at age…"

"Thirty-nine. Remember, I'm a year older than you. And, technically, I played pro basketball."

I gave him a double take as we entered the cove for Marion's apartment. "Technically."

"It's a story."

"You love the tease, don't you? You dance around my questions, throwing out breadcrumbs just to keep me interested, I think."

He wasn't even looking at me.

"Did I get too real for you, Cooper?"

He nodded over my shoulder. "Is that Marion's apartment?"

"Yep," I said, turning around.

"Her front door isn't shut all the way."

I looked closer. The door was probably no more than a half-inch from being shut all the way.

"She was highly inebriated last night."

"I kind of figured that from the way you described those pictures."

"We put her in an Uber and sent her home. I wouldn't have been surprised to see her passed out, leaning against the wall here." I raised my fist to knock on the door, but Cooper grabbed my wrist before I made contact. "What are you doing?" I asked.

He lifted a finger and then stopped moving. "Do you hear something?" His voice was nearly a whisper.

I matched his frozen stature. I picked up birds chirping and leaves skirting across the sidewalk. "You're trying to scare me."

He shook his head and looked at me.

I pulled out my phone. "You want me to text her? I mean, maybe she's still sleeping it off."

"I don't know, Will." He raked his fingers through his hair. "I guess we need to do something before we call the cops."

"Cops? Why are you going there?" I stuffed my phone back

into my purse. Then I knocked on the door at the same time I slowly pushed it open. "Hey, Marion. It's Willow. Are you still sleeping?"

"Hold on." Cooper tried to pull up next to me. We almost got stuck in the door opening.

"Ladies first," I said, wedging my shoulder ahead of his. I marched into the living room and gasped. The cushions from her couch had been shredded. Bar glasses, books, plates were scattered all over the floor. I turned toward a bedroom door that was shut.

"Hey, let me go in there first," Cooper said.

"Don't be ridiculous."

"What are you talking about? Her place has been destroyed. Looks like someone took a knife to it."

I tried swallowing, but my mouth was too dry to pull it off.

"Call the cops," he said, moving around me.

"Why?"

"Is Marion the type to break into a drunken rage?"

"I don't think so."

"So, take out your... Forget it." He pulled his phone from his pocket and walked toward what I guessed was Marion's bedroom door. I jogged up behind him and put my hands on his shoulders. He tapped the green button on his phone as he reached for the doorknob.

The door whipped open, and a man the size of a mountain roared and swung an arm at Cooper.

I was certain that we'd both die in seconds.

Ten

Cooper

My heart exploded into the back of my throat. I dropped my phone, used one hand to push Willow farther behind me, and then stuck my opposite arm up to block the blow from the hooded Sasquatch.

The club, or whatever it was in his hand, glanced off my forearm. I heard a crack. *Great.* Then he roared—all I could see was lots of hair and eyes that were on fire inside of his hoodie. He raised his weapon. That's when I made my move. I lowered my shoulder and plowed into his gut, sending us flying into the bedroom. We crashed into a desk, dropped, and banged into the footboard of a bed, then finally landed on the floor. His entire weight—something that had to be close to two-hundred fifty pounds—was upon me. I grunted out in pain, trying to catch my breath. Before I could get my bearings, he rolled off and swung his club wildly at me. I lifted a knee, and that's where the club connected. That one hurt. Bad.

"Fucker!" I yelled. I kicked him off me. He tumbled back two steps. Willow was right there. *What is she still doing in the apartment?*

He was about to backhand her when she swiped at his face

with her nails. *Since when did Willow Ball have nails?* But I could hear some type of sandpaper sound. He cried out. "Bitch made me bleed. You really going to pay now."

He growled and started going after her, the club raised high. At the same time, my hand found a glass vase. I threw it as his head. Bull's-eye! He yelled out, wobbled a bit. Willow jabbed an elbow into his Adam's apple. He started gagging. I got to my feet, ran, and jumped on his back. He twirled around three times until we were in the living room, and Willow was slapping and punching at him. "What are you doing?" I yelled.

She had this fury in her eyes, as if she were carrying the torch for every woman who'd ever been attacked. A second later, Sasquatch backed into the couch, grabbed Willow, and we all tumbled backward, landing in a heap next to a coffee table on its side.

"Call the fucking cops!"

Willow started crawling toward my phone, but the big guy grabbed her ankle and yanked her backward like she was the end of a whip. He laughed.

"Hey, asshole!" He turned just as I swung my foot, clocking him on his chin. His eyes bounced around, but he let go of Willow. "Get the hell out of here!" I yelled at her. Instead, she raced on her hands and knees for the phone at the opening to the bedroom. That's when I saw a person's legs on the bed. I hadn't noticed anyone on the bed when I was in the room seconds earlier fighting for my life.

I got to my feet and scrambled over to put myself between Willow and Sasquatch. When I turned around, I saw him lumbering out the front door.

"We're safe," Willow said, huffing out breaths.

The operator came on the line. "Nine-one-one operator. How may I help you?"

They talked as I ran to the front door, glanced outside, and made sure he wasn't lingering. I shut the door and locked it, then I walked into the bedroom. Willow was just standing there with the phone next to her side, looking at the person on the bed.

"Is that your cousin?"

The woman was lying with her head on the pillow, her arms by her side. But her skin had this pale-blue tone. It was haunting. Like something you'd see in some Dracula movie.

Tears pooled in Willows eyes as she brought a hand to her face. "Is there any way she's just asleep?"

I walked over, held my breath, and tentatively put two fingers to the side of her neck to check for a pulse. Nothing. Her skin was cold and clammy. I pulled my hand back and felt a quiver ripple through me. I shook my head at Willow. "I think she'd been dead a while."

"Oh, God." Willow started to gasp as if she couldn't catch her breath.

A moment later, she grabbed me, buried her face in the nape of my neck, and cried.

Eleven

Willow

Cooper walked over with a bottled water. "It's not Evian, but are you thirsty?"

I shook my head and toyed with a branch I'd picked up off the ground in the grassy area near Marion's apartment. A uniformed officer cut across the grass and called out to a cluster of fellow officers standing in the parking lot. "People are walking through our perimeter. Get your thumbs out of your asses and do your job."

They ran off and did their thing. Every few seconds, it seemed like another government-issued car would pull up in the parking lot. The standard Dallas black-and-white police cars—there had to be six or seven. An unmarked police car with a cherry on top. A van from the crime scene investigation unit. A hospital ambulance, and another one from the Dallas County Medical Examiner's Office. Having worked as a nurse at Dallas Parkland Hospital for years, I'd interacted with just about every county or city service, but it had never been so personal.

"I'm sorry, Willow." Cooper put his hand on my shoulder. I touched his hand; it was comforting. Something to keep me connected to the side of the universe that wasn't rooted in pure evil.

I went back to twiddling the small branch as officers walked in and out of Marion's apartment. Onlookers gathered on the other side of the yellow police tape. Lots of whispering and pointing. The whole scene was surreal and disconcerting. I looked at Cooper, who for once in his life just stood there without saying anything, as though he were a sentinel to protect me.

"Who was the man who killed Marion and attacked us? And why would he want to kill Marion, of all people?"

"I don't know," he said, running his fingers through his bronze hair. It seemed longer than I recalled. "The detectives will figure all that out. I'm just concerned about you, how you're feeling about being attacked and then seeing your cousin...you know."

I sighed. "I keep replaying the whole thing in my head, but it's all jumbled. I guess I'm not sure how to process it all yet. My adrenaline was racing so fast. Now I feel like someone just popped the bubble, you know? Just drained."

He released a deep breath. "I understand. It can't be easy for you."

Cooper looked at me with kind eyes. Marion was my cousin—and that image of her on the bed was forever etched into my memory—but Cooper had gone through the same shocking experience.

"Hey, how are *you* doing with all this?" I asked, gripping his forearm.

"Ah," he pulled his arm to his chest.

"Did that monster—?"

"He got me pretty good with that club of his on my forearm. But I'll be fine. Just bruised."

"Roll up your sleeve. Let me take a look at it."

"I'm fine. No big deal." He pulled away and looked over his shoulder. "I know we gave our initial statements to the uniformed officers, but I was told a detective would be out here in a moment."

He was deflecting again. I just couldn't understand this guy. It was like he couldn't allow himself to be exposed about anything. And I still didn't know the real story behind his chipped tooth and swollen lip, nor why he'd moved back to the area.

"Cooper," I said.

He turned and looked at me.

"Promise me that when we get past this, maybe in a few days, you'll tell me what's really going on in your life."

"In a few days, you're going to be walking down the aisle and then heading off on your honeymoon."

"The wedding," I said with nothing behind it. "Not sure we can continue after this."

"I get it. Probably something you'll want to discuss with Harvey."

He'd actually said my fiancé's name without making fun of him. Then again, we were at a murder scene. I checked my phone.

"Has Harvey texted you back?"

I shook my head. "I know he's been working like crazy to close this acquisition."

Cooper gave me a quizzical look.

"Oh, he's a partner at an accounting firm, and they're buying a smaller company. It's a really big deal." As soon as the words left my mouth, it just didn't feel right. "Actually, it's not that big of a deal, not compared to this."

I swung my sights to the parking lot, hoping to see Harvey's car drive up. No sign of him or his car, just more gawkers and officers and police cars. I felt a tap on my shoulder, so I turned around.

"Willow, this is—"

"Detective Brouchard," the woman said, reaching out to shake my hand. Already I could see she wasn't bashful. She had raven-black hair and fingernails to match the bold personality. She was statuesque. "I'm sorry for your loss."

It was a standard statement from a DPD police detective. I'd witnessed as much in the emergency room too many times to count. At those times, I thought I could feel the pain for the family and friends of the victim. A teenager dying of a drug overdose. A child gunned down in a drive-by shooting. A husband and father killed in a head-on collision by a drunk driver. The grief of those family members and loved ones was so intense that it felt like it had chipped off a piece of my heart. Now, after going through this, even though I hadn't been tight with Marion, I could see that my attempt at showing empathy toward the victims' loved ones had been like a distant star in the sky. A tiny, almost meaningless twinkle in a sea of darkness.

"So I have the statements you gave the officer, but I thought we could have a more general discussion about what you saw."

"Anything it takes to catch the guy who…" I paused a second—my brain was starting to finally function—and then I snapped my fingers. "I can't believe I didn't think about this earlier. It's got to be Marion's ex-boyfriend. He was overly possessive. She even talked about him last night at my bachelorette party."

"According to your statement, you didn't get a great look at the suspect."

"True. I only saw this huge person wearing a dark hoodie and dark pants. And he had a thick, heavy beard. Could hardly see his eyes."

"I saw the same thing," Cooper said.

"I'm confused." Brouchard reset her feet. She looked a tad annoyed. "You may not have gotten a great look at the guy, but wouldn't you know her ex if you saw him?"

"Oh, sorry. Marion and I haven't been close. I really don't know anyone in her life."

A long, slow nod. "But she's in your wedding party, according to your statement."

Cooper and I snagged a quick gaze, then I looked at the

detective. "My mother insisted. You know, one of those quirky family things."

She nodded but kept her eyes on me.

"You'd have to know her mother to really get it," Cooper said.

Another nod, then she tapped a few notes into her cell phone.

"How about a name? Do you have that?" Brouchard asked.

"Uh…" I searched my memory and came up blank. "Ma would know. I can get it for you." I thought about texting her, but then I realized I couldn't be that callous. "Hey, I need to step away and call her. That's the priority, right?' I asked the detective.

"As soon as you give us a name, we can go question the guy. So, yes, that's the priority. I'll head back in there and see if I can find any pictures sitting around that might match your description."

"By the way, I'm not sure if I said this earlier," Cooper added, "but I'm guessing he was six-six, maybe two fifty. Solid as a rock. A prototypical tight end."

The detective did something with her eyebrows, then said, "Thanks. That helps." She walked off. I called Ma and got her voicemail.

"Dammit!"

"Not answering?" Cooper asked.

"Hell no. She's probably meeting with her neighborhood investment group."

"Could she be telling them how stupid they are?"

"Unfortunately, she hasn't changed after all these years. You know what they say about changing a tiger's stripes," I said, rolling my eyes.

"No offense, but your mom is no tiger. I'm thinking velociraptor with some pretty fierce talons. Kind of surprised that she'd be in any social group."

"She's in another investment group with your mom. Bet you didn't know that."

He stood there in stunned silence.

A second later, I felt arms around me. I knew those arms. It was Harvey.

I hugged his neck and cried for the second time.

Twelve

Cooper

Watching Willow and Harvey hug and kiss and cry was a tad uncomfortable. I turned around and took in the flurry of activity around the front of Marion's apartment. It was like viewing a colony of ants, each one carrying out a task to support the greater goal.

"Wait, how did you know I was here?" I heard Willow saying.

I turned back around and saw her wiping tears from her face.

Harvey said, "Remember that app we put on your phone so we could keep track of each other?"

She swiped a hand across her face. "I guess I forgot."

Harvey offered a half-hearted chuckle.

I took in the full view of Harvey. "Tailored" was the one word that came to mind. A tailored tweed suit, gold cufflinks on his very starched white dress shirt, a fancy watch, and a helmet of charcoal hair where the part looked like it had been in place since he popped out of his mother's womb.

"Come on, Willow," he said with a crooked smile. "You couldn't have forgotten that. I mean, it's not like you're working fourteen hours a day."

My eyes shifted to Will. She wasn't laughing. She just stared at him for a second. I could feel myself tense up. I was waiting for the passive-aggressive punch to his shoulder socket, or maybe one of her patented sharp comments that would clearly reinforce her usual mantra: *don't fuck with Will or her sweet demeanor will quickly turn south.*

"Yeah, I guess you're right. My brain isn't functioning very well right now," she said.

Her lamb-like response floored me. Harvey embraced her again. She seemed to just give in to his way of looking at life and their relationship.

Like you should judge. Look at your relationship history. Maybe you should start taking notes.

Sometimes I hated my inner voice.

"You got that name yet?"

Detective Brouchard appeared out of nowhere. She was so close I could smell her perfume. It had this buttery oak scent. Inviting, yet a tad mysterious.

"Uh, sorry," Willow said, glancing at her phone. "Haven't been able to reach her."

"Any way you could find her? Maybe a friend who lives near her? Or should we send an officer to her home in case she's taking a nap?"

"No, no, no," Willow shot back, holding up a hand. She glanced at me for a quick second. We were both thinking the same thing. Who knows how her mom would respond to a cop showing up at her house, asking about Marion's ex? It could go ten different directions, but it was hard to imagine any of them being less than a train wreck.

Willow punched in a text. "Okay, there. I sent her a text that lets her know she needs to respond, even if she's busy doing whatever."

Willow pushed a curled lock of hair out of her face. That blue vein that ran across her forehead was a little more pronounced. It always was when she was stressed.

"While we wait on your mom to call you back, I want to show you something." Detective Brouchard tapped and swiped at her phone screen about a dozen times. "Did either of you see this when you found the body...uh, Marion lying on the bed?"

Willow and I moved closer to the detective to get a better view.

"What is it?" I asked.

"A question for an answer. Not what I was going for," she said, shifting her eyes to me. "Let me ask again. Did either of you see this?"

We shook our heads in unison.

"Are either of you into birds?"

"Into birds?" Willow asked.

I grabbed the phone and pulled it closer. "Shut the front door! Is that a bird's wing?"

The detective gave a simple nod. "I was wondering if either of you had left it there."

"That's creepy," Willow said, giving her the once-over. "Why would we do that?"

"Did you get along with Marion?"

"Hold on, hold on," Harvey said, taking a step forward. "Do I need to bring my lawyer into this?" He held up a finger to emphasize his point, and I realized Harvey was a manicure man. I almost asked if he also got monthly pedicures, but I took the high road. Another point for me.

"I'm not accusing Ms. Ball or Mr. Chain." She paused a moment, as many had done in our past when they finally put our names together. Thankfully, she shook it off and continued. "I'm not saying they had anything to do with the death at this time. We find this ex-boyfriend, and I'm guessing a lot of questions will be answered. Plus, I'm sure our forensics team will find additional evidence. It's obvious there was a struggle. Someone with a lot of rage cut up those cushions."

"What about that wing?" I asked.

She lifted her chest—not that I was really paying much attention—and released a deep breath. "It's the wing of a dove. We found it partially under the bed."

"I guess it could have fallen off the bed. Sasquatch and I—"

The detective cocked her head to the side. "Sasquatch?"

"He means the man who attacked us, Marion's ex," Willow chimed in.

"Oh, right. Okay..."

"We crashed into the bedroom, falling over the desk. I think we hit the bed too. Hard to remember. I didn't even notice Marion lying on top of the bed, since I was kind of fighting for my life."

She nodded, appeared to be chewing on something. The side of her cheek, maybe?

"What do you think the significance of the wing is?" I asked.

"The medical examiner, while not a vet, believes the wing was pulled off the dove recently. Within the last day. So if the killer left it—"

"Who else would have left the wing?" Willow snapped back.

"Your cousin...uh, she wasn't into birds and taxidermy, was she?"

"I have no idea, but she's never brought it up."

"Look, I'm just asking every question that comes to mind. Most investigations aren't solved by a single affirmative; it's more about that one question that can't be answered. So, we ask a thousand questions, and maybe a handful lead us down the path to find the suspect. As for the relevance of the wing, I don't have any strong theories, nor does any other officer who's been inside. For now, I guess I'd chalk it up to another act of violence. Maybe there's some control issues being played out as well."

This thing was getting more twisted by the second.

"How did she die?" Harvey asked.

Willow and I looked at each other, then over to Harvey. "I can't believe we never asked that question," Willow said, dropping her head onto his shoulder. At five-ten, she was noticeably taller than little Harvey.

"That's the second thing I wanted to ask you guys about."

"Go ahead, Detective," I said.

"You can call me Courtney. I'm not really into the formal titles. We're all just people."

I liked that answer. She continued.

"Ever heard of inert gas asphyxiation?"

I looked to Willow. She was the health care expert. "So?" I asked her.

She shook her head. "It's been a while. I can't say I've heard of that cause of death."

"Well, according to the ME, it's a form of asphyxiation which results from breathing a physiologically inert gas in the absence of oxygen, like helium, nitrogen or even methane."

"You lost me with 'physiologically inert,'" I said.

Courtney shook her head. "I'm just repeating what the ME told me."

"It means that it's a gas that isn't toxic, per se," Willow explained. 'Now that I think on it some more, I *am* familiar with the condition when a gas reduces the oxygen concentration in your blood. It can be very dangerous." She swiveled her head to Courtney. "So what is the ME saying is the cause of death?"

"She doesn't know for certain. In fact, if her guess is right, even doing a full autopsy probably wouldn't give her total confidence to state an exact cause of death."

"Her guess, then?" I asked.

"Apparently, a year back, a few high school kids in a school district near San Antonio made a suicide pact. They used these bags full of nitrogen. They're actually called suicide bags. They're used by people to perform euthanasia."

"To kill themselves?" Harvey asked.

Courtney eyed Willow and me. "So, here comes another stupid question that I have to ask. When you found the body…uh, Marion, did you see a bag of any kind on or around her?"

"Nope."

"Nothing."

She sighed. "The team has yet to find anything in the apartment."

"So are you now thinking it was suicide?" Willow asked. "I mean, that monster attacked us. It was clear he'd torn the place up and was in Marion's bedroom probably setting up that whole macabre scene."

"It's not all a perfect puzzle," Courtney said. "Most murders, or suicides for that matter, aren't really clear cut."

"But it's a murder, right?" I asked.

Courtney put a hand on Willow's arm. "Get me that name of the ex-boyfriend. And fast."

Willow's phone rang. She held it where I could see it. *Mom.*

She pumped out a breath. "Here goes everything." She stepped off to the side and spoke to her mother.

Thirteen

Cooper

The best part about Brandy's weekly pep rally meetings—the ones where she literally has us chanting lame cheers about "happy customers" and "wearing a smile" and "going that extra mile for your teammate"—was when they ended. Not only was I able to escape from the chains of manufactured positivity, but she also left to go buy us lunch. As in free. Free food and a small amount of freedom from the queen bitch herself. I considered it a win-win-win. Until she returned, and then I'd have to settle for eating a free lunch with people whom I found annoying for one reason or another.

I ambled across the store, eager to finally get started on my task list and begin another day of retail drudgery. With each step, the number six started flashing in my mind. It was obvious, of course. I had six more days to come up with fifty grand. Which really meant six more days to be breathing oxygen.

"Oh, nice," I said to myself, instantly thinking about Willow's cousin. I couldn't imagine dying of asphyxiation, even if the term "inert" was how Courtney had described it. Stopping your ability to breathe didn't sound pleasant or inert.

A quick flash from my periphery, but my body didn't have

time to respond. I ran right into a fellow store employee.

"Oh, crap. Hey, Mr. Cooper."

"Ah, damn," I said through gritted teeth, holding my bruised arm. I had no idea if the bone was cracked. I'd refused to let Willow do her nurse thing—*Cooper, keep your mind out of the gutter, dude*—and health insurance was for the rich. Even though I'd iced my arm all night, it still hurt like hell.

"Yo, did I really hurt you that bad? Man, I'm so sorry," the guy said, pacing back and forth in the Games section.

"It's okay, Slash."

That was his name—Slash. No relation to the lead guitarist for Guns N' Roses. Unlike his namesake, he looked more like Billy Ray Cyrus (Miley's dad, for those in the younger demographic) with that mullet hairstyle. He wasn't stupid either. He'd graduated in the top three of his college class, majoring in computer science. But he was hesitant to get a real job, he said, so he just mooched off his parents.

I'd rather end up on the street like the homeless guy from a couple of nights earlier than live with my mom. She was a very sweet woman. And that was the problem. She couldn't understand the real world and had to make a comment about everyone who wasn't clean and wholesome. She went to church religiously— yes, I actually made that pun—and she didn't like to hear cursing or get anywhere near an act of debauchery. And there was a whole lot that was contained in that black box. I'd tried to explain the details of my life, as sordid as they were, but she didn't want to hear them. I was perfect in her eyes. I suppose most parents feel that way about their kids. I should know.

The pain subsided somewhere just south of ten on the pain scale, and I released a slow audible breath. I took another look at Slash. The kid was all limbs, and one of those jagged elbows had just nailed the bruise on my arm.

"You sure, Mr. Cooper?"

"It's *Cooper*. Not Mr. Cooper. It sounds like you're talking to your old high school math teacher or that TV comedian from back in the day."

He nudged his wire-rimmed glasses higher on his nose. "I think that's why I say it," he said. "You remind me of my science teacher in ninth grade. He was pretty cool. Saw a picture of his wife on his desk. Man, she was all that and a bag of chips."

His gaze drifted off like he was trying to catch a dream.

I snapped my fingers. "You with me, Slash?"

He shook himself out of his trance. "Anyway, do you mind working the front for a while? The new graphic novels came in," he said, popping his eyebrows like he was a real player on the girl scene. Slash, I knew, had a fascination with the scantily clad girls in these graphic novels. I tried telling him that if he wanted to look at naked pictures of girls, it took about three clicks on his computer. But Slash dismissed my input. He thought graphic novels were the bomb.

"No problem. I'll work the front. Just don't take too much time. I don't want to get stuck up there."

"You got it, Mr. Cooper."

"It's Cooper."

He was gone before I'd said my name.

I walked up to the front of the store and turned on my fake, high-energy greeter persona. You know the guy, the annoying person who asks how your day is the moment you walk into the store. One of Brandy's rules. She'd once sent in a mole just to put us to the test. So I couldn't blow it off. Not while I still held out hope that my fifty grand was within reach.

Did I mention I enjoy being sarcastic with myself? It's a coping mechanism. Especially helpful when your life has been flushed down the toilet.

I repeated the overly-joyful greeter routine about a dozen times during the next twenty minutes, wondering what the hell was taking Slash so long. I also started thinking of ideas on how to get fifty grand. Rob a bank. I'd probably have to find a weapon, and people could get hurt or killed, starting with me. That option had to be at the bottom of the list.

Here's a thought: I could create one of those Kickstarter campaigns.

"Hmm. You might have something there, Cooper," I whispered to myself.

But what would be my campaign? Then it hit me. I was a writer, at least I was in my former life. Combine that so-called skill with the movie angle that came to mind when the cop found the Sack Brothers and me in the alley. I could put together a convincing description of the campaign, saying I'd written a screenplay for a movie that would tug at people's heartstrings, and that a make-believe friend and I needed the seed money to produce this "indie" movie. You know, really appeal to the tree-hugging, anti-establishment crowd. People a little like me, except those who actually had jobs that didn't automatically put them below the poverty line.

I wondered if that could actually produce fifty grand in six days. And then there was the sticking point about showing the donators some type of finished product. Not sure how all that worked. I needed to do some research.

I reorganized a table of how-to books. One caught my eye: *How to Game the Financial World.*

Everyone had an angle. Another thought hit me. I could convince Slash to hack into some giant company or financial institution and pull out fifty grand. Executives at those places wiped their asses with fifty grand. And it might be safer than exposing myself to the ridicule of hundreds of donators when they realized my movie was nothing more than vapor.

Damn, I was pathetic. Desperate times, though, called for desperate measures. And I desperately wanted to live longer than another week.

The door dinged. "Hi, there. How's your day going?" I said with my head down, rearranging books on a front table.

"So, this is what you do?"

I looked up and saw Willow. I had no words.

Fourteen

Cooper

I knew Willow would eventually find out about my employment situation. I thought she might learn about it yesterday, but an officer had ended up taking me back to work, while Willow and Harvey drove off in their luxury cars.

"You caught me." I could feel my face go flush, and it shocked the hell out of me. I never anticipated feeling so embarrassed, not around Willow. I momentarily considered making up a story that I was actually waiting to meet my new literary agent at the bar in the back of the store. But that would only delay the inevitable.

I looked at Willow. Her majestic eyes could make stone turn to dust, at least from my perspective. But I also saw a sadness. I walked over to her and felt the pull to touch her shoulder. I didn't, though. I couldn't cross that line. She was engaged, for God's sake.

"How have you been since…you know, yesterday?" I asked.

She tilted her head left and then right. "I've been up and down. Harvey's helped…when he's been around."

"Still working on that merger?"

"Yep."

A one word response. She didn't seem pleased with Harvey's

choice of priorities. Then again, I could be reading something that wasn't there.

She scanned the expansive store, then looked at me. "Are you going to have a break anytime soon?"

"Uh…" I could sense an inquisition coming. "Well, it's kind of busy."

She gazed over my shoulder. "I don't see many customers. Are you doing something important?"

How could I lie about that? Not possible.

"Eh. I guess it has slowed down some. Kind of been lost in my thoughts."

"About what?"

I turned and saw Slash's mullet above the bookshelves. He then walked up to the front.

"Good timing," I said to him. "You mind taking over so I can talk to my friend?"

He stopped in his tracks, nudged up his glasses. He looked at Willow, then back at me. A smirk emerged from his peach-fuzz baby face. He leaned in closer to me and not-so-quietly said, "Va-va-voom, Mr. Cooper."

Did he actually believe Willow couldn't hear him?

"Anyway, Slash, thanks for, uh…" I wasn't sure why I was thanking him, really. So, I just gave him a pat on the shoulder. "See you in a bit."

I motioned with my head for Willow to follow me. She caught up as we meandered through the store toward the corner reading section. "Slash. That's his real name?" she asked.

"That's what he wants us to call him. Not sure if that's his real name or if his parents were groupies for Guns N' Roses."

She playfully nudged my arm—yep, my bad arm. I tried not to wince, but I must have.

"Oh, crap. Your arm, Cooper. It's still hurting?"

"Just a bit. Getting better, though."

"Did you get it X-rayed?"

"It's just a bruise."

She grabbed me by my belt loop, yanking me to a stop.

"You almost gave me whiplash," I said, rubbing my neck in jest. "I might have to sue you for, uh, fifty grand."

She put her hands at her waist.

"I'm just saying that you're still a freak of nature. Never understood how you have such strength somehow contained in that lean body."

"Stop it with the praise. You're just trying to divert the attention away from your injury. Push up your sleeve."

"Whoa. I thought you were going to tell me to put my hands against the bookshelf and *bend over*." I flashed my "aren't I witty?" smile.

She couldn't help but grin, and we both laughed for a few seconds. It was an inside joke going back to a mutual friend from college.

I carefully pushed up my shirtsleeve and lifted my forearm.

Her eyes got wide. Really wide. It kind of freaked me out, considering she'd been a nurse for something like fifteen years. She started inspecting the area around the blue and purple bump.

"So, I'm assuming you quit nursing since you got engaged to King Harvey?"

She glanced at me a second then went back to feeling around the bruise.

"Ouch, ouch, ouch. You squeezed!"

"You mouthed off."

"But I always mouth off. It's who I am."

"You want me to squeeze harder?"

I pretended to turn a key in front of my lips.

"Oh, you're not going to fire back one of your funny zingers?"

"Only if you want me to."

She finished her inspection.

"So what's the diagnosis, Doc?"

"I'm no doctor. I'm…" She stopped short and bit at a nail.

"Your chemistry teacher in college said you should get your medical degree. But you chose to be a nurse. It's a gallant profession, but you could have—"

"Coulda, shoulda, woulda. Back to your arm. You have a rather severe hematoma."

"Hema-whata?"

"It's the lump on your forearm. And of course the contusion, the bruising, is quite advanced. With the purple color trailing down your forearm, I have to say I'm a bit concerned that you might have ecchymosis."

"Are you just trying to show off?"

"Sorry. It means that blood from your ruptured blood vessels could have seeped into the surrounding tissues. And then there's the issue of a possible broken ulna."

"I'm assuming you mean a broken arm. You really think it's broken?"

She opened her mouth. I quickly lifted a finger. "Don't bother. My arm is still attached to my shoulder, so it will heal in time." I walked toward two overstuffed chairs. "Have a seat. I'm allowed to get us waters from behind the bar, assuming you're okay with tap water, that is."

She rolled her eyes at me and waved me on.

The bartender was nowhere in sight, so I filled two glasses with ice, added water, and joined Willow in a vacant chair. She chugged the water then retrieved two coasters from a nearby table and set her glass down. Her OCD act couldn't possibly be to protect the table. The darn thing looked like it had been put through a tree shredder.

"Make you feel better?"

She shrugged then stared at the carpet.

"What's wrong?"

"I just can't get that picture of Marion out of my mind. And I'm not sure that I want to."

"Yeah, it's left an imprint on my mind, that's for sure." I waited for her to continue. She didn't, so I spoke up. "I guess you got the ex-boyfriend's name from your mom?"

She slumped in her chair. "Oh, God. Ma. She was…" Willow shook her head. "It's hard to put in words. She was yelling and screaming—I realize, of course, that she'll raise her voice and say something rude to the bag boy at the grocery store—but considering the situation, I thought she might be a bit more empathetic. But she only aimed her vicious attack elsewhere."

"Who now?"

"Marion, at first, for ever being with that loser and for not taking the proper security precautions, and then the cops. As if they could have stopped it. Jesus, she's not only a bitch, her logic is so messed up."

I didn't want to pile on. I could see this was really eating at her. "Sorry."

"Thanks," she said, glancing at me with those knee-buckling, syrupy eyes.

I looked away, sipped some of my water. I gave myself a few seconds to regain my composure. "But you got the name?"

"Ronnie Gutierrez. Detective Brouchard, I mean Courtney, said she'd give me an update when she had one. Have you heard anything from her?"

"Nothing."

"I'm wondering if Ronnie has disappeared. He probably knows the cops are looking for him."

"He might be in Mexico by now. Or he could be hiding out in some sleazy motel. But I've seen the police in New York work a murder case pretty damn quickly. Once they have a suspect, they're like flies on shit," I said with my best country twang.

She didn't smile. My attempt to lighten the mood had failed.

We sat in silence for a minute. "So are you going to tell me what's happened in your life?" she asked.

"I thought we were trying to figure out how to bring Marion's killer to justice."

"Cooper, come on. How long are you going to play this game?"

I could feel my face heat up again. I sat back, crossed a leg over a knee, and sipped my water. "It's not a fairytale story."

"Okay…"

"It's not even worthy of being a Lifetime movie. It's really just…you know, part of life."

She flicked her fingers, her signal for me to keep talking.

I huffed out a breath and secretly wished Brandy would show her face and give me some marching orders. "About six months ago, I got myself in a pickle."

"A pickle. That's what led to you being assaulted?"

"Why would you go there?"

"You're like dealing with a five-year-old, you know that?"

I ran my tongue across my chipped tooth. "I was an investigative sports reporter for the *New York Daily News*."

"Sounds very clandestine. Secretive."

"I just couldn't keep covering sports teams. I'd get the same tired responses no matter what question I asked. It was like they all had four canned answers, and they'd pick A, B, C, or D no matter what I said or asked."

"Athletes. Seems like they're busy building their brand or running from someone."

I leaned forward and rested my good forearm on my good knee—the other knee was still sore from Sasquatch clubbing it. "That's what intrigued me, finding out more about the guys who were running. I mean, not literally running, but the ones who have those demons. I could see it in their faces. I wanted to know their backstory, what made them who they are. And as I started digging,

I found some pretty fucked-up lives. It was challenging, but also rewarding at times to either expose something bad going on, or get some young kid to open up and share his life story. Yeah, those were the days and nights when I loved my work."

"Days and nights. So, you're one of them. Someone who's married to your job."

"*Was.* Anyway, like you should talk. How many overnight shifts have you worked in the past decade because someone's life counted on it?"

She opened her mouth but didn't say anything. Her eyes found the floor again..

"Did I push one of your buttons?" I asked apologetically.

She pushed a loose curl out of her face. "I'm fine."

"You don't look fine. Well, you know what I mean." I couldn't help but wink.

"You just can't help yourself, can you?"

I shrugged.

She tucked a foot under her butt. "So, how did your dream writing job get you beat up and working in bookstore a thousand miles away?"

"I already told you. I got into a pickle."

With the quickness of a cheetah, she grabbed hold of my wrist. "You want me to break your other arm?"

"Are you on steroids?"

"Do I look like I'm on steroids?"

"You don't have the pronounced forehead or the acne, but you are getting upset with me rather easily."

She started squeezing my good arm.

"Just joking," I said in a sing-song voice.

She let go and then stood up. "Cooper, I'm only here because I care. Maybe I shouldn't say that, but I'm worried about you. But if you're just going to be elusive, then I'm going to leave."

Another colleague of mine walked by—Tracy with the red

spiked hair and about a dozen piercings on her face. She gave me that look. The one that said she couldn't wait to tell Brandy about me hanging out with a friend when I should be working. I tried giving her an evil eye, but it wasn't a good look for me. She crinkled her nose, as if she had just smelled something foul, and walked off.

"Hey, Will, take a seat, and I'll tell you everything. If you really want to know."

She sat down and crossed her arms. I rubbed my hands together and studied the pattern in the shades of gray in the carpet.

Before words left my mouth, two hands smacked the table between Willow and me.

"Is this a fucking illusion or what?"

Will and I jerked our heads around, but we both knew who it was. He spread his arms. "I never thought I'd get to say this again, but... How the hell are the old Ball and Chain doing?"

Our old college friend laughed so hard I thought he was going to bust a blood vessel.

Fifteen

Cooper

"We're almost forty years old and this is the best you can do? The old Ball and Chain?" I asked.

He leaned back, put a hand on his belly, and chuckled like Santa. Will and I exchanged a glance. We smiled only because he was laughing so damn hard.

"All this from a guy named Ben Dover," I said.

His laughter ceased as if his near-constant sense of humor had been sucked into a black hole. "Dude, my name is *Benjamin*. I can't help that my parents are clueless."

He was always quick with the defense.

"Alli tells me you're going by your middle name now. Andrew," Willow said.

"Ah, my little sis, Alli. Well, don't believe everything you hear. Uncle Andrew had two teeth and a meth addiction. So, I'd rather go with Benjamin. It's refined. Like me," he said, cinching up his chino pants and flattening his Oxford shirt. I wasn't sure if he was trying to remove the wrinkles or pretend he had washboard abs. Neither was an option that would work.

"Enough about me," he said. "What brings the Ball and Chain together after all these years?"

"Well—"

"Hold on," he said, putting a finger to his mouth while looking at Willow. "I got it, I got it. Before you get married to Mr. Richie Rich, you want to atone for yours sins, heal old wounds, let bygones be bygones." He paused, twisting his lips into a corkscrew—a habit of his from way back.

"For starters, Andrew—"

"It's *Benjamin*, thank you very much, Willow."

"Whatever. I have no sins to atone for, and regarding your other cliché comments, just stuff them up your ass."

He clenched his jaw. "You have to get personal on me? I'm just making an honest observation between friends. We're all still friends, right?" He started laughing before either of us could comment.

Ben was ultra-gregarious and made me come across as a well-adjusted, semi-pleasant man. But he seemed to be on something.

"Hey, man, have you been drinking already?"

He kept chuckling. "This coming from a guy who once drank eighteen cups of trash-can punch and didn't even pass out."

"But he *did* puke," Willow said, moving her sights from Bombastic Ben to me.

I pointed a thumb at Ben and spoke like he wasn't there. "He loves to embellish. Not sure why."

"It was the night we met, remember?"

Was she kidding? I recalled it like it was yesterday. "I was sitting on the front steps of the house where the party was at, wondering if I was going to barf, and then you appeared out of nowhere and just sat down and started talking to me."

"Only after you asked me to put out my cigarette."

"A nurse with a cigarette. There's something wrong with that."

"But you didn't know my major when you asked me to put it out."

"True. I just didn't want to throw up on the prettiest girl on campus."

She gave me a playful eye roll. "Sheesh. You're even into historical charming, but I think you're just distorting things."

"Embellish, yes. Distort? Never."

Her brow furrowed. "Aren't those basically the same thing?"

"You guys crack me up. You really do," Ben said, nodding and smiling.

"So glad we're able to be your comedic outlet, Andrew."

"Benjamin, please."

Willow started flicking her fingers. "Don't you have some deal to make or one of your fifty businesses to run?"

I looked at Willow quizzically.

"Yes, Ben Dover is a high-roller," she said with a snicker.

"It's Benjamin. Can you even remember my name? And I wouldn't go as far as saying I'm a high-roller. I'm not swimming in the kind of money you're marrying into."

Willow rolled her eyes where the world could see it. "I'm not marrying Harvey for his money, just so everyone understands that."

"Yeah, but think about where you've come from in the last year," Ben said.

"Parkland Hospital, right?" I asked. "Or were you working at one of the dozen other hospitals in the area? They're always merging and changing their names."

Willow looked away for a moment.

"Did I say something wrong?"

"Benjamin Andrew Dover! Where are you?" The voice sounded like a woman who'd swallowed broken glass.

Ben went still for a moment. Very still. A squirrel in a tree.

"Who's that?" I asked.

The shake of his head looked more like a body tremor.

"What the hell is wrong with you, dude? Are you possessed or something?"

Willow turned sideways in her chair to face Ben. "I think Alli told me something about you having a new girlfriend?"

"And you don't even tell me?" I said. "Are you trying to cover something up?"

"Nothing like that," he said in a hushed tone.

"Benjamin! The girls and I are ready for our mani-pedis."

I looked toward the front. The voice was close, but still no sign of anyone. "Is 'the girls' a euphemism for her feet and hands?"

"I wish."

"Wish?" Willow looked at Ben and then me. She was just as confused as I was.

Then, out from behind a bookshelf walked a woman who had more strut than a runway model. She wore all purple, had on dark sunglasses, and her hair was up in what looked like a tower on top of her head. A second later, three girls around the age of ten—carbon copies of Mom—walked into our space right behind her.

This had to be a choreographed stunt.

Willow cupped a hand on one side of her face and whispered, "Are they for real?"

I shrugged.

"Who are you talking to Benjamin?" the woman asked.

"Just some old friends. This is—"

"*Old* friends," she said, acting as though "old" was a cuss word. She removed a pair of—you guessed it—purple gloves. "We need to go, Benjamin. The girls are growing impatient."

"But I thought you guys…"

She cleared her throat. It sounded like she'd just started a chain saw. Her voice was lower than Ben's or mine.

"I meant to say 'ladies,' of course," Ben said.

The purple people eaters all smiled in unison. Perfect choreography.

"I thought you ladies wanted to do some shopping in the shoe store down the strip center." Ben, who wasn't a small man, had shriveled into a shell of himself. I wondered what else had shriveled into nothing. Maybe she had those in her purple purse and would only return them if he cowered to her for the rest of the day.

"They were rude. I don't deal with rudeness," she said, snapping her gloves into her opposite hand.

I had to do my best to stick up for Ben, so I stood and extended my hand. "Cooper Chain. Nice to meet you." She gave me a two-finger shake. Who gives a two-finger shake?

"This is my girlfriend, Reva."

"Benjamin, you know I hate that term. I'm your *significant other*. No more, no less. I can't help the fact that my husband died in the line of duty."

"I'm sorry for your loss. Your husband sacrificed a great deal."

"Reva, that's Willow."

"Willow, dear—I feel like I'm speaking to a tree—anyway, my husband wasn't an officer or a member of the military. He died while..." She looked to her daughters. "Ears."

Three girls promptly covered their ears.

"He died servicing me," Reva said with a loud cackle.

I leaned closer to Ben. "Did she just say...?"

He nodded.

"And is she really that...?"

"Uh, yep."

"It was nice to meet both of you. Benjamin, we really must be going."

"Can I finish up with my friends? I haven't seen both of them together in something like eighteen years."

"Do you want your special treat tonight?" she asked with devilish smile.

"Of course I do." He moved right next to her side and held out his arm. She hooked her arm in his.

"Well, it was so nice meeting both of you," she said in the

fakest manner possible.

And with a wave from Ben, all five walked off.

"Did that just happen?" I asked.

"Yes, our friend just got bent over right before our eyes."

Sixteen

Cooper

I refilled our waters and sat back down.

"Before Benjamin and his ladies made their appearance, you were starting to open up. Tell me that freak show didn't wipe out your memory."

I sighed. "About five bad things happened to me at the same time. And all of it combined completely changed my life." I paused a moment and looked up. Her demeanor was less demanding—her hands were clasped on her lap. A glimmer caught my eye. For the first time, I noticed her engagement ring as it sparkled in the overhead lighting. It was the size of a golf ball.

"Keep going." Her voice was kind again. That was the voice I knew from years ago.

More hand-wringing. "I haven't told this story, not the entire story, to anyone."

"But you're going to tell me," she said with kind eyes.

Yes, I saw her "kind" pattern. And as much as I tried to fight it, I knew it was impossible to hold off any longer.

"To avoid getting into all the gritty details, basically I was set up."

"By who?"

"You mean whom."

"Whatever. Answer the question, please."

"The name doesn't matter; you wouldn't recognize him. He was a fringe player, up and down in the Yankees farm system."

"A baseball player set you up?"

My whole body nodded. "It's not like it was a well-planned conspiracy. It just kind of happened." I paused a second and took a gulp of my water. Then I peered over my shoulder, wondering if Brandy had returned with lunch.

"I know your break won't last forever," she said. "So you might want to speed it up."

"The kid was supposed to be the next great centerfielder for the Yankees. But he was always surrounded by drama. An arrest for disorderly conduct at a club. A scene with a girlfriend in a hotel lobby. Multiple confrontations with fans. I took the story to find out what had gone wrong with his career. At first, I found evidence he was taking PEDs. He'd failed two drug tests and was about to be suspended for half the season. When we talked, I could sense something deeper going on. I wondered if it was the mood swings from the steroids. So, I kept digging. And what I found was pretty damn disturbing."

Willow was now the one showing some anxiety. She'd moved to the edge of her chair, her hands in a prayer position just under her chin.

I forged onward. "I showed up at his house at a time he wasn't expecting. I did it on purpose so that he wouldn't have a canned answer ready for me."

"Why did you go over there?"

"Off the record, one of his teammates had said he thought he was into drugs. Cocaine in particular. I was about to write the first major piece of the story, so I knew I couldn't ignore this claim."

"So, you confronted him."

"It's not my forte in my personal life, but when it came to

reporting, I felt like I had this responsibility to get to the heart of the story. Sounds corny, I know."

"It doesn't. But what happened?"

"One of the members of 'Team Perez' answered the door and let me in. It was a pretty crazy scene. Lots of women and booze. The music was cranking. A big party. I found Perez leaning over a glass table, snorting coke. When he saw me, he didn't seem to care. He asked if I wanted a line."

She put a hand on my knee. "Hold on. You're saying you did coke with this baseball player? I can see how bad things would happen after that."

Heat flared up my neck. "Did I say I snorted coke? Shit, you're starting to sound like your mother, always thinking the worst of people."

"Low blow, Cooper."

I shrugged and looked over toward the bar. Anywhere except her face. A minute must have passed.

"You going to stay pissed at me?" she asked.

I turned to look at her. "I thought you were pissed at me."

"I was." She held out her hand like this was some type of business transaction. I shook it.

"Okay, we got over that hurdle," she said. "So, where did your life start falling apart?"

My phone buzzed. I pulled it from my pocket. I didn't recognize the number. Could it be the Sack Brothers, or maybe even Dr. V himself? Fuck it. I tapped the button.

"This is Cooper," I said into the phone.

"Glad one of you picked up."

"Detective Brouchard?"

Willow snapped her fingers as though she'd just recalled something.

"That's me. Your partner isn't picking up her phone, so I'm glad you answered."

I chuckled while looking at Willow. "She's not my partner."

"Oh, right. Of course. I guess I just figured… It doesn't matter. If you can find her, I need both of you to get to the DPD headquarters office ASAP."

"Willow is sitting right next to me."

"And she's not your partner? Whatever. I'll see you soon."

"Hold on. What do you know? Why do you need to see us?"

"We caught the suspect, Ronnie Gutierrez. And we need both of you to try to identify him in a lineup. Can you get to the headquarters building in thirty minutes?"

"I guess so."

"See you soon."

Seventeen

Willow

The last time I'd seen the Dallas police headquarters—officially named Jack Evans Headquarters—was on TV. A few years back, an obviously troubled man had shot out the front glass doors and windows with a semi-automatic weapon. Police later killed him after a standoff in Hutchins, a small city south of Dallas. A placard in the lobby summarized the attack.

"Boo!"

It was Cooper, who'd just walked up next to me. We were waiting for Courtney to escort us into the bowels of the DPD.

I looked at him briefly and then went back to reading the placard.

"I was just getting you back for your little 'boo' act at the sandwich shop."

"I hardly remember. It's hard to recall much of anything before we found Marion—"

"And Sasquatch," he added.

"Well, Sasquatch has a name. Ronnie Gutierrez. And I'm ready to nail his ass in just a few minutes."

"If we can pick him out of the lineup."

I grabbed his shoulder and looked him in the eye. "Do you

want this guy to walk?"

"Uh, no. But do you want to convict a guy who didn't kill her?"

I heard a hissing sound and realized it was me.

"You're pissed again," he said.

"Just annoyed, Cooper. This is my cousin. I didn't know her well, but I'm not leaving here until I know this gutless prick has been charged with her crime. Period."

He didn't say another word, but he started reading a different placard.

"Did you know that Jack Evans used to be the CEO of Tom Thumb?" Cooper asked.

"The grocery store chain? I thought he was the former mayor."

"Well, he was, back in the 1980s. I guess that's why they named this building after him. But I had a high school buddy who bagged groceries at Tom Thumb. He told me that he once met Jack Evans. Said he was a nice guy. Goes to show not all millionaires are assholes." He looked at me. "But I guess you knew that already."

I tilted my head.

"You know…Harvey."

"He's no millionaire." I paused. "Actually, I don't know his net worth. And it's none of your damn business anyway."

Courtney stepped into the space between us.

"But it's my damn business to walk you upstairs." She eyeballed us. "You guys being civil?"

"Of course," I said.

"Whatever she said," Cooper said with his usual dry wit.

As we walked up a set of stairs, I leaned closer to Cooper. "Didn't mean to snap your head off."

"I'm cool."

"It's just that Harvey and I are a little sensitive about that. Too many people think if you have money, you automatically fall into that asshole category. That's not Harvey. And that won't be me."

"I forgot to ask. Is the wedding still on or what?"

"I didn't get much sleep for many reasons."

"Harvey gets frisky at the oddest times."

She pinched the skin on the top of my hand.

"Ouch!"

Courtney glanced over her shoulder at us, but she continued leading the way.

"He's not frisky."

"Is he gay?"

I could feel spears of fire shooting from my eyes. Or maybe I was just envisioning it.

"Okay, I take that back," he said, veering farther away from me. "Seriously, are you guys still going through with it?"

"A lot of people are coming into town, and everything has been ordered. So, I think we're still on."

He acted like he didn't hear me.

"Hello?" I snapped my fingers.

Courtney opened a door and ushered us inside. As I passed Cooper, he said, "I'm happy for you, Will. Hopefully this situation will soon be behind us, and your wedding will be the best day of your life."

I wasn't prepared for such a nice comment. "Thanks."

"Okay," Courtney said. "Six men will be walked into the room on the other side of this glass. You'll be able to see them, but as I'm sure you've guessed, they won't be able to see you. And, of course, they have no idea who you are."

"Not until we identify him. And I'm sure we'll have to testify in court," Cooper said.

"If it gets that far. There's a lot we need to parse through on this investigation. But in the end, depending on the actual charges, plea deals are often struck."

"I'm not sure this guy deserves a plea deal," Cooper said.

Courtney touched his elbow. "Let's not get ahead of ourselves. The main thing we want to accomplish first is to make sure a killer doesn't walk out of this building today. Are you guys ready?"

We both nodded.

She walked over to an intercom system on the wall and asked that the men be escorted into the room.

Cooper and I squared our feet. He started popping his knuckles, and I began to chew on a nail. We both had our vices. Frankly, French manicures and the like weren't my thing, but Harvey thought they added to my sex appeal. I considered that a small sacrifice for our relationship.

As the first man entered the room, Cooper and I drew closer, our shoulders now touching. I could feel my pulse ticking a little bit faster as each man walked into the lineup room. I tried to do a quick scan, but the three accompanying officers partially blocked my view.

Cooper mumbled something. I elbowed him. "What are you saying?"

"Six-six, two fifty."

"That's your guess at the height and weight of the killer, I know. But it's just a guess."

"I've been around enough athletes to know it. I bet I'm not off by more than a quarter inch or ten pounds. And I know his build. Then again, I should. The guy tossed me around like a rag doll."

"You held your own."

We traded a quick glance then turned to face the men, who were now being told where to stand by the officers.

Courtney pushed another button on the intercom system and spoke into it. "Number one, step forward."

I took a good look at the guy. He was tall and broad-shouldered. But he had a military-style haircut.

"He's got to be the plant, right?" Cooper said to Courtney.

She gave him a blank stare.

"I've seen how things are done in New York. They sometimes put a plant in the lineup, and I've heard they'll even throw in a cop if they can't find another person who looks similar. They know that prosecutors don't want this lineup identification process to come back and bite them in the ass. So, you guys try to make it difficult on us. If we can pick out the suspect from a pretty similar group, then that only helps them build their case."

"Didn't know you had experience in this area."

"More than you know," he said.

"Are you guys good on number one?" she asked.

Cooper glanced at me.

"It's not the guy who killed Marion and attacked us," I said as Cooper nodded in agreement.

"Okay. You don't have to give a thumbs up or down on each one. You can wait until the end, if you'd prefer." She spoke into the intercom and asked number two to step forward while number one moved back a step.

"That's a quick no," I said. "His beard is more like the stubble of a teenager. No way it's him."

"Agreed," Cooper said.

I did another quick scan. "Let's not have this drag on. I think it's either five or six."

Courtney and I both looked at Cooper. He said, "I know which one it is. But if you need extra time to look at five and six, that's fine."

Courtney asked number five to step forward. I studied him, then looked at number six. They were practically twins. Dark, thick beards that covered most of their faces. About the same height and build. "I only see one difference. Number six has his hair pulled back in that tight ponytail. The man who attacked us had his hoodie pulled tight over his head." I nudged Cooper. "You jumped on the guy. Do you recall feeling a bump on the back of his head?"

"You read my mind," he said, popping his eyebrows. "Can't be him."

"So you both are saying number five is the guy."

"I'm about ninety percent there," I said. "I think I need a closer look."

"How can you only be ninety percent?" Cooper asked. "Don't get anal on us now."

"Hush, Cooper." I looked at Courtney. "Can you have him step up some more?"

She asked the officer to move number five forward, and I moved closer to the window. I paused and studied his face. "There. I see it."

"What?" Courtney asked.

"I tried slapping him, but my fingernails grazed his face. I can see a small scratch under his beard on his cheek."

"Wait. I don't remember you mentioning that in your statement."

I gritted my teeth. "I think I forgot. I was just too emotional to remember everything." I turned and looked at the man. "Ronnie Gutierrez. You killed my cousin." I could feel my chest starting to heave as tears pooled in my eyes.

Cooper put his arm around me. I didn't fight it.

"You both are certain?" Courtney asked.

We just looked at her.

"It's my job. Better to over-communicate than under-communicate."

We nodded, and I said, "It's number five."

"I'm assuming that's Ronnie Gutierrez?" Cooper asked.

"That's him," Courtney said. Her phone started chirping. "Let me take this. I'll be right back."

She left us in the room, and the officers ushered out the six men.

I felt drained. There were no chairs in the small room, so I leaned against the wall and pumped out a few deep breaths.

"Don't tell me you're already training to have a baby," Cooper said.

"Funny. Not."

"Well, I just thought that Harvey would want to create a fiefdom of kids so he can pass along the family heirlooms."

"I'm not marrying into royalty, and this isn't the 1700s." He was nuts, but at least it helped take my mind off the tension of the moment. "By the way, you never finished your whole riches-to-rags story back at the bookstore."

He chuckled. "Your label fits like a glove. Well, kind of. I didn't start in the 'riches.' But let's wait until another time to rehash my past. More important things to deal with now."

My phone buzzed. I removed it from my purse and looked at the screen. "Oh, crap. Alli's saying that Ma's going off on the manager at the reception location." I released a long breath. "That woman. Sometimes I wonder…"

"If she was born with a heart?"

"I'm trying to think positive here, and you're not helping."

"So, I'm assuming you're using the Holiday Inn off Harry Hines?"

"Not quite."

He seemed to be studying my face. "Stop looking at me."

"I'm just curious about where you're having your reception."

I huffed out a breath. "I'm sure you'll find out anyway. Reunion Tower."

"Cha-ching."

"Harvey insisted on paying for half. He's so noble."

"Noble," Cooper repeated.

I pointed a finger at him. "Zip it." I stuffed my phone back in my purse.

"Seriously, how did you convince Alli to jump in and help out?"

"First, she's been a great friend. We knew there might be some challenges along the way."

"With your mother, you mean."

I shrugged. "Alli told me that her gift to me is to act as a buffer as much as possible with Ma."

"Can't put a monetary value on that kind of gift. I think she might deserve a vacation after the wedding."

"Ha-ha. Ma's not that bad."

My phone buzzed again.

"Drum roll, please," Cooper said as I pulled my phone from my purse.

My chin dropped to my chest.

"Another text from Alli?"

"Yes. She's saying that Ma is nitpicking the pricing of everything and with such a rude tone that the manager just threatened to cancel the whole damn thing. Uggh!" I looked to the door, then back to my phone. "I'm not sure what to tell Alli,"

"Hey," Cooper waited until I looked at him. "I'm not going to say you look stressed because that would be rude."

"But, of course, you just said it."

He smiled and spread his arms. I finally cracked the slightest of smiles.

"It will be okay. Go take care of everything at the reception hall. Don't worry about Courtney."

I patted his shoulder as I walked toward the door. "Thanks. Let me know what happens."

"Your wish is my command."

"Oh, brother."

Eighteen

Cooper

There's nothing like sending a text to your loathsome boss telling her that the police have requested your services in connection with a murder investigation. Perhaps I'd fudged the context just slightly, but I couldn't help but outwardly giggle like a little boy who'd just convinced his mom he was sick and had to stay home from school.

Not that I would ever do that to my sweet mother.

I cracked the lid on my third Orange Crush—courtesy of the DPD—and watched with great curiosity the ebb and flow of movement and emotion in the homicide detective pool.

Over the last two hours, Courtney had three times sent an officer to apologize for her delay. The first time, Officer Mendenhall ushered me to the chair next to her desk and asked if he could get me a drink. I not-so-jokingly asked, "Who's paying?"

He said the DPD would pick up the one-dollar expense since I was taking the time to do my civic duty. *That's me, the poster man for civic service.*

Who was I kidding? If things had gone differently with the DA in New York, I might be serving time right now as opposed to serving my community.

I sipped more of my Orange Crush and released an audible "ah." A detective looked at me over his readers. "Sorry," I said, lifting a quick hand.

I became hooked on Orange Crush back in high school when I had a driving paper route. I'd just gotten my license and was looking to make some money to use for hanging with buddies, going on dates, and yes, even saving a bit for college. It was a mostly rural route. I'd pile the stack of newspapers in the front passenger seat of my very used Toyota Celica and challenged myself each afternoon to see how fast I could finish the route. There was always something more exciting going on, so the motivation to drive at a brisk pace was pretty high. Well, brisk might not be the way some of the locals would describe my driving style. My route was twenty-four miles. Only one lonely two-mile stretch of highway had a speed limit of fifty-five miles per hour. Every other road was forty-five or lower. One of my buddies who rode along one time had said, "You're driving like a fucking bat out of hell."

The very next afternoon, after fishtailing my car onto a gravel-filled road, I looked in my rearview mirror and saw flashing blue and red lights in the front grill of an unmarked car. I pulled to the side of the road. The guy walked up with a hand on his sidearm and his eyes unblinking. "So, you're the crazy-ass paper boy I've heard about?"

I shrugged. "I guess so, sir."

We ended up talking for a good ten minutes. He heard about my plight of saving for college and my family's need for me to work two jobs. Embellishing came quite naturally to me, I'd learned. Before he walked away, he wished me good luck and asked me to try to slow it down just a bit. No ticket. Not even a written warning.

I often think back to those days when Cooper Chain thought he could do no wrong. *Man, times have changed.*

Eventually, life will humble you. And I'd been humbled severely in the last year.

I ran my eyes across Courtney's desk. Lots of sticky notes in different colors. The handwriting looked like something akin to hieroglyphics. "That woman should be a doctor," I muttered to myself.

"I thought about being a doctor when I was in high school."

Her voice made me choke on my Orange Crush, which led to a loud coughing fit.

"You going to keel over right here?" she asked.

After I'd regained my composure, I grabbed a tissue, cleaned off some orange spittle, and said, "Were you serious about wanting to become a doctor in high school?"

"I never got anything under an A in any science class, so it naturally interested me." She dropped a manila folder on her desk and then looked at me, holding her gaze a few seconds. "And then my sister was murdered."

"Jesus, Courtney. I'm sorry."

"It changed my whole perspective on life and why I was spared."

Had to be a deeper story there.

"Sorry I kept you waiting so long." She released a deep breath and wiped her eyes. "And no comments about my face. I know I look like a raccoon."

She was talking about her makeup.

"Looks good to me." I hoped that came across as a compliment. I could see her looking around, so I gave her the scoop on Willow. She didn't seem to care.

"Talking to evasive lawyers is draining," she went on, "but it's part of the job."

"Anything to do with our case?"

She nodded. "Two things happened while you've been sitting here."

I paused a second. "Number one?"

A long sigh as she plopped down in her ergonomic chair. "Ronnie's attorney is claiming—actually, he brought in a sworn affidavit from the person—that says Ronnie has an alibi at the time you and Willow were attacked."

"What's the alibi?"

"He was with his girlfriend."

"Oh, because he's such a charmer, girls just flock to him, I'm sure."

She turned her palms upward.

"You know that's just not true, Courtney."

"The attorney has informed her that it's perjury if she's lying."

"You're still going to check out her story, right?"

She picked up a stack of folders with papers sticking out and dropped them back to her desk. "The answer you want to hear is 'yes.' So, yes, I'll do it."

"Plus," I added, "there's bound to be hair or fiber evidence at Marion's apartment that your hotshot crime scene nerds will find out are his."

"Probably so," she said far too slowly for me not to notice.

"Here comes the 'but.'"

"That was part of the discussion with Gutierrez's lawyer. Ronnie was Marion's boyfriend, so his fingerprints and every other distinguishable marker are all over the place most likely."

"What are you trying to tell me, Courtney?"

"We're not cutting him loose. We still need to talk to Ronnie's current girlfriend, but he's going through the bail process as we speak."

"That's bullshit! He did it. I guarantee you he was the guy who attacked us."

"Maybe."

"Maybe?"

"Okay, probably. I think we can get there."

"Meanwhile, he'll be out on the street. He could kill someone else with his roid rage."

"You think he's on steroids?"

"His face and forehead are dead giveaways. Plus, his temperament. Just needs to be checked out to add to the evidence."

"Right."

She had this overwhelmed expression again.

"Courtney, he could hurt Willow if you let him walk. Have you thought about that?"

"I don't see it. He wants to be a choir boy for now."

"Unless he's a psycho killer," I said. "And really, what kind of killer isn't a little psycho?"

"Two very different types. If he killed Marion, we're assuming it was out of retribution for being dumped. If he's a psychopath, then Marion wouldn't necessarily be his only target."

A loud whistle pierced through the din of voices. We snapped our heads to my right.

"Yo, Brouchard. You going to head out there?"

"Sure thing, Captain." Courtney lifted to her feet.

"What's up?"

"That's the second thing I wanted to tell you. We got word that Irving detectives are working a murder scene where the victim was killed in a similar manner as Marion. I need to check it out." She grabbed her purse and started walking off.

"But I have a ton of questions."

"You can ask them while I'm driving."

Nineteen

Willow

The smooth jazz music playing in the background, supposedly adding a light vibe to the event, was giving me the opposite feeling. Actually, I couldn't blame the music or the people who roamed Harvey's expansive home in the heart of Highland Park. My heart was about to pound outside of my chest, including the little black number I had on—something Harvey had personally picked out for me—because Cooper wasn't responding to my calls or text messages. Add to the fact that Courtney hadn't reached out to me, and I was on edge. Actually, I was almost over the edge.

I hated being ignored. And being ignored when we're talking about the person who killed my cousin was simply unacceptable. I felt completely helpless. Not that it was my job to formally charge Ronnie Gutierrez with Marion's murder and for assaulting Cooper and me, but whatever happened to communication? Hours had clocked by since I'd left the police station. At first, I was wrapped up in the details of the reception, essentially keeping Ma from choking the manager. But after that fun episode, I realized I'd yet to hear anything from Cooper. In fact, after countless phone calls and text messages, the only thing I received from Cooper was the following: *Busy with Courtney. Will call u later.*

I re-read his message on my phone and punched in another reply.

When is later? Call me, dammit!

I convinced myself nothing bad had happened. It was simply my desire to control the situation that had me so riled up. I did some deep-breathing exercises for a good minute, then walked out of Harvey's office and began to nod and smile at all the guests strolling through the home.

If there ever was a house that was made for entertaining, this was it. The home was over eight thousand square feet, with six bedrooms, each the size of my apartment, and eight bathrooms—or were there nine? Didn't really matter as long as I didn't have to clean them. Harvey had cleaners come in twice a week on the regular. If an event was happening, they'd come in before and after.

Tonight was one of those times. A huge event for Harvey and his accounting firm. With the acquisition of the smaller firm officially complete, he was hosting all the big-name clients from that company. A casual setting to get to know them on a personal level. To make them feel like they weren't just a number. When Harvey told me this, he gave me his patented pop of his eyebrow followed by his reassuring grin. Despite his proclivity for numbers and structure, he did have a sense of humor. And early on in our relationship, it was obvious we both shared that need for structure, organization, and pre-planning. It was kind of built into our DNA. One of the many reasons why Harvey and I were meant to be together.

"You have a lovely home." A woman who looked to be in her seventies had stepped right in front of me and taken hold of my hand. She had a warm smile.

"Thank you. I'm so glad you could make it."

I'd already repeated that same line about a dozen times during my first walk-through.

"The funny thing is," she said, taking a slow gaze across the living room with fireplaces at either end, "I don't know how you keep all your kids so quiet. I had three of my own, and they were so energetic. At times during formal dinner parties that my late husband and I hosted, I just wanted to tan their hides for not staying upstairs and out of the way. But now I look back at those times with so much appreciation. Little Tommy even once buried his face in a cake I'd baked."

I hadn't been listening all that closely, my eyes scanning the room for my rock, Harvey. But that last comment got my attention. "That's pretty funny. How old was Tommy at the time?"

"Oh, I think about five years old. Oh, Lord, he loved chocolate. By the time I found him, he was covered in chocolate cake. Of course, later that night, he woke with an upset stomach. I think I was up with him until four or five in the morning. I read him his favorite story, *Just Only Tommy,* about twenty times. I also read to him his Charlie Brown book. It helped calm him. Those are the times you really remember. It's not the big events; it's the small things, you know?"

I nodded.

"So, how many do you have?"

"Oh, we don't have kids. Not yet. In fact, we're not officially married. Getting married this weekend."

"Well, congratulations! Looks like you have plenty of room to add your own batch of rascals." She held up an empty glass. "Looks like I need another glass of that fancy wine." She winked at me and walked off.

Kids. The mommy desire had flared at different times in my adult life. But each time, I was never in the right position in my life, either dealing with a death...or the death of my career. But Harvey and I were on the same page. Sort of. He wanted three kids, unless they were all boys or all girls. Then he'd be open to having a fourth or even a fifth.

"Just want to make sure we're not too out of balance," he'd said with a slight chuckle. "I sound like I'm managing an assembly line. I hope you don't think I look at you as nothing more than a baby maker."

When he'd said those words, I had this odd feeling of not completely owning my body. I wanted kids. Hell, I'm almost forty years old. But I just wanted to have at least a fifty-fifty say in the situation. And did it really matter if we had all girls or all boys? After working the neonatal unit at Parkland for a year and seeing parents and families crumble from watching their poor babies suffer, I just wanted to have healthy kids.

My phone buzzed. Cooper.

Was wrapped up in another case. Call me whenever you can.

Another case? I couldn't get into this over the phone. He'd drive me nuts. I texted him our address and told him to take a cab or Uber.

His response was classic Cooper.

I'm a little short on change. U mind paying for cab when I get there?

I rolled my eyes and punched in a reply.

Fine. Just make it quick. And be ready to talk.

Twenty

Cooper

When the cab stopped in front of Casa de Harvey, the driver looked at me in the rearview and said, "You know people who live in a house like this?"

"What are you talking about? This *is* my house."

"Uh-huh, right. And I'm the Prince of Bel-Air. What you talking about, fool? You think I was born yesterday?"

A second later, a hand knocked on my window. I turned and saw Willow motioning for me to roll the window down. I opened the door.

"Hey, there," I said, still sitting in the car.

"What took you so damn long?"

"I, uh…well, I was just having a conversation with my good friend here."

The driver turned in his seat, gave a quick glace to Willow, and then looked at me. "Va-va-voom. That's why we're here, huh? You're like the pool boy on the side. More power to you, homeboy."

I glanced up at Willow, who'd now crossed her arms across her chest. "Did you hear that?" I asked.

"Uh-huh."

I looked back at the cabbie. "Bad move, dude, and *I'm* going to have to pay the price."

"Well, you just enjoy yourself with that fine piece of—"

"Stop! She can hear you." I started to get out of the car.

"Hold on, homey. You owe me twenty-nine dollars."

I flashed a toothy grin at Willow, who gave me a wad of cash. I passed it along to the driver.

"Fifty bucks! Sweet dog!"

I shut the door, and the cab zipped away. "You're dressed awfully nice," I said before I looked in the windows of the house and saw hordes of people milling about. "Are you having some type of wedding party?"

"Come with me." She grabbed my hand and pulled me along like I was in kindergarten. Even in heels, she was moving faster than I could catch up. I had to admit, though, my head was on a swivel as I took in the majestic landscaping around the mansion. The lighting in the trees gave the area a magical vibe. We made our way around the side of the house—it felt like we'd traveled through an enchanted forest—and marched into a side door. She led the way down a small hallway and into a room adjoining the kitchen. I could already pick up wafts of food that sent me traveling back in time to a swanky party given by a player's agent. His house was almost as nice as this one, from the little I'd seen thus far.

A door slammed shut behind me.

"Where have you been, and why haven't you returned my calls?"

Willow had a hand on her hip. She meant business. Despite her pointed scowl, my eyes couldn't help but traverse the curves accentuated by her little black dress, which stopped mid-thigh.

She snapped her fingers. "Are you staring at my legs at a time like this?"

"Of course not." I didn't believe me, so I doubted she did. I ran my fingers through my hair and noticed wine bottles all around us. "This is a wine cellar?"

"The refrigerated bottles are in there," she said, motioning with her head to a spot behind me. I walked over and looked through a glass door that had an electronic lock on it. The room was dimly lit, like the inside of an airplane on a nighttime flight.

"How many bottles are in there?"

"I don't know, maybe two or three hundred."

"Holy crap. What can you do with that much wine?"

"Hold a lot of big events. Like the one that I'm missing right now. But it doesn't matter. I want to know what happened today with Ronnie Gutierrez. The fact you've been avoiding me has made me more and more anxious."

"It wasn't on purpose. I drank three Orange Crushes and waited a good couple of hours before Courtney showed back up."

"You still drink that crap?"

"I don't have three hundred bottles of wine to choose from. Plus, it was on the DPD's dime."

Her hands dropped against her thighs—yes, my eyes went there again, but this time I caught myself before being chided.

"What's wrong?"

She shook her head in disgust or disappointment. Maybe a combination of the two. "Your money issues, your chipped tooth. I still don't understand what's happened to you, your life."

"Is this really the time to get into it? I mean, it's been a long day. Courtney and I have been—"

"Busy. Right." She nodded as if something was stirring inside that pretty head of hers.

"So, it's really been a grind, to be honest with you. Not sure I ever—"

"Hold on. You. Courtney. A grind. Getting busy. Don't tell me you've been off screwing the detective assigned to investigate the murder of my cousin."

I'd never taken acid before, but I wondered if this was what it felt like. The world literally spinning before my very eyes. "Do whaaaat?"

"I saw you ogling her." She crossed her arms.

"Will, this is nuts. I haven't been screwing Courtney."

"You admit she's attractive?"

"Yes, but why do you care?"

Silence. Then she sighed. "Who said I cared?"

This is the part where I think but don't dare say, *"Surely, women must be from Venus."*

She went on. "I just don't want your flings to impede the process of justice."

"This is ridiculous, you know that?"

"You're calling me ridiculous…in my house?"

"Oh, so now this is your house? I thought this was King Harvey's mansion?"

We were now basically in shout mode.

"Don't call him that," she said, jabbing a finger at my face.

"Don't tell me I'm screwing the detective when I'm not."

Our faces were about a foot apart. I could practically see steam rising in the air—hers and mine.

A knock on the door.

"What is it?" she called out.

The door opened, and a short man with a mustache and wearing a waiter's outfit poked his head inside. "Excuse me, Mrs. Bernstein."

Her eyes shifted to me, then back to the man. "Just call me Willow. Is there a problem?"

"Well, miss, we ran out of the preferred champagne. Should we ask the guests to wait while we run back to our catering shop, or would it be okay to use a few bottles from your cellar? Of course, we'll pay you back."

"You can just use the bottles from the cellar." She bumped

against my shoulder on her way to the glass door. She punched in the code, walked inside, and pointed out the champagne section.

"If you need more, feel free to ask," she said.

The man nodded and scooted out with four bottles.

We stood in silence for a few seconds. Finally, I relented. "I guess I could have communicated better today."

"And I'm sorry if I got carried away about you and Courtney."

I walked over and held out my hand. She shook it…tightly. In fact, she didn't let go. She started squeezing my fingers as a smile spread across her face.

"You still want to play that game?"

"What game?"

"The one where you show off your Wonder Woman strength."

"Super Woman," she said, pulling back her hand and winking. "And don't forget that."

"So, now that we've both blown off some steam, tell me what happened with Ronnie."

I gave her the short version, but she still gasped twice and cussed three times.

"I know. I'm right there with you."

She pushed a few curly locks out of her face that had escaped from her bun. But some hair got caught in her ring. "Ouch."

"Don't move. I can help you." I was close enough to smell her perfume, or her, or both. It was like an aphrodisiac.

"I got it, Cooper," she said, putting a hand against my chest.

I watched her carefully unsnag the hair and ring without creating a major hairdo blowout.

"So, this crazy man is out on the street. No offense, but I still don't understand how that took all day."

"Oh, I forgot to tell you the second part."

"There's a second part?"

I explained about the murder scene in Valley Ranch, in the northern part of Irving but still in Dallas County.

"So, an older woman was found by her son lying on the bed just like Marion? I don't get it. I mean, I could give you ten plausible causes of death because of her advanced age that would show no visible signs of trauma."

"Of course, you're the master nurse. And before you snap back at me, I'm not being sarcastic. According to Courtney, who got on a quick conference call with the ME at the Valley Ranch murder scene and the one at Marion's, they feel like they were killed in similar ways. Of course, it will take a full autopsy to determine if she might have been drugged. But there's also another reason they feel like they're connected."

"What's that?"

"They found a dove's wing in the victim's bedroom."

"Holy. Shit." She paced the room. Her heels clipped the hand-scraped hardwood floors, and her hips swung to and fro, just slightly. But it was enough. The audio-visual combination had me temporarily mesmerized. What can I say? I'm a sensory person.

She stopped and stared me down. "This is really starting to freak me out."

"I'd like to say it's just ironic. But I'm not sure anyone would believe me, starting with Courtney."

"Cooper, the autopsy is one thing. Not sure how quickly the ME can get to it. This is Dallas County, after all."

"About that..." I said, holding up a finger.

"Hold on. This woman in Valley Ranch...when was she murdered?"

"I heard them talking about rigor mortis and how they could narrow down the time of death. Sometime between midnight and four a.m."

"I can't believe I'm even suggesting this, but wasn't our pal Ronnie Gutierrez sitting in a jail cell?"

"You're thinking like a cop. That's exactly what Courtney said."

She made a scoffing noise, then turned her palms upward.

"What does this all mean, Cooper? I don't know how to process it. Is it possible that Ronnie has an accomplice? But why would this accomplice kill this older woman?"

"Well, there's something—"

She jumped in like I wasn't there. "Could there be some type of connection between Marion and this older woman? When is Courtney going to look into that?"

We stood in silence, our eyes trained on each other for a few seconds.

"Did you get all of your questions out of your system?" I asked.

"You act like I'm going through one of those body-cleansing routines."

"Does Harvey make you do that too?"

"Did you just say what I think you fucking said?"

Crap. Where had my filter gone? "No."

"Yes, you did." She started shaking her head. "I don't even know why I bother with you, Cooper. You're a fucking mess. You've got a grudge against my fiancé for some reason, and you're evasive."

"Only on Mondays and Wednesdays," I said with a wink.

She stared holes into my body.

"Just joking," I said. "Look, I'm sorry I made that comment. All your questions make a lot of sense. I was starting to have the same questions myself when I was at the crime scene. In fact, I was pinging Courtney with about a dozen of them. And then she got another call."

Willow brought a hand to her forehead. "Don't tell me there was another murder."

I released a deep breath. "It's probably more than that."

"What are you saying?"

"She ran off pretty quickly, but there was a mass suicide-homicide at some type of commune in far east Dallas. At least that's what I thought I heard as she ran off."

"That sounds…"

"Fucked up. I can say it because I'm not dressed like I'm going to the opera."

She put a finger to her mouth, probably about to start chewing on a nail, but she caught herself and started pacing again.

Suddenly, the door burst open. It was the same mustached man. "Mrs., uh…I mean, Willow, someone told me you used to be nurse."

"Used to be?" I said, confused. "Actually—"

"What's the problem?" she asked.

"One of our cooks. He's having horrible chest pains. I don't want to create a scene. Is there any way you could check him out?"

"Of course."

"He's in the sitting area right off the kitchen," the man said, waving her out the door.

She gave me a fleeting glance.

"Am I supposed to stay in here?" I asked.

She was gone before giving me an answer.

Twenty-One

Willow

When I found the cook, he was sweating and had pretty severe chest pains. I checked his pulse. The beat was irregular, but not off the charts. I gave him an aspirin, and then he started speaking. In German.

Thankfully, Marco, the name of the smaller man with the mustache, knew enough German to serve as an interpreter. It probably took ten minutes to complete the Q&A—something that I'd normally get out of a patient in less than sixty seconds. I learned that the cook had been testing a lot of his recipes throughout the day, even though his doctor had given him specific instructions to lay off spicy foods. He looked embarrassed once that answer was relayed to me and started apologizing for the worry it was creating. I told him, through Marco, that I'd heard much worse excuses over the years and not to worry about it.

I gave him my theory: he was suffering from severe indigestion, and he would be okay. Still, I recommended that someone drive him to a hospital or clinic. One of the busboys eagerly volunteered to take him to a clinic down the road, and off they went.

Emergency diverted. Marco thanked me a dozen times, then apologized twice as many times. No one at the event had noticed anything, anyway. I reassured him he'd still get our future business.

"You and Mr. Bernstein are two of the kindest people I know." He shook my hand with great fervor and dipped his head. For a second, I got this sense he was treating me as though I were Meghan Markle, the newest member of the royal family. The one who represented normal America. And it felt damn awkward.

He walked off with some extra zeal.

"So, are you a nurse, or do you just play one on TV?"

Cooper was leaning against the wall, trying to look cool. Too cool.

I got to my feet and looked over his shoulder. "I think even more people have arrived. I'm sure Harvey is wondering why I'm not out there being social."

"Now who's the one being evasive?" He smiled like he'd just swallowed the proverbial canary.

"Have you not noticed that there is an important event going on tonight? These clients really need to connect with Harvey and his partners on a personal level. Harvey's firm can't afford to pay all this money and have the clients walk."

"By all means, we don't want a few million dollars to get in the way of finding out who murdered two people. Go ahead. Go find Harvey and be his plus-one so he can rake in even more money."

I closed my eyes a second and tried not to let him get under my skin. "Tried" being the operative word. "You're attempting to guilt me into doing…I don't know what. But I'm an independent woman who doesn't need Harvey or any man to complete me. You have no idea what my life has been like over the last eighteen years."

He nodded as if he knew something.

"What?" I asked, even though I shouldn't have.

"You have secrets. Just like me."

"Cooper, I really don't have time for this right now."

"That's cool." He turned and stuffed his hands in his pockets. "Just let me know if you want to talk more about this crazy murder situation."

I'd started to walk past him, but I stopped right in front of him. My eyes went to his lips and the light stubble on his face. I had this odd flashback of feeling that burn of his stubble rubbing against my face…and liking it. I fanned myself.

"Hey, there you are." Harvey had just walked around the corner. He did a double take. "Cooper? Didn't know you were a new client of ours," he said with a lighthearted chuckle.

"I do my own taxes. It's pretty easy. I make zero, so I claim zero." Cooper looked a little out of place.

"Funny, Cooper. I like tax jokes." Harvey elbowed him.

"Ah." Cooper clutched his arm.

"Your arm. You still haven't had it checked out?" I asked.

"I'm good." He turned his head and looked as though he wanted to run off. I really wouldn't blame him. "So, I was just in the neighborhood. Lots of friends in this part of town. But I need to get going."

"Have you had any of our delicious food? You can eat it here in the kitchen, but you've got to try everything. There's plenty to go around. I know. I paid for it." Harvey popped Cooper on the back, then he turned to me. "You got a second? I want to introduce you to—"

"Ha. You couldn't escape from me that easily, Harvey."

Harvey smiled and moved off to the side. "This is who I wanted to introduce you to, Willow."

I stepped forward and took in the full picture. The guy smiled so wide his eyes turned into slits, which looked rather odd on a man shaped like a pumpkin. I shook his hand. He had sweaty palms, so I tried to pull my hand back, but he gripped it extra tightly and then kissed the top of my hand. His lips felt like a scrub brush.

Harvey put his hand on my waist, and the man let go of my hand, although his wide grin stayed etched on his face. "Willow, this is Mr. Khatri."

"All my friends call me Vijay."

Out of the corner of my eye, I noticed Cooper get stiff as stone. His eyes shifted to his right, but he didn't turn his head to look at Mr. Khatri.

"And is this person also in your firm?" Mr. Khatri asked.

"Oh, he's just an old friend of Willow's."

Cooper slowly turned around.

"A friend of Willow's is a friend of mine."

Mr. Khatri started laughing, for some unknown reason. Harvey joined in the laugh-fest, and I tried to do my job of brown-nosing, but I didn't quite get there.

I couldn't stop looking at Cooper. Blood had drained from his face.

Now I had even more questions for my old boyfriend.

Twenty-Two

Cooper

I sighed for about the tenth time in the last ten minutes. Was that a sign of stress or simply frustration at being asked the same question over and over again?

"Cooper Chain, are you going to answer my question, or am I going to have to write you up?"

I was sitting in Brandy's shadow, literally, as she stood over me in the breakroom. The fluorescent lighting created a dark figure that resembled some type of reptilian creature.

We'd started out having a one-on-one conversation sitting across from each other at the only table in the room. When she didn't appreciate my answers to her interrogation—the word "Gestapo" kept coming to mind—she then turned to physical intimidation. Of course, this only worked because I had to keep this job. So, I stayed in my seat, kept my hands folded on the table, as wobbly as it was, and only occasionally looked up.

"Now you're not even looking me in the eye! This is pure and simple disrespect."

I could feel my internal temperature on the rise, so I started counting backward in my mind from one hundred. Anything to keep me from losing my cool. Ninety-nine, ninety-eight, ninety-seven...

"Are you going to answer me?"

"I've answered all your questions, Brandy. For the most part, you keep asking me the same one over and over again, just in a different way. I'll say it again in case you didn't hear me the first ten times. I was at the police station when I left work, and then I went to a crime scene."

"You expect me to believe that?"

"You want to talk to Detective Brouchard? I have her number right here," I said, pulling out my phone and thumbing through my contacts.

A second later, I felt hot breath against my neck. My mind flashed on an image from one of the *Jurassic* movies where the latest lab-mutated beast had nuzzled up next to a man who thought he'd found an adequate hiding spot. Not. Then, he'd pee his pants or tremble with unbridled fear until the dinosaur devoured him like he was an extra-spicy chicken wing.

"Can I help you?" I asked without moving my head, hoping to avoid contact with her face.

"Do I look like I want to talk to your make-believe hussy?"

Hussy. Hadn't heard that one in a while. "Why don't you believe me? Go online and look up the story of the murder, then."

"Haven't had time for something that I know is a lie, or at least a very embellished story."

She had me at "embellished." Yes, I was pretty good at that. But it wasn't required this time. Real life kind of got in the way. "I don't know what you mean."

"I know you can twist the truth."

"Isn't the truth somewhat subjective?" I tried to chuckle, but when I glanced at her one eye, it triggered that same dinosaur flashback. I was afraid she'd roar so loudly that I'd be knocked out of my chair from the concussive impact.

She smacked her bare hand on the table, and I flinched.

"Jesus, Brandy, don't you think you're taking this a bit too far?"

The door opened, and Brandy stood upright.

I immediately saw the lipstick-red locks of Tracy, who leered at me as she walked to the fridge. "Sorry to interrupt. Just grabbing my vegan snack." She acted like she was better than everyone because she was vegan. I wanted to ask how many animals were killed to create that lovely red dye in her hair. But now wasn't the time for wisecracks. She grabbed a paper sack.

"We'll be done one way or the other in just a minute," Brandy said in her fake retail cheerleader voice.

"No problem. I've finished up my tasks, so I figured I'd start on Cooper's closing tasks."

"Well, thank you, Tracy." Brandy nudged my arm. My bad arm.

Through clenched teeth, I said, "Thank you, Tracy (*you ass-kissing bitch*)." I only thought the last part, of course. It was a coping mechanism.

Just before Tracy shut the door, behind Brandy's back, she stuck her tongue out at me.

"Is she for real?" I said.

Brandy wagged a finger in my face. "You should try emulating her once in a while. She's great with the customers, she's reliable, and she works tirelessly around here, unlike you and that freak with the mullet."

"Don't talk poorly of Slash. He's a friend."

"If he's your friend, you've got a lot of problems."

She had a point. But only one.

"Can I go back to work now?" I tried to stand up, but she was hovering so close it wasn't possible. And the last thing I wanted to experience was grazing her body.

"This is your last warning, Cooper."

I swallowed and reminded myself I couldn't quit this gig. Not until I'd worked five thousand hours. Truth be told, it had been difficult to not think about Dr. V all day long. How he'd ended up at Harvey's house was something I still couldn't wrap my head around. Presumably, he was a client of this new accounting outfit Harvey's firm had purchased. "Presumably" did not convince me. It was just too much of a coincidence that he was in town the same week that his muscle, the Sack Brothers, had beaten the snot out of me and threatened to kill me if I didn't fork over the fifty grand by the end of the week.

I'd hightailed it out of the mansion soon after seeing Dr. V. Sleep only made small cameo appearances in the middle of a series of nightmares I'd never repeat to anyone. They had way too much blood, my blood. Dr. V and the Sack Brothers were the villainous stars.

Throughout the day, I'd expected calls from Courtney and Willow. I was hoping to get an update from Courtney. With Willow, I was prepared for an onslaught of calls and text messages that would burn up my phone. I'd actually rebooted my phone twice just to make sure it was working properly. Still, I had to work all day, so it wasn't like I could just run off and chase down Courtney for more information.

"Have you been listening to a thing I've said?" Her arms were now crossed as she tapped her foot to the floor.

"Of course. Just taking it all in. I know I need to be a better communicator."

"Better at everything," she added. She huffed out a breath. "I can't waste any more time with you. Just get your shit together, Cooper, okay? Don't make me have to do something I don't want to do."

She left the room, and I was finally free. I took in a few cleansing breaths. As I got to my feet, the door opened again. It was Slash.

"Glad you're still alive."

"Feels like she cut off my scalp."

Slash touched the top of his head, his eyes glazing over for a moment. Then he snapped to it. "Hey, that temporary bookshelf in the middle of the store, the one Brandy thinks is so cool, just fell over. She wants me to put it back together. I don't know how to do crap like that."

"I don't either. But I'll help you out."

That's what I did for the next hour. When we were done, Brandy walked by and said, "Appreciate you guys working so hard on that."

"Did she actually give us a compliment?" Slash asked after she left.

"On the surface, yes. But when a snake smiles at you, don't forget the fangs are just as sharp and the venom just as deadly."

"Damn. That sounds like a commercial for a movie."

"Hollywood. I forgot to tell you that they called me up and want me to write and direct a new film starring Bradley Cooper and Jennifer Lawrence."

"I know the babe. Who's the dude?"

I thought about telling him what my mom always said about him being my look-alike. What was the point?

I punched out my timecard and headed home.

Twenty-Three

Cooper

Two miles later, I was walking up the driveway of Mrs. Kowalski's house. She hustled out the front door in her robe. "Oh, Mr. Chain, your timing couldn't be better."

"What's wrong?"

"I'm trying to replace a light fixture in the upstairs hallway, and I can't find my Phillips head screwdriver. Do you happen to have one?"

All of a sudden, I was Mr. Handyman. I was more comfortable wearing an apron than wearing a tool belt—and my cooking capabilities were limited at best. "It's awfully late. Are you sure you don't want to tackle this in the morning?"

"You know me. If I start a project, I must finish it."

I held back a yawn and scratched the side of my head. "Let me check a couple of places for the screwdriver, and I'll meet you inside."

"Wonderful. I'll make us some tea while you retrieve the screwdriver."

She went back inside as I made my way up to my apartment. My décor was something between barebones and simple. I guess I could call it "simply barebones."

I turned on the single lamp in the main living area. I knew of only two places where I kept any tools whatsoever. I first checked the bottom of my closet. Lots of sneakers, most of which I'd received from people in my previous sports-oriented world, and a single pair of scuffed dress shoes. I found a box of pictures that I'd taken with me when I was kicked out of my house. I paused a second and considered opening it. *Why rip open old wounds again?*

I moved the box out of the way next to my TV stand, then crawled on my hands and knees, searching for a satchel of tools or even just individual ones. Nothing.

When I pushed up to a standing position, I felt a shooting pain in my knee. I should be used to it by now, but today it felt worse. Probably just age, and a little wear and tear from my basketball days.

I checked the only other likely place in the apartment: my junk drawer in the kitchen. All I found was junk. I should have just dumped out the whole thing right then. But I didn't. I wondered if Willow had a junk drawer.

"No way in hell," I said out loud.

I walked down the creaky wooden steps outside my apartment and spotted my car, a Chrysler LeBaron that was almost as old as I was. It was a convertible. Probably a real babe magnet for some lucky kid back in the day. I'd read somewhere that it was the first American-made convertible in the previous twenty years. Some had hailed it as a classic. Now, though, it was nothing more than a classic piece of shit. The soft cover looked like a patchwork quilt with the various shades of duct tape along with the original tan— a very faded tan.

'Probably the battery," I said to myself, referring to the car's latest issue. "Or it could be the alternator. How the hell would I know? I'm no mechanic." As I walked past it, a thought shot into my mind. The tools had to be in the trunk. I recalled bringing them to the bookstore to help put together some display Brandy had in mind.

I pulled out my keys and opened the trunk. The scratched brown satchel of tools was off to the right. But my eyes didn't focus on that. They were glued to a small, black duffel bag. I didn't own a small, black duffel bag. Or, for that matter, a large, black duffel bag.

I scanned the area. It was quiet, aside from the wind blowing through the old trees in Mrs. Kowalski's expansive backyard.

I could feel my pulse tick faster as I pondered who'd put the bag in my car.

Actually, the more timely question was: what was in the bag? I reached for it but stopped short of touching it. My mind envisioned a snake on the inside. A real snake, not a picture of Dr. V. But putting a snake in my car sounded like something from Dr. V's playbook, one that would usually be implemented by his twin numbnuts, the Sack Brothers.

"Fuck!" I ran my fingers through my hair and paced back and forth in front of the open trunk, my eyes on the bag the entire time. It didn't change shape or move.

The snake could be waiting for you to unzip the bag, dumbass. One quick bite from a cobra or a viper, and you probably wouldn't be able to crawl to the house to get help from Mrs. Kowalski.

"Mr. Chain, is everything okay?"

I turned to see Mrs. Kowalski starting to walk out the back door and onto her deck. I quickly held up a hand. "I'm all good. I just found my tools. You can go inside now. I'll meet you there."

"Wonderful. Tea is getting cold." She disappeared back inside the house.

I took a breath and pondered my next move. Grab the tools, shut the trunk, and then deal with the snake later. *Or* grow some balls and unzip the damn bag right now.

"This one's for you, Willow," I said, connecting my ball-growing comment to the person who'd been razzed about her last name her entire life.

I appreciated my ability to make a joke as I started sweating like I was in a sauna. With my arm outstretched, I used two fingers to tug the loose handles of the duffel bag. It was too heavy to lift with my fingers, but so far, I detected no movement, based on watching the outside of the bag.

I wiped my forehead, moved a little closer to the trunk, and grabbed the bag's handles with my entire hand. I slowly lifted the bag. It was probably twenty pounds. I set it on the cracked driveway, and something shifted against the side of the bag. "What the fuck!" I jumped back a couple of steps.

My heart was thumping like a mad dog. I did more pacing. *What to do, what to do, what to do.*

"A stick!" I called out. I found a sturdy four-foot stick in the back yard and then went back to the bag. I used the stick to nudge the side of the bag. Something moved inside, but it didn't feel like a snake. It seemed like…I don't know, maybe something that wasn't connected to the other parts? I wasn't exactly sure what to make of it, or whether to trust my assessment. Maybe I should just throw the damn thing in the weeds behind the garage.

Out of sight, out of mind, as they say. Like that would accomplish anything. I couldn't keep running from my issues. I had to face them, even if it meant going face to face with a snake.

I forced myself to scoot closer to the bag. I tried to swallow, but it was all cottonmouth. *Wait, isn't there a type of snake called the cottonmouth?*

"Mr. Gloom and Doom, please shut the fuck up," I told part of me.

I leaned down, grabbed the zipper, yanked it open in under a second, and jumped back so fast I stumbled to the ground, landing directly on my bad forearm. "Ah, crap!" I brought my arm to my chest, which was already pumping out breaths like a locomotive.

Nothing had popped out of the bag. I got to my feet, grabbed the stick, and poked the bag again.

I was moving something, but I could swear it wasn't a snake. *Could it be multiple, smaller snakes?*

I stepped closer, my stick at the ready in case something popped out of the bag. About three feet from the bag, I found an angle to where I could see inside the bag.

"Is that...?" I used the stick to open the bag wider, and that's when I confirmed it.

I was staring at wads of cash. I dropped to my knees and took out ten stacks of cash. I thumbed through one of the stacks of bills of various denominations. I even smelled the cash. I looked around the area, wondering if someone was pulling some type of prank that would be shown on YouTube, and I'd look like a real ass in front of millions of anonymous people. No sign of anyone, although I heard a dog barking in the distance.

Back to the bag of money. I ran my hands across the cash, feeling a tingling sensation roll up my arms and through my body.

The cash was real. There had to be at least fifty grand in there, maybe more. I looked up to the sky. "Thank you, Jesus!"

It was a frickin' miracle. Mom always told me to believe in miracles. I'd been skeptical for thirty-nine years. But my string of bad luck had just ended. "Yes!" I muttered to myself. I could finally get those maggots to leave me the hell alone, allowing me to reassemble my life without always looking over my shoulder. The last few months had been the most stressful of my life. Hardly a day went by without me wondering if I was about to be kidnapped, thrown into the back of a van, killed and dismembered, my body parts tossed in a landfill. I wasn't creating that thought out of thin air, either.

I'd heard stories about Dr. V and the Sack Brothers carrying out that exact crime against people who hadn't paid back their gambling debts. Somehow, though, Dr. V had evaded the Feds and local police for years. Or had he simply paid off everyone who held a power position at each agency? Admittedly, that might take a lot of effort and money. From what I'd seen, money was no issue, both through his so-called legitimate businesses (real estate development) and the ones he didn't report to the IRS (illegal gambling, loan sharking, racketeering, and many more). Alibis could also be bought. Fear and intimidation were the tools of his trade, and when coupled with his proclivity for using money at the appropriate time, he seemed to be untouchable.

But I wasn't in law enforcement, and I had no way of exposing his criminal operation, at least not without losing my life in the process. And now it wouldn't matter anyway. I had the money. I would give it to his proxy, the Sack Brothers, then forever wash my hands of that ilk.

My breathing slowed a bit, and oxygen started reaching my brain. I started to think through what had just happened. Someone had broken into my trunk and left a bunch of money. So, why? Why me? Was it just some Good Samaritan? If so, how would he or she know about my debt? Or did whoever left the money now expect something in return?

"Mr. Chain, are you okay?"

Mrs. Kowalski leaned her head out the back door. She sounded concerned.

"All good." I grabbed the tool satchel and the bag of money and walked inside to help Mrs. Kowalski with her light fixture. By the time I finished the task and drank the tea, my mind had completely shifted toward fear. I kept repeating one terrifying question to myself.

Did I now owe my soul to two devils?

Twenty-Four

Willow

If someone you knew slept in past ten in the morning and they were over the age of twenty-one, would that designate them as a lazy-ass? In my book it did.

I'd found Cooper's place by talking to his buddy, Slash, from Books and Spirits. After knocking on the front door of the main house—one of the old classic homes in the Park Cities—I spoke to a Mrs. Kowalski, a sweet woman whose diminutive size made me feel like an Amazon woman. She said she'd yet to see "Mr. Chain" leave the property today. She said his name as if he were some esteemed professor. "Not that I'm nosy or anything," she said, dipping her head slightly out of embarrassment.

She invited me to go ahead and knock on his door, adding, "I haven't seen many women come calling on Mr. Chain. Actually, none that I can recall. At first, I thought he was just being respectful of living in my garage apartment. But now I wonder…" She spoke like it was the 1950s.

"Well, I'm just a friend."

"Darn. I can tell he needs a nice young lady in his life. It might help him with all his issues."

"Issues?"

"Well, it's none of my business, really. He's a nice man who I can see has been put through the ringer. I might be past my prime, but I have good eyes and my instincts are rather spot on. Have you seen that tooth?"

"Oh, yeah."

"I didn't say anything. He already has one mother," she said with a sweet giggle.

Now that I thought about it, if money was such a big deal—and I knew there was a more complex story there—I wondered why he wasn't living with his mom.

Mrs. Kowalski continued. "Between you and me, I think some of his personal issues has to do with a woman leaving him high and dry."

I gave a slow nod, and I found myself curious for some reason. "Did he tell you about what happened with this woman?"

"Oh, no. He doesn't share much about his life. I've tried to get him to share his background, but he just gives me half-answers."

"Been there, done that," I mumbled.

"I'm sorry?" She put a hand to her ear.

"Oh, just remembering something I need to do."

"Anything to do with that rock on your finger?" She grinned like a little girl.

I held my hand up. It was difficult not to smile. "I'm getting married this weekend, so I have a few things on my plate."

"I bet you do. But you're still finding time to help a friend. That's nice. Mr. Chain can still use a good friend, even if it's a platonic relationship."

"Definitely platonic." I said it so fast it seemed to take her a moment to process my words. I started to walk around to the back, but I stopped. "Do you have any insight into his issues, other than this woman? I mean, I have my own thoughts, but he's not very good at opening up."

"Nothing specific, sorry. Although it's obvious he's been in a fight of some kind," she said, waving a hand in front of her face. "I think I have something burning in the oven. Got to run. You two have fun."

I waved goodbye, realizing that fun wasn't in the equation, not this week and not with Cooper. The steps up to his apartment wobbled so much I wondered if they might give way. I knocked on his door and waited. I repeated that exercise three times. Then I started banging my fist.

Cooper opened the door while rubbing his eye with the palm of his fist. "What the fuck are you doing?" He coughed twice.

I put an arm over my face. "You sound horrible. Are you sick or did you party too much last night?"

"Party?" He tried to laugh, but that turned into a coughing fit, and he started shaking all over. Or parts of him did. He was only wearing boxers.

"You need to…" I flicked my hand toward his midsection.

"Need to what?" He was back to rubbing his eye. He was either oblivious or trying to tease me, or something like that.

"Can you put on some damn clothes?"

"Well, shit, I'm so sorry. I just happened to get out of bed," he said with a fair amount of attitude. "At least I'm not naked."

I giggled—a little nervously, to my surprise.

He opened the door wider. "You want to come in while I get cleaned up?"

I took two giant steps inside, ensuring I was far from his body. That said, I couldn't help but sneak a quick glance. He seemed to be in a decent shape. I doubted he worked at it. Probably just in his genes. My mind actually spelled that j-e-a-n-s.

I closed my eyes and spoke to myself: *Harvey, Harvey, Harvey.*

"Did you drop by just to wake me up and give me shit for sleeping in?"

He shut the door, then raked his fingers through his hair. I hated to admit it, but he did kind of have the Bradley Cooper look, the one with the longer hair. Now that I wasn't in the middle of dealing with wedding dresses and hangovers and police lineups and even Harvey's important social event, I took him all in. And I was hit by his piercing blue eyes. I could feel myself wobble a bit, so I reached for a wall.

"Your arm, Cooper," I said, looking for some kind of flaw to point out. Then I did a quick scan of his place. If you Googled "pigsty," his apartment would be the first image. Shit was everywhere. "This place, your life is a mess."

"Is that your way of volunteering to be my life coach?" he asked, raising an eyebrow. "Don't answer that. I don't need any help from you or anyone else. I'm doing just fine on my own."

This is what he calls "doing just fine"? Part of me wanted to fire off a zinger in response, or at least counter that argument in a major way. But I was a nurse. Or at least I used to be a nurse, so my empathy factor was usually pretty high. "Don't worry about it. Forget I said anything. It might look like I'm living this privileged life, but it hasn't always been that way."

He looked at me and didn't blink. "You have your own dark secrets, don't you?"

"You sound so...dark."

We waited two seconds, and then we both broke out in laughter.

"I'm such a dork," I said.

"Still, even after all these years," he said as he disappeared into the bedroom.

"At least I'm not a slob!" I called out.

He came back not even two minutes later, and he looked like a different man—jeans that fit him perfectly, a casual V-neck sweater that showed off a hint of chest hair, and that mischievous smile.

"You never said why you dropped by."

"Have you heard anything from Courtney?" I asked.

"Hell no. I was hoping you had. You know I would have called you, right?"

"Same here," I said.

"Ooookay." He huffed out a breath. "You want a drink?"

"Booze at this hour?"

"What? Are you still thinking I was out partying last night? Far from it. I came home, helped Mrs. Kowalski install a new light fixture, then hit the bed. I just happened to stare at the ceiling a while."

"One of those nights?"

"Uh, yeah."

"You still thinking about seeing Marion's body?"

He looked away for a second. "That and many other things."

I blew out a frustrated breath. Mainly frustrated at myself for giving a damn about those "many other things."

He walked to the fridge and pulled out a bottle of Orange Crush. "Want one?"

"No, thanks."

"I also have water," he said, pointing at the sink with a smirk.

"I'm good."

"So what's going on?"

"Look, I'm here because I'm...because of a lot of things."

"Like?"

"I start to get into thinking about my wedding day, and then I feel guilty. Someone died, and here we are planning a party."

"Makes sense. But you didn't kill her."

"I know that, Cooper. We thought we had this ex-boyfriend identified as the killer, but now he's not even in jail, and he has this alibi. So, I'm kind of pissed."

"Kind of?"

"Very. Very pissed."

"I am too." He took a swig of his drink, then the two of us ran our eyes across the floor. Crumbs were everywhere. I tried to ignore the urge to find a broom and sweep it all up. Then again, something told me he didn't own a broom.

"So what are we going to do about it?" I asked.

"Seems to me you already have an idea. That *is* why you're here, right?"

"I guess. This commiserating thing only lasts so long. I need to see some goddamn progress."

"We."

"Huh?"

"*We* need to see progress. I want this fucker arrested just as much as you do."

"Are you still thinking it's Ronnie?" I asked.

He shook his head and moved his shoulders in no discernible direction. "I wish I knew for certain. But let's think about this a moment. We know Ronnie is the one who attacked us."

"Right."

"So, is this alibi claim one way of saying that when we caught Ronnie there, he had *not* just killed Marion?"

"I guess I'd just made an assumption that he had."

"Me too," he said.

My eyes found what looked like a burn stain on the wall behind the toaster. I blinked it away. "But we ID'd the guy, so we know he was there at that time. Could he have come back to set up that creepy scene with her lying in the bed?"

"It's possible, I suppose."

We were both in deep thought for a moment. All I could hear was water dripping out of a leaky faucet. It began to give me a headache. I rubbed my temple and said, "I think we're missing something. We need to know what the ME is estimating for time of death."

"And we should also corroborate this story about Ronnie's alibi with his supposed new girlfriend."

"His new girlfriend," I scoffed. "Can you believe that monster has any girlfriend at all? What was Marion thinking?"

"Who knows if any of it's the truth? We could find out this new girlfriend suddenly traveled to New Zealand to take care of an ailing aunt."

"Or maybe Ronnie threatened her into giving an alibi."

"That was my first thought," he said.

"But, ultimately, it all comes back to the timing."

"Exactly. Where was he at each hour during the broadest window of time for when Marion was killed?"

I tapped a finger to my lips. "You know what? Janice, an old nurse friend, had a brother who worked in the ME's office. Not sure if he still does, though."

"Can you call her?"

"I'm not bashful." I pulled out my phone and paused. "Wait. Can't we just go straight to Courtney and get all this information?"

"Haven't you heard about the drug suicide-homicide in east Dallas?"

"No."

"Well, it's all over the national news. How could you not see that?"

"Oh, I don't know. Maybe because I'm planning a wedding, holding events for Harvey's clients, trying to keep my mom from pissing off everyone in the wedding party." I could hear the pitch of my voice on the rise. I took a breath then blew a loose curl out of my face. "Sorry for going off on you."

"I might have forgotten to mention it. My bad. When I last saw Courtney, she was running off to that crime scene. That could be why she hasn't contacted us."

I just shook my head. "What the hell is going on in this city? It's like some type of murder plague."

"Sounds like something I would say. You're a nurse. You're logical. You don't speak in those terms."

Maybe I'd changed more than I knew in the last few years. Actually, I knew I'd changed, but I wasn't sure how it had all manifested. But I wasn't into having Cooper do a psyche evaluation right now.

"I'm calling Janice," I said, tapping her contact. Cooper pretended to clean up the kitchen while I turned my back to him. Janice picked up on the third ring, and we spoke for five minutes. When I got off the phone, Cooper was standing right there with a kitchen towel in his hand.

"He's still working at the ME's office," he said as if reading my mind.

"How can you tell?"

"You're smiling. You always smile when you're proud of yourself."

"Whatever. She told me that her brother, Earl, eats lunch every day at the same time at a diner off Harry Hines. She thinks we should just meet him there so he'll be more open to giving us the information. And we should tell him she's asking for the favor."

"Sibling pressure. I like that strategy."

We rushed out the door.

Twenty-Five

Cooper

The place smelled like cow manure. Not the actual diner, of course. It came from the home next door where they'd set up a small goat farm. Right in the middle of the city limits, no less. I looked at Willow, who was pinching her nose.

"I think I'm going to throw up," she said.

"You're a strange bird," I said, glancing to the restrooms for any sign of Earl. Our conversation had lasted all of five minutes before he said he had to use the restroom.

"Why am I always the strange one?"

"You're a frickin' nurse. How many gross things have you smelled, seen, or touched?"

She twisted her lips. She hardly wore any makeup. That's the way I'd always remembered her all these years. Not that I thought about her constantly. Something, though, would invariably trigger a quick image of Willow once every few months, and it was always with this natural, casual look.

"Okay, you have a point. I guess when I'm in that setting where I have this duty to take care of sick people, I just...I don't know."

"You forget about all your anal issues."

She tried to give me flat eyes. Her eyes could never be flat.

"I'm just giving you shit, Will."

"And I'm smelling it," she said with a quick wink. She looked at the time on her phone. "Earl's been in there a while. You think everything's okay?"

"You want me to go check, don't you? Like he's a five-year-old."

She half-smiled.

"I don't have all day anyway. Can't be late for work. Brandy will chop me up into tiny bite-sized pieces and then fire me."

I got up before she could throw more questions at me and walked to the bathroom. Once inside, I was hit with a stench that stopped me in my tracks. I waved a hand in front of my face. I could see Earl's shoes under the stall. I knocked on the door. He opened it, smiled, and then we both joined Willow at the table.

Her eyes quickly narrowed.

"Earl, do you have something you'd like to tell us?" I asked.

"I love my weed, what can I say?"

Willow and I exchanged a shrug. "It's your life, Earl. We're not here to judge," she said.

"But you are here because you want inside information."

I couldn't take my eyes off Earl's sideburns. Not only were they black as coal, but they reminded me of Elvis Presley's sideburns. I'd seen pictures of him in his heyday. Come to think of it, Earl's face was oval with that same prominent chin. Maybe he was a distant relative.

"I've been thinking about what you asked before I went to…you know." He brought two fingers to his lips as if he were smoking a joint. "Normally, I'd tell you to fuck off. I mean, I might only be an autopsy tech, but if I get caught giving away information like this, I'll get canned. My reputation will be ruined."

Willow brought up his sister. I winked at her perfect timing.

"Oh, damn. Janice knows I can't say no to her." He started squirming in his seat like a little kid with a bony ass sitting on a hard wooden bench in church. Yep, that had been me all right.

"So, you'll give it to us?" Willow prompted.

He scratched his sideburn, then glanced at the restrooms. "Look, I love Janice. I'd do anything she asked of me. Anything." His eyes shifted to me and then to Willow.

"But you'd like something in return," Willow said.

"Dallas County doesn't pay like some of the other big cities. And you know, my habit costs me some money."

Willow pulled a fancy leather wallet out of her purse and opened up a sleeve of cash. Nothing like one of those stacks in my little black bag, but still a significant amount of "walking around" money. I felt certain it was a Harvey protection mechanism.

"How much to give us this information, Earl?" she asked.

He held up two hands. "Giving me cash...well, it just doesn't seem right. Too seedy."

"I'm confused. I thought you needed a little side bonus to help us out with information on Marion's time of death."

"Well..." He started squirming again.

"Just spit it out, Earl," I said.

He looked at Willow. "I actually knew you two were coming. Janice warned me, and I started asking questions. So, I know who you're marrying."

Willow's back got very stiff. "What are you implying?"

"Oh, it's nothing bad. I wish you and your fiancé nothing but happiness."

"What is it, then, if you don't want money?"

"I could use some quality shit. You know what I mean?"

Willow tilted her head. "You mean high-end weed?"

"Bingo."

"Why would you think my fiancé or I have any drug connection?"

He smiled and pointed in my direction. "Actually, I was thinking *he* might know someone."

I looked at Willow while speaking to Earl. "Why would you think that?"

"I don't know. Maybe just how Janice described you, I guess."

"Wonder where she got that description?" I kept my hardened gaze on Willow.

"She asked me lots of questions. I didn't say anything wrong or not true," she said as pleasantly as she could muster.

I rolled my eyes then turned back to Earl. "I think I know just the person who can hook you up."

"Cool. You get me the connection, and I'll turn over the information."

"You don't know it off the top of your head?"

His eyes bulged out of his head. "You know how many bodies have shown up in the last couple of days?"

"The drug homicide in east Dallas. What happened there?"

He leaned in closer. "It's not public knowledge, but the word is that someone sold these folks some bad heroin. And it killed all of them in one night. Feel bad for those guys. I think most, if not all, were homeless."

I was sure Courtney was neck-deep in that investigation.

"Okay. I'll have your weed connection by the end of the day."

We traded contact information, and then Willow and I got into her car. "I'm not sure what you told Janice about me having this drug connection."

"She must have inferred it. I never said those words."

I could have quizzed her more, but I knew my life from the outside looked anything but stellar. I blew it off.

"I think I know who you're going to talk to," she said.

"Who?"

"Slash, of course."

I nodded. "I'll talk to him as soon as I get to work. But we also need to figure out who Ronnie's girlfriend is…the one who gave him that alibi."

"Want to try Courtney again?"

I already had my phone in hand. I sent her a quick text, hoping she'd find that less intrusive.

It dinged back a response before Willow had pulled out of the parking lot.

"What did she say?" Willow asked.

"She said was very sorry for not getting back to us and that the drug homicide was eating all of her time. Then she gave us a name and address."

"Cool. Tell me where to go," she said.

My phone dinged again.

"What now?" Willow asked.

"Courtney's saying if I tell anyone that she gave me that information she would personally kick my ass."

Willow pulled her eyes off the traffic for a moment and gave me a quick once-over. "Apparently, the line forms at the left for that one."

Twenty-Six

Willow

Cooper and I had been sitting in my car three doors down from Lucy Gallardo's house for a good thirty minutes. The skies had opened up and unleashed a serious storm. The drops of rain sounded like tiny pebbles bouncing off the hood of my car, the howling wind bending large trees like they were made of rubber. For a moment, I feared that we were in the middle of a twister.

There was a clap of thunder followed immediately by a flash of lightning right in front of my BMW.

"Ooh!" I chirped.

"Fuck!" Cooper shouted.

Then we looked at each other. A smile slowly cracked his stubbly face.

"What?" I asked.

"Oh, that just reminded me of when we used to, uh… I guess you could call it 'hitting our peak' whenever we had sex."

I swung the back of my hand at him before he could start laughing.

"Ah! Dammit, Will! That was my bad arm."

"Oh, shit. I'm sorry. I forgot." I reached over and gently touched his hand. He took hold of it and caressed my fingers. I didn't pull my hand back, and that shocked me so much that I kept it there another few seconds.

With our eyes locked, he said softly, "I was just joking. That isn't my bad arm."

I smacked him again. "You're incorrigible."

"Hey, that hurts. And I'm supposed to be the one using the fancy words."

"But it fits you perfectly."

"You really think I'm irredeemable?"

I rolled my eyes.

"I can see you have hope for me."

I just shook my head. "Do you think this rain is ever going to let up so we can make a run for it to the front porch?"

"Eventually. Patience is the key to a happy life."

"That's your mom talking."

"I know. Isn't it disgustingly sappy?"

"She's a good woman. You might want to try to live your life more like her."

He let his hands drop to his jeans. "You can't be serious."

"A little religion might help you with your…issues."

"I don't have any issues. Just normal everyday stuff, Will. Not all of us have been lucky enough to suck from the golden teat."

"Don't be gross. And I told you before, it's not true."

"I just think you're afraid to admit it to me."

"Afraid? Yeah, right. This coming from a guy who looked like he was about to pee his pants at Harvey's work party." Cooper didn't respond. I pulled my eyes off the driving rain and saw him fiddling with a shoelace on his sneakers. "No snarky comeback?"

"What do you want me to say?"

"Why did you freak out when that man, Dr. Khatri, walked up to us at Harvey's party?"

"I have no idea what you're talking about. Maybe I was thinking about work, about getting my ass chewed by Brandy.

Which, by the way, did happen."

"I see your ass is still intact."

"I wondered if you noticed," he said with a wink.

"There you go with that incorrigible quality again."

The rain finally let up, and we made a run for the front porch of Lucy Gallardo's home. We both got soaking wet anyway. Of course, Cooper with his longish bronze hair looked like one of those shampoo models. *God, did I just think that?*

His hair was darker when it was wet, but his streaks of blond, to me, symbolized the rebel in him.

"You going to ring the bell?" I asked while trying to fix my hair, which I knew looked scary.

"I would if it was there."

I looked up and saw him pointing at two wires dangling out from a hole next to the front door. There was a screen on it…well, on half of it. The top part was mostly intact, aside from a few gashes and holes, but the bottom part was nothing more than an open wooden frame.

"I don't have a good feeling about this," Cooper said, trying to peer into a front window. "Can't see a damn thing. Shades are pulled all the way down."

"We're here to verify Ronnie's alibi, so let's get it over with."

Cooper put his knuckles up to the door, then he turned around and looked me.

"What now?"

"It just hit me. What if Ronnie is here?"

"Crap."

"Double crap." I thought for moment. "But doesn't he have incentive to leave us alone, since he's out on bail?"

"I guess it depends on what his motivation is—to be Mr. Nice Guy or to destroy anything in his path."

I looked out from the porch. The rain had intensified again to the point where I could barely make out my car. "I don't know,

Cooper. Do what you think is best, but make sure it doesn't get us killed."

He put a fist in the palm of his opposite hand.

"What are you doing?"

"Rock, paper, scissors."

"What is that going to decide? Who knocks on the door?"

"I was thinking the one who loses could sacrifice himself, or herself, and then the other one would make a run for it and call the cops."

"I know you're joking."

He shrugged. "I try to lighten the mood as much for me as for you. Glass half full," he said, and then he knocked three times.

The door opened about three inches.

"What do you want?" a woman said while sniffling.

"Lucy?"

"Who's asking?"

"We'd just like to ask you a few questions," Cooper said, pointing to me. I walked up next to him.

"You selling something? Cuz I don't have any money."

"Can you let us in, and we can talk about it? The weather is pretty nasty out here."

"I don't let strangers in my house."

"You want to step out on the porch?" I asked. "I promise it won't take more than just a couple of questions."

The door shut, and I heard metal sliding. Then the door opened all the way. A small woman in baggy sweats stood there. Her red nose practically glowed in the darkened space.

"Are you going to come out on the porch?"

"Nah. I'm good talking to you through the screen." She used a crumpled tissue to wipe at her nose.

"Okayyyy," Cooper said, looking at me with raised brows.

I began with, "So, I know you must be going through a difficult time right now with Ronnie being arrested."

"Don't you say his fucking name."

Was she pissed *I* was saying his name, or that it was mentioned at all? I had no idea. I could only draw on my experiences of watching cops and detectives question people when I worked in the ER.

"Are you upset about him being arrested?"

"Yeah, sure."

That wasn't very convincing.

"Well, we'd like to verify a couple of things," I said, looking at Cooper.

He picked up on my nonverbal cue. "Can you share with us if you were with Ronnie two nights ago?"

"Who's asking?"

"I'm Cooper."

"And my name is Willow. It was my cousin who was murdered."

"And tell me why I should care."

My breath hitched at her callous response. But I'd dealt with a lot of assholes over the years. What's another one? "Were you with Ronnie or not?"

"I haven't seen any badges. Are you two cops?"

"Not exactly," Cooper said.

She started to shut the door.

"Please hold on."

"Why? I don't have to talk to you."

"Did you hear what she just said? Her cousin was killed. And we were assaulted by Ronnie."

"I don't believe you or anyone else! You're just flapping your gums, making shit up as you go along. I said I was with him. Did you fucking hear me?"

Cooper shook his head. I studied her more closely. Something was off. Her head was twitching, her eyes were bloodshot, and her emotional state was obviously on edge.

I whispered, "Is he here...right now?"

"Don't act like you give a shit! No, he's not here. Only stopped by once he got out of jail." She squeezed her eyes shut and started trembling—her whole body.

"Lucy, what's wrong?"

She shot through the screen door, screaming, flailing her arms. Her hand smacked Cooper's face. I jumped back a step, knowing it was dangerous to try to stop a person who was losing it. "Lucy, get a grip on yourself!"

"I don't have to do a fucking thing!" she cried out, now pummeling Cooper with punches and kicks. He covered himself. I knew he couldn't hit a woman, even a troubled person like Lucy. But maybe I could do something.

I swung out my arm and grabbed hold of her wrist just before she connected another punch. Her arm came to a standstill. She looked at me as though she might unleash her fury on me. Then she screamed like she'd been stabbed, shook her body until her wrist was loose, and ran inside.

The screen door snapped back to the frame. I put a hand on Cooper's shoulder as he uncovered his face. "You okay?"

"That woman is on something," he said, touching his face. "Shit. I think she might be a frickin' werewolf with those damn claws."

That's when I saw the three bloody scratches on his cheek.

"We need to clean out those wounds."

"True. I might get rabies or tetanus or something."

I just shook my head. "You don't know what you're talking about." I gently touched the area around the scratches, felt his beard and the outline of his jaw.

"I'm so sorry," a meek voice said.

Cooper and I both startled and turned quickly toward the door. Lucy was on the floor, her knees pulled to her chest. "I'm so fucked up that I attacked you."

I got down on one knee. "Lucy, is there something you'd like to tell us?"

She lifted her eyes. "I'm scared. For me, but especially for my daughter."

Twenty-Seven

Cooper

My best guess was that most people who knew me thought I didn't give a rat's ass about anyone other than myself. Being a bit of a wise-cracking smartass probably had something to do with that opinion. And it's not like I participated in protests or walked around waving a flag for the oppressed.

But in all reality, I was nothing but a softie inside.

"Do you mind if I have my receipt?" A middle-aged guy who wore a purple bow tie extended the palm of his hand.

I'd been working the register at Books and Spirits and, once again, found myself drifting off into a hundred other directions, not the least of which being the state of mind of one Lucy Gallardo. After practically losing her marbles on me, she'd fallen into a deep abyss of depression. It took Willow and me a good thirty minutes for her to share the details about her fear. Actually, her multiple fears. Willow took the lead in interacting with Lucy, which made sense because of her experience in dealing with people in severe mental health situations. But her sensitivity and strength left me in awe. And we learned some very disturbing information.

Ronnie had taken Lucy's ten-year-old daughter and told her that if she didn't claim to be with him the entire night Marion was murdered and the next morning, then he would harm her daughter. Lucy had no idea where Ronnie was at the time, and at first, she didn't want me to contact authorities. We obliged her request temporarily while Willow asked her more questions. Lucy finally told us that she had been with Ronnie most of the night. He had left the house at around five in the morning, ostensibly to find them some heroin. They were both addicts.

But he never returned, and then he was arrested later that day.

Once I convinced Lucy she'd be protected, I put in a call to Courtney. I got her voicemail. Lucy said she wouldn't approve me to call anyone else. So, Willow and I left Lucy's home feeling very torn. We had more information—a window of time when we knew Ronnie had no alibi—but we were fearful of what Ronnie might do while we waited on Courtney to call back. I'd had another sleepless night.

"Oh, sorry," I said, handing the man his receipt, taking another look at the book he'd purchased. It was a new book about the Dallas Cowboys by Gary Myers, an old colleague of mine at the *New York Daily News*. I knew he'd covered the Cowboys during their Jimmy Johnson years in the 1990s.

He touched his face and nodded toward mine. "You look like you got in a cat fight. Literally."

"Yeah, something like that. By the way, I think you'll love that book. Gary's got some great insight, and he's a damn good writer. I used to work with him back in the day."

"It's actually for my son. He just started high school, and all of a sudden, he's found a real interest in the history of sports."

"Football player?"

He chuckled. "He played when he was young. Skinniest, smallest kid on the field. I held my breath each time he got hit, but he kept getting up and taking the punishment. Then we moved to the burbs, and the coaches of the little league team we put him on were..." He scratched the back of his mostly-bald head while exhaling.

"Not very good?" I finished for him.

"Actually, they were the biggest pricks I'd ever met. But I put my thoughts aside because Mason really wanted to play. Then my worst fears came to fruition. These coaches started keeping water from them, and on the first day of pads, they made the boys—we're talking about eleven-year-old boys with necks the size of my forearm—hit each other like battering rams. Each hit made me cringe, wondering if my son would be paralyzed. After three weeks, even against Mason's wishes, I pulled him out of it. I just couldn't take the risk."

"Damn," I said, exhausted from the stress in his voice.

"Funny part to that story. Just in this last few months, one of the coaches was a scorer at the place where my son plays basketball."

"Ah. Hoops. It's the sport for intellectuals. I bet you didn't know that."

"Sounds like you might be talking about yourself."

"Maybe. Keep going with your story."

"Anyway, this guy's son is playing on the other team; I was coaching my son's team. I recognized him right away, but I didn't say a word. Halfway into the game, though, he starts talking trash to me...about Mason."

The guy was poking a finger into his chest as his veins popped from his expansive forehead.

"What did he say?"

"He said, 'Your son is just a fucking quitter and has no guts.'"

"Damn. What did you do?"

"I tried ignoring him, but he kept on. Inside, my blood was on fire, and I was about ready to blow. But then I thought, if I do that, what kind of example would I be for the kids, you know?"

"Take the high road. Wish more people would do that these days."

"I'm not done yet."

"Oh. So, you shoved your fist down his throat?"

"Actually, a league official saw the guy jawing at me, came over, and removed him from the scorer's table. Then the guy kept chirping from the stands...well, until the fourth quarter."

"You went into the stands and kicked his ass? Hell, I might need to write a book."

He paused a second, then continued. "Actually, Mason hit four three-pointers in the fourth quarter, scored twenty-three points overall, and we won by two. The asshole disappeared, and I've never seen him again."

"I love that story."

"Truth is stranger than fiction."

"Ain't that the truth," I said.

"You seem to know a bit about sports."

"A little."

"Just a little?"

"Okay, more than a little. I used to cover teams in the New York area. Then I got bored with the mundane answers, so I branched out."

"If you don't mind me asking, into what?"

"Deeper stuff. Seedy stuff. Investigative feature stories."

"The real meat of sports journalism."

"That's what I thought."

Brandy squawked out my name from the other side of a bookshelf. I hollered back, "Be there in a minute. I'm helping a customer."

The man leaned closer. "If you're a big-time writer, why are you working in a bookstore?"

"Long story."

"I'm still here..."

My phone buzzed as Brandy called for me again. I held up a finger to the man and looked at the screen. It was Courtney.

"I have to take this," I said, punching up the call.

Brandy walked around the bookshelf with her arms spread. I turned away from her, my phone pushing against my ear.

"Courtney, what's going on?"

"You fucking tell me!"

"What? I've been calling and texting you for two straight days. I know you got your hands full, but…"

"Cooper, you need to take your calls on your own time," Brandy blurted. "Plus, I need your help over here. Slash can take over."

I saw Slash walking up to the man at the counter, who was waving his hand, trying to get someone to help him. Slash was droopy-eyed and giving me the peace sign. Yeah, he was stoned.

"What's got you so upset, Courtney?" I walked around the corner, away from the devil woman.

"You left me four voicemails and something like ten text messages with all this urgency around Lucy Gallardo. I'm over here right now with two officers, and the only thing I see is a malnourished cat prancing around."

"She not there?" I stopped dead in my tracks.

"Nope."

"Dammit. She told us she wouldn't leave. She knew we were reaching out to you. She didn't want us telling anyone else."

"You said in your voicemail that you didn't think she was very stable."

I touched the scratches on my face. "I have personal knowledge on that front. But if she's telling the truth—and my gut says she is—Ronnie has her daughter and has threatened to harm the child."

"That's why I left everything at the warehouse—"

"Where all those people died from a heroin overdose?"

"Six dead, two in critical condition. We think they were sold a bad batch of heroin."

"I didn't know there was such thing as a good batch."

"Okay, smartass."

Brandy appeared right under my chin. "Cooper Chain, get off that phone right now!"

"Crap. I need to run, Courtney."

That didn't stop the questions. "So, you're sure that Lucy never told you guys she might visit a friend or family member?"

"Nothing."

"And did she give you any indication of Ronnie's whereabouts?"

"Nope, but I got the feeling she didn't know."

"I'm calling that fucking lawyer right now," she said. And then I heard her barking out orders to her officers.

"Please let me know what happens. There's a lot riding on getting Ronnie back in custody, starting with this little girl's life."

"Okay. Will do, Cooper."

The moment she hung up, I realized I'd forgotten to mention Lucy's revised alibi time, which would then lead me to ask about the ME's approximate time of death for Marion. But right now, my thoughts were mostly on finding Lucy's little girl.

"Did you not hear me?" Brandy was moving her hands all around.

I blinked and stepped back. I'd completely zoned out. "Sorry."

"What the hell is wrong with your face?"

"Oh, just a little scrape."

"With a lion?"

I popped an eyebrow. "I like that you're embracing your sarcastic side. Studies show that finding humor in things will help you live longer."

She just started shaking her head. "Whatever. Can you restock every shelf here on the left side before we close? We have a book signing in here tomorrow, and I want us to be prepared for the big crowd."

I hadn't seen any notice of an author book signing. This could be the opportunity I've been waiting for. Maybe the author's literary agent would show up, and I could do some Cooper schmoozing. "Okay. I'll get right on it."

She started to walk off but turned around. "How do you know Archibald?"

"Who's Archibald?"

"That's the guy you were talking to at the counter, dimwit."

I turned to look at the counter. The man was gone. I recalled him talking about his son and the pitfalls and triumphs of youth sports. He seemed like a good guy.

Slash was holding up something, but Brandy got my attention instead. "Archibald?"

"I don't really know him. We were just talking about his son and sports."

"Well, it's *his* client who will be here tomorrow."

"Client?"

Slash was now flicking his finger against a business card.

"Yeah," Brandy said. "He's a literary agent. One of his authors is a guy who used to tour with Journey. Lives locally, so he thought it might be a good way to kick off his memoir book launch."

"Cool."

"Yeah. We just have to be ready. Should have a big crowd." She finally walked off, giving me a chance to breathe.

"Yo, Mr. Cooper."

"Slash, will you please—"

"Cooper."

"That's better."

"This guy left you his business card."

I walked over, and he handed it to me. "Archibald Motta wants me to talk to him?"

"I guess so. He just dropped it on the counter and whispered for me to give it to you."

I put it in my pocket, my heartbeat picking up. Something to look forward to tomorrow.

Slash leaned against the counter, pulled out a graphic novel from under the counter, and started ogling the pictures. He looked up after a few seconds. "Am I doing something wrong?" he asked innocently.

"You're good."

"Why are you staring at me?"

"I'd like to ask you a favor."

"What kind of favor?"

"I need for you to hook me up with your weed contact."

The paperback dropped from his hands. He scrambled to pick it up. I could see the red lines in his eyes, and his breath had a hint of that unique smell. "Dude, if you want some shit, you gotta keep it on the down low. I've got some stuff in my bag in the back. You want to smoke during your break?"

"No, I need your contact."

"My contact?"

"The person who sells you the weed."

"Ah. Dizzy."

"As in Dean?"

"Who's that?"

"An old baseball pitcher."

"You and your sports. Dizzy as in Dizzy Gillespie."

"So, you do know your music."

Slash smiled. His teeth pointed in every direction except straight down.

"Can you get me his contact information?"

"I'm all about freedom of expression." He started chuckling, showing off those teeth again. He looked like he was so high he might just topple over right there.

"Cool. Me too. So, the contact?"

"You're in a rush."

"It's for a friend. Kind of. Anyway, this could help us catch a killer."

"You fucking serious?"

I nodded.

"Break out the Five-O alarm. Dano's all over this shit."

Slash/Dano gave me the contact info, and I forwarded it to Earl. Before I was halfway done with restocking the bookshelves, Earl had replied with a time of death for Marion. And it shocked the hell out of me.

Twenty-Eight

A diesel engine roared down the nearby street, causing the man to jerk his head to the left. His heart pummeled his chest as he realized the truck wasn't turning into the alley.

He took two deep breaths.

A dog barked somewhere behind him. He could hear paws racing through a bed of leaves. He looked between the two dumpsters and noticed the silhouette of what looked like a greyhound hauling ass across darkened lawns. Was that a leash flapping in the wind behind the dog?

The man didn't have the time or fortitude to worry about anything on four legs right now, even though he feared the dog might very well get hurt running across the busy streets in south Dallas, where there were more busted lights than ones that worked.

Something bumped his foot. He looked down and saw the pained eyes of one of the kindest women he'd ever met. Her jaw trembled as if she were choking on the strands of her black hair that were caught in her mouth.

A quick glance around him, and then he lowered himself down to one knee and pulled the hair out her mouth.

"I'm so sorry that I had to hurt you, sweet lady."

She mumbled and groaned, her chin flapping like one of those automated Halloween skeletons that people used to scare trick-ortreaters. As a kid, Halloween was one of the few times of the year that he was able to feel a true high, a wonderful endorphin release so many runners speak about. His high came at the expense of the most annoying creatures to walk this earth: rabbits. All they did was shit pellets, eat up the grass, and dig holes in your yard, and mate like...well, rabbits. A nuclear bomb could go off, and if any living thing survived, it would most likely be rabbits. There were too damn many roaming the landscape, at least in Dallas-Fort Worth.

So, he viewed his teenage hobby as a way to help control the pet population, just like good old Bob Barker used to direct his audience at the end of his game show. "Don't forget to do your part in controlling the pet population. Make sure to have your pet spayed or neutered," he would say just before signing off.

The man implemented his own form of controlling the population of rabbits. He fucking choked the life out of them. Then he would cut them into tiny bite-sized pieces and feed them to rabid dogs in the neighborhood.

What the hell did Bob Barker know, anyway? He acted like he was some philanthropic do-gooder, and then he'd go bang one of his hot "showgirls" sixty years his junior. Whatever.

The woman groaned louder, and the man knew he couldn't sit here forever and admonish himself for making such a grave mistake. She'd found him hiding behind the Community Health Clinic on her way to her car. He'd seen that she was frightened, and she immediately darted toward the back door. He got to her just as she reached for the doorknob and tossed her in between these dumpsters. He'd put his hand over her face and begged her to be quiet, promising that she would die as peacefully and humanely possible.

That, unfortunately, came as quite a shock to the nurse, whom he'd personally witnessed show tremendous care and empathy for those who were sick or wounded. The moment he pulled his hand off her mouth, she bit his thumb and screamed at the top of her lungs. Over and over. He wasn't angry at her, more at himself for being so clumsy in stalking his latest victim. But that didn't mean she could walk away unscathed. Buoyed by an adrenaline rush, he had slammed her to the ground, crushing her back. He heard the vertebrae snapping like twigs and, undoubtedly, cutting into her spinal cord.

He lifted her arm and released it. The arm flopped down to the wet concrete. Yep, she was paralyzed from the shoulders down. Her lungs probably had difficulty expanding. It was time to put her out of her misery.

He pulled the bag out from his coat pocket. Her eyes shifted and stopped blinking. Did she know what it was?

He cupped the side of her face. "You've given so much to this world, Janice. I'm sorry I had to harm you. It wasn't my intent, I assure you. Just know that suffering will soon end. Not just the anguish of being paralyzed. You're a saint, and saints don't belong in this fucked-up, mean-spirited world."

He placed the bag over her head and pulled the cord, releasing the nitrogen gas. When her eyes shut, he removed the bag and checked for a pulse. There was none. He placed her arms across her chest and stared at her face. She was at peace. Finally and forever.

A tear rolled off his cheek and fell onto her face. It was a tear of joy. He'd once again fulfilled his promise to protect a good, kind person from the evils of the world. Now, he had to make her final resting spot as comfortable as possible.

Twenty-Nine

Willow

We were officially one hour into the pre-wedding party, and Ma had already thrown out a dozen insults. Of course, she didn't see them as insults. They were either categorized as "normal advice any idiot would take" or "just a simple observation."

Florence Ball—yes, she'd kept my father's last name, even though flames would shoot from her eyes whenever his name came up—had made quite an impression with the forty or so folks in attendance at Harvey's home. Through it all, though, Harvey was steadfast in his ability to not focus on the negative and seemingly lead our group toward happiness. And his unwavering positive attitude was one of the reasons I'd fallen in love with him.

I'd been in social mode throughout the evening, shielding everyone from Ma as much as humanly possible. My younger sister, Jennie, and the youngest Ball, Kyle, usually stayed out of the fray. Jennie was more of an introvert, while Kyle just rolled his eyes and tried to ignore Ma.

"Here, you need this."

Alli had just walked up holding a full martini glass.

"Thanks, but I've already had two."

Ma cackled from the other side of the living room as she

conversed with an aunt and uncle of Harvey's.

I grabbed the glass from Alli. "Actually, I'll take it now." I sipped the martini.

"And I got you two olives from the bartender."

I ate both of them as my sights stayed glued to the scene on the other side of the living room.

"You going to run over and try to break it up?" Alli asked.

"I've been doing it all night. I think it's too late, anyway. Ma is…Ma. No changing her now."

"I can try it if you want," she said as if she were bracing for a slap to the face.

I put my arm around her. "You're sweet, Alli, but you've been in the middle of these frays so much you probably have PTSD."

She tilted her head. "Let's just say it's not my favorite thing to do."

Just then, Ma lifted the man's tie and started flapping her gums. "Oh, God. I think she's going to comment on his tie," I said.

Alli took hold of my hand. "Get ready for something really bad to happen."

Ma said something and then laughed. The look in the couple's eyes was one of horror. Of course, Ma didn't notice that.

"Jesus, does she not have any sense of reading other people?" Alli asked as we watched the man and woman stiffly walk away from her.

"Only if you're talking about money. Actually, her money. She turns into this high-stakes poker player where her radar is at an intensity of about one thousand. She reads every twitch or muscle movement, ready to counter—or should I say pounce?—if they try to, as she calls it, 'screw me over.'" I'd used my best Philly accent on the last phrase.

"Nice one, Willow. You sound like you were born and bred in the city of brotherly shove."

We both giggled, and then I sipped my martini. Hard.

Harvey entered the room with a rather stern look on his face. He was stopped for a moment and drawn into a conversation.

"That toast that Harvey gave to Marion to kick off the dinner party was really poignant," Alli said.

"I know. He hardly knew Marion at all, but he always knows the right thing to say. Come to think of it, Ma actually didn't have anything negative to say about it."

"If that's the case," Alli said, "we can probably rank it as one of the top toasts of all time."

My thoughts drifted back to that morning when Cooper and I had stood over Marion's bed. She looked so much at peace, yet she'd been murdered. She was too young to die, yet someone—I still presumed it was that beast, Ronnie—had taken her life. And for what reason? We really didn't have any answers at this point, and it seemed to have grown more complicated since Cooper and I had spoken to Ronnie's girlfriend, Lucy. Actually, it was more tragic than anything else. Lucy was on the edge of that emotional cliff. She'd lost it on Cooper, but that wasn't a one-time thing. Ronnie had her daughter, and Lucy was a heroin addict.

Cooper had assured me when I dropped him off at work that he would reach Courtney somehow, someway, and then she would be able to help Lucy with both of her problems. I could feel my insides rumbling, thinking about Ronnie and all the damage he'd done. Deep down, I was worried about Lucy's daughter, about Lucy, about anyone who came in contact with that maggot. For now, though, I could only trust that Courtney and her DPD colleagues would put the necessary effort and resources on this case and end the killing.

I saw Jennie walk over to Ma. They seemed to be talking quietly about something. Anything to deflect her for even a few minutes was a welcomed gift.

A second later, Harvey approached and kissed my cheek. He liked to kiss my cheek. It was sweet, but I kind of felt like his grandmother when he did it. I always told him I wanted more lips, less grandma-type kisses.

"Hi, sweetie. I think our little party is going rather well, all things considered," I said, nudging my head toward the other side of the room.

He gave me a forced smile. "No wars have broken out, only minor skirmishes from what I can tell. But you have a visitor at the back door."

"Huh?" My eyes had been observing Jennie and Ma, who was simply standing there and listening…without interrupting. Her expression bordered on docile.

"Your old friend, Cooper, is at the back door. Actually, I let him inside."

"What's he doing here?"

"Not sure. I invited him to the party, but he wanted no part of it. In fact, he was very apologetic for interrupting our get-together. Said he'd been trying to reach you."

"My phone. Dammit, it's stuck in my purse in your bedroom."

"Our bedroom," he said, trying to pop his eyebrows in a suave manner. "Is everything okay?"

I hadn't had time to get Harvey up to speed on everything that had occurred. "It's just more drama around that person who attacked Cooper and me."

"He hasn't threatened you again, has he? Do I need to hire private security to make sure you're safe when you're not with me?"

"That's way over the top. I'm not on anyone's hit list. I was in the wrong place at the wrong time. I just want to see this guy arrested and put in jail for good, so he can't hurt anyone else."

Harvey exhaled. "It would be nice for everyone to have closure."

"Let me talk to Cooper. Maybe he as an update. You okay for a few minutes without me?"

"I'll survive," he said, glancing across the room. Then he looked at Alli. "What do you say we make a trip to the bar?"

They walked off while I snuck into the kitchen. Caterers were hustling around. To a degree, it was odd seeing other people essentially taking ownership of your kitchen, or rather, Harvey's kitchen. But I was almost at a point where I was getting used to it. Probably because I was juggling so many other things.

I walked down the corridor where the back door was, but I didn't see Cooper.

"I'm in here."

I looked inside the wine cellar to find Cooper giving me a round wave, and I walked into the room.

"Sorry. I had no idea you were doing this pre-wedding party tonight."

"I forgot to mention it. There's a different event every night leading up to the wedding."

"You excited?"

"Kind of."

"Only kind of?"

"No, I'm actually very excited. Thrilled to be honest. But there's the distraction of Marion's death and trying to get that piece of shit, Ronnie, off the street." I grabbed Cooper's arm. He didn't flinch, so I knew I had his good arm. "Tell me you have good news about Lucy and her daughter."

He opened his mouth then shut it. No words.

I could feel emotion crawling up my throat. 'Dear God, Cooper, Ronnie hasn't hurt Lucy's daughter, has he?"

"No, it's..." He tried to pry my fingers from his arm.

"Sorry."

"No problem. You don't know how strong you are." He raked his fingers through his hair and looked away for a second. "The truth is, I really don't know."

"Tell me, tell me now."

"Okay, okay. Courtney finally made it over to Lucy's house with two officers, and Lucy wasn't there."

"Where did she go?"

He shrugged. "No idea. Courtney was seething. Last I heard, she was going to call Ronnie's lawyer and demand that Ronnie turn over Lucy's daughter. She said she'd reach out to me when she had an update."

I lowered my head for a moment.

"Hey, I'm really sorry about your cousin, all this crap, especially during this week."

"Not your fault. Who can predict the timing of a maniac?"

"But I do have some news to share."

"Do I need to get another martini?"

"Eh."

I turned and walked toward the door, then flipped my head around. "You coming?"

"I'd rather not."

I grabbed his hand and led him through the kitchen.

"You know I feel like your child when you do this."

I let go once we entered the living room.

"That's more like it," Harvey said. "Glad you could join us, Cooper. Let me get you a drink. What's your drink of choice?"

"Do you have Orange Crush?"

Did he really just say that? I just shook my head as Harvey chuckled. "Good one. Seriously, what can I get you?"

"Eh. Jim Beam and Coke, I guess."

"Not sure we have Jim Beam. But I'll find a whiskey that will be the best you've ever had."

"I'm game."

"And another martini for my beautiful fiancée?" he said, kissing my cheek...again.

"I think I'm good for now. I need to be able to walk a straight line for the next couple of hours."

He returned with Cooper's drink and then ran off to talk to some buddies. Just as I was about to interrogate Cooper, Alli came up to say hi. "Do you feel awkward or what?" she asked Cooper.

"Alli, give him a break," I said. "This is a festive atmosphere...well, if you don't count my mother." We both giggled.

"Wait, your mom is here?" he asked, scratching his chin like a nervous teenager.

"She won't bite," Alli said, then she looked at Cooper more closely. "Actually, it looks like you've already been bitten, or maybe attacked by a werewolf."

He touched his face. "Yeah, it's just the hazards of the job."

"That's right. I hear you're working at Books and Spirits."

"Good old Ben. He's a great communicator," Cooper said, looking more unsettled by the second.

I asked Alli if I could speak to Cooper alone. She obliged and walked over to the appetizer table, where my brother was scarfing down lemon cheesecake.

"So, tell me this not-so-good news."

Cooper had just sipped his drink. He held up a finger, then said, "Your husband, I mean fiancé, knows how to pick his whiskey."

"He likes having the best of everything."

"True. He's got you."

I didn't say a thing for a second. Cooper sipped more of his drink and kept his eyes on me.

"I'm going to pretend you didn't say that."

"Never happened," he said, gazing across the room of people.

"So, can we get back to this information you have?"

"I gave Earl the name of Slash's weed contact."

"Oh, right. I totally forgot. And has Earl gotten back to you with Marion's estimated time of death?"

"It's not what I expected. He said, based upon the state of rigor mortis, they're estimating between midnight and three a.m."

I reached for his arm again.

"Ah!"

I quickly let go. "Wrong one?"

He nodded while taking in air like he'd just hiked Mount Everest.

"Sorry. Are you ever going to get it checked out? It's probably broken, you know."

"Can we get back to more important questions?" he asked, pressing his arm against his chest.

I'd dealt with a lot of stubborn patients over the years. I'd used various tools to get them to comply with medical advice, including bribery (food) and guilt (relatives). But Cooper, I knew, was in a stubborn class all by himself.

"Fine. Is Earl certain he's talking about Marion? I mean, he did say they've had a lot of bodies come through his office in the last few days."

"I didn't question him. I assume he's good at his job."

"You sure about that? Isn't he basically a pothead?"

"Canada just legalized it."

"I'm not having this argument with you right now."

"I'm not arguing," he said, way too calmly.

"So, do you think Lucy was just so out of it that she got the time wrong about when Ronnie left her house?"

"Possibly, but probably not. She seems to be so scared of the guy. I think she'd remember the exact time when he left."

"Okay. If we assume she's right, then what does this say about Ronnie killing Marion?"

"Let's just look at the facts as we know them. He was at Lucy's until five a.m., and then, supposedly, he went off to find more heroin. Then, we show up at around ten a.m., and Ronnie's in Marion's bedroom. After he tries to maul us, we find Marion's body on the bed. So, could he have an accomplice who did the actual killing?"

"An accomplice," I repeated, closing my eyes a moment. "So, we're supposed to believe that a jealous boyfriend has an accomplice. Who would commit murder because of someone else's jealousy?"

He crunched a piece of ice, then said, "Hadn't really taken it that far. But I guess you make a good point. Still, though, Ronnie was there when we showed up, and he didn't seem to be in despair. Is it possible he knew about her death, even if he didn't have a direct hand in it, and he was there to gloat or maybe put the finishing touches together?"

"Like the bird's wing."

He nodded. "Yeah, there's that freaky detail."

"What about the second victim? We still haven't looked into where Ronnie was during that murder…"

Cooper held up his drink, "Or, if she—her name is Irene Washington—is connected to Marion in any way."

"Crap," I said, folding my arms. My eyes caught someone quickly approaching us.

"What's wrong? I can see it your eyes," Cooper said.

"Incoming."

"Incoming what?"

"Cooper Chain. I never thought I'd see your gutless ass near my daughter again."

He turned, extended his hand. "Oh, hi, Mrs. Ball. Nice to see you after all these years."

And then the doorbell rang.

Thirty

Cooper

I swear I saw red pitchforks in Florence's dark, soulless eyes. But it was her cold scowl that made me quiver.

"You just going to stand there and stare at me, or perhaps you'd like to tell me about your failed writing career," she said, sneering as if she'd just unveiled the secret location of where Al Capone was buried.

"Oh, Ma, how could you be so rude?" Willow said, turning her head to the front of the house for a second.

Without thinking it through, I pulled out the business card of Archibald Motta and flashed it in front of the evil one. "My literary agent might have something to say about that."

"Hold on," Willow said, bringing her attention back to me. "You have an agent? Cooper, why didn't you tell me? That's incredible news."

"Well, I, uh, didn't want to brag or anything." I didn't like how that sounded. I also immediately started regretting the fact that I'd just lied to Willow.

"It's not bragging. That's just conveying news about your career, your passion. I couldn't be more proud of you," she said, gripping my shoulder.

"Literary agent," Florence muttered, while rolling her eyes so far back I wondered if she'd been temporarily possessed by the devil. Well, maybe not so temporarily. "It's either a fake card or this schmuck agent hasn't sold a book to a publishing company in forty years. Probably some guy that Cooper met while he was begging for money on a street corner."

"Ignore her," Willow said. "She doesn't like to see other people succeed or be happy."

"Why are you giving this guy any credit, Willow? He's a loser who knows one thing: how to cut and run, just like someone else we both know," she said with a knowing nod.

Florence was obviously referring to Willow's dad, whom Willow hadn't seen since she was a little girl. Why would she bring up that memory to her daughter, especially during this week? I just looked at her and started shaking my head.

"Got something to say, wise-ass?"

"Ma, that's it. You need to drop it right now. Why don't you go over and talk to Jennie again?"

Florence huffed out a breath and started to turn away.

The doorbell rang again.

"Can someone get the front door?" Harvey called out from across the room.

"I've got it," I said, eyeing Willow, who mouthed *sorry* to me.

"Skin like an elephant," I said with a wink.

As I turned to walk toward the front of the house, I noticed Florence hadn't slithered off. It was as though she wanted to fake me out. Whatever. It was better for me to walk away. As I made my way into the foyer, I was in awe of the detailed tapestry on the side wall. Probably some original from fifteenth-century France. The front door had to be ten feet high. I wondered how much it weighed. I pulled it open while I sucked down the last of the most expensive whiskey I'd ever imbibed.

"Excuse me, but is this the home of Harvey Bernstein?"

The man had silver-tipped hair and wore a dress shirt and vest—no coat. He might have been making a trendy fashion statement, although I guessed he did his shopping at the Big and Tall shop. "Yep. Are you here for the wedding party? Well, they're officially calling it a pre-wedding party."

"Why yes, I am."

"Come on in and join the fun."

He walked into the foyer as Willow came around the corner. "Are you from the bride's side or the groom's side?" I asked.

Willow stopped next to me. She slowly lifted a finger to point at the man.

"The bride's side. Definitely the bride's side." I followed his gaze over to Willow, who started shaking her head.

"Is that really you?" she asked the man as her chest expanded with deeper and deeper breaths.

"Who?" I said, suddenly feeling like I shouldn't be there.

"It is, little Willy."

"Little Willy?" My brow crinkled as I looked over to Willow. She wasn't confused, but her chest and neck now had red splotches. She was still shaking her head, and her eyes had become glassy.

"Are you okay?" I whispered.

She didn't hear me. She appeared to be falling into some type of catatonic state. I moved next to her and touched her arm. It was ice cold. "Will, do you want me to do something?" I had no idea who this guy was. My thoughts went to the absolute worst-case scenario. Maybe this guy was some long-lost relative or family friend, and he'd harmed Willow as a kid. And now he'd shown up at her wedding party just to have her regurgitate all the painful, suppressed memories.

"Hey," I said, moving in between Willow and the man. "I'm not sure you were invited, and it doesn't look like you're wanted here. Maybe you should just leave."

The man looked me in the eye. There was something familiar about him, but I wasn't sure I'd ever met him. He then stepped to his left and opened his arms toward Willow. "I didn't mean to shock you. I just thought you'd want me to be part of this."

I heard the clatter of heels off the hardwoods. Someone was quickly approaching the foyer. I was hoping it was Alli, who had a calming effect on Willow and might even know this guy.

A second later, Cruella DeVille—a.k.a. Florence—marched around the corner and came to an immediate stop. She didn't look at me, thank God. Her eyes were pinned to Vest Man. There was a moment of silence. Actually, more than a moment. No one moved except me, as I swiveled my sights from one person to the next, looking for a clue as to who this guy was and, more importantly, if I should start the uncomfortable process of escorting him out of the house.

I tried to be patient, but this standoff was making me want to have another high-end whiskey and Coke. Just as I opened my mouth, Florence raised a hand—it was wrinkled and veiny. Her face had lost all color. For some reason, my mind went straight to an image of Emperor Palpatine from *Star Wars* fame. Not a flattering comparison, I knew. But who can control their own thoughts? At least I hadn't said anything out loud.

"You…" Florence said as her hand trembled. She looked like she could bite off a snake's head and eat it for dinner. So…just slightly more pissed than was her normal disposition.

"It's me, Florence. How have you been? Wait," the man said, holding up a hand. "Don't answer that. I'm here for one person and one person only. Little Willy."

My mind started putting together some puzzle pieces. But it couldn't be him, could it? I stared at him, and then looked over to Willow. *Ho-ly shit!*

"Is that…?" I asked Willow.

She nodded once. "Dad," she gasped.

My hunch was right. Her dad had shown up after thirty years. What the fuck was this guy thinking?

Tears poured out of Willow's eyes, and my heart felt a crack. Then her breathing cadence took off like a runaway horse. "How...why...?"

Suddenly, she started to fall. I let go of my glass. I heard it smash against the floor as I lunged to catch Willow just before she collapsed.

Thirty-One

Willow

I never actually blacked out, thanks to Cooper running off and finding a paper sack from the kitchen. I breathed into the sack, slowing the overflow of oxygen into my brain.

"Dear God, I made her faint. I'm so sorry," a man's voice said.

I blinked and pulled the bag away from my face. Propped up against the foyer wall, I was still lightheaded, but my brain seemed to be functioning as my eyes swung to the man in the vest. My father.

"Dad…" I said.

He smiled, and my eyes momentarily fixated on his teeth. They were so white and straight. My memory was something different. I recalled his teeth having yellow stains and being crooked.

Harvey appeared at my side. He was trying to wrap his arm around my shoulder, but it was making me uncomfortable.

"I'm okay," I said, pushing his arm away.

"I was just trying to hold you," he said defensively. "What else can I get you?"

A bottled water was lowered in front of me. "It's Perrier. I found it in the fridge." I looked up and saw Cooper.

"Thanks." The top had already been cracked, so I chugged a few sips.

Someone was cleaning up the broken glass on the floor, and more people started crowding around me. I didn't just feel awkward, I felt smothered. I heard whispers of "Is she all right?" and then "Is she pregnant?"

I couldn't let that one go unanswered. "No, I'm not pregnant."

Harvey wiped a hand across his face. He looked stressed. I touched his hand. "I'm fine. Really, I am. Can I stand up, and we can continue our party?"

"Are you sure?" he asked.

About ten hands pawed at me, presumably to help me up. I felt like I was being groped. Then I saw one hand in particular just two feet in front of me. I grabbed it. Cooper and I used our body weights as leverage—something we had done a million times in college—and I was standing in the blink of an eye.

"Be careful," Harvey said.

I patted his shoulder. "I'm doing good. Thank you for caring."

He leaned down and kissed my cheek in front of everyone. I heard a few *aww*s. I tried not to roll my eyes. Why was I embarrassed by that?

"I'm fine, everyone. But I'll feel better if you will go back to having fun. The next round is on me," I said with a giggle. The crowd around me slowly started to disperse, and then there before me was my father.

"Where have you been? Where did you go? Why are you here now?" I could feel a lump in my throat.

"It's a long story, Willy. And I don't mind sharing it with you. Truly, I just want to support you and to witness your marriage to this fine young man." He nodded at Harvey, who gave a half-smile.

I looked down at the floor, my brain still trying to process everything. My chest felt like it was wrapped in steel bands.

Ma walked right up and smacked Dad across the face. I

flinched from the violent act. The echo of the smack seemed to linger in the air. "You show up at this party like some kind of white knight in shining armor, but you're nothing but a fucking loser who gave up on his family three decades ago."

Jennie and Kyle stepped in front of Ma as Harvey stood nearby. I could see such disappointment on his face. I—my family—had ruined this event.

"Woo! You still throw a good punch, Flo, I'll give you that much," Dad said with a laugh. I remembered that laugh. It was so unique. It sounded like a digitized clap. He'd laughed a lot when I was young—that was something I'd never realized until this very moment.

Ma calmed down, and Kyle escorted her out of the room. I released a long sigh.

Jennie, standing next to Cooper, had this sheepish look. Dad walked over and put his arm around her. "It will all work out. It's already looking better, just like I told you it would."

Her eyes went to me.

"Wait, you knew Dad was going to show up after all these years?" I said, moving a step in her direction.

"He found me, started texting me, Willow. What was I supposed to do, just ignore him?"

"Hey now. We're a family. We might be a bit dysfunctional, but we're still a family. We need to get along and let things work out naturally." Dad, who still had his arm around Jennie, wrapped his other arm around my shoulder. I was tall, but next to him, I felt like six inches of my height had been chopped off.

Someone called out from the kitchen. Harvey said, "Hey, since you're kind of tied up, I need to run and check on things." He gently squeezed my arm and then walked away. I sensed he wanted no part of this crazy family. I couldn't blame him.

Dad said, "Hey, Cooper. That's your name right?"

He nodded.

"Get a quick picture of me with my girls, will ya?"

Cooper pulled out his phone, then stopped and looked at me as if he were waiting for my permission. I could see concern on his face, but not judgment. That meant something to me, even in the middle of such chaos.

"It's okay, you can take it." My voice sounded meek, and that pissed me off. If there was one thing I'd become over the years since Dad left, it was independent and strong. Ma often worked two jobs to put food on the table for three kids. That was at least one thing I admired in her. But it had also left me alone in the house with my two siblings. I made sure they stayed close to home when they played outside, helped them finish their homework, made sure they ate their meals, even if they were TV dinners, got them to bed at a decent hour, and generally kept the peace.

"Just a quick one, Cooper. I need to get back to the guests," I said, reinforcing my position of inner strength.

Cooper took the shot and said, "I'll text it to you."

"Hey, go ahead and send it to me right now," Dad said, moving next to Cooper, who seemed uncomfortable with the whole scene. Dad didn't notice. He was all smiles. He gave Cooper his phone number and then I heard a ding. "Cool, I just got it. Thanks, Coop."

I wondered how he knew Cooper's name.

"I'll just blend in with the crowd, Willy. We can talk tomorrow or whenever you like. I'm sure you'll want to speak to the priest about including me in the ceremony."

I gasped but not loudly enough for others to hear. My father walking me down the aisle? The image had been so foreign to me, it wasn't something I ever thought about leading up to the wedding. Thirty years had passed.

"I guess," I said, looking to Jennie. "How long have you and Dad been in contact?"

Dad stepped in between us. "Don't get upset with Jennie. I showed up in town four days ago and reached out to her. It wasn't easy on her, just like it's not easy on you. Believe me, I'm sorry for not being in touch all these years. But I learned that you can't keep beating yourself up over things. Sure, I made mistakes. I'm sorry. You know that right, Willy?"

"Yeah, I guess." Was he trying to brush off thirty years of absence in our lives in one little speech? And what was up with him calling me a nickname from when I was five? I looked over his shoulder and locked eyes with Cooper. I think he sensed my unease and growing displeasure with this whole scene and Dad's attitude.

"So, Mr. Ball—"

"Raymond. Just call me Raymond, Coop." He popped his shoulder and leaned in closer, but looked at me. "It's pretty cool, Willy, that you invited your old college boyfriend to your wedding. Shows a lot of maturity. Something I didn't have a lot of over the years."

"How would you know who I dated in college?"

"I've been around. Sometimes, I'd come back in town, and you know...."

The room started spinning, or maybe it was just my mind. I put a hand to my head. "You know...what?"

He shrugged but didn't say anything more.

I could feel my neck and ears getting warmer. "You passed through this area like some type of vagabond, and you never reached out to me, to us?" I said, pointing at Jennie. "You never thought that we might need to have a dad around to help us out when times were tough, or maybe even just be there to share some of the good times? Growing up isn't easy, Dad. I hate to break it to you. But I'll give you this much, you certainly gave me purpose in life. I had to be the leader of the house while Ma was off working *two jobs* to support us."

His head dropped. In fact, his posture sagged a couple of inches. Then he walked two steps forward and took hold of my shoulders. "Willow, I'm so sorry for putting you in that position, for leaving you, Jennie, and Kyle. A day hasn't gone by when I haven't thought of you and your siblings and regretted not having those experiences with each of you. It's just that…"

He looked down as if he were in deep thought. I was about to rip into him again—my inner Florence was trying to make an appearance—but I squashed the notion.

"You see, when you make mistakes in your life, big ones, like I did, then time becomes this double-edged sword. It helps you heal a little, but you also find yourself coming up with excuses to not make amends for your mistakes. After a while, it just became this snowball effect, and it became harder and harder for me to reach out."

A swell of emotion surged inside. Part of it was anger. I was so mad I could just punch him in the jaw. Part of me just felt sad…for me, for Jennie and Kyle, even for Ma. But I also saw sadness in Dad's eyes. Regret. Still, it was difficult for me to reconcile a thirty-year absence.

I took another drink from my bottle of water. I could see he was waiting for me to respond. My mind was swimming with thoughts, and just when I was about to speak up, the next thought would contradict the previous one.

"Hey, you're shaking," Cooper said quietly in my ear. "Give yourself a break. You don't have to figure all this out tonight."

I released a long sigh. "Dad…"

"Say no more. I've put you in a tough pickle. Hey, Jennie, what do you say you escort me around and introduce me to everyone?"

"Sure." She shrugged. "Why not?" And with that, they walked off.

"You ready for something stronger?" Cooper asked, pointing to my water.

"I don't want to keel over again." I watched my sister parade around with my father. "That girl is so easygoing, I'm not even sure she knows she can question Dad's decision to just show up out of the blue."

"It's pretty crazy." Cooper ran his eyes across the crowd, then he looked at me again. "This is a lot to take in. You going to be okay?"

I gave him a light punch in the shoulder. "I'm tough."

"Don't I know it." He set his drink on a tray. "I think I've had enough drama for the night."

"Call me whenever Courtney gets back to you."

He gave me a mock salute and scooted out the back door.

Thirty-Two

Cooper

As I walked up the driveway, I could see that Mrs. Kowalski's bedroom light was on. Other than that, the house was dark. The moon had made a quick cameo earlier, but quick-moving clouds now blanketed the dark sky, reducing the visibility.

The walk home hadn't cleared my mind as much as I'd hoped. Instead, the night's events had only stoked similar regrets from my past, which at the moment felt very present.

I kicked through a few weeds, walked up to my LeBaron, and put my hand on the trunk, remembering the stash of cash that was now up in my closet. It seemed like a lifetime ago that I'd found the money bag when, in reality, it had only been about twenty-four hours. So much had happened with Lucy's disappearance and then with Willow having to deal with her father showing up unexpectedly. Through it all, I'd put some of my other worries to the side. Now, though, in the stillness of the night, I questioned the legitimacy of the money magically appearing in my car.

Good Samaritan's just didn't exist. Not to the tune of fifty grand. I'd actually never counted the money, just assumed it was at least fifty grand based upon thumbing through one stack. The total sum might be more, or it could be less. The strange thing was, even though I had severe doubts about the money's origin and why it was placed in my car, I'd subconsciously convinced myself that it was my meal ticket to hand over to the Sack Brothers. I could rid myself of one of the greatest mistakes of my life—getting into the betting game with some very seedy people, even if I had been basically tricked into doing so.

What if I turned the money over to the brothers and then the real owner of the money showed up wanting it back? It was possible someone had just stashed it in the car as a temporary hiding spot, and they would show up at any time to...

I froze when I heard shoes crunching through leaves and sticks. I hurriedly scanned the back yard. Was there something moving back there? During the three seconds I gave myself to assess the placement of the noise, the thud of my heart made it more difficult to hear clearly.

I was certain the noise was coming from behind the garage. Maybe.

I lifted a foot and slowly brought it to the ground. Quiet as a bird. I continued my heel-to-toe movement as I made my way to the side of the garage and took hold of the corner panel. I paused and listened. The crunching sound wasn't as prominent, but it was still audible. Could it be an animal? Most dogs in this neighborhood were kept inside or behind fences. Maybe it was an armadillo digging at the foundation of the garage. One of those little fuckers had done major damage to my mom's house when I was in high school.

But something told me this was no four-legged creature. Well, maybe it was a creature, or even two of them, but I had a feeling it was human. My first thought was the Sack Brothers. If so, I could hand over the money and watch one problem walk out of my life. Of course, that would likely soon be replaced by another problem—the owner of said cash.

Another thought hit me so hard it took my breath away. What

if Ronnie Gutierrez had found out where I lived?

I swallowed, and the crackling noise in my ears was almost deafening. I glanced around. Of course, I had no weapons, no real way of defending myself. But I had my phone. I could call Courtney. What was I thinking? She was never available. Okay, I could just dial 9-1-1.

But what if I was wrong and it really was the Sack Brothers? Cops would ask way too many questions, and Elan and Milo would get very pissed. I couldn't picture a good outcome.

I went with the one-foot-in approach. I took out my phone, punched in the three digits, 9-1-1, and restarted my walk toward the back side of the garage. If it was anyone who would harm me, I'd simply tap the button to dial, and the operator would hear everything.

Damn, Cooper, you're such a super sleuth.

I got to the back, touched the corner of the garage, and leaned my head forward. A man was jumping up and down.

"Ben?"

"Fuck!" He jumped even higher. "You scared the shit out of me, Cooper."

"What are you doing?"

"My zipper is caught on my shirt."

"Why was your zipper down?"

"Dude, I was taking a leak, why else? Can you give me a hand?"

"Not in a million years. Finish whatever you're doing, and I'll meet you by my car."

A minute later, he came around the side, and the bottom of his white Oxford shirt was sticking out of the fly of his chinos.

"Nice look."

"Yeah, whatever. Some friend you are."

I laughed. "Why are you here at this time of night, Ben?"

He looked up at the sky and took in a deep breath. "Seems like we're both back at college. You're getting home late, I'm drunk—"

"You're drunk?"

"At least I'm admitting it. And honestly, Cooper, if you lived my life, you'd look for every opportunity you could to get out of the house."

"Wait, you and Reva are married?"

"Nah, dude. I'm over there a lot. But can't you see it's inevitable? I mean, I'm not getting any younger."

I chuckled. "I think you get to decide if you want to get married or not. Unless…"

He motioned with his hand for me to continue my thought.

"Unless she's basically your sugar momma."

"Ha!" He looked away, then turned his sights back to me. "Wait a second. You're making me sound like a loser."

"She's loaded, right?"

"Actually, her first husband had money. She says she got screwed in the divorce."

"I thought she said he died while 'servicing' her?"

"Oh, that was husband number two."

"So now she's leaning on you?"

He huffed out a breath. "Some. And the financial stuff isn't that bad…well, up until the triplets started having weekly mani-pedis."

"She's demanding."

"So, you kind of picked up on that?"

He was serious. "Kind of, yeah."

"A man's got to have his space, kind of like going commando-style—just let it all hang loose. Know what I mean?"

I nodded. "And that's why you went out and got drunk."

Ben's head sunk into his shoulders. "Reva thinks I was meeting my new business partner."

He'd dabbled in a lot of things over the years, at least from what I'd heard. "So you lied and got drunk instead."

"If I tell her the truth, she'll cut me off!"

"It's that good?"

"Dude, I think Bissell is her middle name."

"Thanks for sharing. I'll never look at Reva the same way. What are you going to say when you get home—that you accidentally fell into a pool of beer?"

He popped his fingers off his forehead. "Wow, I think I was just struck by a bolt of lightning. I can say *you* are my new business partner."

"You're obviously joking. I mean, I don't think I qualify in her mind as a legitimate business partner. I don't have the résumé for it. On top of that, you already have a business partner, right? So, she might find out, and then your little drunk-excursion lie would be exposed."

"That's the lightning bolt. *You* could be my *newest* business partner."

"Me?" I snorted, poking a finger at my own chest.

"Why not you?" He crossed his arms and tried to give me a serious look. It just didn't work with his shirttail sticking out from his fly, flapping in the breeze.

I was waiting for him to snap out of it and realize the lunacy of his idea. After a while, I heard an owl hooting. Ben's posture hadn't changed.

Then a thought hit me. "Hold on. This so-called partnership…would it require me to invest thousands of dollars of my own money and would I see the word 'Ponzi' included in the company description?"

"Funny, Cooper. Very fucking funny. Seriously, hear me out. This could be a huge win-win for both of us."

"Win-win" meant *here comes the sales pitch*. I leaned against the LeBaron and crossed my arms. "Yeah?"

"Goat."

"Goat what?"

"You ever hear of G-O-A-T, all caps?"

"The Greatest of All Time, like LeBron."

"And that's how we came up with the name of the company. Ingenious, isn't it?" He bounced his fingers off his head and made an explosion noise.

"Mind-blowing. Truly. What the hell are you selling?"

"Let's just say our competition will be Nike, Adidas, Puma."

"You're selling sneakers?"

"Dude, it's all about the name. And we market the company in all caps, G-O-A-T, just so everyone knows we're not talking about the animal." His eyes drifted to the top of the trees. "Actually, I can envision the first set of commercials. We'll use an actual goat...you know, just so people see we can make fun of ourselves."

"Everyone will make fun of you."

"Us," he said, pointing to me and then to himself. "They'll be making fun of *us*. Wait. They won't be making fun of us, because everyone will think we have the flyest sneakers out there."

"Fly," I said, trying not to laugh. "And you haven't mentioned what my role would be in this new sneaker giant."

"It's all about your connections."

An image of Dr. V's crooked smile came to mind, and I almost shuddered. "Do what?"

"Listen, you know coaches and players in college and the pros. You've just got to convince them to wear our shoes. You do that, and it's our golden ticket."

"Ben, you do realize that professional athletes—hell, even college coaches—go with a brand of shoes for money. It's called an endorsement deal. You, or I guess GOAT, pays them money, and they endorse the shoes, wear the shoes."

"And that's why you'll hold the title of executive vice president over marketing."

"How will a fancy title help?"

"Well, you'll have full autonomy to figure out creative solutions to get the first big-time schools and pro athletes to wear our shoes. They'll be in on the ground floor of something huge."

I sighed. I was tired, and this business wet dream of Ben's was only further draining my body of energy.

"I'll think about it."

He pumped his fist like he'd just won a national championship. "Hot damn!"

"I said I'll think about it. I might have another coal in the fire."

His smile evaporated. "That loser retail job?"

"I'm not going to get into it now."

"I see, you don't want to jinx it." He walked over and patted my upper arm. "I can accept a little competition, Mr. Cooper Chain. Just don't accept anything until you talk to me. Got it?" He pretended to pull the trigger of his hand gun.

"Got it."

He put his hand on the LeBaron. "This puppy still run?"

"Not at the moment."

"I remember you telling me one time back in college about you and Willow and the back of your car." A smile split his face.

"That's nuts. I don't kiss and tell, even to you."

"Hmm. Okay, maybe that was someone else, but the two of you looked kind of chummy at the bookstore."

"Chummy? You're going Hardy Boys on me now?"

"Ha-ha," he said in mock laughter. "Seriously, you think she's going to drop tall, dark, and rich just days before the wedding for *you*?"

I didn't like how that sounded. "First, he's not very tall."

"Whoa. Point for you."

"Dude, it's not like that between Willow and me. We're just friends helping each other out."

He started grinning again, but I held a steady gaze.

"All right, I see how you're playing this. I respect that."

"Okay, whatever. I'm beat."

"And I'm calling Uber." He started to walk off. "See you soon, Mr. Executive Vice President."

"Later, Ben Dover." I laughed all the way up my steps as he cussed me out from the street. And then I started to recall that night with Willow in the back of my car in college.

Thirty-Three

Willow

Other than a couple of folks cleaning up the kitchen, the house was nearly empty, and I was sitting on a chair, rubbing my foot. A second later, Harvey was down on one knee, and *he* was rubbing my foot.

"You're so kind."

He winked. I'd never considered Harvey to have James Bond's suaveness, but it was still cute.

"You're beautiful, Willow."

I touched his cheek. "You're rather dashing yourself, Harvey."

"I know this night wasn't easy for you. But you handled it with such grace."

"Not sure about that. I nearly fainted, and then I almost came unglued on, uh, *Dad*. Still hard to say that word."

"But you didn't come unglued."

"Probably because Ma beat me to it."

He shrugged. "We're all one big happy family."

"Who are you kidding?"

"Okay. I'm joking. But isn't it just amazing that your dad showed up after all these years?"

"Amazing. That's one word for it." I pinched the corners of

my eyes. "The whole night was kind of a blur. I know what happened, but my mind keeps flashing back to a lot of childhood memories. It's a little of surreal."

My eyes gravitated to a painting on the far living room wall. I was sure it had a title, and it probably cost Harvey more money than I'd ever made in a month, or multiple months, but it captured my attention. Why? The nature scene showed ominous clouds and lightning in the background, and a single bird was ascending into the sliver of light seemingly glowing down from Heaven. I was a little baffled at the symbolism. Was it supposed to reflect eternal hope or pending doom? And I only asked all those internal questions because the bird on the canvas was a dove, the very bird whose parts were found at the murder scenes of Marion and the other woman, Irene Washington.

"You're stressed, and my foot massage isn't helping," Harvey said

"The massage feels great. Don't stop. But there's just so much going on, and not just with Dad showing up and Ma embarrassing me."

"Marion?"

I caught Harvey up on everything that had occurred, trying to remember every last detail. When I finished, he nodded and looked away for a moment.

"What are you thinking?" I asked.

"While you'd told me about this Ronnie fellow, I wasn't aware of what he'd done with Lucy's daughter and now possibly Lucy herself. The timing of the murder is difficult to resolve, but he's a very bad person."

"'Bad' doesn't begin to describe this guy. He's killed at least two people that we know of—or, at least, he's been associated with the murders. He might have harmed Lucy and her daughter. And the police aren't giving me much confidence right now. In fact, I'm pretty pissed."

"I'm just sick about Marion's death. But I'm also worried about your safety. And to top it off, it's all coming down this week, our wedding week." He paused, and so did his foot massage.

"You look like you have an idea. That would be very welcomed. Cooper and I can't figure this crap out, and we're not exactly professionals."

"I have a couple of thoughts." He pulled out his phone and walked away while I stared at the dove painting. Was it some type of sign from the Universe? If so, it was speaking a different language. I still felt just as confused and upset as earlier.

Harvey returned about five minutes later, interrupting my near-catatonic gaze.

"Do you know a city power broker who might light a fire into this investigation?" I asked.

"Something like that."

"That's vague."

"Who knows if it will work? Let's give it twenty-four hours and see if something breaks."

I released a long sigh, then ran a finger along his cheek. "Thank you, Harvey. You are my white knight."

He made a scoffing noise. "I'm no great athlete or crime fighter, but my logical brain has its moments." He gave me another awkward wink.

He removed my other shoe and started massaging that foot.

"Ooh, you know just what I need."

He popped his eyebrows. I knew that signal.

"I'm just kidding, you know," he said. "It's been a difficult night for you. I think you need a nice long night of sleep. No going back to your apartment tonight. You need to stay here where it's safe."

I relished lying in his arms, feeling the warmth and comfort of his body against mine. My life experiences—Dad leaving notwithstanding—had driven me to be an independent person and to not rely on anyone else to take care of me in any form or fashion. Some might disagree with that notion, considering my circumstances when Harvey and I first met, but you can't really know what's in a person's mind. Not my mind. And one thing I felt rather sure of was that any successful relationship required trust and commitment. Maybe that epiphany had come with age. I knew I couldn't stay inside my protective cocoon and expect us to grow our relationship.

I brought Harvey closer and kissed him softly on the lips. "Thank you for being such a rock in my life." I got to my feet and hooked my arm in his. "Now, what do you say we go take care of that other rock?"

He smiled and walked a few steps, but then he stopped me and held my hands. "This is going to sound quite old-fashioned, but we have only a few days until the wedding. Don't you think we should, you know...save ourselves until the big night?"

My jaw dropped open, but I didn't speak.

"I don't mean to disappoint you. Believe me, I love our romps in the bed. But let's have something to look forward to. The guest bedroom is all ready for you. What do you say?"

"Sure, Harvey. Anything you want."

Thirty-Four

Cooper

For the first time in my illustrious tenure, there was a buzz inside Books and Spirits, and it had nothing to do with the amount of spirits being served. Actually, since it wasn't even noon yet, the bar wasn't officially open. But Brandy had allowed our bar staff—basically one guy—to serve soft drinks and water in plastic cups. She even sprung for some prepackaged appetizers from the local grocery. Not exactly the same quality found at Willow and Harvey's lavish party last night, but for a B-list author book signing, this was pretty high end.

The author, a guy named Brett Murphy, had just finished reading a portion of his memoir to the crowd, which consisted mostly of women in their fifties. They'd apparently turned back the clock. Partially because of the scintillating details and partially because he had that 1980s rocker look (glorified spiked mullet while wearing an old Journey tour T-shirt), the ladies cooed and squealed at every salacious detail. And then they cheered and whistled when he sung a snippet of a lyric. They were so excited you'd think he was Steve Perry, not a backup guitarist who had toured with the band after they released their *Escape* album.

From our safe spot behind the register counter, Slash and I

watched Brett being escorted through the crowd. Archibald Motta, his agent, played more of a security role, as some of the women became rather handsy as Brett passed by. Finally, Archibald and Brett reached the table Slash and I had set up earlier. It was positioned behind green velvet ropes that established a barrier from the crowd. Two assistants to Archibald were set up at either end to help with the crowd flow.

"Hey, dude, check out Brandy," Slash said, nudging my arm. My bad arm.

I winced a bit and then found her beaming smile on the other side of the raucous group, where she stood next to a sign that said if a person was in line to get an autograph, they had to have purchased the book.

"You'd think she personally got a portion of the proceeds from each sale," I said.

"Maybe she does," Slash responded

I knew that was ludicrous. This was the world of retail— bookstore retail at that. Books and Spirits wasn't in one of the massive DFW malls that were shrinking or declaring bankruptcy every other week, but the profit margin in anything that touched the book world was razor thin. While the journalism profit margin wasn't much better, there were a few in my profession who'd developed a large enough platform to make some serious bucks. And before my glorious downfall, I was on my way. My writing gig had netted me just enough money to make some good bets, which of course, we can see where that led. Enter Dr. V and his Russian goon squad.

"When are you going to make your move, Cooper?" Slash asked, nudging my arm again.

I made an audible gasp.

"Dude, your face is turning red."

"My arm is bruised." I refused to say it was broken. Out of sight, out of mind.

I noticed Brett's interactions with the book buyers was now in full swing. He would sign a book and then, when asked, stand up and take a quick picture with the reader—or were they more like groupies? He obliged, even if some of the ladies grabbed his waist as if he were a slab of meat.

"So?" Slash asked, this time without touching my arm.

"I have to be patient. Don't want to appear too eager. Apparently, Archibald knows about my writing prowess, so he might have an idea in mind."

"But he also knows you're working at a bookstore," Slash said with a chuckle.

Whatever confidence I carried had just been…slashed. Damn, I could throw out a pun even if it was at my own expense.

Ensuring Brandy wasn't watching, I passed the time by munching on a few crackers with cheese. They tasted like salted cardboard with a hint of cheddar. But it was a change of pace from my regular meal of chicken or beef Ramen.

After a while, Archibald moved to the near side of the front table and watched the assembly-line book signing and picture session work flawlessly. He was within striking distance, so I meandered in his direction.

Two of the women who'd just had their books signed were gleefully walking past me, then one dropped a bookmark, a (cheap) free gift from Brandy. "Excuse me," I said, leaning down to pick up the bookmark, "but you dropped this." I handed it to the woman, who stopped for one second to say a quick "thanks" before she went right back into gab mode.

Archibald turned to me then and smiled.

"Hey," I said. "Looks like you've got quite a strong book and author on your hands. That will make the publisher happy."

"It's the buzz I was looking for. This is his hometown, and I knew he'd throw in some stories to get the crowd going."

"I like the name-dropping as well. Don Henley lives at least part-time in Dallas."

He straightened his bow tie—today it was red, white, and blue—and smiled. "You don't think I know that? Plus, I've been trying to get face time with Henley, hoping he'll want to do another book."

I nodded. "Sounds like a good idea." I waited a few seconds, wondering if he was going to steer the conversation to me.

I waited five minutes, and he said nothing. Then, I thought, maybe he wanted to focus solely on Brett and ride that Journey wave today. At least my ego convinced me that had to be his position.

The signing went on for another hour. I did my best to stay noticed by making a few comments here and there, but Archibald wasn't really into small talk. Part of me wanted to say, "Hey, I listened to your story about your son. Remember?" But I knew that wasn't exactly a great way to show off my maturity, as fleeting as it can be.

With about ten readers left in the line, I removed his business card and flicked it against my hand. I can't say it was a subconscious move, but I really didn't have a plan.

"Oh, I see you got my business card," Archibald said.

I felt like a ten-year-old kid who'd just gotten the attention of Michael Jordan. "Oh, right," I said, acting as though the card had magically appeared in my hand.

"You got kind of busy yesterday juggling your boss—she seems a bit demanding—and that phone call. I hope everything is okay?"

"Why wouldn't it be?"

"You just had this serious look on your face."

"Well, it's just, uh…" I pondered my next thought. "I'm looking at a number of business opportunities right now." I was playing hard to get. Yep, that seemed like the most prudent strategy.

"Business opportunities." He nodded and glanced back at the author table. "Hey, I mentioned to my son that I ran into you. Being the new sports nerd in the house, he did his homework and found some of the articles you've written. He's pretty impressed. That makes two in our family."

My breath left my lungs. I was suddenly floating so high I couldn't even see cloud nine well below me. "Yeah?" I said, showing off a calm demeanor when I felt the exact opposite.

"Hey, Archibald, this young lady says she's written a romance novel," Brett said from near the table, where he was having his picture taken next to a woman wearing a shirt with a puppy stitched on the front. "Says she'd love it if you could recommend her to an agent."

Archibald half-turned to me and muttered behind his smile, "Cozy romance. Just what the world needs."

"Right," I said, looking for a quick bonding moment.

He walked over and introduced himself. Damn, had Miss Cozy Romance ruined my best shot?

"Dude," Slash said.

I reflexively jumped two feet to my left. Self-preservation. "Yeah?"

"Did you just nail the deal, and now he's going to nail that babe?"

"No nailing of any kind, Slash. He was distracted by Miss Cozy Romance—that's my name for her."

"Oh, my. I'd like to cozy up to her romance."

"Huh? You're talking gibberish now."

"I can't think straight. She's a hottie."

"She's at least twice your age. On top of that she's wearing a dog shirt."

"I'd love to get hold of those puppies," he said as his eyes bulged for a second.

"You need to go back to your graphic novels."

He sighed. "Probably right. What lady in her right mind would want to be with a douche bag like me?" He chuckled and walked off.

I turned and tried to figure out a way to get Archibald's attention again. He had a strained look on his face, so I knew he wanted a way out. Maybe I could walk up and say I knew an agent in New York City. I'd appear to be connected to people in the biz and save Archibald from pretending to the woman that she had a chance at getting published.

Creative solutions, brought to you by Cooper Chain.

What about the part that you don't know such an agent?

Live in the moment, Cooper.

I took two steps, and then my phone rang. I'd forgotten to flip it to vibrate. All eyes looked at me. "Sorry," I said, fumbling with my phone. Earl Grant's name was on the screen. I almost forwarded the call, but I could see Archibald talking again to his prized author, so I peeled back and took the call.

"Hey, Earl. Don't tell me you need me to bail you out of jail because you got busted buying weed from Dizzy."

A second later, a car rammed into a No Parking sign just out front, and again, I jumped two feet in the air. "Damn!"

"Did you fucking hear me, Cooper?"

Earl sounded like he was crying.

"What's going on, Earl?"

"My sister, Janice. She's dead. They think she died just like the other two."

For the second time in the last few minutes, air rushed out of my lungs. Just then, the door flew open. It was Willow. She spotted me and ran in my direction, her face glowing red.

"Earl, I'm so sorry. I just…I don't know what to say."

Willow grabbed my shoulders. "Janice is dead. Janice is dead. Did you hear me, Cooper? Janice is dead. Oh my God, I just can't believe what is happening."

It took ten minutes for emotions to calm, most of that focused on Brandy. And then we finally had a conversation about what this all meant.

Thirty-Five

Willow

I sat in the overstuffed chair by the bar in Books and Spirits, my hands covering my face. My gut felt like it had been split open with a fork.

Janice. Dead.

"Hey, you should drink this."

I looked up to see Cooper holding a glass of what looked like a soda. "I'm not thirsty."

"Will, your hands are shaking. Just have a sip."

I took a whiff. "It's booze."

"Beam and Coke. My—"

"I know. Your go-to drink for the guy who'll gladly go to the store to get his Beam."

He gave me a half-smile. "You still remember some of my idiotic mantras."

"I didn't know I did until you showed up."

I sipped the drink and released a deep breath. "Is this legal? I mean, the bar doesn't look like it's open."

Cooper looked over his shoulder. "Brandy was cool with giving me a break. But she won't know anything about the booze. It's not like you're going to run off to the TABC and turn us in for serving booze fifteen minutes before it's legal."

"I think people might wonder if I've been drinking all morning, given what I did to that sign out front."

"Uh, yeah...about that."

"Don't worry. Harvey will pay to get it fixed."

"That's not it. I was more worried about your state of mind."

My eyes found Cooper's phone resting on the stained table as he took a seat. "I was out of it. Earl's calling us back?"

"Said he would. We'll see. Sounded like he might have more information, but he was pretty upset."

I slurped more of my drink, then set it on the table. It sloshed over the side. "Sorry."

Cooper pulled some napkins out of his pocket and cleaned up the mess.

"Who wouldn't be upset, Cooper? Think about it..." I swallowed back a lump in my throat as tears pooled again in my eyes.

He reached over and put his hand on my knee, and I rested my hand on his. Our eyes locked for a moment, and I could feel some type of pull. It made no sense. But I also knew that trauma could excavate emotions that you never knew were there.

"How did you find out about Janice?" he asked, pulling his hand back.

"I got a call from another nurse friend who also works at the clinic."

"The clinic?"

"The Community Health Clinic in south Dallas. Janice had decided to use her skills and wonderful compassion to help those who really need the help, who can't afford to see a doctor. She worked part-time at Parkland, but the clinic was her passion." I cleared my throat and ran through a flurry of images of Janice and me and our many other nurse friends having too much fun during our nightshift at Parkland. "All the crazies seemed to show up at night."

"At the hospital?"

I wiped my eyes. "Yeah, the overnight shift at Parkland. On some nights it was like a scene from the *Rocky Horror Picture Show*. That kind of bizarre, unexplainable stuff that you somehow get through, and then you can only laugh about it later."

"Sounds like you and your friends were tight."

"You save lives, you see lives end way too early...you have to bond with someone. For a while, they were all I had. In my old life." He looked at me with both curiosity and concern. "I'm fine, Cooper. Talking to you helps, believe it or not."

"I'm wondering about this 'old life.' You're not simply referring to just before you met Harvey, are you?"

I shook my head. "How do you read my thoughts?"

"Because I care."

His eyes stayed on me, unblinking. I felt another tug from somewhere deep inside. "Please don't. I've done so much to put my life back together." I could feel tears bubbling again, and Cooper handed me a napkin. I dabbed my eyes.

"You want to tell me about your former life?" he asked.

His phone started buzzing, and we glanced at each other, then back to the screen. It was Earl. Cooper punched up the line.

"Hey, Cooper. I have a couple of minutes before the cops show up."

He sounded much more mellow.

"Willow is here, and I have you on speaker."

"Can you fucking believe it, Willow? Janice. The kindest soul on this fucked-up planet. Who the hell would do this?"

I closed my eyes for a second to maintain some composure. "I'm so sorry, Earl. I know you must be hurting."

"It's..." He paused, and I heard a sucking noise. Cooper held up two fingers to his mouth. Earl was probably smoking a joint. One way to calm down, I supposed.

"It's just tough. All I can think about right now aren't the great times I had with Janice, but the times I was too busy for her or didn't give her a call back. In fact, I can't even remember the last time I told her I loved her. How sad is that?"

He was really hurting. We both were. "You're just living your life like the rest of us, Earl. Don't beat yourself up. We just need to remember Janice's kind spirit. You remember the way she laughed so loud?"

He chuckled. "Yeah, that was one obnoxious laugh. It was that way even when we were kids." He released a long sigh, maybe even took a good puff on his joint. "The detective called me. That's how I found out."

"Courtney?" Cooper asked.

"Nah. Another guy I know who has worked with me here at the office before. He was pretty torn up himself."

Cooper said, "Where does she live, Earl?"

"An apartment off Greenville. But that's not where she was found. They found her body behind the clinic, right next to a dumpster. A fucking dumpster, can you believe it?"

I held up a hand, motioning for Cooper to not get Earl riled up. I wasn't sure he saw me because he continued talking about it. "It fucking sucks. And we're going to do everything we can to figure out who did this and stop them."

"You? You're not even a cop."

"When you said she died like all the others, what did you mean?"

"Well, it's not exactly the same. Before I called you back, I got more details from Remy."

"Remy?"

"Yeah, she called me. She's an ME here at the office."

"And what did she share?"

"Janice's spine was crushed like a tin can." Earl's voice started to crack.

Cooper and I shook our heads in disbelief. "Is that how she…?" Cooper asked.

"Given what we saw with the two other victims, Remy's initial assessment is that she died from some type of gas asphyxiation, probably nitrogen. It would fit with the others."

I was trying to make sense of it all, but Cooper plowed ahead. "How was she found?"

"What do you mean 'how was she found?'" I shot back, offended that he'd ask Earl such a callous question right now.

"It's okay, Willow. He's just trying to understand if or how these murders are connected. The detective said she was on the ground, her arms across her chest, real peaceful-like. Oh, and her head was resting on an old cereal box."

Brandy walked up. "Cooper, sorry to interrupt, but…" She tapped her wrist.

"Hey, Earl," he said, picking up the phone. "We have to go."

"Oh, one more thing. They found a bird's foot resting on her chest."

Thirty-Six

Cooper

It turned out Brandy did have a heart, even if ninety percent of it was crusted over like hardened lava. I'd taken her to the side and explained how Willow's friend had died. She was so happy about the haul the bookstore had made from the book signing, she said I could take an extended break. Just like that.

I walked outside with Willow and saw the front end of her BMW wedged into the bent metal pole.

"Looks like I'll have to get the car fixed too." She handed me the keys. "You drive. That one drink made me a little woozy."

I got behind the wheel and took in the new car smell. "How old is this?"

"About six months, why?"

"Nothing like a new car, especially a puppy like this." I ran my hand down the leather steering wheel and then along the dash.

"It's not a real dog, you know. It's just a piece of metal and plastic with an engine."

"An engine that purrs like a panther ready to race across the African prairie."

She shook her head. "Why are you so fixated on animals?"

I shrugged.

"Do you need a four-legged companion?"

"I'm fine. I can talk to Mrs. Kowalksi whenever I'm looking for a conversation." I fired up the car and pulled out of the parking lot. "Where am I going?"

"I don't know. Just drive for now. Maybe we'll get inspired."

I headed east toward White Rock Lake on Mockingbird.

"Hey, didn't we eat pizza there once?" She was pointing at Campisi's.

"Right after the TCU-SMU game. You were heckling the SMU fans."

"Huh? That was you."

"No way. Not my style."

"You're kidding, right?"

"I make fun of people, I don't heckle."

She snorted and shook her head. "Who were you texting on our way out of the bookstore?"

"Courtney, of course."

"Because…"

"Because this is getting bat-shit crazy, that's why. Did you hear Earl? A bird's foot. If I had to guess what kind of bird that foot came from, it would be a dove. That's what I think we've been overlooking all along."

"What do you think the significance of this dove is?"

"No clue. That's why I texted Courtney. They must have been working this angle. Hopefully, I'll hear back from her soon."

There were a few minutes of silence as we passed the northern tip of White Rock Lake, then veered onto North Buckner and drove along the east side of the lake.

"I ran the Rock a few years ago," she said.

"Before the Dallas Marathon, it was called the White Rock Marathon."

"Yep. Froze my titties off." She was laughing before I could gasp.

"Are you drunk off one Beam and Coke?"

"You fixed the drink. I think it was ninety percent Jim Beam."

"I only did it so I could drive your car. It might be the closest I get to real money. Especially now."

"You know, you never finished telling me what went down with the cocaine and the baseball player…one of the bad things that you said happened to you."

I sighed. "Do we really have to get into this now?"

"What else can we do? We're waiting on Courtney to call back." She motioned with her hand. "So, spit out. Can't be that painful."

My chest felt tight. "Not so sure about that."

"The wound is still fresh?"

"At times, it feels like the surgeon is still prying away under my skin and I'm fully awake."

Her whole body quaked. "That's a morbid thought."

"I know I shouldn't complain. People have it much worse than I do."

"It's good for all of us to reflect on the positive and not dwell on the negative."

"Amen." I turned south onto Garland Road and drove by the Dallas Arboretum, heading back toward Central.

"Cooper, you're not talking."

"Oh, I thought we'd moved on."

"Not until Courtney calls back. So, come on and give it up. Unless you want me to squeeze the arm you refuse to get X-rayed." She started to reach over.

"Okay, okay. Here's the quick-and-dirty version. Cops raided the party. The athlete and his buddies said the coke was mine."

"That's uncool. You convinced them it wasn't yours?"

"I tried. My very expensive lawyer tried. But the player and his buddies stayed aligned on their story. So I was screwed."

"Screwed?"

I shot her a quick glance. "I had to plea to a felony. In the state of New York, it's called a Class D non-violent felony. No jail time, but I was put on probation and had to do community service and pay a fine."

"Damn, Cooper. That really sucks."

"Donkey dicks."

She snorted. "That's when the tough times started?"

"Kind of."

"Mr. Evasive returns."

I wiped a hand across my face. "I lost my job over it, and no one would hire me. My relationships went to shit. I just couldn't catch a break. But I couldn't really blame them. I was a fucking felon. I *am* a felon. I can't even vote, you know?"

She didn't respond, so I looked to my right, and her eyes were staring straight ahead.

"We're getting way off topic here. Too much about me. This is your week, and now we have all this murder crap screwing it up."

She still didn't say anything. Everyone had their own way of dealing with drama and grief, so I gave her some mental space and focused on driving the BMW in and out of some traffic. I eventually turned right onto North Henderson. We passed through an area where some of the homes had couches sitting in the yard. Barbed wire surrounded dilapidated structures. Two blocks later, we drove by art galleries and trendy restaurants. I thought she might make a comment, but she kept her gaze on the window. Maybe I'd said something that had sparked a bad memory, or we'd driven by a place that reminded her of Janice.

We crossed over Central, and the road turned into Knox. As I slowed to stop at a red light at McKinney, I saw Chuy's on the left, home of the best margaritas in the country. It was packed, and it was only lunchtime.

"You hungry?" I asked, breaking the silence.

"I don't know if Harvey is right for me, Cooper."

I didn't move for a second. My mind replayed what I'd just heard, or thought I'd heard. I slowly turned my head in her direction.

"The light is green. Go!" she said.

I pressed the gas and eased forward. Traffic was always heavy on Knox, at least any time before midnight.

"You want to share more?" I asked.

I saw her wipe a tear from her face. There wasn't a place to park along the road. Instead, just beyond the Katy Trail, I hooked the BMW down an alley, stopped the car, and put it in park. I leaned over, and we embraced. Her hold on me was, not surprisingly, strong. But she wasn't just showing off her strength.

"It'll be okay. It's just pre-wedding jitters," I said softly.

"How would you know?"

"Didn't I mention that I used to be married?"

"Another one of those five things?" She sniffled.

"Eh, but who's counting?"

"You."

"True. But it's time to start a new count. A positive one."

Just then, our car was bumped from behind. Not hard, but enough to make me realize another vehicle had hit us. I whipped my head around to see two men sliding out of a red Ford pickup.

"Shit."

"What's going on, Cooper?"

I put my hand on the gearshift, ready to throw the BMW into drive and punch it, but there was a delivery truck stopped a hundred feet in front of us. "Double shit!"

"Double shit? Why double shit?" She swung her head around. "Who the hell are these guys?"

I thought about playing keep-away in the car for as long as possible in this hundred-foot space, but they'd probably inflict heavy damage on Willow's car, and it would piss them off even more, which would likely be followed by inflicting heavy damage to my face. Which, frankly, was fine with me. I just didn't want them touching Willow.

There was a knock on my window. "It's all right," I said to Willow with very little conviction. "They're former business associates. I'll just talk to them for a second, and we'll be fine."

"Oookay," she said, glancing at the beast looking at her through the passenger window.

I punched down my window. "Hi, Elan."

"It's Milo, dickwad."

"Of course, I should have been able to tell." I sounded like the ice cream guy. "What can I do for you?"

"Want to make sure you'll have our money in two days."

I considered telling Milo about the bag of money just showing up in the trunk of my LeBaron, but that would raise questions I had no answers for. "Yep. No problem on my end."

"You sound mighty confident for a loser who works at a bookstore." Milo looked over the roof of the car and shared a good laugh with his brother. Was that supposed to be funny? I just couldn't keep up with one-celled organisms. I chuckled a couple of times. I could see Willow out of the corner of my eye looking very concerned about me...not them, but me.

"Anything else I can help you with today?" I asked as if I were still at my loser job.

Milo put his arm on the rooftop—for a second, I thought he might crush it—and then he looked inside and ran his eyes up and down Willow. "Yummy, yummy."

It was at that moment I noticed a black-and-blue bruise under his left eye and a cut on his nose—the same nose I wanted to punch.

"Can I help you?" I asked, snagging his attention.

"Not like she can. Va-va-voom."

Had some entity sent out a notice to all single-threaded guys to ogle my...uh, Willow when they laid eyes on her for the first time?

"She doesn't know how to cook, and she's a lesbian."

His face looked like he'd smelled something foul. "She can't even cook? What kind of woman is she?"

Willow heard that. "The kind that will kick your ass if you—"

"You're so funny!" I yelled, trying to distract Milo from what she'd said.

Milo rubbed his face, then winced a bit as if he'd forgotten about his facial injuries. "Sounds like she's a loud-mouth jerk, just like you."

I heard Elan from the other side grunting something about jerking off. The pair made hand motions and laughed. Now it was Willow who looked like she'd smelled something foul.

Elan lowered his head again. "The money. Two days. This is your final reminder."

"Just what I needed. Thanks."

"No problem." He started to walk away, but stopped and pointed a finger at me. "By the way, for the favor we did for you, you might owe Dr. V big time. Just sayin'."

They laughed some more, got in their truck, and drove off.

I turned to Willow. She had steam coming out of her ears.

Thirty-Seven

Willow

Peering through the back window of my BMW, I watched Ogre One and Two back out of the alley and then turn west on Knox.

"Get out of here. Now!" I smacked Cooper's arm.

"Doh!"

"I would say I'm sorry, but after that shit…" I could hear my breath hissing through my teeth.

"I know, I know," Cooper said, holding up a hand. "There's more I need to tell you."

"Not here. Get the hell out of this alley. It's making me claustrophobic."

Cooper backed the BMW up and was about to turn west.

"Don't go the same direction they did. Go left."

He waited for traffic, then turned east.

"Now where?" he asked.

I looked over my shoulder, ensuring there were no signs of the red pickup. "Take a quick right down Cole."

Cooper did as I said without saying a word. Miracles do happen. But he might need one of his own after I peppered him with my questions.

We drove about a mile and approached Cole Park. Cooper started to slow down, glancing at me. "Want to take a walk through the park?"

"Are you fucking nuts? There's hardly anyone in the park. That's just inviting those beasts to mug us for the fun of it. Keep going."

He continued south on Cole, passing the old North Dallas High School. We reached Blackburn.

"Now where?"

"Take a left."

Again, he did as I said. His dog-like obedience was a sign that Ogre One and Two were not business associates, and their threatening tone and posture wasn't a joke.

"Take another left on McKinney."

"But that's taking us north, back to the alley off Knox."

"Just do it."

He did.

"Pull in here."

"Sip Stir Coffee House," he said. "If you wanted coffee, we already passed a Starbucks."

"Not a fan of the big chains. And this place gives me a good vibe. I need more good vibes right now."

Before he'd put the car in park, I slid out the door. I walked inside the coffee shop and ordered my usual double espresso. Cooper pulled up next to me. "Want anything?" I asked.

He stuffed his hands in his jeans pockets and looked around. I pointed at a menu on the counter.

"Do they have Orange Crush?"

"Seriously? Orange Crush in a coffee house?"

"That's a real classic," a woman from behind the counter said.

Cooper grinned. "See? Someone who appreciates great drinks. And it's a lot cheaper than these fancy coffees. I'll just have an Orange Crush, please."

The woman put a hand to her mouth and giggled. "We don't have Orange Crush. I was just thinking about my grandparents. They have those drinks all the time. But they live in Denver and love the Broncos."

Cooper's grin disappeared.

"Just get something, please," I said.

He asked for a water cup. I picked up my espresso and walked toward a table in the corner of the shop.

"Want to sit on the couch? Looks kind of comfy," he said.

I needed a table with space between us. "I want the corner booth so I can see the front door."

"Oh, right."

I sat in the high-back leather booth facing the rest of the room, but my eyes were glued to the front door and parking lot, specifically on the lookout for a red pickup.

"You going to drink your espresso?"

I shifted my eyes to Cooper. "You…" I took in a deep breath, trying to get my pulse under control. "What the hell have you gotten yourself into, Cooper? And I want to know the whole damn story. No bullshit. Right now."

"Please."

"Huh?"

"If you say 'please,' it will help create that positive vibe you were talking about earlier."

I didn't blink.

"Okay, forget I said that." He sighed, took a sip of water, and glanced at the few patrons also in the restaurant. More delays. What a piece of work.

I strummed fingers on the table.

"Never thought you'd have a French manicure. Not really your style," he said.

"Cooper…"

"Okay, okay. After what you just witnessed, I suppose you deserve to know what's going on." He spun his water cup a couple of times. "Based upon a recommendation, I put in some bets. And I won. That was the worst thing that could have happened." His eyes momentarily lifted to the ceiling.

"Are you addicted to gambling?"

"Hell no."

"That was a quick answer."

"It's the truth."

I sipped more of my espresso. "I dealt with addicts at the hospital. Alcohol was the worst, believe it or not. Then again, I never witnessed anyone addicted to these newer drugs, the ones that have all sorts of shit laced in there."

"You've seen a lot, Will. Helped countless people, I'm sure."

I wasn't about to let his praise divert our focus. "So, you claim not to be addicted to gambling."

"It's not just a claim. It's more about the who, not how many times."

"Who?"

"The two goons."

"Okay. I'm starting to follow you, although you said you won, so you kept gambling."

"You're still implying that I'm addicted. That's not the case, I assure you."

I couldn't be sure of anything right now. "The who. It's not just those two muscle heads, is it?"

He huffed out a breath. "They work for another gentleman."

"I'm guessing this guy doesn't run a legitimate business."

"Not really."

"Not really? He sends those two guys to collect his money, Cooper. How can you say he has a legitimate business?"

"Okay, the gambling business probably isn't registered with the Better Business Bureau. But he has other businesses."

"To launder his dirty money?"

"Damn, Will. You been watching *Ballers* or something?"

"I'm not ignorant." He pressed his lips shut, which was a wise choice. "How much do you owe?" I reached for my purse and sifted through it.

"You're not writing me a check, Will. Absolutely not."

I stopped what I was doing and looked up. "I'm just trying to find my phone. So, how much you owe?"

"Fifty."

"Thousand?"

He nodded as my hand found my phone. I pulled it out.

"I was in the hole for thirty grand, but they've added interest."

"That's one hell of an interest rate you got there."

"Kind of funny, but I didn't have a lot of say in the terms and conditions."

"Man, you can really pick 'em, can't you?"

He sipped his water. His ears were glowing a shade of red. He wasn't happy.

"Do you really think they'll harm you once they realize you can't pay the fifty grand? I know they're built like Russian tanks—"

"So you noticed the Russian-Jersey accent?"

"Huh? Whatever. You get my point."

"I do." He started tapping his chipped tooth.

"They gave you that?"

"It was an extra incentive for me to pay up by week's end."

I shook my head at him. "That's just great. And I'm assuming you don't have the fifty K."

"We might have no reason to worry, because I think I have the money."

I put my hand to my head. "*Might* and *think*. Can you be any more cryptic? You don't know if you have the money?"

"Well, you see—"

I raised a hand. "Hold on. Did you get a loan from another criminal to pay off this one?"

"Do you really think I'm that stupid?"

I just stared at him.

"I guess I know your answer to that question," he said, slouching in his chair.

"Tell me about the money you think you might have." Damn, that sounded ridiculous coming out of my mouth, *but look who I'm talking to.*

"Kind of a strange thing happened the other night, and I've been trying to figure out if it's a gift from the Man upstairs or someone's just trying to play a cruel joke on me."

I almost spit out a mouthful of my espresso. "On you?" I asked, grabbing a napkin and wiping my mouth. "This is the week of my wedding."

"About an hour ago, you weren't even sure you wanted to marry little Harvey."

"Don't call him that. And I shouldn't have said that. It was just nerves or something."

"Or something."

"Dammit, Cooper, look at what's gone on the last few days. The murders of people I know, my dad showing up like he's some hero, and now these goons making threats to collect on your gambling debt. It's just too much."

He stuck out his jaw but didn't snap off a snarky comment. Not right away. He sipped more of his water, and I did the same with my espresso. One minute turned into two. After a while, it felt like standoff.

"You know I'd do anything to ensure you weren't hurt," he said with sincerity.

"I won."

"Won what?"

"You talked first." I stuck my tongue out at him.

"You're really mature."

I snorted out a laugh and smacked my hand off the table. "That's a good one. You even said it with a serious face."

"Willow, I am being serious. I know I've made some stupid

mistakes, but I wouldn't knowingly put you or anyone I care about in danger."

He didn't crack a smile. The manic jokester wasn't joking. "Maybe I was a little rough on you. But you're still in deep shit, unless this pot of gold you're referencing is legitimate money."

"Don't know about legit, but it's not counterfeit. It's real cash."

I straightened my back. "So, you actually have the fifty K?"

A slow nod. "I found it in the trunk of my car."

My phone buzzed in my hand at the same time Cooper reached for his back pocket.

"It's a text," I said.

"From Courtney," he said. "A group text."

I read the text out loud: *Call me now!*

So we did, from my phone.

"Meet me at headquarters," Courtney said with little preamble. "And if you're a little squeamish, you might want to bring a barf bag."

Thirty-Eight

Cooper

Two officers escorted a handcuffed man right by our chairs. The man's shirt looked like it had been a target at a gun range. And he smelled like he'd been swimming in a vat of garbage and BO. Willow removed some perfume from her bag and held it to her nose.

"You think this is why Courtney told us to bring a barf bag?" she said.

"Hardly."

"What do you think is up?"

I saw Courtney from across the detective bullpen. She was waving us over.

"We'll soon find out."

Courtney escorted us into an interview room and shut the door. A manila folder was on the table.

"Did you find Ronnie Gutierrez? And is he the person who also killed my friend Janice?" Willow asked.

"Have a seat." Courtney extended a hand and then pulled out a chair for herself.

Willow took a defiant step back. "I don't need to have a seat. I don't want to play any more games. Three people have been killed, there's a crazy man on the loose who might have Lucy and her daughter, and we're not even sure Ronnie is the killer. We need answers, Courtney. I know you're spread thin working multiple cases, but this matters too. Don't you see that?"

"Ronnie's dead."

Willow and I glanced at each other, speechless.

"I know he's not your best friend, but he's still a person, and he didn't deserve *this*." Courtney lifted the manila folder and let it drop to the metal table.

More stunned silence. Courtney soon filled the gap. "Can I get either of you a drink?"

Willow ignored the question. "Is it possible that all of this is over?"

I knew that was hopeful thinking. Then a thought burrowed out of my soul that brought bile to the back of my throat. "Tell me Lucy and her daughter are okay. Please tell me Ronnie or some other desperate addict didn't kill them."

She held up a hand. "They're alive. Found them in a shed on some remote farm south of the city. They were tied up, and...well, they'd both been assaulted. But they're alive and will be okay, at least physically."

Willow grabbed the top of a chair. "I want to know more about what happened to them. And their condition."

I chimed in with a question before Courtney could respond. "Was it Ronnie who assaulted them?"

Willow shot a glance at me. "What do you mean? Who else would have done it?"

"Maybe it was the person who killed Ronnie."

"Okay, okay, you don't have to play Nancy Drew and the Hardy Boys," Courtney said. "I'll tell you everything I know."

"Joe Hardy," I said. "I'm more of a Joe than Frank."

Both ladies rolled their eyes, and then we each took a seat.

"According to Lucy—and she didn't say much—it was Ronnie

who assaulted her and her daughter. She's basically in shock. So is the little girl. When I arrived on the scene, the girl was still shaking, even with about a dozen cops there and repeatedly being told she was safe. She's only ten years old."

She shook her head and closed her eyes a second as if she were trying to scrub her thoughts. Then she took a deep breath and folded her hands on the table.

"Where are they?" Willow asked, thumbing a tear out of the corner of her eye.

"They're at Parkland and being given the best care possible."

Willow looked at me. "I want to go see them."

"Why? It's not like they're stuck in that crack house."

"You don't get it, Cooper. Everyone else is dead. Lucy is alive, and so is her daughter. I just feel like I need to talk to them, let them know it's okay. They might still be scared. Maybe I can help a little. I want to help."

I didn't really get it, but I saw that look in Willow's eyes. "Sure. We'll do it."

She touched my knee under the table as we both turned to Courtney.

"Do you have the person who killed Ronnie in custody?" I asked.

Willow snapped her fingers. "Maybe he was Ronnie's accomplice. You know, the whole timing of Marion's murder didn't quite fit with what Lucy had said about Ronnie being at the house."

"Wait a second," Courtney said with her eyes shifting between us. "I haven't shared with you Marion's time of death. Hell, I didn't know it until yesterday."

"We were desperate for information, Courtney. We had to start digging on our own."

"You're not going to give up your source?"

"Does it really matter at this point?"

She gave a half-shrug, then looked at Willow. "Your theory about an accomplice is an interesting one. We're poring through Ronnie's digital footprint right now. Phone calls, text messages, emails. But if that theory is correct—you know, being killed by his murder accomplice—then there might be more than one accomplice."

"How would you know that?" I snapped back.

"Lucy saw two people wearing masks."

"Where? When?"

"That's why I asked you down here. This is going to be a little unsettling." She placed the palm of her hand on the folder.

"What's in there?" Willow asked.

"Pictures. Now, I don't have to share them with you, but it's what Lucy and her daughter saw, and that has just added to their trauma."

"Hold on," I said. "You were talking about two people who might be Ronnie's accomplices."

She released a slow breath. She looked beaten down. Her hair didn't have the same radiant sheen, and her clothes were wrinkled, but she was still stunning. She glanced at me—did she think I was ogling her?

Come on, Cooper, get your head in the game.

"According to Lucy, Ronnie had just finished assaulting them and tying them up when they heard something outside the shed. Ronnie went to check it out. A minute later, Lucy heard yelling and then scuffling sounds, like there was a fight. And then after a few minutes of silence, she heard a scream that..." She paused.

Her eyes appeared glassy, so Willow and I both waited a moment.

Courtney swallowed, then said, "Lucy and her daughter both screamed themselves, they were so frightened."

Willow shook her head. "That child will be tormented the rest of her life. She needs counseling."

"There's more. Much more," Courtney said, her eyes shifting to the folder.

Willow placed both hands on the table as if she were bracing for a direct blow. "What now?"

"This is the part where I mentioned you might need a barf bag."

Willow again smacked her hand on the table. I flinched. Courtney didn't. She was the cop, so I wasn't surprised. But, damn, Willow was on edge.

"Just frickin' tell us, Courtney."

"Ronnie's scream had to be related to him being cut up."

"He was knifed to death? How many stab wounds?" I asked.

"You're not hearing me. He was cut up. Decapitated. His body cut into pieces."

I was happy I'd only had water earlier. Willow's face had lost all its color. "You going to lose it?" I put my hand on her shoulder.

She peered at my hand and then my eyes. I quickly pulled my hand back.

"I've seen a lot, Cooper. And this isn't about me." She turned to Courtney. "What else can you share?"

"Lucy and her daughter saw all of this." She popped her fingers off the folder.

"The body parts?" I asked.

"The two men." Willow nodded at Courtney. "You said Lucy saw two men in masks."

"I did. Apparently, these two men opened the shed door. Lucy noticed one of them holding a metal saw. It had blood on it. She thought she and her daughter were about to be killed."

Willow brought a hand to her mouth.

"Then, all of sudden, the other guy dumped the contents of a trash can right there on the shed floor. And then they left."

My eyes went to the folder. "The contents were…"

Courtney cleared her throat. "Ronnie's body parts."

Willow's chin dipped to her chest as I shook my head. My mind was racing with who could have done this and if it could be connected to the other murders.

"Courtney, what are we supposed to make of all this?" I asked.

"Our forensics team is still at the crime scene. We're hoping to find hair, fibers, blood, whatever will lead us to the two men who apparently killed Ronnie."

"But what about the other murders?" Willow's face had morphed from ghost white to beaming red. "Marion and Janice, and the other woman, Irene Washington?"

"The bird parts," I said. "Were there any bird body parts found at Ronnie's crime scene?"

Courtney bit into her lip. "Nothing has turned up so far. But the scene is not exactly an ME's lab. It's very messy, so they have a lot to sift through. Maybe they'll find something."

"More maybes," Willow scoffed. "When the hell are we going to have real evidence and then a suspect in custody?"

I could sense Courtney was about to snap off a biting response.

"Willow is just upset by all this, and I am too."

"No, Cooper. Upset sounds like I'm going to go home and crawl up in a corner and cry. I'm pissed. The lives of people we care about aren't the priority of the DPD. I guess we'll have to figure out who killed everyone on our own." Willow pushed out of her chair.

Courtney arched an eyebrow. A hurricane was building in the warm waters of the Gulf, and it was about to hit land. "That's not fair, Willow. Yes, we had this mass drug-related killing. I've been juggling the cases. But I've juggled this type of workload before and still caught the bad guys."

Willow gripped the back of her chair so tightly I saw white knuckles. "Cooper just asked about the bird parts. Have you or any of the hundreds of resources at the DPD figured out if or how these bird parts connect to the deaths?"

"Not yet. We're working on it."

Willow marched to the door. "Cooper, you coming?"

I looked at Courtney and turned my palms to the ceiling. "I don't know what to say. Just let us know if you guys come up with something."

"We're trying. We're doing the best we can."

"Not good enough," Willow said.

I followed Willow out of the building.

Thirty-Nine

Cooper

I finally took the opportunity to take in the full damage to the BMW. My first thought: an accordion. With all the scratches on the front and back ends, it looked like it had gone one round in a smash-up derby—one made for luxury cars, of course. Willow didn't notice or didn't care. She only instructed me to drive her to Parkland Hospital. Once inside, she found a nurse that she knew, and they talked for a good ten minutes. That led to a conversation with a doctor and more nurses. Then she walked over to me.

"I'm going to talk to Lucy and her daughter in the corner lounge area on floor two. It's basically empty. Apparently, they don't like to be in an enclosed room. Makes sense, I suppose. You're welcome to come up—Lucy met you at her house. But it's probably best if you sit off to the side and let me talk to them on my own."

"No worries there."

We made our way to the second-floor lounge. She was right. It was empty and quiet, aside from the low-volume sounds from a TV.

"You okay with talking to them about such a grisly thing?" I asked Willow. "I mean, they're probably going to see a bunch of counselors, right?" I didn't really know how it all worked.

"I'm connected to this, to them. I can't really explain it. This is who I am. This what I do, Cooper," she said, looking over my shoulder.

I saw a perfect seat for me in the corner. "I'll just be over there. Let me know if you guys need anything."

She turned around as a nurse walked up with Lucy and a little girl holding a stuffed animal in one arm, her hand clutching her mom's shirt. The girl's deep-set eyes looked hollow, as if her mind were in another place. I tried to show a caring smile. She didn't smile back, so I calmly took out my phone and tried to look as non-threatening as possible.

As they talked, I settled in to my seat and opened up Google in my phone browser. I started thinking about how exactly I wanted to do my online search. Before I punched in any combination of keywords, my mind flashed to the image of Courtney thumping that manila folder. We never saw the pictures of Ronnie's diced body, but I couldn't keep myself from forming my own set of visuals. A few hours ago, I hated that guy more than almost any person on the planet. For what he'd done to Marion, for what I feared he'd been doing to Lucy and her daughter. If given the opportunity, I might have killed the guy. I wasn't really the physical type, but everyone had their breaking point.

Colors splashed across a TV screen in the corner. It was the movie *Finding Nemo*. I turned toward Lucy's daughter, whose gaze was set on the screen. She hardly blinked. I stared for a good couple of minutes, hoping I'd witness her laugh. Heck, even a slight smile would prove there was still a little girl's gleeful spirit buried deep inside.

I knew it would take time and probably a lot of counseling. If my mom were here, she'd say a prayer right at this moment. "Can't waste time with the Lord, Cooper," she'd said more times than I could recall.

I couldn't help but think about another little girl—that's how I'd always addressed her, even if she wasn't so little anymore. But the pangs of guilt and shame and regret quickly swirled into a dust storm, essentially choking off my oxygen supply. I coughed a couple of times, cracking the silence. Lucy's daughter jerked her head in my direction while nuzzling up against her mom. Lucy put an arm around her, and I took a deep breath.

I watched Willow for a while. She seemed so engaged and caring, and Lucy appeared to really connect with her. It was one of those moments when you feel like you're invading something really personal, but part of me felt…I don't know, maybe proud of Willow? It was cool to see her in her element, doing what she was best at, and how people responded to her caring soul.

I took in a few seconds of the movie, basically cleansing my mental palate, and then I turned my attention to the Google search bar. My mind could have raced off in about ten different directions. The threads in this drama were almost endless, and none appeared to have definitive ties.

I thought about some of the investigative stories I'd taken on for the *Daily News*. The amount of time I spent hunting down leads and confirming information with at least one other credible source was difficult to calculate. I'd typically discuss the initial idea— usually something I'd come up with—with my editor, and he'd give me a two-week deadline.

Invariably, I'd learn more information than I ever imagined, and the story would pick up new angles that I'd be compelled to investigate. Sometimes, that list would be as long as my arm, with small branches sprouting almost every day. So, just before the two-week deadline, I'd amble into my editor's office, explain the situation, and ask for a two-week extension. It happened on so many stories that we joked that my over/under for the number of extensions I requested for each story was four.

I later recognized the irony of using a betting term to describe my writing process. Despite what Willow inferred, I was no addict. If anything, I'd been purposely blind—just riding the roller coaster of life, having fun, and thinking I was a bit untouchable. Not at the same echelon of the athletes I covered, but my head was definitely in the clouds. Actually, some might say my head was stuck up my ass, but I ignored them.

Damn, Cooper, you were pretty fucking stupid. And look at everything it cost you!

I couldn't afford to fall into a pity party, so I dug a fingernail into my wrist, successfully executing another mental misdirection play.

Figuring I'd start with a wide net—that was my natural approach to this type of research, just in case I might find something new—I punched a search term into the phone: bird symbolism.

I ignored the fact that it took .79 seconds to return 139 million results, and focused on their top results, which was a section labeled "People also ask." The first question caught my eye: which birds symbolize death?

It noted crows, ravens, vultures, and black swans. Wasn't there a movie called *Black Swan*? My significant other at the time had forced me to tag along. I only recalled that it was disturbing, and I'd tried to take my mind off it by sneaking glances at my phone to catch up on football scores. She took my phone away, saying it was rude. I'd normally agree, but we were the only two people in the theatre.

Two rows down on the search results another question sparked my attention: what bird is the symbol of hope? Sparrows. They also happened to be a sign of fertility, intelligence, ancestral knowledge, and rejuvenation of the spirit. That seemed like a mixed bag.

Had the person who killed Marion, Irene, and Janice left the bird parts because of death or hope? Logic said it had to be death.

If you murdered someone, it would make sense to leave a symbol of death. I tapped the back of my phone. Something about this logic gnawed at the back of my mind.

I scrolled down two more rows: what do birds symbolize? Okay, this might be the one to enlighten me. I tapped on the arrow to show the answer. *Hmm.* Basically, it said that birds are symbols of freedom, and because they fly high into the sky, some consider them to be messengers of the gods, providing people with a bridge between the mundane and spiritual life.

That last part confused me. Were we supposed to think that the killer was simply bored, and by leaving the bird part by the murdered body, that was their ticket to an everlasting life?

Just saying it to myself sounded strange, yet plausible. There were too many people in this world who could twist even the most benign phrase into a case to murder someone.

I read through about a dozen more questions and answers, and quickly found myself wrapped around the proverbial axle. The volume of data available via the Internet was dangerous for a mind like mine—one that asked lots of questions.

I glanced up and saw the girls still talking. I noticed Lucy's daughter glancing at the movie and then quietly saying something to her stuffed animal, a little hippo. The normalcy of the scene was almost surreal. She'd come around to feel more at ease—it had to be a result of Willow's caring nature—and that warmed my heart, which could normally be categorized as jaded.

I rubbed my hand across my face, then remembered I was in a hospital. Smooth move, Cooper. I got up and went straight to a hand-sanitizer dispenser. I rubbed the foam substance thoroughly in my hands. As I sat back down, I noticed an ad on the back of a magazine in the chair next to mine. An ad for Dove soap.

Duh! Wings from doves were left at the first two murder scenes. While I was unsure of the type of bird associated with the foot left on Janice's body, starting my search with a dove would have been the smarter play. Whatever. I typed in "dove symbolism" and tapped go. All the results seemed to go in one direction. The Christian symbol for peace. One site elaborated a bit, saying that a dove serves as a spirit messenger that helps people go about their lives with calm and purpose.

Purpose. Maybe that's what this was all about. Ronnie, or his accomplices, needed a purpose in life, and murder was their way of sharing it with the rest of the world.

Sick. But this could be something.

"You ready to go?" It was Willow.

My breath hitched. "Didn't see you walk up."

"Carpeting," she said.

As I got to my feet, I saw Lucy and her daughter walking away. The little girl turned her head and locked eyes with me. And then she waved. I waved back and smiled.

I caught up to Willow, and we walked toward the elevator. "Damn, you're a miracle worker," I said.

Forty

Dark, menacing clouds churned just above the top of Parkland Hospital. A pattern formed in the gray palette, and it seemed as though a hand was about to reach down and pull in another victim. And just as quickly, the hand was sucked back into the ominous cauldron. Maybe there was some symbolism there. The man knew his mind was an uncontrollable, unpredictable organism.

Actually, his mind wasn't singular at all. He recalled a *National Geographic* documentary he'd watched on TV, where colonies of Dorylus ants in Africa would creep onto a sleeping lion, sting him hundreds of times and then eat his flesh, muscles, and tendons. That was more like his mind.

He glanced up at the sky through his windshield again. The spinning and twisting of the clouds continued. He closed his eyes for a moment, and he heard the pulsating motor of a blender. That was it. The sky was like a blender, crunching and shredding thick shards of glass, sucking in loose fingers, devouring bone and ligaments and flesh. The red splay of blood mixed in with the other ingredients, and the toxic mixture appeared to grow in volume and strength.

He pounded his fists against the steering wheel and screamed. "Shut the fuck up!" he yelled. Who was he talking to? He had so many voices in his head, and one had produced and directed that little short film.

It was sick and twisted. And he knew it would never cease.

He opened his center console, grabbed the container, and eyed the pills through the blue-tinted plastic. "You get me through every day. You've done this for thirty years, and today will be no different."

He didn't like the sensation after he took a pill, but what choice did he have? The pills were the only things that kept him from going crazy.

Going crazy?

He chuckled. "You're beyond the crazy stage, and you know it." He removed the cap on the container, then shook out a pill and swallowed it.

He released a long breath and momentarily rested his head on the steering wheel. He had a list. Yes, there were a few tasks on that list that some would call "normal." Actually, that's why he was in the hospital parking lot. He knew that in a few minutes he'd have to flip on that kind, charming, compassionate personality to complete the work he was getting paid to do. Some people felt like their jobs were the moral equivalent of selling their souls to the devil. But he'd passed that stage long ago. He used his job now as a window into the community around him, to seek out those who deserved far better than to be subjected to the cruelty the world dished out like an all-you-can eat buffet.

And through that window, he'd already identified his next project. He'd get to it later, after he finished his day gig. The joyful anticipation sent a tingle through his arms and legs. It was always best for him to have something worthwhile to look forward to.

He lifted his head as raindrops pinged the hood of his car. It was light, but he knew a downpour was imminent.

Just then, he spotted a couple walking briskly out of the hospital. The man he recognized almost instantly from his homeless stunt he'd pulled off a couple of nights earlier. The stunt had proven two things: one good and one evil. But right now, his mind snapped back to eighteen years ago. Could it really be them? Could they still be together after all these years? He rubbed his eyes with the palms of his hands and leaned forward for a better look. They were obviously older, but he'd never forget those faces of kindness. He felt a flutter inside, and he put a hand to his chest. He couldn't take his eyes off them. He was mesmerized by every step they took, how they interacted with each other. They had apparently survived all the temptations that couples faced on a daily basis. They were still together.

Everything that had occurred was all meant to be. This serendipitous moment was also very symmetrical in his life. This could be the perfect bookend to what had occurred eighteen years earlier.

He drew in a quick breath. It was difficult to contain the concoction of emotions racing through his body. Tears pooled in his eyes, and adrenaline made him want to jump and dance around.

He had to be near them. He pushed open his car door and hopped out with more energy than he'd felt in years. He eyed their path and cut through a row of cars, then snagged a quick glance in their direction. They were deep in conversation about something. The woman was using her hands a lot as her mate nodded quite a bit. For a quick second, the man wondered how many kids they had and why they were at the hospital.

No time for a mental debate. He changed his angle slightly and slid between two more cars. They were twenty feet in front of him and closing. He put his hands in his pockets and fingered the coins and cash that he often would give out when he saw donation boxes at his various stops.

"So, it's really more about listening," the woman said. "But at the right time, you remind the patients that their lives are worth so much more than they ever imagined. That God or the Universe or some higher power has a plan for them and to expect to feel and see unlimited opportunities for joy and happiness going forward. It's about hope, Cooper."

The man bumped into the woman's arm, stumbling a bit. "Oh, sorry, I wasn't looking at where I was going."

"That's okay." She reached out and touched his shoulder.

"You all right?" Cooper asked him.

"I'm fine, thanks." He turned to walk off.

"Hold on a second."

The man stopped in his tracks and glanced back. Was there any way they were reading his mind?

"Hey, you dropped this." Cooper reached out and handed him a twenty-dollar bill. "It fell out of your pocket."

"Oh, right. Thank you." The man couldn't help but stare into Cooper's blue eyes. He was more certain than ever that he was the college boy from eighteen years earlier. Then he turned his attention to the woman. She had that same caring vibe.

"Need to get out of this rain," Cooper said. He turned to the woman. "Hey, Willow, I've got to talk to you about the research I did."

"Have a great day," the man said with a wave.

They waved back. "You too," Willow said with a smile.

The man practically skipped into the hospital. A new task had just been added to his list.

Forty-One

Willow

As Cooper pulled into the parking lot at Books and Spirits, the front fender scraped off the concrete. His shoulders bunched up. "Damn, I'm sorry."

I waved a hand. "It's just a car, Cooper. They can be fixed. That's what Harvey would say. And he's right."

I thought I noticed his eyes roll as he turned into a parking space.

'You don't like me bringing up Harvey, do you?"

"It's not that."

He didn't elaborate, and I didn't care to dig any deeper. I was emotionally drained.

"So, do you have any more thoughts about my research project?" Cooper asked.

He'd given me the full rundown of his Google searches on birds, and doves, in particular.

"Not really. I guess your theory on Ronny or his accomplice needing a purpose in life makes sense. Kind of."

"Kind of. You're waffling."

"I wouldn't call it waffling. I'm trying to picture a group of people sharing this purpose of killing people, and then using the dove parts to symbolize some type of spirit messenger. Beyond that, does it really help us figure out who's behind all this killing?"

He raked his fingers through his hair. "Who knows? I'm no expert at this. Maybe I was hoping that once we figure out why the killer is leaving these dove parts, a flashing red arrow would point us to the perp, or perps."

I made a scoffing noise. "Perps? You're trying to talk like a cop."

"I heard a detective use that term at the police station while I was waiting on Courtney the other day."

"Hey, maybe you can apply to get into the police academy and then become a real cop. Maybe take your Google search skills to a whole new level."

He gave me flat eyes, then said, "I doubt they let convicted felons into the police academy."

"Oh, right." I glanced out the window

"You're wringing your hands. Why?"

I looked down. He was right. "No I'm not."

"Okay, whatever."

A boy and girl wearing SMU sweatshirts walked by. They were joking with each other, playfully nudging the other one.

"That was us back in the day."

"Way back in the day," I reminded him. "And we were different. We wore the purple of TCU, not the blue and red of SMU."

I got the feeling Cooper was stuck in the past, afraid of living in the moment. My mind was flooded with the series of events just from the last few hours. And while the conversation with Lucy and Tiffany had reminded me why I loved nursing, I couldn't stop thinking about the two thugs who'd cornered us in the alley. They had been threatening in the way they spoke, how they looked at me. I could feel a chill crawling up my spine just reliving it.

"Who's Dr. V?"

"Do what?" Cooper had this look on his face like I'd spoken a language from another universe.

"I might have been shocked, but I heard what that one brother—I'm guessing they're brothers, based on their looks—said as he walked off. Something about how you might owe Dr. V some type of favor."

Cooper scratched the stubble on his face. He looked pained. But instead of pinging him with another question, I counted to ten to see if he'd respond. He didn't last until seven.

"He's kind of the boss," he said with a quick glance at me before looking out the windshield again.

"Of the two brutes?"

"The Sack Brothers, yeah. Lots of stuff."

"You're speaking in tongues again."

"Okay. He's the big cheese."

"Meaning, he's really the guy you owe the money to and the Sack Brothers work for him. Is he like a mob boss?"

"Look, I don't want you to worry about it. I'll take care of it."

"That plan hasn't worked so far."

He looked at me. "I'll take care of it."

"With the money that magically showed up in your car."

"Maybe. I think that's the best way of getting them out of my life."

"Trade one problem for another. Not sure any of this makes sense. And what about this favor?"

"No clue what that was about. But once I deliver the fifty K, they'll probably run back to New York and harass someone else."

He started scratching his stubble again as his eyes seemed to fall into some type of trance. I snapped my fingers. "Earth to Cooper."

"I'm still here," he said without looking at me.

I paused, hoping he'd elaborate. He didn't. "Something is stirring in your mind. You don't sound confident about what you just said. You're anxious about something."

He released a sigh. "I'm fine."

The Talker had gone silent. Yep, something was definitely off. "Hey, do you think we should just tell Courtney and the cops about this Dr. V person and the Sack Brothers? That's what normal people would do."

He slowly turned his head in my direction. He had this look, like he'd just heard the craziest idea. "Were you not right there with me in the alley?"

"Okay, okay. I guess you're right," I said. "I'm just afraid they might think of another reason to keep you on the end of their leash."

"I got it, okay? You don't need to worry," he said, waving a hand. "What you did back at the hospital with Lucy and her daughter was pretty cool."

"They're not healed, Cooper. They just opened up and became a little more normal. It's like rebuilding a house one brick at a time. I might have helped add a brick."

"I think you added a whole wall, but that's just me."

I tapped my chin.

"Now what are you thinking?" he asked.

"Something Lucy said under her breath to me while Tiffany was taking in the movie."

"That's her name, huh? Tiffany. Anyway, go ahead with what you were saying."

"She said that the guys who came into the shed were wearing pro wrestling masks. You know, like those fake wrestlers on TV?"

"As in The Spoiler?"

"Never heard of him. Anyway, she just said they were really big and muscular."

A hand smacked against Cooper's window and both of us jumped. "Crap!"

He punched the window down, and I saw a familiar face and

mullet arching backward in laughter.

"Funny, Slash. I'm just rolling on the floor laughing my ass off," Cooper said with his dry wit.

"Mr. Cooper, nice ride." He tilted his head to the front and rear of the car. "Although I think it needs some work."

"It's Cooper, not Mr. Cooper, remember?"

I snorted out a laugh.

"What can I do for you?"

"It's Brandy. She's starting to ask a lot of questions about you."

"Like?"

"She's wondering if you're connected to the freaks."

"What freaks?"

"Didn't say, but I'm guessing she thinks you're into the drug scene with all your covert conversations and running off all the time. And I'm not just talking about a little weed," he said with a wry grin.

"Yep, I'm the illegitimate child of Pablo Escobar."

"Who?"

"Doesn't matter. Brandy must have too much time on her hands to create these kind of delusional stories."

He shrugged his shoulders. "I'm just giving you the inside scoop, homey. You can try to talk to that hurricane if you want." He lowered his head and looked at me. "Mr. Cooper, you never formally introduced me to your, uh, friend."

"Oh. Slash, this is Willow. Willow, this is Slash. Good enough?"

I gave a round wave. "Hey, Slash. Cooper and I just need a couple more minutes to talk, okay?"

"This is your car, isn't it?"

"My fiancé only lets me take it out twice a week when I'm not chained up in his dungeon."

He looked like he'd stopped breathing. Then he nudged his

glasses up his nose and took a step back.

Cooper wrapped his knuckles on the side of the door to get Slash's attention. "She's joking, Slash."

He paused a second. "Oh," he said, back in laughing mode. "I get it. You were chained, as in Mr. Cooper Chain. You made a pun because the two of you are knocking boots."

"Excuse me?" I said.

Cooper jumped in. "You have it all wrong, Slash. No pun, and we're not knocking boots."

"Okay. Cool. See you inside, Mr. Cooper."

"It's Cooper, dammit!"

Slash was already out of earshot. Cooper sighed and shook his head. "That fucking going-nowhere-job is going to be the end of me."

"Don't be so dramatic."

"Says the woman about to marry her way into never having to worry about money again."

I reached over and pinched the skin of his neck.

"Ow!" he said.

"Feel lucky that I didn't go after your arm. And here I was about to ask you to my wedding."

"Eh."

"You're saying you wouldn't come?" I wasn't sure why I'd gone down this path.

"I don't know. Just...eh."

"You could bring your mom as your plus-one."

"Now that would be a great comedy, seeing my mom and your mom in the same room again."

We shared a quick chuckle.

"Hey," Cooper said. "Have you talked any more to your dad?"

"A little."

"Too painful?"

"Some, I guess. I don't like how he drops in just days before my wedding. And I'm still pissed at Jenny for not telling me. Should be an eventful wedding rehearsal. And just to get it out of your system now, we're holding it at Fearing's."

"Isn't that in the Ritz-Carlton?"

"We got a good deal. Harvey knows Dean."

"As in Dean Fearing?"

"Stop."

My phone buzzed, and I plucked it from my purse. I turned the screen to where Cooper could see it.

"Speaking of Daddy Warbucks," Cooper said.

I tried to reach over for another pinch, but he leaned away from me. I answered the call.

"Big news," Harvey said. "Father Tom came down with the flu."

"You've got to be kidding me."

Cooper glanced at me and leaned closer to the phone to where I could smell him. I didn't push him away.

"Sorry, Willow, I know how much you liked him."

"Aren't there another four or five priests at St. Barnabus?" I asked.

"They're all busy Saturday night."

"Dammit!"

Cooper's eyes got wide. I ignored him.

"It'll be okay, Willow. I've already worked with the church wedding coordinator, and she's found a very nice priest who works for the church in Denton."

"In Denton?' My eyes went back to Cooper only because I recalled him telling me old party stories of Denton and Texas Woman's University.

"His name is Father Moses Hoffman."

"Moses is the name of our new priest?"

Now Cooper's eyes narrowed, and he said, "You're joking, right? Your new priest is Moses? If he can keep the Red Sea at bay, maybe he can do a number on your mom."

I held back a laugh.

"Is that Cooper?"

"Yeah."

"What are you guys doing now?"

Harvey sounded slightly irritated. He probably should be.

"Lots to share with you, honey. But I got a chance to speak with Lucy and her daughter. I think I helped them just a bit."

"Wonderful."

He still sounded short.

"Thank you for taking care of the priest issue. That's a big load off my shoulders."

"You're welcome. You want to meet for a drink in a bit? Our final peaceful moment before we're engulfed by family and friends?"

"Sure. Our same spot?"

"Meet you there in thirty minutes."

"Love you, Willow."

"I love you too, Harvey." I ended the call with my sights on the floorboard.

"Well, I think that's my cue to jump back into the shark waters with Brandy," Cooper said. He wasn't smiling, but he wasn't frowning either. It was just this pure, unfiltered look into Cooper Chain. A silence fell over us. For a quick moment, I wondered if he'd started leaning toward me, and my eyes flashed to his lips.

Who's living in the past now? He's your fricking ex, not your current man.

"You know, it's possible that with Ronnie dead, the killing has stopped."

That's not what I'd expected to hear. "I guess. I hope."

"I know. Lots of questions. I'll keep digging."

"Using Google?"

"That and anything else I can think of."

"I'll do the same, as much as I can around all this wedding stuff."

We heard the squawk of a voice shouting Cooper's name.

"The warden is calling. Keep in touch."

And then he was gone.

Forty-Two

Cooper

I took the thrashing I received from Brandy in stride. Apparently, an "extended break" did not equate to four hours. Having callouses on my ass from previous beatings certainly helped. I was also distracted by the sensation that someone was drilling into my skull. It felt so real I actually scratched the back of my head.

"Do you have fleas too?" Brandy asked with her arms crossed in the breakroom.

Her latest insult temporarily knocked my anxiety to the back of my mind. "I take a shower at least once a month."

"Ew! You're so gross." She whirled around and marched out of the breakroom.

"Well, Cooper, I guess you're not the babe magnet from years gone by," I said out loud to no one.

Magnet? I was more like a bitch magnet, considering the method by which my marital status had changed. Just another branch to the tree of life that I'd yet to fully share with Willow. I saw no need to drudge up my own painful memories, especially when Willow was trying to push through the recent drama and marry the man of her dreams.

Did I just think that? Harvey didn't seem like her kind of guy.

Not a bad guy, just not her kind of guy.

I sighed, tried to step back and chill for a second. Who made me the resident couples guru? My track record showed that I was the last person who should judge which couples were meant to be together.

Stay in your lane, Coop.

So that's what I did. I found a list of menial tasks where I'd interact with as few people as possible—starting with restocking the children's books—and kept my head down for the rest of my shift. It gave me time away from the mental noise to think through the potential epiphany that had hit me earlier like a Sack-Brother punch to the gut. This breathless moment took place when Willow had shared what Lucy told her about the physical features of the two men who walked into the shed. Pro wrestling masks (creepy). Tall. Muscular.

I, more than most, knew there were lots of people in this world who fit the bill of tall and muscular. I'd been around a fair number in the athletic world. The latest rookie phenom from the New York Jets was a defensive tackle who stood six-eight and weighed three hundred ninety-five pounds. I figured his actual weight topped four hundred, but the team didn't want him to seem like a freak show. But pro athletes were freaks of nature, either from their sheer size and strength, their cat-like reflexes, or their breathtaking quickness. The super freaks, though, were the ones who had it all. LeBron James in basketball. Walter Payton in football. Tiger Woods in golf. Serena Williams in tennis.

The physical stature alone wasn't why I felt like I'd been stunned with a Taser, however. One of the two men had been holding a bloody saw. The same one presumably used to chop Ronnie to pieces. When Courtney had initially shared this fact with Willow and me, the dots didn't connect. Not until I heard Lucy's somewhat generic description of the killers. That's when the first ripple hit the bow. And then another one a second later. The repetitive swells toppled over the edge of my mental boat. And try as I did, I couldn't bail the water fast enough to stop from sinking toward the ocean bottom.

What does that second-rate analogy really mean? The sum of all the facts had triggered memories from my time in New York— the kind that were so disturbing your mind can only deal with them by not dealing with them at all.

It started with Dr. V—a.k.a. Vijayakumar Khatri. He'd reportedly earned his medical degree in India before moving to Russia. His medical emphasis was pathology, as in studying dead bodies. But the underground rumor mill, the one associated with illegal gambling, had suggested that Dr. V had a fetish for cutting up people *before* they were dead. And then he'd even feast on some of the pieces of the corpse before having them disposed of by his loyal henchmen.

Dr. V had never been arrested or charged with such horrific crimes. But the rumors, unsubstantiated as they were, created this aura of brutality that made everyone who entered his sphere of influence shudder.

Except for those of us who were either too full of ourselves or too naïve to even consider the notion that bad people were probably associated with something that we all knew was illegal.

And now, even as I lost myself in the mindless minutiae of stocking bookshelves, my mind was running rampant with images of Ronnie sliced and diced. I couldn't help but wonder if that would be the ultimate payback for not paying off my debt to Dr. V. And would they even stop with me? Now that the Sack Brothers had seen me with Willow, would they go after her?

"Hey, old man, you look like one of those creeps from the *Walking Dead*." I turned to see Tracy the Tattletale stop by my aisle.

Not sure what to say unless it started with the letter F and ended with "off," I simply shrugged.

She chuckled. The kind of chuckle that only seemed to embolden her evil spirit. She turned to me, hands at her waist, giving me the Wonder Woman power pose.

"Seriously, Cooper, you look like Dracula just sucked all the blood from your face. You about ready to lurch or something?"

"Not until you showed up." I couldn't help myself.

Her lips twisted into prunes, and her nostrils flared. "You have the fucking gall to mock me? You're working in a bookstore, and you're as fucking ancient as King Tutankhaten." She considered herself to be the female version of Indiana Jones, the preeminent expert on all things archaic. She always blabbered on and on about searching for the real Ark of the Covenant. From her "extensive studies," she believed it was buried in the Amazon jungle somewhere. She was only waiting to find the right partners and funding before she set off on her wild adventure.

"Don't you have anything better to do? You know, maybe crack a mirror or two or make little kids cry?"

She hissed through the gaps in her teeth.

I continued. "You just crossed the line. I am afraid of snakes. Can you slither away, please?"

She stomped her foot, then reached over and tossed an entire shelf of books to the floor. "Ha-ha!" she barked and snapped her head back as though she'd just pulled off the greatest heist in history.

"Have a great day," I called to her as she walked off. She flipped me the middle finger.

As I lowered to a knee to clean up the books, I heard the sound of crushed gravel. That was apparently bits of cartilage floating around under my kneecap. It not only hurt, but it made me feel like an ancient artifact. I brought my leg in front of me and sat on my butt, my mind circling back to the theory of Dr. V and his two ogres being the ones who had murdered Ronnie.

I asked myself one important question: if that were the case, then what conclusions could I make?

I scratched the stubble on my chin and stared at the mound of kids' books. But instead of conclusive thoughts, I found myself coming up with more questions.

Was it possible that Ronnie's accomplices in this series of murders actually were Dr. V and the Sack Brothers?

Taking it a step further, were the victims not murdered by some loner but instead by a collective effort of like-minded lunatics?

I thought about the information I'd learned about a dove representing a spirit messenger. Was I supposed to believe that Dr. V and the Sack Brothers felt this calling to connect with any spirit that wasn't the God of Greed?

The more questions that came to mind, the more skeptical I became. At the same time, I couldn't ignore the facts. Well, a combination of facts, along with the unproven gossip about Dr. V essentially being a butcher.

Outside of asking the Sack Brothers if they were partners with Ronnie or had recently taken part in a pumpkin-carving contest that had gotten out of hand, how could I prove this theory, or even disprove it?

"Ask Courtney, dumbass," I muttered quietly to myself. She'd said they had a forensics team sifting through the bloody mess to try to find evidence of Ronnie's killer. But had enough time passed? If so, would she even share it with me after Willow and I had walked out of the station so abruptly?

I had my doubts, but I had nothing to lose, so I thumbed her a quick text.

Hey there! Any info yet on who killed Ronnie? Inquiring minds want to know.:)

My subtle attempt at humor would hopefully loosen her up some.

Yeah, right. It was more lame than subtle.

Time flew by as I placed more books on the shelves; it seemed like I was restocking our entire catalog. I checked my phone for a response from Courtney about two dozen times. And, to be candid with myself and no one else, I was somewhat hoping that Willow would reach out with her own epiphany, or maybe that she'd conducted her own research that would align the stars and put the killers behind bars.

But I struck out twenty-four times with both Courtney and Willow. In fact, my phone was deathly quiet.

Then, Brandy barked out instructions for starting the close-down procedure, seemingly waking up my phone from the dead. It buzzed from my back pocket. The number wasn't one of my contacts, which made my stomach twist into a million knots.

"Cooper here," I said.

"You mean a dickwad is there, right?"

It was Elan or Milo, and he was laughing.

"Dickwad. Funny. Who writes your jokes, Milo?"

"This is Elan, dickwad. And this isn't some comedy show, unless they're showing a picture of a dick growing out from your ugly face." More baritone grunts from Elan and his twin in the background.

I knew if I continued down this path, I'd start having flashbacks to the fifth grade.

"Can I help you?"

"You sure ca-an," Elan said in a sing-song voice. This was really creeping me out. Had he inhaled some type of laughing gas?

"It's time to put up or shut up, dickwad. Tomorrow night, you give us the fifty K at 11:59 p.m."

"Why not just say midnight?"

"Damn, you're such a—"

"I know, a dickwad. So…?"

"Because if I said midnight, then that wouldn't be tomorrow night. Technically, midnight is the following morning. You've got to be the dumbest dickwad in the northern hemisphere."

"Western hemisphere," I corrected him.

"I say it's northern!"

Whatever. "Where's the meet-and-greet taking place?"

"We'll text it to you beforehand with just enough time for you to get there. We don't want you setting up cameras or telling any cops where we're at."

"Okay. Fine." I thought a moment, then decided to go for it. "What can you tell me about this additional favor I might owe Dr. V?"

They laughed until the line went dead.

I slipped the phone into my back pocket and felt this sense of dread slowly consume me. The kind that makes your brain feel like it's being squeezed in a vice. I ran my gaze across the bookstore, but I didn't see people or books or chairs or display tables, I only saw two men in colorful masks, one of them holding a bloody chainsaw.

Could my imagination get any more morbid?

I rubbed a hand across my face and started to question every decision I'd ever made. Earlier, when talking to Willow, I thought I'd convinced myself that I was going to use the money from the black bag to pay off my debt to Dr. V. And now that my own version of the *Texas Chainsaw Massacre* was growing roots in my mind, the thought of not turning over the money to the Sack Brothers made me want to lurch—even without looking at Tracy. But I couldn't continue putting my head in the sand when it was convenient. As Willow had said, by using money that no one had really bequeathed to me, would I be trading one set of issues for another set that might have an even worse result?

"How could it be worse than being chopped up and devoured by some crazed cannibal?" I whispered.

I released a long sigh, leaned over, and put my hands on my knees.

Maybe I could drop everything and leave the area without telling anyone where I was going. Leave the money behind, leave the Sack Brothers behind, and just disappear into the ether. I could find a job serving drinks at a beach club in San Diego, or head to Vegas and take some overnight job as a casino cashier. I could figure out a way to get a new name, change my identity, even my appearance, and just wash all my problems down the drain.

I was pretty much describing the FBI Witness Protection Program. Not exactly an option at this moment. Then again, wouldn't the FBI love to get their hands on real evidence that connected Dr. V and the Sack Brothers to a litany of crimes? Surely, all of them had to be on the FBI's radar. But how would I go about accomplishing that task? Just walk up to an FBI office, knock on the door, and say, "Hey, how do you want to use me to take down a crime boss who, rumor has it, eats people who don't abide by his rules?"

And that wasn't going to happen in just over twenty-four hours.

"Fuck!" I yelled out.

"Cooper Chain, is that you?" Brandy's voice bounced off the ceiling.

"Uh, no, it was just some customer who walked out."

No response. Maybe a book had fallen on her head and knocked her out.

I felt my phone buzzing again. *Crap.* It was probably the Sack Brothers again, wanting to change the time of our money exchange or add interest.

I pulled the phone out of my pocket. I saw the name on my screen and felt instant relief. I'd never been so happy to see the letters M-O-M.

"Hi, Mom. How are you?" I said with surprising vigor.

"Cooper, did I bother you at a bad time?"

I heard stress in her voice. "No, Mom. What's going on?"

"Well, I hate to be a bother to you. I'm a very independent woman. Have been really my entire life. You know that, don't you?"

How many times had she gone through this with me? "Yes, Mom. They should put your picture on a billboard at Central and Mockingbird as the most independent woman of the last century."

"I know you're joking. You're very cute when you do that, always have been. I remember when you were about six years old, or was it eight? Anyway, that's when your teachers and I realized you had a gift for sarcasm."

"A gift," I said with a hearty laugh. "Not sure you called it a gift back then."

"I'm sure I didn't. But as time passes, you realize those challenges are just another flavor of happiness."

Her wise thought made me pause. "I'm not sure many others would agree with you, but you won me over. So, you called because you need something?"

"Well, I kind of did a bad thing today."

A bad thing for mom was jaywalking. "What can I help you with?"

"I drove here to the church—you know I help run this outreach program here at St. Barnabus."

"Yes, Mom. You were saying…?"

"Well, my front right tire is nearly flat, and I drove on it anyway. I knew I should stop and get it fixed, but I said a prayer and the good Lord got me here safely."

"Glad you're still on His top ten list, Mom."

"Oh, don't say that. He loves everyone equally."

Right now, I could put a serious hole in that theory. "So, do you need me to change your tire?"

"Oh, I hate asking you for a favor. It's late and…well, I really don't know what you do since you don't open up to me."

A guilt complaint. *Uggh.* "I'm fine, Mom. Just don't want you to worry. You worry too much, and your heart can't take a lot of pressure."

"Oh, be nice to your mother, now."

How was I not being nice? Double *uggh*. "I can change your tire for you, no problem."

"You're such a good son. I tell the ladies here at church that you're a good son, although there are a few who are a little more judgmental. Did I tell you that Dorine has a daughter who's just moved back? She's about your age and the nicest young lady."

Not only did Mom talk nonstop, but she was always trying to fix me up. "I'm good, Mom. I'll be there shortly. Stay inside the church since it's dark outside."

"The good Lord will keep me safe. That much I know."

Forty-Three

Thank God the church's congregation was rich enough that it owned two buses. That was the man's most prevalent thought as he huddled inside the dark bus in the back parking lot at St. Barnabus. He looked out the side window and spotted a basketball goal with the front rim bent lower. Probably some kids who had nothing else better to do.

He knew exactly what he wanted to do, what he *had* to do. His gaze focused on the blue Honda Accord, the one that belonged to a woman who could only be called a saint. She had a heart of gold. But he knew that over time that gold would become tarnished, just like everyone else who tried to do good in this fucked-up world.

He shifted his eyes to the lighted office just to the right of the back door. As usual, the woman had outworked everyone else at the church. Always the last to leave. He was familiar with her outreach program, one that asked for donations to send people to drill for water wells in the African nation of Cameroon. He'd learned recently by speaking with one of her colleagues that she had gone on one of those mission trips.

An amazing woman who'd given so much to people. And now, he was called upon to end her life before the harsh world devoured her. The timing, he thought, couldn't be more perfect.

He flipped around and momentarily eyed the resting place

he'd assembled on the floor. It was only a simple pallet, but he didn't want to make the same mistake he had with the nurse. Breaking her back still gnawed at his conscience. The last thing he wanted to do was bring pain to those who didn't deserve it.

He had personally witnessed acts of tremendous kindness as well as unbelievable cruelty.

Cruelty came in many forms, and depending on your age, even the simplest acts could puncture your heart. Take his half-brother, for example. That man was the ultimate do-gooder. Or so he'd convinced the public. He'd fooled so many people for so many years, it was hard for the man to fathom.

As children, his stepbrother had ridiculed him, called him names, and basically made him feel like he was worthless. Reeled him in with mind games, gave him hope, and then crushed him.

The memory of his half-brother's barrage of hatred caused the man's eyes to tear up still to this day.

"Look at the fucking baby. Cry, cry, cry. You going to go tell your mommy, little baby?"

"This is the real world, you stupid little shit. No one gives two cents about you."

Boom, boom, boom, knuckles rapping on his skull. "Hello? Is it just hollow inside there? Jesus Fucking Christ, you're stupid."

"I'll be damned if you didn't just break some type of record for being most pathetic loser in the whole fucking world."

"I'm not being mean. This is normal. And you're the one who makes me act this way."

Punches, punches, punches.

A wad of spit landing on his cheek. "Pathetic. Fucking. Loser. A PFL. That's all you are and that's all you'll ever be."

The man gasped, and then air shot out of his lungs. His fingernails were digging into the plastic bus seat as rage rippled through his extremities. It took a couple of minutes for him to regain control of his breathing. But as his mind became clearer, he knew he couldn't let that part of his life go unanswered. Up until now, he'd been compelled to complete his acts of mercy out of love and admiration for those who'd blessed others with kindness. Not everyone would agree with his approach, but they hadn't lived his life.

But these last shots of memory had been his most vivid in years. There had to be a reason for that. Even though he'd shied away from acting on hate thus far, he now understood that he had to take that next step.

Vengeance. A new purpose.

He could hardly wait until he finished the task at hand, so he could do his homework and come up with a fresh plan—this one for revenge, not mercy.

Headlights snagged his gaze. Another car was entering the parking lot just as the sweet lady exited the building. What was going on?

Shit! He hunkered lower to make sure he stayed hidden.

Forty-Four

Cooper

Leave it to Mom to wave at me like she was directing a 747 on a darkened runway. I punched the car window down.

"Hey, Mom, everything okay?"

"Of course. Why wouldn't it be?"

I got out of the car and looked at the tire on the front right side of her Accord. "Got your keys on you?"

"Wait a second. What is this all over your car?"

I wondered if she'd notice. "It's not my car."

She brought a hand to her chest and spoke in a hushed voice. "Tell me you're not destitute. You don't have to steal cars to put food on your table, do you? Your mother just couldn't take that. But if you did, I'd forgive you. Don't you know, son, you just have to ask for a favor?"

She said all that in one breath.

I put my arm around her shoulder. "Mom, it's okay. I'm not destitute, and I haven't gone off the deep end and started stealing cars."

Just saying that made me wonder if I'd ever get that desperate. Given my tumble down the rocky slopes of life, part of me questioned if I was at the bottom. Or was I simply teetering on the edge of a jagged rock about to fall even deeper into the abyss?

She stood on her toes and kissed my cheek. "I'm not sure why I went there. Cooper, you're one of the good guys, you know that?"

She'd repeated that phrase a million times over the years. *One of the good guys.* At times, I felt like giving her an example of why I was the opposite of a good guy. Right now, I wasn't really sure how to respond, so I went with a neutral comment. "If you say so, Mom."

She patted my back and looked up at me for a second. I knew she had questions, lots of questions. She always had questions. But something stopped her this time. Maybe she didn't want to know the real answers. Regardless, I was thankful for the reprieve.

She went from studying me to studying the car. I'd borrowed Slash's car, an old-model Corolla that had been painted with a dull gray primer. But that only served as a backdrop.

"What on earth are all of these?" she exclaimed, spreading her arms while walking around the car like it was some type of new-age art exhibit.

"They're bumper stickers."

"Then why aren't they on the bumper?"

I walked around back and pointed at the bumper. "Slash—"

"What kind of name is that?"

"I don't know. He's just someone I work with. He has bumper stickers on the bumper too. I think he just ran out of room," I said with a chuckle.

She leaned closer to the passenger door and then turned her gaze to me. "Is this someone eating a bat's head?"

"Ozzy Osborne back when he was in Black Sabbath. You probably heard of them back in the '70s."

"Black Sabbath?" She shook her head and then crossed herself. "You know that's pure blasphemy."

"Mom, I thought you had an open mind."

"I do, but Black Sabbath? It's heresy."

"Come on, Mom. You sound like one of those religious freaks who says that kids who listen to a certain kind of music will go to hell."

She exhaled slowly. "I'm just a little shocked, Cooper."

"I bet you didn't know Ozzy was also called the Prince of Darkness," I said, knowing it would rile her up.

She tilted her head and gave me a half-smile.

"Keys?" I asked, extending a hand.

She tossed them to me, and I caught them in my left hand without looking.

"You should try out for the Dallas Mavericks, you know that? You still have better hand-eye coordination than anyone I've ever known."

Mom was either the most gullible, naïve person on planet Earth or blindly loved her children—I have a brother and sister, both of whom live out of town. Probably the latter. At times, her off-the-wall comments were funny. At other times, however, I'd rather stick my hand down a running garbage disposal.

"As soon as I'm done changing your tire, I'll run over to Mark Cuban's house."

"Mark who?"

"The owner of the Mavs."

"Oh, that gentleman on *Shark Tank*!"

"That's the one."

"Okay, let me know what he says."

"Are you serious?"

She came up and nudged my arm. My bad arm. I pulled back quickly and she said, "Oh, dear! Are you hurt?"

"Doing just fine."

That seemed to satisfy her, miraculously. While I changed the tire, she regaled me with stories about the Mission of Mercy outreach program. By the time I was done, my hands were coated with grease and I couldn't remember a word she'd said.

"Oh, I need to grab my papers from inside. You can wash your hands. Follow me."

I did. Once I finished washing my hands, I met her in the church office and found her trying to scoop up a heap of pamphlets, brochures, and loose papers. Her desk was buried somewhere under the mess, which actually spilled onto the floor around the desk.

I knew where I'd gotten my organization skills. Willow would probably have a cow right about now.

"Let me help you, Mom." We each grabbed a pile. She turned off the lights, locked up, and walked outside to her car. When she opened the back door, a mound of books and papers poured out onto the concrete.

"Do you think we can put this stuff in your friend's car for tonight? I can drop by tomorrow and pick them up once I clean up this mess at home."

How painful could this get? Then, it seemed like a shooting star had just carried a message to my frontal lobe.

"Mom, I didn't forget. Tomorrow is your birthday."

"Well, at my age, I just thank the good Lord for each day He gives me."

Which was code for "please celebrate my birthday."

"How about I pick you up and take you to dinner?"

"Oh, Cooper, you don't have time for that."

All that money was just sitting in that black bag at home. I felt certain there was more than fifty K in the bag. I had to count it to make sure. If so, I'd fix my car and take my mom out. If not, then I'd still figure out a way to celebrate with Mom, even if I had to borrow Slash's car. Those are good things, which removed at least some of the guilt. The part about using fifty thousand dollars of it to pay off a gambling debt to a lunatic crime boss, though, was all about saving my ass. Life is, after all, nothing more than a balancing act.

"I know I haven't been very available since I've been back..."

"You're certainly right about that, mister," she said, wagging a finger at me but smiling as she did so.

"So, let me take you out for a birthday dinner. You can tell me more about your outreach program."

She brought her hands together under her chin. "You make your mother so proud." She hugged me. "Thank you for rescuing me. You know, I'm an independent woman and have been for decades."

"I know, Mom. Very independent," I said while walking to my car.

"By the way, when we go out tomorrow, I'd love for you to tell me more about what's going on in your life. Hopefully, you've met a nice young lady."

Help. Me. "I'll pick you up at seven, Mom. Have fun cleaning out your car."

Forty-Five

Cooper

I spent most of the night counting the money in the black bag. Each time, I came up with a different number. I tried to sleep, but I couldn't stop thinking about who had put the money in my trunk. The "how" part was also a question—how they got into my trunk without the keys—but that concern was a distant second. Some people might feel personally invaded if their car had been broken into. My car was a piece of shit. I should feel honored. But again, I wracked my brain on who had left the money in the trunk and why.

I probably came up with two dozen theories, all of which were pure fantasy. Not a single one had any merit, but sometimes the mind goes where it wants to go...especially at three in the morning.

As I stood behind the register at Books and Spirits and waited for the customer's credit card to be approved, my tired eyes glazed over. If drool was dripping from the corner of my mouth, I wouldn't be surprised. I was picturing the digits on the calculator from the last time I'd counted the money at home: $55,555.

Five fives. There had to be meaning in that, right? So, I'd stayed up another hour and used my top-notch researching skills to find out if that was some kind of sign. The answer? Yes and no. I found nothing about five fives. But take the number five by itself, and there was plenty of data. Some positive, some not so much.

One site said the number five meant maintaining balance between the material and spiritual aspects of your life. That balance would lead to happiness. Of course, my mind interpreted that as the following: my mom had enough spirituality for both of us, and with my focus on the material side, there was my balance.

I knew better. But still, all in all, that insight had given me a positive vibe about the money. And then I'd tapped on the second site. It talked about how, in Chinese, the number five is associated with good luck *and* bad luck.

Something about that didn't sit right. Probably the word "bad." I didn't need more bad anything in my life.

I heard someone clearing their throat. Oh, the customer.

"Your receipt. Right. Here you go." I tossed it in the bag and then gave the bag to him. His eyes went to my hands. I still had grease on them. I shrugged, and the man walked out of the store.

The grease, this time, had come from changing out the battery on my piece-of shit car during my break earlier. So, technically, I no longer had the perfect set of fives in the money bag. The front door dinged as I checked the time. Only a few minutes until I was supposed to pick up Mom. Part of me was looking forward to the evening. The thought of getting out and about, although it was using this gifted money and I'd have to act interested in mom's stories for a few hours, was strangely appealing. Yet I knew that when the bell tolled midnight, or one minute before it, I'd be in the process of paying off the fifty K.

And then there was the thought about the additional favor. Again, I erred on the side of blind hope. The hope that the Sack Brothers would be wetting their pants over getting their cash and that this "favor" would be long forgotten.

A bag was dropped on the counter in front of me.

"There you go," Slash said. "This is all the religious crap you left in the back of my car."

"Oh, right. Sorry about that."

"It's cool."

I peeked inside the bag about the same time the door dinged. I ignored it again, even though I was supposed to say something cheerful. My mind had already jumped forward in time, envisioning life after the payoff.

"Hey, have you seen that literary agent in here since the book signing?" I asked Slash.

"Motta?"

"Good memory. Archibald Motta is his full name."

"It's a no-go."

"Meaning you haven't seen him?"

"You got it."

"Wonder why he left his card," I said, sifting through the bag of Mom's ministry stuff.

"Have you thought about calling the dude?"

The song-and-dance routine of working with an agent. How could I explain that to someone? My talent as a writer would result in the agent getting paid, but the agent would act like I worked for him or her. Yeah. The upside-down world of publishing. As for the courting process, on the day of Brett Murphy's book signing, I'd tried to chat it up with Archibald, but he just treated me like just another retail clerk.

I shrugged. "I'll think about it."

"Suit yourself. But while you're thinking about it, he could be talking to two other guys just like you. Live the dream, man. Do what it takes to become a famous novelist."

I looked at Slash, surprised. There was some wisdom behind his metal-rimmed glasses.

My phone buzzed, and I quickly pulled it out to see a text from Courtney.

Forensic team found another blood type at Ronnie's crime scene. DNA testing has started. Will hopefully get a hit in next couple of days.

Cool. Some progress had been made. I just hoped the killing had finally ended.

A hand smacked the counter. I jumped ever so slightly.

"Ha! Got you, didn't I?" My buddy, Ben Dover, smiled and pointed a finger at me.

"You did indeed."

"Hey, I just got a minute here." He peered out the window over my shoulder before bringing his eyes back to me.

"Speaking of ball and chain..." I could hardly finish my thought without cracking up.

"Very fucking funny."

"Dude, chill out on the cussing. We've got customers around here."

Ben made a dramatic production out of rubbing his eyes. "Did you just give two shits about what goes on at Books and Shit?" He laughed at his own joke. Slash joined in and I soon followed, although he didn't know we were laughing as much at him as we were with him. He seemed to slowly realize those dynamics, and his zealous enthusiasm subsided.

"Seriously, the female contingent in my life are picking up coffees. So, have you decided to take the leap into the most awesome business anyone could possibly experience?"

I hadn't given his idea much thought. The murders and figuring how out to stay alive were higher on my priority list. "I don't know, Ben. I know you came up with this fancy title and all, but the way you described it pretty much makes me sound like a sleazy sales guy."

"Whores."

"Huh?"

"Sales guys. We're called whores. We embrace it. You should

too. It becomes part of who you are. And once you do, then man oh man, you can rake in the big bucks. Think about all those commissions."

Not having to live on Ramen and tuna fish would be nice. A few ideas on how to use larger sums of money came to mind, and most weren't very material. Most importantly, though, I could have a job making big money, something I'd probably never have the opportunity to do with this felony conviction permanently tattooed on my face. Ben didn't care because we went way back. Loyalty meant something. But still, sneaker company representatives who'd been courting college coaches and young athletes had recently been indicted and were on trial in a very messy scandal, exposing under-the-table payoffs and lying to federal investigators. Just what I'd need, somehow getting sucked into another crime-infested rat's nest.

But who said you have to follow their path? Make good, ethical decisions, and you'll be fine. On top of that, consider what you could do with that money, who you could impress.

"I'll think about it."

"That's what you said last time when we were standing next to your piece-of-shit car. We need to get hopping on this, Coop. It's time to let the world know about GOAT."

"What is GOAT?" Slash asked.

"You'll find out," Ben said, spreading his arms like he was a bird about to take flight. "The world will find out once we launch our global marketing campaign."

"I want in," Slash said.

Ben ignored him, then tapped his fingers on the counter again. "A couple days, Coop. Need to know by then if you're in or out."

"Well, for now, I'm out."

His eyes bugged out. "You already made your decision?"

I picked up the bag of mom's papers and hoisted it over my shoulder. "I've got a date with my mom. It's her birthday." I turned to Slash. "You mind punching me out?"

"No prob. I just want to know more about this goat business."

I glanced at Ben, who shook his head, then turned back to Slash. "It may not be your thing, but I'll give you the scoop tomorrow."

Ben met me at the door, and we walked outside. "Taking your mom out on a date, eh? Golly gee, you really are Mr. Apple Pie."

"Nobody's ever said that about me. It's her birthday, so she deserves a little attention."

"Seriously, that's very cool. You can think about all the things you can do for her with the big bucks you're going to make."

I rolled my eyes. He didn't notice.

I stopped at my car, and he snapped out a laugh. "You got this thing running? I thought you could barely pay for your next meal, working at this bookstore and all."

I shrugged, and he ran his hand along the ragged-out convertible top. "You remember my Mustang in college?" he asked with a nostalgic smile practically lighting up the parking lot.

"Oh, yeah. How many times did the cops catch us racing other hot rods?"

"Hey, we won every time," he said, popping his eyebrows. "All because of...the Beast."

His car's nickname.

"How could I forget? Life was all about the Beast."

"And girls," he added.

"True. But that's how we got the girls."

"This old classic here," he said with his eyes back on the LeBaron, "I've now christened it. Are you ready?"

"Hit me."

"The Converta-Beast."

"The Converta-Beast. Very original. Not."

I tossed the bag into my car, and the papers and brochures fell across the back seat. Oh well. "Can't be late picking up Mom.

We've got reservations."

"Mr. Apple Pie. My future executive. Tell Mom hi for me. And tell her you'll be giving her a very nice gift next year."

Forty-Six

Willow

Taking a breather from the near-constant interactions, I stood near a huge potted plant and sipped some champagne. A moment to myself. A moment to reflect on my life and the path I'd chosen, although my focus came in spurts. I was distracted, even as I felt that internal nudge to reconsider my marriage plans.

Every time I tried to take a step back and look at things logically, my mind would start swimming with countless concerns and theories about the murders. Marion had been lying on her bed, looking so peaceful, almost as if it were her choice to die. But it wasn't choice, of course. Someone had murdered Marion and set up a bizarre vignette deathbed. For what reason, I had no clue. Neither did Cooper or, more importantly, the cops.

And then I thought of my old friend, Janice, and all the other mayhem that culminated in Ronnie being dismembered, his body parts dumped right in front of Lucy and Tiffany.

My emotions ran the full gamut as I peered inside the Sendero, one of the many glamorous rooms within Fearing's restaurant, which was the most prominent feature of the Ritz Carlton in downtown Dallas. There was plenty of happy chatter among the invitees to our wedding rehearsal dinner. A pianist played a montage of feel-good love songs. Everyone was smiling. Yes, even Ma—despite my dad making the rounds like a proud father who'd raised me all on his own. The general vibe in the room couldn't get any happier.

But I wasn't very happy. And I couldn't determine if it was because of the horrors that had taken place in the last week or if my body was flashing a red light that told me to reverse course and not get married in less than twenty-four hours. To stop before it was too late. Before I hurt Harvey.

"Feeling the nerves?"

Alli had just walked up.

"I'm fine."

"That means you're not fine. Do you want to talk about it?"

I sipped more champagne, staring at the bottom of the flute to see if it carried any answers. Nothing. "Not really."

She put a hand on my shoulder. "Has your dad shared his life story with you yet?"

"Hardly. But I only asked once. He gave me the runaround. I think he doesn't want to hurt me anymore than he already has."

"Eh."

"You think it's more than that?"

"Do you trust him?"

"About as far as I can throw him. But he's harmless, all things considered."

"The murders. First Marion, then the others, including your friend, Janice. It's absolutely insane. And for it to happen the week of your wedding...I'm so sorry."

"It's not really about me, though. I can't sit here and pretend I was close with any of them. I hadn't spoken to Janice in something like two years. You know, ever since..."

She nodded. "Willow, you have a huge heart. You hate seeing people hurt. So, even if you didn't know them well, I know why you're in pain. We all are shocked. But we think it's over, right? I mean, that Ronnie guy is…you know…"

"Dead. You can say it."

"You're right. Let's just call it like we see it. He's dead. And whether he killed Marion or these crazy people with saws are behind all the killings, isn't the consensus that it's done and behind us? I'm only saying that so you can stop feeling guilty and try to find a peace about this time of your life."

She put her arm around me, and I rested my head on her shoulder. "If only it were that easy, Alli." I could feel a tear bubble in the corner of my eye. I didn't think it was because of any specific reason, only the culmination of so much drama over such a short time span. Part of me still had the urge to sneak off, find Cooper, and continue brainstorming on how to identify the killer. Just because two guys might have killed Ronnie—potentially on top of the other three victims—that didn't mean we should stop trying to find them. In fact, it just showed me how dangerous they really were.

The new priest ambled across the room and stood with his hands clasped next to a table of flowers.

"Okay, this is meant to be funny…" Alli nudged her shoulder, and I lifted my head. "But that new priest looks like he's on Prozac. You know, like he's not all there. And did you see the way he walks and carries himself? No offense, but I'm wondering if for Halloween he dresses up as the Grim Reaper." She giggled quietly as I studied him for a moment. "And he's not exactly small. I mean, how many priests look like a… I don't know. He's just really big."

"But he's nice," I said, suddenly defensive.

"Really? I thought he was kind of aloof."

"Okay. Well, he's not mean. Maybe he's a bit of an introvert."

"Yeah, it was just an observation. And with a name like Moses Hoffman, he's got a lot of power in his words. Might be a sign," she said, popping her eyebrows playfully.

I smiled, then shifted my eyes back to Moses. He seemed uncomfortable in the setting, as though he'd rather be in any other place. There was something else about him that gnawed at me, but I couldn't figure it out.

"Ready to head back in?"

Just then, Harvey strolled over to us. "Hello, future wife and Alli," he said.

"Hey there," I said, holding his gaze for just a quick second. He knew I wasn't all that happy. He probably thought it had to do with him blowing me off earlier when I wanted to talk about the murders.. He'd actually been a bit curt with me, saying, "Are you going to obsess over this throughout our entire wedding weekend and honeymoon? Ronnie is dead. That should be the end of it." Then he'd marched off.

But he hadn't read me correctly. I was in the process of trying to get to my point—building up to a pointed question, actually. But he never gave me the time or space to get there. And that was another reason why I wondered if this marriage was a good idea.

"Mind if I have a moment with my future wife?" he asked Alli.

"Of course I don't mind. It's time for me to get a refill anyway. Talk to you later, Willow." She walked off. When I looked up at him, he planted a kiss on me—on my lips, no less. It shocked me.

"Harvey, I'm…"

"Gobsmacked?"

I touched his cheek and looked at him.

"I'm sorry if I was insensitive earlier," he said. "It's just been a lot to digest. I feel so bad for Marion and your other friend. But through everything you've shared with me, I can see how much you care about people. How you connect with people who no one else might care about, like Lucy and her daughter. I'm impressed."

Impressed, as though I'd completed an office project on time and on budget. "Thank you, I guess."

He hugged me, kissed my forehead, and then held my

shoulders while looking into my eyes. "We can't forget what has happened, Willow. But if we live in fear or stay so focused on the negative, we'll never fully commit our time and energy to each other. And that's what is most important, don't you think?"

I thought about it a second. "Yeah. It makes sense. I guess I have a tendency to not let go of something until I know it's perfect. Maybe I'm a little OCD on things."

He chuckled. "You're perfect just the way you are. We just need to have faith that the police will do their jobs. That's why I pay all those taxes, right?"

"Hey, Harvey!" One of his buddies was waving him over to a cluster of friends. Looked like they had a few shot drinks lined up on the bar.

"Go have fun. I'll join you in a second."

"Cool. This is a special night. I can feel it." He kissed my cheek and headed toward his friends.

I held up my champagne glass. "You need another one, Willow," I said to myself.

Before I took a step, I felt my purse vibrating against my waist. I pulled out my phone, but I didn't recognize the number. "Hello, this is Willow."

"You won't believe what the fuck I just found out."

"Is this—"

"Earl Grant. Janice's brother. You know, the person who everyone thinks looks like Elvis."

"I—"

"It doesn't matter. I just learned something about all these murders, what might be the connection point."

I turned my back to the party room and put a finger to my ear so I could clearly hear Earl. "I'm listening."

"Well, it all started when I was reviewing the data on the Irene Washington autopsy, and as I was sitting there—"

"Earl, you don't have to walk me through every step. What is it?"

"The Community Health Center. Irene Washington was a patient there. Of course, Janice worked there."

I could feel my pulse thump faster. "But what about Marion? She was younger, had a job. She had no reason to use the CHC."

"I just got off the phone with a colleague of Janice's at the CHC, a woman named Kelly. Turns out she knew Marion came by the CHC."

I wasn't sure how to process what I'd heard. "I don't understand. What was Marion doing—"

"Kelly knew Marion. Turns out working with homeless people was something Marion did in her spare time. She would sometimes bring in people who had health issues."

"This can't be a coincidence. Could the person who killed them be someone at the clinic?"

"Don't know. Look, detectives just drove up to my apartment. I'll keep you in the loop. Later."

He hung up. Without thinking, I put in a quick text to Cooper.

Forty-Seven

Cooper

I was twenty steps in front of Mom, looking for someone in a uniform. I swung my sights to the left. Found him. Within seconds, the bellhop finished giving me directions to the party room.

"Appreciate it," I said, turning to cut down a hallway inside the Ritz-Carlton.

"No problem," I heard him say from behind me.

"Cooper, can you wait up for your mother?"

I flipped around and walked backward, giving Mom an encouraging wave. "You can do it, Mom."

"Where are we going again?"

"Something called the Sendero Room inside Fearing's restaurant."

"Dean Fearing. This is like a culinary dream come true," she said with a breathy giggle. Her gaze wandered like a little kid at Disney World. I'd gone there when I was eight, and it was magical. This was her Disney World.

A man holding two enormous trays of food darted out of a side door. "Mom, look out!"

She spun around but never saw the man, who somehow dodged her while keeping everything on the tray.

I rushed up to her as she wobbled a bit. "You okay?"

"Maybe I had too much wine at Del Frisco's."

Her birthday dinner had been at Del Frisco's Steakhouse, considered one of the best in Texas. I'd "withdrawn" three hundred from the magic pouch at home and decided to live it up for her birthday. "Mom, I think you only had half a glass."

"For your mother, that's a lot of wine."

The bottle had cost over a hundred bucks, and we'd left three quarters of it sitting there once I'd received the text from Willow.

I started marching down the corridor again.

"Don't leave your mother all alone."

I slowed down to a snail's pace, and she caught up.

"I think it's just around this corner," I said.

"Why are we going to see your ex-girlfriend at her wedding rehearsal?"

Earlier, without much time to think it through, I'd told her that Willow and I had recently crossed paths at a bookstore and struck up a friendship. Purely platonic, I emphasized. And Willow wanted me to meet the priest. It was a lame excuse, but Mom didn't question it.

"To meet the priest, Mom, remember?" I strained my neck, trying to locate Willow's hair amongst a crowd of folks loitering in the hallway.

"I know that, son. But why Willow?"

"I thought I already explained it to you," I said, my eyes still looking ahead, semi-wishing I could just take off so I wouldn't have to maneuver my way around her questions about my private life. Hell, I wasn't even sure I knew all the answers.

"You did, but I worry. I want you to move forward with your life, not backward. That's what the good Lord wants for you. I can feel it."

I felt a spark of annoyance ignite inside of me. I counted to ten, hoping I could restrain myself from telling her to mind her own business.

We made the turn, and I spotted Willow standing alone next to a lush green plant. Almost instantly, I felt the same knee-buckling flutter as I did when I'd seen her in her wedding dress days ago. She looked stunning. But I also knew it wasn't about her blazing eyes or taut figure. There was something that drew me to her like a beacon on a dark beach.

"Hey," I said.

She looked at me a second, the kind of look that said, *"Why did you bring your mother?"*

"Mom and I were just celebrating her birthday over at Del Frisco's."

"Just across the street?"

I shrugged.

"That's a pretty special birthday dinner. It's so nice to see you, Doris. You look amazing."

"Why, thank you, Willow. Your mom has been gushing about your upcoming wedding in our monthly investment club meetings. I guess she's here, too?" Mom peeked inside the room. A sparkling glass chandelier caught my eye. It had to be as big as my car.

"Yes, Ma's in there. You want to go say hi while I talk to Cooper a second?"

Mom brought a finger to her lips. She was apprehensive. Who could blame her?

Just then, Willow's dad popped out of the room. "And who is this lovely lady?" he asked with a slight bow to my mom.

Willow made the introductions.

"Let me give you a tour of this place. It's amazing," he said, extending his arm. My mom hooked her hand inside the crook of his elbow and giggled. "I guess I'm being taken hostage, Cooper. See you in a bit."

She waved goodby, and Willow and I watched them walk into the Sendoro Room.

"I have no words," Willow said.

"Pretty bizarre," I said, running my fingers through my hair.

And then we looked at each other. I took a deep breath. "You look amazing," I said without thinking.

Her mouth opened, but she didn't speak. I quickly bailed out the both of us. "So, what's the urgent news?"

"Earl called."

"Elvis? Is he okay? Does he have any news for us?"

"He's upset, but I think he's made a connection between the three murders."

She told me how the Community Health Clinic appeared to be the center point for all three victims.

"That's fucked up."

"I don't know what to make of it, but it's a huge lead. Earl was about to tell the cops about it when we got off the phone, but—"

"We don't trust them to follow up. We have to do it ourselves. I guess we need to start with all the people who work there. Anyone there you have a connection with?" I asked. My eyes caught a glimpse of my mom and Raymond making the rounds. She looked almost giddy.

"Not directly. But Earl knows someone. A woman named Kelly."

"Cool. So, maybe you can talk to Kelly since you nurses speak the same language and—"

"Cooper, I'm about to get married. I just can't keep putting all my focus on this."

"Oh, right. Sorry. I guess…" My voice faded off as I peered into the room, purposely avoiding eye contact with her.

She touched my arm. My good arm. "Cooper, this isn't personal."

"The part about you getting married or about you not having time to find out who killed two people you know?"

She frowned. "Please don't make me feel guilty. I have to

commit to Harvey. You know that, right?"

"Sure." I sounded dismissive, and I didn't like it, but I also didn't know what else to say.

"Cooper," Mom called out from inside the room, "Raymond says you've got to try this cheesecake. It's incredible. Come on."

I held up a finger, acting as though I'd join her in a moment .But there was no way in hell I was going in that room.

"I'm sorry I texted you," Willow said.

"Why are you saying that now?" I sounded annoyed. I was.

"I think we might have been too quick to dismiss what the cops will do."

"You thought the opposite a moment ago."

"You said that, not me."

"But you're the one who had this urgent news. One minute, it's urgent; now, not so much. Damn, you're fickle."

"What did you just call me?" She balled her hands into fists and leaned toward me. I leaned just as far back. I could swear those majestic eyes now had flecks of red rage.

An elderly woman walking into the party room stopped, looked at both of us, but settled her eyes on me. "Don't fuck with the bride. I don't care how important you think your argument is. Got it, mister?"

"Yes, ma'am," I said.

She ambled into the room, and I turned to Willow. She had a hand over her mouth, but she couldn't hide that grin.

"I'm glad I can entertain you," I said, running my fingers through my hair.

"Why do you wear your hair longer now?" she asked.

"Huh?"

"I just wondered. Your hair was shorter in college."

"I guess it's probably because I can't afford to get haircuts. Go ahead," I said, flicking my fingers. "Hit me with another kick to the nuts."

"I'd never do that." She tapped her hand against my cheek and giggled, though she seemed to be trying not to. "Hey…" She waited until I was looking into her eyes.

"Yeah?"

"Sorry if I'm a little histrionic about everything."

"I forgive you," I said in quick order.

She twisted her lips. "Look, if you want to reach out to Kelly at the CHC, you have my blessing."

I bowed with my hands in a prayer position. "Can I kiss your ring, Mrs. Corleone?"

"You can kiss my sweet ass."

"Sweet indeed."

She glanced into the room for a second, then punched me in the shoulder socket. "Want me to find that old lady to really kick your ass?"

I rubbed my shoulder. "You seem to have this fixation with the word 'ass.'"

She tilted her head.

"Okay, I'm kind of being one. I'll reach out to Kelly. If nothing else, it'll be a good check to see if the cops followed up with her or anyone else at the CHC office."

"You could also try to reach Courtney," she suggested.

"Dead-end Girl. That's my new nickname for her."

"Ooh. That's mean. But I understand why you chose it."

"Maybe this new information will give her some incentive to direct her time to this case. Let me text her real quick."

I thumbed out a text and tapped "send" just as Willow grabbed my hand and yanked me along like I was on the end of a leash. "What are you doing?"

"You can deal with all this murder stuff tomorrow." She dragged me into the Sendoro Room. About seventy heads turned in our direction. I felt my face glowing, so I veered off to the side.

Willow caught up to me. "You're allowed to be here. I have

some pull, you know."

"I guess."

A waiter walked up and offered me a glass of champagne. "No thanks," I said with a quick shake of my head.

He started to walk off when Willow grabbed a glass from the tray and handed it to me. "This is good champagne."

"I'm sure it's the best money can buy." I took a sip. I was right.

"Why are you so bitter?"

I opened my mouth at the same time someone started clinking a spoon against a glass.

"Excuse me, everyone," Raymond called out. He was standing next to the dessert table. "I'd like to give a toast to the happy couple."

Willow looked horrified. Harvey approached us, gave me a curious eye, and draped his arm around his future wife. I wanted to hide under the table, but I nodded, shrugged, and slid to the back of the crowd.

Raymond's toast was more like a speech. It went on for five minutes. At the end of it, he led a cheer. "Hip, hip, hooray!" he yelled, pumping his fist in the air. "Come on now, let's not be bashful. Let's show Willow and Harvey our support." He orchestrated five more rounds of the cheer, and then everyone drank and laughed. Did he know they were laughing at him?

I tried to exit stage left, but Mom grabbed my arm and stuffed a forkful of cheesecake into my mouth. It felt like I was five and she was forcing me to eat my spinach.

"Isn't that the best cheesecake you've ever had in your life?"

With Mom, everything was the best.

"Hi, Doris." I turned to see Willow's mom walk up. She gave me the once-over, her face in a semi-permanent scowl.

"Florence, it's nice to see you." Mom's pleasant demeanor was dialed back about fifty percent.

"Did you take the lunatic's advice and invest in that

pharmaceutical stock?"

Mom looked up at me. "We're in an investment club together. Doesn't that sound exciting, Cooper?" She was trying to change the topic.

I didn't have a chance to respond.

"Oh, I guess that means you did. Whatever. If you want to lose thousands of dollars, that's your decision. No one listens to me," Florence said as her hands dropped to smack the side of her legs.

Mom blinked rapidly. "Oh, Florence, I'm so happy for you and, of course, for Willow and Harvey. He seems like a very nice man."

"You can say it, Doris. He's loaded. That's not a bad thing. People think having money is some big sin. Screw that. But yeah, he's a pretty good guy." She looked at me like I repulsed her. The feeling was mutual.

I heard another spoon clinking against glass. This time, Alli was standing next to Willow and Harvey. The two friends wrapped arms around each other. Willow looked much more comfortable now. Alli's toast was more like a homage to their long friendship. It lasted a couple of minutes, and when she was done, there was a chorus of *ahhh*s all around, and a few even wiped tears from their eyes.

From my observations over the years, all the sentimental gestures at weddings seemed misplaced. Many of them had to do with healing old wounds more than creating a supportive, realistic picture of what married life was all about. I'd always wondered if people realized how they were setting up the young couples for disappointment, starting with how they rationalized spending huge money on things the couple could never afford on their own. Well, everyone except Willow and Harvey. I think Harvey's fondness for extravagance was built into his DNA.

Then again, my perspective might be jaded.

The parade of toasters went on and on. I grabbed a second

glass of champagne and did a lot of people watching, thankful the focus wasn't on me.

"Hey, Cooper," Raymond whispered in my ear.

I flinched. *Why do people keep sneaking up on me?* "Raymond." I kept my gaze looking to the front of the group. I didn't feel comfortable doing anything more than simply acknowledging his presence next to me and at his daughter's wedding.

He smiled, popped on me the back. "It's a magical night, isn't it?"

"Yep."

Another toast was being given, but Raymond kept talking. "Did you find that money?"

Forty-Eight

Cooper

I was mid-swig on my champagne, and I coughed until I cleared my air passage. He hit my back twice just to make sure.

"What money?" I said nonchalantly, turning toward him.

The big Raymond smile twisted into something not quite as easygoing. "Come on, Cooper. Your mom told me all about your big night at Del Frisco's. How could a guy working at a bookstore afford that, especially when your car doesn't run?"

Heat raced up my neck and practically exploded out my eyes. "How the hell would you know that?"

He gave me an aw-shucks smile. "It's my business to know."

His business. "You put the money in there?"

He showed me his pearly whites.

"Why?"

He put his arm around my shoulder—I couldn't help but eye his hand. With my pulse already doing double-time, I was just about to push his hand off. But he pointed a finger toward the front of the group.

"Willow? What does she have to do with you putting fifty thousand dollars in the back of my car?"

"I love my daughter, Cooper. I assumed you knew that."

"How would I know that? You left her, her siblings, your whole family thirty years ago without saying a word. You never contacted them once. And now you show up out of thin air expecting everyone just to shrug and move on like nothing ever happened? That's pretty fucked up, in my mind."

The grip on my shoulder tightened. I was sick of the intimidation, both from him and the Sack Brothers. I looked him right in the eye. "Take your hand off me. Now."

He patted my shoulder once just for good measure and let go. "No need to get testy, Cooper. I did give you that fifty grand."

"You never said why."

A waiter walked by, and Raymond snagged a glass of champagne off the tray and took a sip. "It's a way for us to help each other out."

I wasn't following him. I shook my head in confusion.

"It's pretty simple, really. Jennie and Kyle don't hold grudges. They've already accepted me. But Willow can be a little stubborn. Probably gets that from her mother."

"And so you think that I can—"

"Convince her to allow me back in her life. That's all I want. Nothing shady or mysterious about it."

He'd been reading my mind. "Shady" and "mysterious" were there, but so were a few other choice words. "I'm not your PR firm, Raymond."

"You're as untrusting as she is."

"I see this from her perspective; let's just put it that way."

He nodded, then took another gulp. One of Harvey's buddies was up front telling some mundane story about their college days. I noticed the priest standing off to the side. He had a solemn look on his face, as if his thoughts were in another place. Regardless of his state of mind, his demeanor contrasted sharply with all the smiles and laughter. Maybe he looked at most of this like I did— nothing more than a contrived display of affection and support.

I swung my sights back to Raymond, who was engaged in a conversation with one of the many people at this event I didn't know. My thoughts snapped back to the night he had shown up at Harvey's mansion and what he'd said about how long he'd been in the area. One week. That was roughly about the time of the first murder.

My stomach clenched into a knot. I blew out a slow breath. What would be Raymond's motivation for killing anyone, let alone someone from Willow's wedding party? And then there were Irene Washington and Janice. Earl had figured out that the intersection point of the victims was the health clinic. Why would Raymond have any association with the clinic?

Raymond finished his conversation with a hearty chuckle and gulped more of his drink, then held up his glass. "This is the best, isn't it?"

"The champagne or the fact that you've somehow wedged your way back into Willow's life enough to be part of this event?"

His smile dropped like a bag of lead as his eyes shifted to me. Another person walked up, gave him a pat on the shoulder, and just like that, he flipped his happy face back on. He seemed rather adept at changing his personality on a dime. *Hmm.* I couldn't get that earlier question out of my mind: why would Raymond have any association with the clinic?

"Cooper, there's something you need to know about me," he said.

"You've finally learned how to use a phone?"

He ignored me. "Family means everything to me."

I almost spit out my mouthful of champagne. "You're kidding, right?"

"Stop it with the jokes, will you? I do mean it. I gave you the fifty K for a reason. I think you're my best hope—maybe my only hope—for getting Willow to forgive me. I messed up. All I want is a chance."

"And what if I don't agree to be your mouthpiece?"

"Then I guess I'd have to take back that fifty thousand dollars. And I'm not sure Dr. V and his minions would appreciate that."

I went still.

He chuckled. "Got your attention now?"

I tried to speak, to move, but something invisible had paralyzed me. Fear? Maybe. Loathing, for certain.

He whispered into my ear. "Enjoy your night, Cooper, and we'll talk soon." He patted my back and started to walk off. I swatted at his arm, but my reflexes were mired in sludge and I whiffed.

I gasped out a breath and replayed the last few minutes. What the hell was going on? How did Raymond know Dr. V and the brothers? My whole body broke out in a sweat.

A second later, Mom grabbed my hand. "What are you doing, Mom?" I asked as my eyes scanned the room for Raymond. I had to find out his connection to Dr. V and the Sack Brothers. Was he part of their operation? I'd theorized that the Sack Brothers were the ones Lucy had seen with the bloody saw, the ones who'd dismembered Ronnie. But the DNA test Courtney was waiting on would make that final determination.

My mind went back to "one week." Raymond's time stamp for being in the area. Maybe he, like myself, owed money to that maggot, Dr. V. And maybe he'd been forced to commit murder in exchange for paying off his debt. But then why would Dr. V want to kill Marion, Irene, and Janice? And how did Raymond still have fifty K to give to me?

I felt myself drowning in my own thoughts. My mom tugged on my hand. "Bow your head, Cooper."

"Huh?"

"Prayer," she said, nudging her head.

I followed her eyes and saw the priest up front. I lowered my head, but I didn't hear a word he said.

Forty-Nine

Willow

Harvey gave me two quick hand squeezes. I blinked away from Cooper and his mom and flipped my sights over to Harvey.

"Prayer," he whispered.

"Sorry," I said, quickly bowing my head.

Had Harvey seen me staring at Cooper? It wasn't what he thought, or might have thought. But at this point, did it really matter? I pinched the corner of my eyes as the priest's voice played like elevator music. It was nothing more than white noise in my mind. I chewed on what I'd witnessed seconds before Doris had grabbed Cooper's arm: my dad and Cooper having a moment.

During the last toast—was it number six or seven?—my eyes snagged my father approaching Cooper. For whatever reason, even as Harvey and I laughed at the story and made occasional eye contact, my sights quickly swerved back to Cooper and Dad. I saw Raymond drape his arm on Cooper's shoulder and then Cooper eyeing it like it carried a disease. They had some sort of conversation. Seemed mostly one-sided, although Cooper got in his shots. He always did.

Until that one comment. Dad had whispered a brief statement into Cooper's ear, and for a second, I thought Cooper had suffered a stroke. He didn't move. Not even his jaw, and that was saying something.

Then, as Dad walked off, he gave Cooper one last slap on the back. Normally, that type of thing wouldn't even register with me, except for two things. First, Dad and Cooper were not exactly chums. Cooper, I was pretty sure, had the same opinion of Dad as I did. I'd unloaded my life story on Cooper back in college, and my loser dad was at least partially responsible for creating the Willow that Cooper knew. Second, and most notably, Cooper swung his arm out as if he wanted to smack Raymond's arm. It was so slow-moving you'd think that Cooper had just downed ten cups of trash-can punch. But even from across the room, I saw his face lose all color.

Dad had said something to Cooper that rocked him. I could feel my insides twisting into a millions knots. I was worried about Cooper, while at the same time more than curious about what Dad had told him. I could feel my nostrils flaring. I was pissed. With every passing second, the intensity of my anger grew that much more. But even in those few seconds, I wasn't completely blind to the origin of my fury. My father had abandoned me. He didn't give a shit about me for thirty years, and now he showed up to—

A shooting star flew across my mind, carrying a message as clear as the thick bed of unruly curls on my head. Had Dad only reentered my life because I was marrying someone who was swimming in money?

A flurry of questions peppered my brain, but they were mangled together like the roots of a hundred-year-old tree. I swallowed, took in a breath, and tried to clear my mind.

The priest said, "Amen."

I paused as the volume of chatter slowly increased. I thought about the last line of the priest's prayer. I looked up at Harvey. "Did he just say, 'And may God have mercy on our souls'?"

"Uh, I think so. I wasn't paying that close attention. Why?" he said with a lighthearted chuckle, and then he turned and fell into a conversation with someone else.

My eyes shot upward and found the priest. There was something about him that reminded me of someone. Had I met him previously? I wracked my brain until it hurt as I watched his mannerisms. He was a large man, and he lumbered when he walked. But it was his face that seemed familiar. But as much as I tried, I couldn't place it.

I sifted through my personal database of people I'd seen recently. Still, nothing hit, although it seemed to be just out of my mental grasp. I clenched my jaw, irked that my brain didn't seem to be functioning at an optimal level.

Father Moses had a small bag in his hand, and he was handing something out to everyone in attendance. Alli broke free from a small group of people and walked up.

"What did he just give you?"

"Father Moses?"

"Yeah. What did he give you?" My tone was abrupt, I realized.

"Just this little twig," she said, spinning it between her thumb and forefinger. "I think he called it an olive twig."

"Why?"

"What's got you so upset, Willow?"

"Why is he handing those out?"

Out of the corner of my eye, I saw the priest slip outside through a side glass door into the dimly lit gardens. "Where's he going?" I asked her before she had a chance to answer my previous question.

"Kind of funny. Said that his only vice is smoking cigars. Says he walks and smokes one cigar every night. Doesn't drink much alcohol, but he has to have his cigar." She giggled and touched my arm. "Willow, are you sure you're okay?"

"I'm fine." I wasn't. The area just behind my one eye started throbbing, a telltale sign that a migraine was coming on. I rubbed my eye, and I was certain I had just smeared my makeup. *Hello, drunk clown.*

"Can I get you another drink?" Alli asked.

"Sure," I said, without thinking much about it. I tried to find the priest through the glass, but with him wearing all black, he'd seemingly disappeared into the night.

Alli went off to the bar, so I walked over to the glass door. I pushed it open and slipped quietly into the dark garden.

Fifty

Cooper

I intercepted Alli at the bar. "Where's Willow?"

She shook her head. "What's with you two?"

"What are you talking about?"

"You're both so uptight."

My eyes were roaming our space. From across the room, even while speaking to a group of folks, Raymond locked eyes on me.

Fucker.

Back to Alli. "What's with the little sticks?"

"I guess you didn't get one because you weren't officially invited." She gave me flat eyes, and then she smiled. "I'm just screwing with you, Cooper. The priest was handing out the olive twigs after his prayer. He said he does that at every wedding rehearsal." She held up her stick.

"Olive twig," I repeated while taking hold of the stick.

I felt a hand on my back. My brain was no longer stuck in quicksand. I lifted my elbow, prepared to jab it backward, but then I realized the hand was small and gentle. I turned to see Mom.

"Make sure you don't drink too much, Cooper," she said.

"Someone's got a drink limit," Alli whispered to me, teasing. She twirled around on her heel while holding some type of martini. But she stopped before walking away. "Benjamin said you're going to join his business as a marketing executive."

"Marketing executive?" Mom asked, putting her hands together as if a prayer had just been answered.

It was more like a marketing whore—Ben had even said as much. I tried not to roll my eyes. Did I really have to deal with this now? "Alli, I'm not sure—"

"Oh, Cooper, I'm so proud of you," Mom said. "An executive. No wonder you've been so coy with me. You didn't want to brag. My humble son."

She took hold of my arm—my bad arm—and squeezed. I knew it was done out of love, but it felt like I was being tortured. It took everything in my power not to scream. I gently pulled my arm away.

Alli snorted out a quick laugh at Mom's praise and walked off. I was left twirling the olive twig.

"That was so nice and thoughtful of the priest to hand those out. We all need to remember these symbols of peace and have mercy for each other in these times," Mom said.

"Reminds me of your Mission of Mercy," I said, my mind starting to recall some of the brochures from the bag that was in my car.

"The olive twig is carried in a dove's mouth. That's the symbol of mercy. We all need to show each other mercy in this day and age. That's why we named our mission the way we did."

I thought about the MO for the killer—leaving parts of a dove at each murder. Maybe that foot left at Janice's side was indeed that of a dove. And this olive twig fit right into that theme.

"Didn't you love that prayer by the priest? It's like he knew I was part of the Mission of Mercy."

"Huh? Why are you saying that?"

"Didn't you hear him?"

"Not really. I was busy."

"Busy?"

"What was this prayer?"

"Well, it's not anything new, but he finished by saying, 'And may God have mercy on our souls.' I knew he was speaking to all of us, but it felt like he was speaking to me. It only validated my work on the Mission for Mercy."

I'd been so hyper-focused on Raymond—and for good reason—I'd not paid a lot of attention to the priest. There was something about him, about the way he carried himself, that seemed familiar.

I did another quick scan of the room for the tall man in black. "Did he leave already?" I asked Mom.

"Father Moses? You know what? I'm not sure. Everything okay, son?"

"All good," I said, my eyes still shifting left and right.

Mom squeezed my arm again. I couldn't help but jerk my arm away this time.

"Did I hurt you?"

"No, I'm fine."

"You're not fine. Your mother gave birth to you thirty-nine years ago, and there's never been a time when I didn't know you were suffering. Tell your mother. I can help."

She pawed at my arm. Little did she know my list of issues was as long as my arm. "Really, Mom, it's nothing I can't handle." I continued to search for the priest. I replayed everything I'd learned in just the last few minutes, starting with Raymond's extortion attempt and his stunning connection to Dr. V and the Sack Brothers. That had felt like a kick to the sac.

But my mind couldn't stop thinking about this new information—the prayer, the olive twig, and the dove connecting to mercy, the possible familiarity of the priest. Then again, it could all just be a coincidence. Priests discuss peace and mercy all the time. The phrase Mom had recited from Father Moses…well, I'd heard it (or zoned it out) a thousand times in my life. So why did it feel different this time?

It was the priest's face, maybe his aloof demeanor at the same time. Willow had said he was a late substitute for their regular priest. Speaking of Willow...

"Hey, Mom, have you seen Willow?"

"She's around here somewhere. Well, if you're busy doing your thing, I'm going to go have a conversation with Raymond. He was talking to me about his most recent trip to some amazing spa in Arizona."

She started to walk off. No way I wanted her near Raymond. "Hold on. Uh..." I spotted Florence nearby.

"Hey, Florence, can you talk to Mom about your latest investment strategy?" I put a hand on Florence's elbow. She immediately shook it off and gave me the evil eye.

"But we already meet with our club members on a monthly basis." Mom's voice had a nice but pleading tone.

She'd have to deal with Florence, who was relatively harmless as long as words and tone meant nothing to you. I gave Mom one last carrot. "Maybe the two of you can brainstorm on a safe financial plan for me."

"Oh, that's a great idea," Mom said, holding up a finger. "It's so nice to see you thinking ahead. You're just so mature...my little executive."

"Executive?" Florence cackled. "You call working at a bookstore an executive job? He might as well be cleaning toilets for a living. Pays as much."

Mom looked confused.

"You didn't know, did you?" Florence said.

I help up my hands in defense, but I couldn't deal with this now. "You two have fun."

I flipped around as my mom called out my name. I had to ignore her. I cut through a number of folks while on the lookout for the priest and Willow. I stopped and did a three-sixty. Still came up empty.

Wait a second, dumbass. Alli already told you that the priest had stepped outside to smoke a cigar.

I felt like an idiot. So where was Willow? Bathroom. She always had to pee a hundred times a night.

I headed for the exit and almost ran over Harvey.

"Hey, have you seen Willow?"

He paused a second, as if he questioned my intentions.

"I just want to pass along a funny story about our two moms interacting."

He looked across the room, then snapped his fingers. "You know, I think I saw her walk outside earlier."

"With the priest?"

"I didn't see the priest. I figured she just wanted some clean air. It's a little stuffy in here."

Tell me about it.

"Thanks." I began to turn around, but he grabbed my bad arm.

"Crap!" I said, pulling his hand away.

"What's wrong, Cooper?"

"Nothing, I don't think." Out of the corner of my eye, I spotted Raymond. "Hey, keep an eye on Raymond until I get back."

I spun around and headed for the glass door.

Fifty-One

Cooper

I had no idea how badly my senses were being assaulted until I slipped out the glass door and stepped into the garden. The volume of chatter and music in the Sendoro Room had made my brain hurt. Florence was number one on the assault list.

Right now, though, the only thing I could hear were the rhythmic sounds coming from the three-level water fountain. The edifice was adorned with ornate carvings, as though it belonged in a museum. But it was a functioning fountain.

I looked from side to side. Soft, hidden lights illuminated colorful flowers and a variety of tasteful shrubs. Behind them was a dark green wall of Foster hollies. I opened my mouth, prepared to call out for Willow, but I stopped myself. If the priest was out here smoking a cigar, I would smell it. I'd smoked my fair share of cigars in my life, mostly back in my party days. Cigar odor was distinct, and it carried a good distance.

But I only smelled the outdoors, plus a hint of exhaust.

A horn honked, which reminded me that Olive Street was just beyond that wall of hollies. I took a breath and raked my fingers through my hair. No cigar odor. No sign of Willow or Father Moses. I turned and looked through the wall of glass at the party-goers. Everyone was in their own world. I was hoping to see Willow and the priest, thinking they might have reentered without me noticing. But I didn't see them.

There was a shriek. I jerked my head around. I hadn't heard that shriek in eighteen years, but I knew it was Willow. I moved in the direction of the noise in the middle of the cluster of hollies, each step quicker than the last. By the time I left the stoned patio, I was in a full-on sprint. I busted through the thick green wall of limbs. A second later, I dropped like a sack of cement. While midair, my brain tried to process what the hell I'd tripped over— it had some give to it. It was too damn dark to see a thing, even the ground. I barely got my arms up in time. My forearms took the brunt of the force. Yes, on my bad arm, and on a tree stump.

"Fuck!" I said, rolling over while praying that I hadn't fallen over Willow's body.

"Cooper!"

I looked up and saw a silhouette of curls dancing in the breeze. "Willow?"

She fumbled with something in her hands, then a light flashed in my face.

"What are you doing?"

She crouched lower to the ground. "You okay?"

"What was—" I stopped short, scrambled to my knees, and saw a body sprawled on the ground.

"Who is that?" The thump of my heart pounded my chest like a drumroll on a tympani.

"It's Father Moses. I stumbled over him myself and had just taken out my phone. He's not moving. I think he's dead, Cooper. Can you believe he's dead?"

I snatched the phone out of her hand and shined the light on his face. Willow shrieked and bile shot into the back of my throat. "What the…?"

"What is stuffed in his mouth?" she asked.

I bent over as if whatever it was might jump up and bite me. "Holy shit. I think it's the head of a bird."

"A dove, right? It's got to be a dove."

"I guess."

"Who would do this?" she asked. "And why Father Moses?"

"It's got to be the same person who killed the others."

"Or people." She put her hand on my shoulder. "The Sack Brothers. Could they be behind this?"

"I don't know, Will. They're ruthless, but they're also dumb as nails."

I moved the light upward. The priest's eyes were wide open; he had a pained expression on his face, as if he'd been frozen in a glacier.

"There, do you see it?" I could hear a quiver in her voice as she pointed at his forehead. I saw a small hole rimmed by a trace amount of blood. I touched the side of his neck. It kind of grossed me out, but as expected, he had no pulse. "I guess he was shot, maybe from point-blank range. The person who did this was motivated by something."

"Hate."

"But this one is different. The others were killed using inert gas and laid to rest in a peaceful manner."

"But Janice's back was broken."

"Yeah, I can't figure that out yet."

Just then, someone honked their horn, long and hard. I lurched, nearly banging my head off Willow's nose.

"Hey, mister, get the hell out of the road," someone yelled.

The street was much closer than I'd imagined. Holding my arm to my chest, I got to my feet and directed the light behind us. More hollies.

"Did you see anyone else?" I asked Willow.

"If I did, do you think I'd still be here?"

"Love your sass. You're learning," I said, prying my way through another wall of hollies. Willow gripped my shirt from behind.

"These damn bushes are too frickin' thick." I was so entangled, I began to feel a little claustrophobic.

"Just get through!" Willow plowed into my back, essentially using me as a battering ram. I stumbled through the bushes, nearly falling against a wrought-iron fence.

"Damn, what's into you?" I asked.

"Look!"

I followed her finger to a man jogging down the sidewalk, moving west on Olive. Every few steps, he looked over his shoulder in our direction. He was the only visible pedestrian from my vantage point.

"You think that guy was in the garden?" I asked.

"You see anyone else?" She snapped her feet, and her shoes went flying. Then she hopped over the fence like it was a speed bump, all while wearing a short party dress.

"You're a badass," I said.

"You're a slow ass." She took off in a sprint. I crawled over the fence and tried to catch up.

Fifty-Two

Willow

The man wasn't very fast. In fact, his stride was more like a pattern of awkward lunges, his legs seemingly out of sync with the rest of his body. But he had a big head start on me. He swerved into the street, and a car almost hit him. A horn blared, and the man was back on the sidewalk. He turned, snagged a quick glance at me, and then kept running.

He reached the Cedar Springs intersection where there was a lot more traffic, but he never slowed his pace. He lunged into the middle of traffic. An SUV swerved right, popped over a curb, and cracked the side of light pole.

I took a breath but kept churning my legs.

Just then, a sports car roared up from the south. Horns blared then tires screeched. The car, a Lexus of some kind, fishtailed as smoke billowed from burning rubber. The car slammed into the back of a truck, which then shot forward and rammed a car crossing the intersection. I jumped in the air from the horrific sounds of ripped metal, busted taillights, and tire blowouts. Six, maybe seven cars ended up crashing into each other or some immovable object.

A hand touched my shoulder. "Remind me never to chase after you again," Cooper said, pumping out breaths while holding his arm against his chest. "Is the man we're chasing nothing more than tire print now?"

I stood on my toes and tried to look for the man through the haze of smoke coming up from accordion-shaped hoods. "I don't see him. I can't say for sure."

"Need a better angle. Follow me." Cooper crossed the street and jogged up to the northeast corner where five roads intersected—a combination of one-way and two-way streets. The lighting was better, and there was less smoke from this angle. I noticed that all the drivers were outside of their cars, either cursing or on their phones. One was doing both.

"Hey, is that him?" Cooper flicked his fingers at my arm and pointed up McKinnon, which went in a northwesterly direction from Cedar Springs.

I didn't bother answering Cooper. I just took off. I veered a good fifty feet north of the wreckage to ensure my bare feet didn't hit glass. When I looked up, I couldn't find the guy. "Dammit!"

I slowed down, but then Cooper zipped right past me, yelling, "He must love Rolex watches!"

"What?"

He pointed and kept running. He looked really strange with one arm seemingly glued to his torso. On the other side of Moody Street, I saw the glass Rolex Building. Could the killer have a car stashed in the parking lot?

I spotted the man again and bolted out of my stance, making sure to not divert my gaze. He made it to the front of the Rolex Building where spotlights gave him an eerie glow. I noticed he had a backpack over his shoulder. He turned and saw us still chasing after him. He followed the curve of the front of the building until it reached a side alley. And then he disappeared.

"Did you see where he went?" I asked Cooper as we approached the front of the building.

"No clue," he said, breathing hard.

"Remember, he could have a gun."

He stopped on a dime. "Crap."

We were both at the edge of the building. Just beyond the alley was a small park.

"Which park is this?" I asked.

"Not a park. I think it's like Fearing's, some type of garden connected to the building at the far end of the trees. I think it's another five-star restaurant. Surprised Harvey hasn't taken you there."

I ignored his dig and ran my eyes up the building. "There might be a restaurant on the first floor, but those are condos up there. We might know where the killer lives."

I started walking across the street toward the garden.

"Hold up," Cooper said. "Don't you think we should call the cops?"

"Stop wasting time. We have no idea where he is. We may not get this chance again." I reached the edge of the garden. It was dark and thickly wooded.

Cooper sidled up against my hip. It felt oddly comforting. "I'm not sure this is wise, Will." He scratched his face.

"If we let him get away, he'll just keep on killing. We have to stop this now."

"But he'll hear us coming, if he's in there."

Suddenly, it started to rain. No wind or storms, but a hard, driving rain. I nudged Cooper and said, "I think someone upstairs just evened the odds."

Fifty-Three

Cooper

Willow and I were both drenched within seconds. Her matted hair and smeared makeup made her look like a character out of a B-list horror movie. She was still cute, though. And true to the woman I knew, she didn't care how she looked.

We tiptoed to the edge of the garden and gave each other a glance. I took a hard swallow. It was amazing how dry my throat was while I was essentially standing under a shower. A chill crawled up my spine. I had a bad feeling about confronting this guy, especially in a space with little visibility and no other people around.

"Hey," I said to Will, touching her arm.

She ripped her arm away and marched forward.

Dammit!

I followed her into the garden, and immediately we were engulfed in darkness. I could only see shapes, most of which were trees, creating a canopy from most of the rain.

Willow raised her phone. I put my hand on her arm and shook my head. "He could see us coming," I whispered.

She nodded, and we moved forward, our elbows touching each other while we carefully maneuvered around one tree at a time. We walked through the grass and mud as though there might be an explosive device hidden underground. Our heads were on swivels. My eyes were adjusting to the darkness, but all I could hear was the smattering of raindrops on the leaves.

While keeping my gaze in front of me, I leaned toward her ear. "You see anything?"

She shook her head.

I heard a cracking sound. I spun around, wiped water off my face, and stared into the sea of dark trees.

"What was that?" Willow asked.

"No clue." I took a few steps forward, and Willow stayed right with me. My shin then ran into a branch. I lifted my arm to stop her progress and keep her from hitting the same branch. "I think it just snapped off the tree," I said, glancing up. "You think he climbed into one of the trees?"

"From what I saw, he didn't look like he could climb out of bed without tripping over his own feet. Plus, he's on the large side. Not sure these limbs could hold him."

"Good intel," I said.

"You think you're some SWAT stud now?"

"You got the stud part right. I was thinking Navy SEAL."

She rolled her eyes. We turned and continued our trek through this mini city forest. After another twenty feet, I could see the soft glow of an outdoor light by the rear of the building. "He may not be in here," I said.

"Could be in a condo, or maybe he had his car parked in their garage."

Just then, I picked up another distinct odor. It wasn't a cigar. It was weed.

"You smell that?" I whispered into her ear.

"Yep."

"You actually think this man, a possible killer, has stopped to smoke a joint?"

Did something just move? I turned to look closer and…

"It's him!" Willow darted out of her stance, but I was just as quick this time. Too quick to see the tree. I rammed my shoulder into the trunk, bounced off like a pinball, and tumbled into an unsuspecting Willow. I fell into a mud pit, and she fell on top of me, straddling me.

"Uh…" I muttered as we both slid around in the mud to try to gain traction and get back to our feet. One second seemed like one minute.

"Get off me," she said.

"You're the one straddling me."

"Don't say that. You can't say that."

Huh?

Just as we reached a standing position, I heard a pained scream.

Was the man killing someone?

Fifty-Four

Willow

The scream pierced my chest. It was a man's voice, although it sounded like he'd just been castrated.

Cooper and I raced toward the noise. I dodged trees and Cooper to make sure we didn't crash into each other. I saw a light just beyond the edge of the tree line. Was someone moving?

Just as we broke out of the dark canopy, the man with the backpack was trying to get to his feet. Under him, his victim was flailing on a small patio.

"Stop!" I yelled.

The man flipped his head toward me. I saw something in his hand.

"It's a gun!" Cooper yelled, jumping in front of me.

Did he think he was made of steel?

I still couldn't see the victim. The killer's enormous frame made him invisible. But I know I picked up a groan. He was muttering something indecipherable.

The man grabbed the victim's neck and put the gun against the guy's head. "Don't come any closer!" the killer said, pulling the victim upright like he was a puppet.

"Ben Dover?" Cooper blurted.

Air rushed from my lungs. Benjamin was rubbing his head and smacking his lips. "I was run over by a fucking train," he said as his eyes fluttered open only momentarily. I wasn't sure he knew the killer had a gun against his head. He might have been both high and suffering some type of concussion.

"Ben, don't move," Cooper said.

"If you don't back off and let me out of here, I'll kill him," the man said.

Cooper and I got very still. My eyes went to the pistol; it was unlike anything I'd seen before. The barrel was long and thin, but it connected to a larger metallic pipe. Even the trigger mechanism looked strange.

"Did you hear me? I swear to God, I'll kill him!"

Ben started acting as though he had no control of his limbs, and the man struggled to keep him upright.

"It doesn't matter what he's done in his life," the man said. "I'll make one sacrifice. I'm allowed that. I have more work I have to do."

"What kind of work?" Cooper asked.

I gritted my teeth, wondering if quizzing this maniac was the right tactic.

"You should know by now...Cooper."

I swung my sights to Cooper. "You know him?"

"What are you talking about? I've never met this guy."

"Yes, you have," the man said.

I was about to punch Cooper in the arm, but the man continued. "I know both of you. You're good people."

Cooper and I snagged a quick glance. He had to be thinking the same thing. This man was insane. But then I looked closer at the killer's face. The width of his marble eyes seemed familiar, even the crow's feet.

"Ben is good too," Cooper said. "Just let him go, and you can walk away."

A siren whirred in the distance. Had someone alerted the cops? I recalled the series of crashes a block away. That was their likely destination.

The man slammed the gun against his own forehead and screamed like a coyote. Blood poured down his face as he started crying. "It wasn't supposed to end this way. I needed to save you, just like I saved the others."

Save what? Was he equating saving with killing?

Cooper continued to engage the large man. "Why do you think we need saving?"

The man was gasping out breaths, his face coiled into madness and misery. "The world...it's fucked up. It's full of hate. Most people are mean, so fucking mean. The good people shouldn't have to deal with it, so I did them a favor and sent them to a better place. I killed them in the most peaceful way possible."

"The dove parts. You were trying to show us that you killed those people out of mercy," Cooper said.

The man wiped tears from his face and nodded. "See, you get it. You understand. I knew some people would understand." He paused, gulped in some air. He started waving the gun around. Benjamin blinked his eyes. He was starting to break out of his slumber a bit.

"Who the fuck are you?" Benjamin shouted.

Crap! Couldn't he just keep his mouth shut?

The killer looked at him with disdain as he brought the gun up to Benjamin's chin. My heart leaped into the back of my throat. "Please, don't kill him," I said.

The killer looked at me and then Cooper. "Both of you gave me hope."

"When? How?" I asked.

"It's been eighteen years, four months, and twenty-seven days. I saw the two of you making out on the hood of a car as I walked across a lawn. I was on my way to kidnap and kill a girl."

I gasped. What was he talking about? He paused and stared at me for a second before continuing. "But you thought I was homeless, and you gave me twenty dollars. You were both so nice to me. I've never forgotten you."

I scanned my memory and came up empty.

"But both of you deserve better than this world. So, you are on my list. And don't worry, I'm not going to kill you with this hydrogen gun."

"Is that what you used on the priest?" Cooper asked while inching forward.

What was he doing?

Then I heard more sirens. I prayed that the cops were on their way to our location.

The man started seething. "My half-brother, Moses. He deserved to die in the most painful way. He treated me like shit when I was young. It's his fault that I have so many demons in my mind. So, killing him was not done because of mercy." He looked at his weapon and chuckled. "This hydrogen gun shoots out bullet-shaped ice at a speed of sixteen thousand kilometers per second. Shot at point-blank range, it creates a massive ballistic shock to the brain. Killing him, stuffing that dove's head in his mouth...well, it just seemed like the right thing to do."

This man was truly demented. "But why Marion, Irene, and Janice?" I asked.

"I sell pharmaceuticals. I saw them all show such unbelievable kindness at the Community Health Clinic. And I knew it was time to start my project. I'm just sad that I caused Janice pain in the process. She deserved much better."

My chest started to burn. His justification made me sick.

"I just want you to know that if I'm able to walk away from this, I'll eventually have to find you again and do the same to you as I did to the three ladies," he admitted.

"Okay. But just don't harm Ben, please," Cooper said, taking a step forward.

I wanted to reach out and pull him back. This psychopath's odd affection for us could flip in a second if he thought Cooper was going to charge at him. I just couldn't let that happen.

"I remember you from eighteen years ago," I blurted out.

"You do?" He was staring at me again, the timbre of his voice suddenly calmer.

"I've always wanted to know your name and your story."

"I'm Terry. Terry Spencer."

"Well, Terry, I guess we got it wrong. You weren't homeless. But as I think back, I can see that you had a kindness about you."

His face contorted as if he couldn't believe such a notion.

"And honestly, I can see it now. You want to be caring and compassionate to people."

Terry shook his head and wiped sweat from his face. "I've tried to be, but I just don't think I have it in me. I'll kill myself after I give mercy to all the good souls in this world. At least the ones I'm aware of. I just hope that someday people will appreciate what I've done. But make no mistake, I know I'm not a good or caring person." His breath stuttered, and then he started sobbing full force. "There's no hope for me. And it's all because of Moses. What a name, huh? Moses. The original Moses supposedly parted the Red Sea to save a tribe of people. My half-brother split me in two, ruined my life." Then Terry screamed out loud. "Fuck him! Fuck the world! I just can't control myself." He waved the gun around. He was going to shoot someone, I just knew it.

Cooper took another step in his direction.

Terry suddenly stopped moving and locked his eyes on Cooper. "You want to hurt me, don't you, Cooper?"

"I want to help you, Terry."

Terry shook his head. "I don't believe you. You want to stop my mission of mercy. But I can't let you do that."

"Now, Ben!" Cooper yelled.

Benjamin lunged upward and smashed his head into Terry's nose. Blood gushed, but Terry didn't fall. Cooper sprang in their direction, and then the gun went off. Cooper fell to the patio.

More blood spurted into the air. Terry was fumbling with the gun while Benjamin tried to pull away. Cooper was writhing in pain.

I took three steps, jumped into the air, and kicked Terry in the face. He screamed, and the gun finally dropped. I snatched the gun off the patio and aimed it at Terry, my arms shaking. He fell to his knees and cupped his hands over his face.

"Cooper, you okay?" I asked.

He rolled over. I saw blood snaking down his hand. "It's just a flesh wound," he said, using a British accent.

Benjamin clapped out a laugh. "You're such a smartass, Coop. But dammit, you're my GOAT. I just can't wait for us to work together. I'm going to make you a rich man."

Cooper tried to laugh, but he sounded like he was in pain.

Terry fell and curled up in a fetal position.

A minute later, cops showed up, and I quickly checked on Cooper's wound.

Fifty-Five

Cooper

I didn't like people doting over me. I'd been that way as long as I could remember.

But if I were being completely honest with myself—and that wasn't always the case—I kind of enjoyed Willow touching me with her gentle hands, even if the wound burned as though a blowtorch was being held up to my forearm. The same damn forearm that had felt like it was broken for days now.

Willow had found some napkins and was pressing them against the wound to slow down the bleeding. She'd already admitted the frozen ice had only grazed my arm.

"You straddled me earlier," I said, unable to contain my smile.

"You did what?" Ben said from behind me.

She didn't punch me or squeeze my broken arm, but she did gaze into my eyes. "Hush. You're not supposed to say that."

"But you did."

"Only because you're a klutz and ran into me."

"I swear, the tree moved."

She snorted out a laugh and glanced at Ben. "Maybe he's not the only one who's high right now."

I arched my head back a bit. "Ben, what the hell were you

doing smoking weed out here?"

Two cops who'd handcuffed Terry looked in my direction.

Ben scooted closer to Willow and me. "Reva and the triplets are inside the restaurant. I needed a mental break." He rubbed the back of his head. "Was all that true…that you knew this lunatic?"

"It took a while, but I remembered giving some guy twenty bucks a long time ago," I said.

"So you actually remember him?" Willow asked.

"You don't?"

"I was making it all up. We mugged down on or in your car so many times, it was kind of a blur."

"You're such a stud," Ben said, flicking his hand off my shoulder.

Willow gave Ben a glance. Her eyes looked like they were shooting darts at him.

He quickly scooted away.

Minutes later, paramedics arrived and took over for Willow. Then Courtney showed up, which led to a lot of questions. We answered each one thoroughly.

"So, you're saying that Terry Spencer admitted to every murder except for one. Ronnie Gutierrez," Courtney said.

"I thought you were waiting on DNA results to make the confirmation," I countered.

She curled her lips inward. "Got some bad news tonight. They can't find the DNA sample."

"I don't understand," Willow said. "How can a crime lab lose a blood sample?"

She shrugged and huffed out a breath. "I spoke to the director myself. He can't explain it. Says they've never lost a sample in his six years on the job."

I felt my phone buzzing in my back pocket as a paramedic approached us.

"You finally ready to go to the ER and get your arm tended

to?" he asked.

I was staring at the text message on my phone. It was from Milo. Said I needed to meet them at the Stevens Park Golf Course, on the green of the seventeenth hole.

"Cooper, you are going to the ER," Willow said.

Just then my mom walked onto the patio, followed by Florence, Harvey, Raymond, and a host of other faces I didn't recognize.

I saw the time on my phone: 12:30 a.m. I was already thirty minutes late. I got to my feet. "I can't do that now. There's something I have to do."

"You selling drugs on the side?" Florence asked.

Everyone ignored her. Mom doted over me for a good minute. But I pulled away from her clutches. "I have to leave," I said as I watched Harvey take Willow in his arms. She looked at me and mouthed, *Sack Brothers*. I nodded. "I'll go to the ER later. I promise."

As I walked away, part of me wondered if I'd ever make it to the ER.

Fifty-Six

Cooper

I raced back to my car, each footfall feeling as though a hammer was slamming into my forearm bone. The ulna bone—that's what Willow had called it. I couldn't stop, though. I was late, and I had no idea how the Sack Brothers or Dr. V would respond to my tardiness.

I reached my car and broke every speed limit on the way to my apartment. Once there, I kept the car running, ran upstairs, and grabbed the bag. I'd already ensured that the required amount, fifty K, was in the black bag. I'd hidden the extra five grand in a shoebox in the apartment. I skipped down the steps with the black bag. Even though Raymond had admitted to giving me the money, I had no clue where he'd picked up this cash. I'd have to find out more tomorrow. For now, I just wanted to live to see the light of the morning.

I backed the Converta-beast out of the driveway and headed for Oak Cliff. Stevens Park was probably the nicest public course in the area. Why they'd chosen that location, I had no idea, other than I knew it was closed at this hour and there was probably no other person nearby. They could kill me and toss my body into one of the ponds. Or they could dismember me while I was still breathing.

Oh, the joy.

As I zoomed across town, I thought about what Courtney had shared. The blood sample had disappeared. Were the Sack Brothers connected to that crime? I suspected they were behind Ronnie's murder. But now I wondered if Raymond was somehow connected to any of this. He didn't seem like the murdering type, but my judge of character was flawed. And the timing of his arrival in Dallas still chewed at the back of my mind. I'd have to confront him tomorrow. He might want his money back. But I had one goal—to live and try to get this particular nightmare behind me.

I parked on the side of North Montclair and walked through the parking lot and onto the course. No other cars were in the lot, and I felt my stomach seize up.

I made my way to the seventeenth hole. No sign of anyone. I turned on my phone flashlight and scanned the area around the green. I saw two squirrels prancing near a tree, but no humans.

I waited thirty minutes. Finally, I sent a text message.

Where are you guys? I have the money, and I've been waiting for over an hour.

I took the chance that they were also running late.

A response hit my phone a minute later.

You're lying. Dr. V doesn't like liars. We waited for 30 minutes and took off. U now owe him 2 favors.

"Fuck!" I yelled out loud. I thought about trying to explain what had happened with chasing after Terry, but I knew it wouldn't hold any weight.

Another text came in.

U get 1 more chance Cooper. We'll text u tomorrow with location and time. Be ready to move or get ready to eat your arm.

They were fucking cannibals. But I had to be compliant, so I responded one last time.

I'll be ready, don't worry.

I went home, pulled out some cash from the shoebox, and went to the ER, where they treated my wound, X-rayed my arm, and then put me in cast. They gave me pain meds, which they said would help me sleep through the pain.

The meds didn't work, and I stayed awake the rest of the night thinking about my mortality and Willow.

Fifty-Seven

Cooper

The text came in at seven a.m. Milo said to meet them in the parking garage of American Airlines Centre, home to the Dallas Mavericks and Stars—at 11:59 *a.m.* I was actually relieved. It was daytime, and people would likely be around.

Hoping to revive my tired brain, I took a cooler-than-normal shower, and I even remembered to wrap a plastic bag over my cast. I put my face full into the water. To a degree it soothed me, but my anxious mind fought back and eventually wrestled control of my thoughts. My biggest concern now was the nature of the two favors Milo said I owed. Something told me these favors wouldn't be anything like picking up their laundry or taking care of their pets while they went out of town. Of course, I doubted they had pets, at least ones they hadn't tortured.

I finished getting ready, put the money bag in my car, and drove to Books and Spirits to start my morning shift. Brandy noticed my arm cast right away, but she didn't offer any commentary. She told me to work the register, so I did just that. Despite every effort to focus my thoughts on anything but what I was about to experience, the pace of my thumping pulse picked up with each passing minute. I closed my eyes and tried to find some peace.

I heard knuckles rapping on the counter, and my eyes shot open. It was Archibald Motta.

"Doing some meditation?" he asked.

"Something like that."

His eyes shifted to my arm. "Did you break it in some type of pickup game against a bunch of younger guys?"

I almost offered the same response, but I kept it neutral. "I'm just a klutz."

"I doubt that. My son tells me you played for Canisius back in the day."

"Not sure how he knows that, but he's right."

"Remember, he's a sports historian now. He actually showed me the video from the year you guys made it to the Dance, when you hit the game-winning shot. I think they called it 'the shot of gold from a Golden Griffin.'"

"He really knows his stuff."

"YouTube helps," he said with smile.

I noticed he still wore a bow tie. Today, he'd gone with gold and black.

He continued. "I'm surprised I haven't heard from you."

I was confused. "Why are you saying that?"

"Well, I told your friend, the one with the mullet and glasses, that I wanted you to call me when you had some free time."

My high-speed pulse now had veered toward the light. This could be the break I'd been waiting for. "I saw you the next day at the book signing, though. You didn't say anything about signing me."

"Oh, this has nothing to do with being your literary agent. It's practically impossible to get a publishing deal unless you've got a recognizable name or you're promising to share big-time dirt."

I had the market cornered on dirt. So much dirt on so many people. But I also wanted to live. "No dirt from me," I said, my hopes suddenly deflated.

"Look, I'm not sure how much longer I'm going to be an agent anyway, so I recently started a side business. It's a new sports blog called *The Wire*. And I wanted to see if you'd be interested in writing for us."

"Sounds kind of interesting, but honestly, I'm not sure I can be a beat reporter again. I'll get sick of hearing the same answers to my questions."

"That's not what I had in mind. I want you to be our *investigative* sports reporter. You've been there before. You'd get free reign on the topics and prime space on our home page whenever you post a story. But it's got to be thorough and noteworthy. No fluff."

I felt a new jolt of energy. "I hate fluff almost as much as I hate cozy mysteries."

"Here's the only thing. We can't afford to pay you very much for the first six months, until our ads start generating some decent cash."

"Hmm," I said. This couldn't be like Ben's new company, could it?

"I think this is really going to catch on. But you might need to keep this bookstore job for a while. You think you can do that?"

It could be a lot worse. Hell, it could be fucking awesome. I would get to write and be paid for it, the type of reporting I lived for. I extended my hand, and he shook it.

"Very cool. We have a deal," he said.

I wanted to scream in excitement, but I just said, "Thanks." I had the strong urge to share the good news with someone.

Mom? I was thirty-nine years old. I already wasn't thrilled that she poked around in my life as much as she did.

Ben? Normally, he'd be the right type, but he still had that crazy idea of me running marketing for his new company. I didn't want the confrontation.

Willow? That's who I really wanted to tell. But she was getting married later today. As she told me earlier yesterday, she needed to focus on her relationship with Harvey. If I cared about her at all, I needed to honor her request. In the big picture, my little job wasn't very important.

The door dinged, and few seconds later, I saw Ben's face. Archibald was still standing at the counter. "Hey, partner," Ben said.

Partner. He was implying that I'd accepted his offer to become his marketing officer for GOAT. "Hey."

I could see Archibald's brow furrow, so I looked to Ben and said, "Hey, I told you I'm still thinking about it."

"Thinking about it? You basically told me you were jumping on board the GOAT train last night."

"GOAT, as in the Greatest of All Time?" Archibald asked Ben.

"Damn straight. It's a new sneaker line. You want to invest in our company, or at least walk around in our shoes and brag to all your friends about it? Word of mouth is the best kind of marketing. Well, I guess I should defer to my partner, Cooper, since he runs the marketing arena."

Archibald turned to me. "I had no idea you had this other great job offer. Sounds like it might be your best move."

"No."

"What do you mean, no?" Ben said. "And what am I competing against?"

"Nothing, because I already took a job as an investigative sports writer for a new blog."

He frowned as though his dog has just been stolen. "Wow, Coop. I thought we were best buds. I guess not."

"Ben, it's not like that. You're cool, but I'm not sure the job is a good fit for me."

"So, you'll still think about it? Man, you're a damn good negotiator."

I was about to shoot him down when his phone started blaring a song. "Is that a George Michael tune?" I asked.

He looked like he wanted to crawl into a hole. "Reva put this ring tone on her phone number."

"What's the name of the song?"

"Do I have to tell you?"

"Yep."

"It's called, 'I Want Your Sex.'"

I knew that, but I wanted him to say it loud. Slash walked up. "Not exactly Guns N' Roses," Slash said with a hearty chuckle.

Ben shook his head, then turned his back to us and took the call.

Archibald said, "You sure you're not going to back out on me? I want to know you are taking this seriously."

"Ben's harmless. I'll break the news to him later, when we're alone. Count me in."

Another phone chimed. It was mine. I'd set my alarm to make sure I wouldn't be late for my meeting with the Sack Brothers.

"Slash, I'm taking my lunch break. It's all yours."

"Rock and roll, dude."

I looked at Archibald. "I'll let you know when I have my first story idea."

"You do that. I'm excited about what you're going to bring to our little outfit."

I headed out the door with an extra skip to my step. By the time I reached my car, though, anxiety had returned with a vengeance.

Fifty-Eight

Cooper

I rolled into the AAC parking garage and found the Sack Brothers waiting by their truck on the top level. I was relieved not to see Dr. V.

"You bring the money, jerkoff?" one of the brothers asked the second I slid out of my car.

"Hold on." I opened my trunk and tossed the bag at him. I then walked back to the driver's-side door, hoping I could make a quick exit.

"Not so fast, jerkoff."

"Milo, I've got to get back to work. Some of us have honest jobs."

"I'm Elan. Yeah, like you're the commish of the Honest Police. Give me a break, jerkoff."

He unzipped the bag and removed one of the bundles of cash. I looked around for any folks walking around in the garage. There were cars, but no people on this level. He started thumbing through the bills as his brother popped his knuckles. It took Elan about five minutes to count the bills in one bundle, and he was mouthing the numbers the whole way.

"Do you need a calculator?"

"Shut up. You're making me lose count."

"Seriously? Aren't you aware that ten comes after nine?"

"Still a wiseass. Right, Milo?"

"We'll see how long that lasts."

Elan grunted and then popped his neck. It gave me the creeps.

It felt like I'd just watched an entire baseball game by the time Milo finally said, "Okay, the fifty grand is all here."

"Okay, have a wonderful trip back to New York."

"Hold up, jerkoff."

A second later, a door opened from the Cadillac parked next to their truck. It was Dr. V.

My stomach flipped.

"Cooper, it's nice to see you again." He pulled up next to the brothers, his hands folded in front of him.

"Likewise. Well, you have a great trip. Enjoy spending your money." I put my hand on the door handle to my car.

He laughed, something I'd never heard from him. It sounded like a nasally hiss more than a laugh, actually.

"We need to talk about your payback."

"What are you talking about? I gave you the money, even all that absurd interest." My voice sounded more irritated than I wanted it to.

"But you owe me."

"Why do you think so?"

"Two reasons, Cooper. First, you didn't make our meeting last night."

"I was chasing down a freaking serial killer! He almost killed me and two others." I immediately regretted providing an explanation, something I knew he'd simply call an excuse.

He laughed again, his nasally hiss sending a chill up my spine. The Sack Brothers joined in the fun with a series of mocking chuckle-grunts.

"Okay, okay. What's this second egregious act that you think

I committed?"

"It's not what you did to us; it's what we did for you."

I pinched the corners of my eyes. "I haven't asked you for anything. I just wanted to pay you the money so I can move on with my life."

"*You* didn't ask us for a favor Cooper, but someone else did."

He thought I still owed him something big. More money, maybe? I had more questions before I'd agree to anything. "Tell me, Doc, what big favor did you do for me?"

"We found Ronnie Gutierrez and took care of a problem. He could have harmed you; he could have harmed your friend, Willow. We knew he'd already harmed Lucy and her daughter. The world is a better place without him walking around."

I couldn't disagree with his last statement. But the fact that I shared anything in common with this vulture was difficult to process. "You killed him by chopping him up into pieces. But do you know the mental and emotional damage your two ogres did to Lucy and her daughter? They saw these numbnuts dump his body parts in the shed."

The Sack Brothers grunted like angry bears, and then they started moving toward me.

"Not yet." Dr. V raised a hand, and they stopped about six feet in front of me. "Cooper, that is an unfortunate consequence, but we did save their lives. So, for that, they must be thankful."

"Like I said before, I never asked you for anything. You can't put this on me."

"I disagree."

"Fine, we agree to disagree on that one. So, for being tardy last night, you want some more money? How about a thousand bucks?"

"You're not my boss, Cooper. I've determined that you owe me two favors. And that is non-negotiable."

"Tell me who the hell gave you the task of killing Ronnie?

Because in my mind, he or she can pay you back."

"You actually know this man."

I waited for more, but he didn't continue. "Is this going to be some type of game? I'm tired of dealing with your shit."

"So rude," he said.

"No one disrespects Dr. V like that," Milo said. "Can we just go ahead and kill this bastard?"

"Let's give Cooper one more chance."

I wasn't about to let them see me shaking on the outside, but I could feel my gut quivering like a tuning fork. "Who is this mystery person?"

His lips turned up at the edges. For a man who was worth a lot of money, he had the ugliest set of teeth I'd ever seen.

"Someone who wanted to make sure this Ronnie person did not harm his fiancée."

"Harvey? You're saying the man who will do your taxes asked you to kill a person?"

"He cares about his woman. And he was willing to do anything to ensure she was safe."

I felt like I'd been stabbed in one of my lungs. I coughed for a good minute.

"Need us to do the Heimlich on you?" Milo grunted. "That way we can break a few ribs in the process."

"Milo, I'm not your type. I'm not going to let you 'lich' any part of my body."

His eyes narrowed. "Please, Dr. V, let us teach this wiseass a lesson."

Dr. V ignored Milo and kept his gaze on me. "So, now you see why you owe me."

"Actually, I don't. You can get your payback from Harvey."

"I've already taken care of that. But you have skin in this game. And for that, I want to use your considerable connections in the sports world to be our point person for setting up some investment opportunities."

"What kind of investment?"

"Some people call it point shaving."

"You're nuts. I don't want or need another felony on my record."

"Again, this is non-negotiable."

"And if I refuse?"

"A pity that you're so hard-headed. But let's just say you refuse. Then I'd be forced to perform the same type of surgery we did on Ronnie to someone close to you."

"Who?"

"Willow Ball, of course."

"Fuck. You!"

"Cuss all you want, but you know that you can't turn down my offer."

Not Willow. It just can't happen.

I suddenly felt lightheaded, as if someone were choking me. I bent over as my mind painted a picture of Dr. V using his saw to cut up Willow. Now I wanted to hurl. I put a hand on my car and stood up, thinking I might have it in me to choke Dr. V until he wasn't breathing. But I knew the Sack Brothers would pound me into the ground the moment I touched their ruthless boss.

"I could go to the cops, tell them all about your extortion plans."

"Ha! You really think they would believe you? I've dodged every type of charge for twenty years. You have to know, Cooper, that I have contacts everywhere."

"The DNA. You had someone lose it?"

He nodded at Milo, who came up to me and patted down my body. His hands felt like steel wool. He was checking to make sure I wasn't wearing a wire.

"He's clean," Milo said.

Dr. V continued. "I wasn't about to have me or my two

employees take the hit for carrying out a task for someone else."

"For Harvey." I had to say his name out loud just to convince myself it was him.

Dr. V gave a slight nod. "We can talk about the details of our investment plans later. But I think with this new job at *The Wire*, you'll develop even more contacts to help us with that. And if you were to also accept the job at this new sneaker company, then you'll open the door to even more opportunities."

My life had been completely invaded. "How the hell do you know about those jobs?"

He smiled again. It was revolting. "I told you I have contacts."

"So, you won't tell me who?"

"Maybe someday I'll share it with you. But I'll have to trust you first. For now, you need to focus on these two favors."

"You never told me the second one."

"I have a nephew, Ishaan. He's very interested in sports writing. I want him to shadow you as you research and write your stories for *The Wire*."

Is he fucking kidding? Now I have to be a babysitter? "How old is your nephew?"

"A freshman at SMU. He's a very talented writer."

Says the butcher.

"He just needs some experience. Hopefully after learning at your side, he'll be given the chance to write articles for this new blog. You can make that happen, right?"

I was at a loss for words. "I'll try."

"Don't try, just do."

That internal quiver made its way up my throat. It was as though I was trying to control a wild animal.

"So, I'll have Ishaan reach out to you," Dr. V. said. "It will be a great experience for both of you."

I just stared at him, unsure if I could accept being tied to his family and setting up a point-shaving scam. "Right," I said. "Can

I go now?"

"Of course. I'm so glad we've come to an amicable agreement. And I'm sure Willow will appreciate your sacrifices as well," he said, smiling.

Bile crept into the back of my throat. Without saying another word, I got in my car and drove off, wondering if or how I should tell Willow what kind of person she was about to marry.

Fifty-Nine

Cooper

During the drive back to Books and Spirits, I rolled down the window and let the cool fall air slap my face. Anything to keep me from thinking that I would forever be indebted to Dr. V.

As my mind cleared, my thoughts turned to Willow. Dr. V had warned me that if I didn't follow through with setting up this point-shaving operation, Willow would be next on his hit list.

I knew that Dr. V's threat had to be taken seriously. So, as much as I hated the idea of committing this crime, I couldn't take the chance of him killing Willow.

I'd have to figure out the next steps on setting up this point-shaving scam. For now, though, I wondered if Harvey could be trusted. He'd essentially asked Dr. V to kill someone—if I were to believe everything that Dr. V had told me. I was both shocked that he had that in him and that Willow would be married to the man in just a few hours.

I didn't want to be that guy—her old college boyfriend, no less—to stop her wedding. But at the same time, how could I not warn her about what Harvey had done? And what was he capable of? Was this his first time to break the law, or just the most recent? I couldn't predict how her life would be impacted by Harvey's approach to resolving issues, but she deserved to know the truth. Then she could make her own decision.

I pulled into the lot just outside the bookstore and tapped Willow's number on my phone. It rang five times, and then it rolled over to voicemail

"Crap!" I said out loud, wondering if I should leave a message or just call her back. It beeped, and I quickly ended the call. She was busy getting ready for the wedding. She didn't need this shit right now.

Still, I decided to try her two more times in the next couple of hours. If she didn't answer, I'd be forced to leave her a voicemail. Shit or no shit.

Slash caught me a few seconds after I walked into the store. "Dude, you frickin' caught a serial killer last night."

"Eh. I didn't really catch him, but he's in the custody of the police."

"You're a fricking superhero. Spider Man or Iron Man?"

"Neither. And how do you know about all that?"

"I saw the cast on your arm, and I asked your buddy Ben about it. He filled me in. He thinks you're more of a Captain America, but I just couldn't see it."

Like it mattered. "Where's Brandy?"

"She took off, said she'd be back later. Time to party. You want me to grab you a drink from the bar?"

"Not today, thanks."

"Hey, man, just means more for me."

He walked toward the bar while I tried to stay busy. An hour passed, and I put in my second call to Willow. It rang five times and went to voicemail.

"Double crap," I said, punching the end of the call.

Another hour passed. Brandy had yet to return to work, so I called Willow a third time. It rang only three times before it went to voicemail.

I considered running off to the church to try to intercept her before she walked down the aisle. But I may not get access to her. Hell, Harvey might have people guarding her, so I decided to leave a voicemail. I summarized everything about my meeting with Dr. V within a minute. And then I closed with, "Sorry about all this. Let me know if you want to talk through it with me. I'll be available whenever you need me."

I hung up. I was concerned that I'd just delivered news that would devastate Willow. I hoped like hell she'd call me back. I checked my phone every couple of minutes for the next six hours. Nothing.

As I made my way back to my apartment, I wondered if she'd ever gotten the message. Or maybe she had received it but didn't want to believe my assertions.

Willow, from my experience, wasn't the kind of person to blow off reality. So I hoped for the best and waited for her to call me.

One day passed, and then another day passed. I thought about trying to reach out to Raymond to learn more about his connection to Dr. V and the Sack Brothers, but I didn't have his phone number. Yes, I could have asked Ben to ask his sister, who could have reached out to Jennie, but for some reason, I had no desire to go down that path. Not now anyway.

My optimism on Willow returning my call slowly waned, and by the time I reached work on Tuesday, I found myself wondering if she was enjoying her honeymoon. Had the message I left not meant anything to her? Maybe she'd changed over the years?

I ate my lunch in the breakroom, a plain turkey sandwich I'd brought from home. Two bites into it, the door busted open. It was Slash.

"Dude, come quick. That hot babe friend of yours just showed up. She wants to talk to you."

I left the food on the table and walked to the front of the store,

Slash right on my heels.

"Where is she?" I asked.

"In the bar."

I twirled around and headed toward the bar, Slash again following me. "Hey, can you give Willow and me a few minutes alone?"

"No prob." He walked off as I marched forward. When I came round the final bookshelf, I saw Willow in her jeans and a sweater. She was pacing by the chairs. She looked up and saw me.

"Are you okay?"

She walked up with tears pooling in her eyes. She punched me in the shoulder socket, and then she hugged me with everything she had.

My heart broke in two.

Sixty

Willow

After a few seconds, I could feel Cooper's embrace tighten. Then I held him even harder.

"You're choking me," he said.

I quickly let go.

"Just kidding," he said with a wink.

Now that we were separated, I looked into his eyes. Neither of us said a word, but our gaze didn't waver. Part of me wanted to reach out and touch the scruff on his face, then grab hold of his hair and pull him closer. And kiss him.

But I knew my pain wasn't a good excuse to hurt him.

"I didn't know your honeymoon would be so short," he said.

"Never went on one." I dug my hands into my pockets

"Planning on a trip around the world in a few months? You know I spent a season in Turkey."

"Huh?"

He dipped his head. "That year of professional basketball I was telling you about a while back."

I exhaled slowly. "I got your voicemail."

"You did?"

"About an hour before the wedding."

John W. Mefford

"Ah. I wasn't trying to judge you or Harvey. I just wanted you to know all the facts."

"You were worried about me. You can say that."

"Okay, I was. Actually, I am. You don't look so happy."

"I called off the wedding."

"Are you kidding? Weren't people already on their way?"

"Yep. Harvey offered to go into the sanctuary and tell everyone. But I did it instead. It was time for me to take control of my life and not rely on anyone to save me or do the uncomfortable thing."

Cooper nodded for a few seconds as if he were trying to process what I'd shared. Then he said, "So you and Harvey broke up?" He had hope in his voice.

"We agreed to push back the wedding indefinitely. But we're going to still date each other. I moved most of my stuff out of his house. We're just going to take it slowly."

A long nod. "Okay. If you think that will make you happy, I'm fine with that."

"I wasn't asking your permission."

He held up two hands, and I took note of his cast. "Your arm still hurting?"

"It's better every day."

"I'm just glad you finally took care of it." I looked away, my eyes roaming the bar area.

"You want a drink?" Cooper asked.

"Not really. I need to…well, I want to share some things with you."

"Why me? You still have Harvey."

"Because you deserve to know the truth."

"I'm listening."

I started to feel a little wobbly in my knees, so I plopped down in an overstuffed chair. Cooper sat in the other chair and waited for me to talk.

"The life story of Willow Ball isn't comprised of you walking out of my life in college and then me meeting Harvey."

"And here I thought you mourned me leaving for eighteen years."

"Sarcasm. Not really my thing right now."

"Sorry. It's kind of baked into my personality."

"Believe me, I know."

"So…" He motioned with his arm for me to get to it.

"I've been married before."

He extended his neck. "Really? And that's why you were hesitant to commit to Harvey? You don't trust men."

"The events aren't connected."

"How couldn't they be? But, then again, after learning about what Harvey pulled off with Dr. V, you're probably scared of a lot of things."

"Harvey told me he was sorry, that he had no idea Dr. V was going to kill Ronnie. He only wanted to keep me safe."

"And you believe him?"

"Mostly."

He opened his mouth as if he wanted to rebut my comment, but he didn't go there. It was a miracle.

"My first marriage didn't end in divorce. My husband, Scotty, died."

"Jesus, I'm sorry, Willow. Do you mind telling me how?"

"Prostate cancer. It was a tough last three or four months. After he died, I poured myself into my job."

"You're a natural caretaker."

He reached over and put his hand on my knee. I wanted to knock it off my knee, but I also wanted him to grip it harder. I was torn about a lot of things.

"Thanks, I guess. But my life got turned upside down."

"How?"

"I was working at the hospital, and I, uh…"

Emotion clawed at the back of my throat. Cooper waited for me to get it together. It took a few seconds, but I eventually felt confident I could go forward with this.

"I was naïve, Cooper. A so-called friend convinced me that her back pain was something that ruined her life on a daily basis. She asked me to write a prescription, so I forged the name of a doctor. I was caught, and that's when my world cratered."

"What happened to you?"

I looked him in the eye. "You're not the only one with a felony on your record."

"Seriously?"

"And that pretty much doomed my ability to get any kind of nursing job. I ended up working at a Waffle House as a waiter. Not only had my confidence been gutted, but I was barely able to pay my bills. Eventually, I worked my way into a waiter's job at the Old Warsaw."

"Another five-star restaurant."

"I was working there, not eating there. After I pulled myself out of a depressive state, I really thought that my life would improve. I just wasn't sure how. And that's when I met Harvey. He came into the restaurant three times before he asked me out. On our first date, I told him everything, but he didn't run away. I really thought I'd found an incredibly kind and compassionate person."

"I don't know what to say, Will."

"I suppose that's why I'm giving him a second chance. He gave me a second chance, knowing that his rich friends would probably find out the truth. He always believed in me and protected me. Over time, though, I realized I didn't want or need protection. It felt like he was controlling too much of my life."

He looked confused. "I'm not sure why it took this news for you to break it off."

"Honestly, I'm not sure either."

We sat in silence for a minute, and then I asked. "Can I get a water now?"

"Sure thing." He walked over and poured two glasses of water. I chugged half my glass pronto.

"I need to tell you a couple of things," Cooper said. He then recounted his meeting with Dr. V and his ogres.

I just shook my head. "Cooper, we need to figure out what to do about Dr. V so you're not being held hostage by him."

"Nothing I can do since he's holding these threats over my head."

"I don't want you to protect me."

"I know he's not afraid to follow through with those threats. Don't worry about me."

Damn, he was stubborn. "I'm really happy about you getting this writing gig, but it sucks that you have to babysit that butcher's nephew."

"I'm not thrilled about it. Maybe I can figure a way out of all this."

"You can bounce your ideas off me," I suggested.

"Harvey won't mind?"

"It's not his decision."

"So, what are you going to do for money?"

"He wanted to give me an allowance. But I couldn't let that happen. Yesterday, I dropped by the CHC and told the director, Joan, about my life and how much I missed nursing. She was desperate to hire an experienced nurse, so much so that she said she'd ignore my felony. The job doesn't pay much, but I think I can handle it."

"Congrats, Will. I'm really happy for you."

I got out of my chair. "Need to go buy some new scrubs. Keep me in the loop with your life." I lifted a closed hand to give him a fist bump. Instead, he pulled me closer and hugged me. I didn't fight it. He kissed the side of my neck. I felt a tingle ripple through my body.

"What's up, Ball and Chain?"

I looked up and saw Benjamin standing near us.

"We're just catching up," I said, putting some space between Cooper and me.

"Alli gave me the details. You must feel really embarrassed," he said.

"Dude, can you give her a break?" Cooper spat out.

"My bad."

"She's now going to be working as a nurse."

"Yep, I know that. Also heard the pay sucks."

Cooper shook his head and looked at me. "Ignore him."

"I'm a big girl."

"Hey," Benjamin said, "I've got a great idea on how you can make some extra cash on the side."

"Don't fill her head with your crazy GOAT idea," Cooper said.

"It's not crazy. This is solid advice for both of you. Cooper, you might need to supplement your income while GOAT takes off."

"My new writing gig will do just that."

"Still may not be enough. Do you want to quit this bookstore job?"

"I'm willing to hold on to it for now."

"But my idea is even better."

I jumped in. "We're listening."

"We are?" Cooper asked.

I shrugged and looked at Benjamin.

"Start your own company and call it the BCDA."

"Sounds like an insurance company," I said.

He lifted his arm into the air as if he were unveiling a new painting. "The Ball & Chain Detective Agency."

Cooper and I both broke out in laughter.

"You guys are a couple of bad-asses. Look how you took down a fricking serial killer."

He was clearly delusional. "You must be higher now than you were three nights ago," I said.

"So you're saying you'll think about it? That would be wise. And the fact that I came up with this brilliant idea and can help you launch it, I'll only charge you twenty percent of your revenue for the next year."

Cooper and I nearly tipped over from laughing so hard. I gave him another hug on my way out the door. "Meeting Harvey for lunch. Talk soon?"

Cooper nodded and winked at me. "You bet."

Sixty-One

Cooper

By the time I got home, I was tired and, admittedly, lonely. I checked the time. It was ten o'clock on the East Coast. I paced in my apartment for ten minutes as I pondered if I was ready to get shot down again.

Finally, I picked up my phone and dialed a number.

She picked up on the second ring.

"Hey, sweetie. It's Dad. I miss you."

Dear Reader,

I hope you enjoyed that first taste of Ball & Chain. In some respects, it was more like a four-course meal. Pop in an antacid pill and get ready for Book 2.

In this next adventure, Willow and Cooper are drawn into finding a missing person—for two very different reasons. The hunt corkscrews into an impossible maze of events...their lives threatened by a swarm of twisted deviants and social misfits.

Emotions run rampant, stoking one savage response after another. A spark ignites the hate, but what is the real fuel for this wave of brutal crimes?

Can Willow and Cooper save a family from the torment before it's too late?

Grab *FEAR* and find out!

Best,
John

Next In The Ball & Chain Thriller Series - FEAR

Excerpt from FEAR (The Ball & Chain Thriller Series, Book 2)

One

One week ago

Gunmetal gray skies gave way to the last bit of sunlight as the enraged man jerked the car to a stop a block away from the park.

Take a deep breath, and then exhale slowly.

He repeated the exercise three times.

It didn't work a damn bit. The side of his neck pulsated as though some type of beetle-like alien was trying to punch its way through his skin—it had freaked out his wife the first time she saw it. But she'd never seen him in this kind of condition. No one had.

He glanced in the rearview and caught the edge of his right eye. He turned the mirror for a quick inspection. He almost didn't recognize himself. Blue and green veins outlined every stress mark—and there were too many to count—but it was his eyes that stole his gaze. He saw in his eyes exactly what he was feeling.

Pure. Fucking. Hate.

He picked up the Glock 19 G5 9mm pistol and let the weight rock his arm up and down a couple of seconds.

He slid out of the car, quietly shut the door, turned up the collar on his barn coat, and walked into the park. He spotted an old sign: *Opportunity Park, Built 1966.*

Someone will be receiving the ultimate opportunity in a matter of minutes.

The twenty-acre park had it all. Lots of grass, although it was a dormant brown right now, playgrounds, areas of thickly wooded trees, and...

He spotted the cage. It was the backstop to the softball field. The very same field in which Tasha had played her last game. She was only thirteen years old at the time. He was nine. He recalled her final game—she had two hits, including the game-winning RBI in the bottom of the seventh inning. They exchanged high-fives, and Mom took them out for ice cream.

Two days later, Tasha was dead.

Died from a drug overdose. A goddamn drug overdose. Some fucker, whom they'd never caught, sold her the coke in a park just like this one. She'd snuck out of the house and met an older high school friend who said they needed to have real fun that night. Turned out her so-called friend was connected to some thugs who sold drugs to kids on the southeast side of Dallas.

Kids.

The man knew he was about to right a wrong that was thirty years old. He had two kids of his own. He would do anything to protect them, even if they didn't know it.

He circled around the softball field and stopped near the edge of the playground.

"Come out, come out, wherever you are," he sung to himself as his eyes scanned the darkness.

He'd been tipped off by a like-minded online friend, who had given Rashad the scoop: he'd seen a group of guys selling drugs to kids at the park around this time of night near the edge of the woods. Three punks who wore saggy pants and red bandanas. Tattoos on the side of their necks: two dice and the words "Black Jack" etched just above the image. Some type of drug-dealing symbol, he was certain. Sitting in front of his computer at home, Rashad didn't waste another minute. He thanked his online buddy, grabbed his pistol out of the safe, and drove over here.

It was time to right a wrong.

A hand touched his shoulder. He swung around while he pulled out his Glock in one rapid motion.

He gasped out a breath. It was just some older guy with his dog.

"Yeah?"

"I…" The older guy raised his arms, yanking the leash on his little poodle, and stared at the gun.

"Sorry," he said, putting the gun back in his waistband. The man, who wore an overcoat and fedora, didn't lower his arms. In fact, he wasn't blinking.

"Yo," he said, snapping fingers. "I'm no banger. You just scared me."

The older guy continued to stare at him.

"Seriously, put your arms down. I just carry the gun to, uh, you know…"

"Protect yourself."

"Yeah, that's it."

"I get it." The man patted his coat. "I carry a semi-automatic myself."

"Really?"

"I'm just joking. No one pays us much attention. Right, Barney?" he said to his pooch.

He swung around, looking for any sign of the dealers. Was that something moving over by the tree line?

"Hey, sorry to bother you."

That's exactly what you're doing, he thought. He looked over his shoulder. "What can I do for you?"

"Well, I'm kind of new to the area, but my daughter tells me there's a Waffle House less than a mile from this park. Do you know—"

"Yep," he interrupted. He'd do anything to get rid of this guy. The fewer people around, the better. He turned and pointed toward the street at the end of the park. "Basically, just take Pine Street right here down about a half mile, then turn left. You'll see the Waffle House sign just beyond the car wash on the left side of the street."

He felt a prick in his arm. As he whipped around, he lost his balance, stumbled off to the right. He looked at the older guy—there were two of him. No, three of him. The older guy smiled. Or were his own eyes blurred? He tripped, moving a step toward the older guy. "What did you...?"

And then his head bounced off the ground.

The man lifted his head two inches off the ground, then let it drop. "Fuck!" That was concrete. It was so dark, he couldn't see where he was.

He tried to move his arm to scratch his head, but it was restrained by something metal. Some type of wrist lock. Both wrists were bolted to the floor. His ankles too. His heart leaped into the back of his throat, and he screamed, "Where am I?"

His voice bounced around, but there was no response. Panic gripped his insides as his mind worked through the sludge. He recalled giving the man directions, and then...

He heard some movement. "Someone there?"

No response. He held his breath, hoping to pick up a clue as to where the sound had originated and maybe who or what it was.

But he heard nothing. He blinked a few times, trying to adjust to the darkness. There might have been a wall nearby. Other than that, it was a blank screen.

A thought hit him. The older guy at the park with the dog must have been a setup. Those fucking gangbangers had paid off the man to distract him, and then someone had snuck up on him and stuck him with a needle. Who knew what kind of shit was in that syringe? Once he got ahold of them, he would put a bullet in their heads. No questions asked. No apologies. Fucking dead!

A spotlight flipped on. It was so intense and hot that it felt as though the sun had been placed five feet from his face.

A second later, a figure appeared. He or she was covered in some type of head-to-toe outfit, wearing a welding screen. "Who are you?" He could feel his entire body trembling.

A blowtorch snapped on. The person held the lit blowtorch against his little finger.

He yelped and screamed until his voice cracked.

Then the flame went away, and the light turned off.

Writhing in pain, he struggled to hear through his own whimpers. A minute went by. Or was it an hour?

Then he heard a slight chuckle. A man or a woman? He couldn't tell, but it was a laugh just the same.

A door shut.

All was quiet.

He waited.

And waited.

And waited.

Two

Present Day

Cooper

The knock on the apartment door wasn't just loud, it vibrated my rib cage. It was an insistent rapping. My first thought: not a welcome visitor.

Could it be the Sack Brothers?

My pulsed ticked faster as I swiveled my head to the front of the apartment.

It was quiet for a moment, although I could feel a silent, onerous energy on the other side. I hadn't gotten back to Milo and Elan Sachen yet, and two weeks had passed since I was given *the directive*. They hadn't given me a specific date for showing them proof that I had indeed set up an illegal point-shaving scheme, but they knew my track record: cut and run. A few more seconds ticked by without another knock. Maybe it was a service technician, and he'd just given up. My eyes diverted back to the blinking cursor on my laptop. I'd just spent another two hours researching the topic of my first story for *The Wire*, a new sports blog, and I had actually started the opening paragraph. The oddity of the exercise was that I'd yet to speak to the person I was profiling, a former

NBA first-round pick who'd reportedly blown through millions of dollars over his career. While I was eager to interview him and those within his universe, I could already envision how I was going to approach the lead. It had to be a serious hook, and I was in the middle of writing it.

Which is why that pulsating cursor carried beats of creative verve. My zest to unleash all the ideas that had been floating in my mind the last week made my mouth water. I was slightly anxious—I hadn't written a story since my untimely fall from grace almost seven months earlier—but also excited. The thrashings I'd endured recently, both physical and mental, were (hopefully) behind me. This keyboard was my turf, my sanctuary.

I closed my eyes and released an audible breath to find my mojo.

Two more loud bangs.

"Dammit!" I pushed up from the chair, accidentally knocking the rickety card table. I paused, put a hand on the table as though it were a pet. Didn't need my laptop crashing to the floor.

I yanked the door open. "Yes?"

A finger and a nose. That's all I saw at first.

"Do you have any idea what you've done to this street?"

I looked curiously at a man who was easily twenty years my senior. I was thirty-nine. I guessed he was one of Mrs. Kowalski's neighbors, the nice woman from whom I rented her second-floor garage apartment.

"I'm sorry?"

"You're sorry, that's for sure. You're just another one of those mooching, ne'er-do-wells," he said, looking at me down the slope of his nose, his eyes nothing more than dark slits.

Ne'er-do-wells? I'd last heard that term in a black-and-white 1950s Humphrey Bogart movie. "I'm not really following you."

"Then pay attention, you hippie."

I raked my fingers through my hair—something I'd

instinctively been doing ever since I let my hair grow out a bit. (My mom thought I looked like Bradley Cooper. Go figure. Classic mom.). Truthfully, my long hair was only a repercussion of not having much money.

"Hippie. Ne'r-do-wells. Is this your strange way of coming on to me? I'm not really into that. but I can recommend an upscale S&M place on—"

"I heard you were a smartass. Goes with the look. You're all the same," he said with the kind of disdain that might normally be directed at someone who'd committed a felony. Hold on—I'd committed a felony. Let's make that a serious, violent felony.

I crossed my arms, leaned against the door frame. I was growing tired of his antics and eager to jump back into creating the ultimate hook for my story. "Is there a reason you knocked on my door?"

He walked right past me and into my apartment. Momentarily stunned, I didn't try to stop the man who had decent quickness for his age.

"Can I help you with something?" I said, now turning around.

"Just looking for drugs. I'm sure you're into that kind of thing. You going to show me or am I going to have to take this place apart?"

I waited a beat. My mind was trying to process what this guy had just said. Yep, he was being a complete asshole. "This isn't your place. You need to leave."

He glanced over his shoulder, snickered, then opened my lone closet door and started riffling through my things.

"Hey, dude, have your heard of personal property?" I walked over, put my hand on the door, but he still ignored me. So, I put my hand on his shoulder.

"Assault! Assault!" He jumped back, holding his shoulder as if he'd just been pounded into the ground by a Cowboys defensive tackle.

"What the fuck, dude?"

"You assaulted me," he barked, growling like an injured bear. Was he really going there? "What's your name?"

"Myron Little, former Marine."

"So, because I touched your shoulder, a former Marine is claiming I hurt him? Give me a frickin' break."

"Doesn't matter what you think, punk," he said pointing both his finger and his nose in my face. "Your car downstairs is a disgrace."

"The Converta-beast?"

"Say what?" he snarled.

That was the nickname my buddy Ben had given my "classic" LeBaron, which was nothing less than a classic piece of shit. You see, I can admit my faults.

"My LeBaron is a little old, but I recently got it running. And Mrs. Kowalski has no issues with me parking it in front of the garage."

"She's not the only one who lives in this neighborhood." He swung around to the closet. "Where do you keep your stash?"

"Stash?"

"Your drugs. I've smelled things coming from this lot that I haven't smelled since 'Nam."

This guy was like a watchdog. Sounds like he was on patrol when my buddy Ben had dropped by a couple of times.

"You fought in Vietnam?" I asked.

He flipped his head to look over his supposed injured shoulder. "Got a problem with that?"

"None." I held up two hands. Being a former—well, I guess, now current—investigative sports journalist—I was naturally curious by people and their stories. Everyone had one. Some had more than one.

A second later, shoes were being tossed at me like they were being shot out of a cannon. "Too much crap in there to find all your stash," the nosy neighbor growled.

"Can you stop looking through my stuff?" I swerved left and then right to avoid the onslaught of sneakers. I felt like a boxer dodging punches. I probably had twenty pairs in the closet, most of which were gifts from athletes or coaches I'd interviewed in the past.

He stood upright, rubbed his shoulder again.

"Myron, this mission of yours has come to an end. I need you to leave. I've got stuff to do." I extended my hand to the front door.

"Ha! I'll stop when I find your stash."

Could this guy get anymore paranoid? I still didn't understand his obsession with me being the next El Chapo. I moved a step closer. Bad idea. He swung his elbow back, clocking my chin. Momentarily stunned, I stumbled, falling over an old chest that served as my coffee table.

Now he'd pissed me off. I jumped to my feet, took old of his arm, and started to pull him toward the door.

"Get your hands off me you drug-dealing buttmunch."

"Myron, you need to update your insult vernacular."

He hurled about thirty more lame insults at me while taking five steps. After that fifth step, he jammed his foot against the wall and did some kind of back flip.

A clip of *Teenage Mutant Ninja Turtles* flashed across my mind. A second later, he chopped his hand down across my forearm, just above my cast. (Long story on how I broke my arm.) As nimble as Myron was, the chop carried the power of a…turtle.

"Get out, Myron!" I yelled.

He went in for another chop, this one aimed at my neck. I juked left, and he swiped nothing but air. Still determined, he grabbed an empty bottle of Orange Crush off the floor that had never made its way into the trash and swung his arm across my space. The bottle brushed the whiskers on my chin.

"That's it!" I grabbed both of his shoulders, and we wrestled for control.

"Hold up!" a woman shouted.

Myron and I swung our heads to the doorway.

"Hey, Courtney."

"Detective Bouchard," she said, flashing her badge.

"It's the fuzz," Myron said.

"The fuzz?" She gave me a quizzical look as Myron and I released our grip.

"Arrest this drug-dealing buttmunch," Myron said, pointing a finger at me.

She looked at me again. I just shook my head.

Five minutes later, Courtney and I watched from my second-floor landing as a sulking Myron Little plodded his way home.

"Man, I really know how to make friends, don't I?"

She turned and looked inside my apartment, which I knew was a catastrophe. Organization wasn't one of my strong suits. But my eyes stayed on her raven black hair that had the shine of a seal's wet fur.

"So," she said, turning to meet my eye. "You ready to give this date thing a try?"

My eyes didn't blink. I'd forgotten all about it.

Three

Willow

The first swing of the blade ripped through the sleeve of my scrubs.

"He cut you?" Stacy yelled from the hallway just outside exam room 3.

"Not yet."

Ollie Randolph circled me like a drunk lion. He'd exploded into a fit of rage the moment he came out of his latest addiction slumber to realize I wasn't his dealer and couldn't give him what he coveted more than anything in the world: another fix of heroin.

"Ollie, put the scalpel down," I said, my knees bent, rotating to meet him straight on while scanning the room out of the corner of my eye for a way to protect myself.

"Not until you give me my fucking heroin!"

Blood snaked down Ollie's cheek. He'd already cut himself just to prove he was willing to do anything, including all forms of manipulation, to get his next fix. It wasn't necessary. I'd already seen his desperation. From the first time I saw Kelly open the door to the Community Health Clinic exam room, Ollie was trembling as though he were trapped on a glacier. His eyes were glassy and splintered with red lines. Without any input on his situation, I knew he was starting the process of a heroin withdrawal. A new batch of the vicious drug had hit the streets of Dallas in recent weeks, and the rate of deaths had skyrocketed. And not just from the opioid itself. According to a cop friend of mine, violent crimes, including murder, had also ticked upward.

When I'd tried to take the blade from his hand, he lost it and came after me. I was pretty nimble on my feet—this, according to my running buddy, Cooper—but that would only get me so far. Ollie had me trapped inside this small exam room and outweighed me by at least a hundred pounds.

"Have you called the cops?" I called out to Kelly. Thankfully, in Ollie's world, Kelly didn't exist. He was singularly focused on me. Lucky me.

She held up her phone. "Called twice in the last minute. Someone's on the way." A second later, she disappeared out of the hall. Had she gotten scared and run off to find Dr. Alvarez, or was she letting the cops in?

I was alone with this guy—that's all I knew. My eyes were dry because I hadn't blinked in the last three minutes. They shifted between the scalpel and Ollie's enraged face, which sprayed spittle from his seething breaths.

"Ollie, you know you don't want to injure anyone, right?"

"I don't give a shit who I hurt. Get me a needle of the Black Pearl, do you hear me?"

"Ollie, you're not thinking straight. I'm a nurse, not your dealer. This is a health clinic. We don't have heroin here. But I think Dr. Alvarez has a methadone pill that will help with your withdrawal until we can get you to a detox center. That's what you need, Ollie."

"Fuck the detox centers! They don't help. They just lock you in a room until you go batshit crazy. I've done it, and look where I'm at."

Sadly, Ollie's case wasn't uncommon. Over ninety percent of

people who complete a detox program relapse. Ninety percent! I'd been a nurse on and off for almost fifteen years, and I still found that number to be staggering.

"Ollie, I know you're in a lot of pain. I want to help. Let us give you that pill. It will help you, I promise. Then I'll personally drive you to the detox center."

"I told you that I'm not going to no detox center! Can't you fucking hear?" He swiped the blade horizontally. I hopped back—my sneakers squeaked hard off the linoleum—and watched the metal blade nearly rip through my torso.

"Hey, Willow. Catch," I heard Stacy say from behind Ollie.

A metal tray flew over Ollie's shoulder. I caught it with one hand and brought it up just as he hurled his whole body at me. His arm and the scalpel smashed into the tray, denting the middle. But he didn't stop.

"You're just like those fuckers at the detox center. I want to kill you!" He screamed at a falsetto pitch while banging the blade and his arm harder and harder against the metal tray. Each blow sent me lower, but I somehow kept the tray upright, protecting my face. My butt was nearly on the ground.

"Stacy!" I called out.

"They're on their way," she said, her voice fading down the hall. I didn't blame her for not jumping in. Only a crazy person would do that.

But a crazy person—actually, a very sick person—was about to slice me up like minced onions. His screams turned into wails. If he hadn't been about to kill me, I'd have tremendous empathy for the guy. But it was a game of survival right now.

The banging stopped. I opened my eyes, and from under the tray, I saw his legs back up three steps. He was preparing for a running start. If there was one thing in my favor, it was his current lack of dexterity. Almost like a bull stomping its hooves, Ollie stutter-stepped and came after me with an enraged yelp that could melt the polar ice cap. Just before he reached me, I swung the metal tray at his forehead. He threw up his arms while still moving, which is what I was hoping for. I kicked out my foot, which tripped his legs, and he dropped like an oak tree. On the way down, though, the blade tore through my sleeve and grazed my arm.

"Hold it! Police!"

Two cops paused at the door, then barreled into the exam room and pounced on poor Ollie, who dropped the scalpel as he grunted from the force of an officer's knee in his back. Kelly ran up and saw that I was bleeding. "Dear God, you're going to bleed out!"

Stacy was our main administrator and had worked at the clinic for years, but she wasn't a nurse.

"He grazed me, that's all. I'm just sweating a lot."

Her shoulders relaxed. "Well, I'm going to get Dr. Alvarez. That chicken shit was hiding out in his office. He'll treat your wound, or I'll cut off his dick."

The officers snickered. And so did I.

John W. Mefford Bibliography

The Ball & Chain Thrillers

MERCY (Book 1)
FEAR (Book 2)
BURY (Book 3)
LURE (Book 4)
PREY (Book 5)
VANISH (Book 6)
ESCAPE (Book 7)

The Alex Troutt Thrillers

AT BAY (Book 1)
AT LARGE (Book 2)
AT ONCE (Book 3)
AT DAWN (Book 4)
AT DUSK (Book 5)
AT LAST (Book 6)
AT STAKE (Book 7)
AT ANY COST (Book 8)
BACK AT YOU (Book 9)
AT EVERY TURN (Book 10)
AT DEATH's DOOR (Book 11)
AT FULL TILT (Book 12)

The Ivy Nash Thrillers
IN DEFIANCE (Book 1)
IN PURSUIT (Book 2)
IN DOUBT (Book 3)
BREAK IN (Book 4)
IN CONTROL (Book 5)
IN THE END (Book 6)

The Ozzie Novak Thrillers
ON EDGE (Book 1)
GAME ON (Book 2)
ON THE ROCKS (Book 3)
SHAME ON YOU (Book 4)
ON FIRE (Book 5)
ON THE RUN (Book 6)

The Booker Series
BOOKER – Streets of Mayhem (Volume 1)
BOOKER – Tap That (Volume 2)
BOOKER – Hate City (Volume 3)
BOOKER – Blood Ring (Volume 4)
BOOKER – No Más (Volume 5)
BOOKER – Dead Heat (Volume 6)

To stay updated on John's latest releases, visit:
JohnWMefford.com

Made in the USA
Middletown, DE
21 August 2020